Holly

SEASON ONE
ASH FALLS STORYVERSE™

WILLIAM AIME

Holly, Season One (An Ash Falls Series)
By William Aime
Print Edition Copyright © 2019 by Fiction Vortex. All rights reserved.

This novel is a work of fiction. Names, descriptions, entities, and incidents included in the story are products of the author's imagination. Any resemblance to actual persons, events, and entities is entirely coincidental.

ISBN: 978-1-947655-30-0
Published by Fiction Vortex, Inc. (FV Press)
Nampa, ID 83651
http://www.fictionvortex.com

cover by Daniel Priego

Published in the United States of America

For Dad
and everything he did

NOTE TO THE READER

Holly is a series from within the *Ash Falls* StoryVerse™ of the Fiction Vortex™ (http://www.fictionvortex.com). You may have gathered that this project involves a growing handful of uncouth authors bent on creating a ruckus amongst the publishing establishment. Shame on us, but kudos to you for boldly stepping into the Vortex.

Ash Falls is a StoryVerse™. That means many different authors are creating many different series within a shared story world. Fiction Vortex publishes these series via weekly (or even daily) episodes. An episode will typically range anywhere from 30 to 60 pages.

You may choose to follow any or all of the series within a StoryVerse. Each series is designed to be enjoyable independently of the others. Of course, the series will enhance each other and shed light on the story world as a whole.

Holly is a series. What you are holding is a season's worth of episodic stories in the *Holly* series. These episodes each tell a story. Together, Season One is a novel's worth of great episodic stories.

No one knows exactly how long each series will end up or how long a StoryVerse will remain open (actively publishing regular content). We promise that once we start a

StoryVerse, we'll end it eventually. No leaving everyone hanging like a certain Fox Studio (cough, *Firefly*, cough, cough).

I suspect that *Ash Falls* will easily require a few years' worth of continual episodes to draw to its climactic closure. But if it balloons in popularity and scope, who knows where it will go before it's all over. This is, after all, a live process depending in no small part on your participation.

Ash Falls currently consists of the following series:
Inheritance, by Jeremy Schofield
Reborn, by Corinne Kunz
Holly, by William Aime
Coven Ascending, by J.D. Mankowski
Fallen, by Steven Cotterill
A Dead Sun Rises, by J.M. Koczwara
The Perpetuals, by K. Edwin Fritz

Find these titles by searching Fiction Vortex or *Ash Falls* in your favorite online retailer, or by asking for them at your favorite local bookstore. For now, enjoy *Holly, Season One*.

Episode One: Hatchet Job

Trwe mon trwe restore;

Þenne þar mon drede no waþe.

If the true are repaid with truth
Then they need dread no test.

ONE

Emma Bosk first hiked this trail with her father a week before her twelfth birthday. Back then, as now, hunting within five miles of the city was illegal. But five miles was a long way for her to walk, even if she was unusually tall for her age, so they only went far enough for the roar of engines, people, and river to be obscured by the trees. They walked until they found the place her grandfather taught him to hunt—a mountain lake, which fed a creek, which fed a river, which fed an ocean.

There, underneath the boughs of an ash tree, she waited for a day and a night with her father. They stayed absolutely still, letting their smells become the smells of the forest, so that their skin was the dusty soil, their sweat the sweet pine, and their blood the clear water of the ice melt. There, under the careful guidance of her father, she watched a buck step gingerly to the water. She drew a bead on him as the beast checked his surroundings. She fired as he bent to drink.

Tonight she smelled like the gas of big tankers powering upstream. She smelled like the stale clay of a riverbank poorly dredged. She smelled the way steel tastes. Out here, these smells made her feel alien. They reminded her of why she stopped hunting.

Emma followed the same path that her father showed her. Even ten years later with only the full moon to light her way, she could remember its every bend and climb. She remembered dragging that buck on a makeshift sled her father built, its legs trussed and its offal left by the lake for the coyotes. She remembered all the trail markers along the way—the place the sled snagged on a rock, the place a crow tried to steal some of her prize. She remembered her relief when she saw the truck.

Behind her, there was the scuff of a boot sliding along dirt, a thud, a cry, and then a louder thud. "Goddamnit," Kevin said.

"Watch your feet," Emma told him.

"It's the middle of the dag-blasted night," Kevin said, trying to push himself off the ground. "How the hell am I supposed to watch my goddamned feet?"

"By using your eyes," Emma said.

"Bite me."

She waited a little farther up the path while he struggled to his feet. Once he managed to get himself up, he brushed the dirt off his pants and shirt while still muttering to himself. When he saw Emma watching him, he growled, "The hell you looking at?"

Emma pressed her lips tighter together. "You should go back," she said. "We both don't need to be here."

Kevin raised an eyebrow, his face dimly illuminated by her flashlight. "And leave you alone with that thing?" he asked. "You've got to be kidding me. I saw it, same as you. We all saw it. I'm still furious Ian didn't come too."

"He made the smart choice."

"There's nothing smarter than all three of us facing it," Kevin countered. "Safety in numbers."

"I don't think numbers will do us much good, honestly," Emma said. "I think you should go back."

"Shut up," Kevin said. "Not one chance in hell I'm letting you go alone."

"So you can play the hero?" Emma asked.

Kevin spat on the ground. "No," he said.

"Then why?"

"Because you're my boss, that's why. Because you stuck your neck out before Ian and I had a chance to even think about it. Loyalty," he spat again, "loyalty, that's why. Something you damn millennials don't know a damned thing about." He spat a third time. "Goddamn," he added for good measure.

Somewhere in the woods, a pack of coyotes began to yip and bark to each other, a sound that moved like the swaying of the trees.

"Keep your mouth closed while we walk," Emma said, turning. "You're getting all clogged up. That's why you're spitting."

"Yeah, thanks," Kevin said sarcastically, "I've hiked before, you know." He spat a fourth time.

After a mile, they crested the next ridge. Emma could see their destination, a teardrop of pale moonlight inexplicably reflected in the mountainside. They weren't far, maybe three quarters of a mile. Taking a moment, Emma was certain she could even point out where she had killed the buck. "Find me in the holiest wild you know," the thing had told her. This seemed to fit the bill.

"What is it?" Kevin asked, noticing her pause. "Do you see something?"

"No," Emma said. "We're close." Turning to look at him, she saw something in his right hand. He had it raised, but close to his body. Prepared, but easy. "What the hell is that?" Emma asked.

Kevin shrugged sheepishly. He held his hand out toward the flashlight, revealing a small hatchet, its head made of darkened steel. "I figured that thing likes axes, why not bring one along?"

The cries of the coyotes had moved off, but now seemed to be coming closer again. Whatever they were hunting was giving them a good chase.

"You really think that's going to do much good?" Emma asked.

Kevin shrugged. "Can't hurt, can it?"

Emma smiled, then reached to her own waist. "I guess not," she said. The pistol was heavy, a solid hunk of cold metal. She showed it to Kevin and he grinned.

"You better keep that," he said. "I haven't had steady aim since I quit drinking."

They set off again. The path stayed at the same altitude while the crest continued to rise. Eventually they were three-quarters down the side of the ridge, then two-thirds, then half. The valley formed by the two hills loomed all around them, the sky a sliver of stars. The lake came into view, its feeder stream a trickle of silver in the hills beyond. The surface was smooth as varnished wood, seemingly undisturbed by the slight breeze that ruffled the leaves. The path came to an end on the banks of the lake, disappearing into its depths.

The coyotes were getting closer, their cries and calls growing insistent. Hungry. A shiver crawled down Emma's spine.

"Why here?" Kevin asked.

Emma shrugged.

She walked along the bank, careful to step over the brush without making much noise. Heedless, Kevin followed, tromping on every shrub and fern in his way. Emma winced, but said nothing. It only mixed with the sounds of the coyotes, and anything waiting probably already knew they were there. The flashlight had seen to that.

She found the ash first. Kevin, who didn't know what they were looking for, had his weapon cocked, the blade reflecting starlight. Emma looked at the old tree, found the spot where she had waited for two days. Then she walked on. It didn't feel right.

"Where is he?" Kevin whispered. "Is he bringing those damn dogs?"

Emma snorted. "I doubt it," she said.

"Then why are they getting louder?" Kevin asked. It sounded as if the coyotes were just over the hill, about to pour over the crest and drive them into the lake to drown.

"They've probably found a deer or something," Emma said.

"Poor thing."

"Yeah." Emma's mouth was dry.

She saw it ahead of her now—the hawthorn, unchanged as the rest of the valley. She felt her chest constricting as she approached. The bullet came from the ash, but it found its mark in this tree's shade. Here she came upon her first kill, saw the lifeless eyes and the fat, pink tongue hanging out at an odd angle. Her father showed her how the bullet went through the buck's eye, out the back of its skull, and buried in the thin brown trunk.

"Good thing it's spring," her father said with a wink. "Bad luck to cut a hawthorn when it isn't."

That's strange, she realized, noticing the white flowers that adorned the tree. *Hawthorn doesn't bloom this late in the year.*

A high, keening screech echoed across the valley, the coyotes howled in excitement.

"Goddamn," Kevin cried.

Another low and pained cry followed. It lasted longer, turning from a bellow to a moan and then a gurgle, the last notes echoing in Emma's ears. She stood stock-still.

"Are you ready?" a soft voice asked from the darkness.

Ash Falls Police Department - Field Report
Rank: Detective   *Name:* Lydia Pike
Date: 08/08/2017   *Time:* 1230 hrs.
Location: Umpqua State Forest
Report:

At approx. 0950 hrs., Lt. Lake received call from OSP Tpr. Andrew Larkin stating that he and his partner OSP Tpr. Gary Rice had identified the body of Cmdr. Leonid Ellwood, 14th AFPD Precinct. As I was only on-duty detective in squad room, Lt. Lake instructed me to go secure scene and make sure 14th Precinct got the lead on the investigation. I immediately left and arrived on scene at approx. 1030 hrs.

Met first with Tpr. Larkin and Tpr. Rice and collected statement. Tpr. Larkin told me that at 0900 hrs., he and Tpr. Rice responded to 911 call from Charles Smith (age 30) in Umpqua State Forest. Smith informed 911 that he and (12) minors discovered body one mile from Sequoia Trailhead. Upon arrival at scene, Tprs. Larkin and Rice found (12) minors who appeared to them to be a boy scout troop and Smith in clearing around body. Tpr. Rice noted that none of the minors had gone near the body and that it didn't look like there were any footprints around body. Tpr. Larkin noted that Smith was vomiting on north side of clearing. Tprs. Rice and Larkin cleared minors and Smith from area. Tpr. Rice waited with troop while Tpr. Larkin checked body for identification. Tpr. Larkin discovered: (1) cell phone, (1) brown leather wallet, (1) key ring with (8) keys, (1) car fob, and (1) bottle opener, (1) 9mm Glock handgun, and (1) AFPD badge. Based on badge, Tpr Larkin identified body as belonging to Cmdr. Leonid Ellwood and, after conferring with Tpr. Rice, decided to contact 14th Precinct. Tpr. Larkin then secured scene while waiting for my arrival.

After brief discussion, Tprs. Larkin and Rice agreed to hand over case to me. I called Lt. Lake at 1100 hrs. asking for two squad cars and ME. Lt. Lake asked about the state of the body, and I informed him that body had been decapitated. Lt. Lake instructed me to wait at scene and keep boy scout troop, Tprs. Larkin and Rice, incoming AFPD officers, and ME at scene until joined by Det. McDonagh, who would take lead on investigation.

After hanging up with Lt. Lake, I instructed Tprs. Larkin and Rice to set up checkpoints on trail and then took statement from Smith. Smith stated that he and (12) minors had found body at approx. 0845 hrs. Smith and minors were supposed to hike another (4) miles that day and spend the night at Silk Creek Campsite. Smith did not know the victim and had not ever heard of him. Took contact information from Smith and asked him to contact parents and stay at scene until parents arrived. Smith agreed to do so.

Conferred with Tprs. Larkin and Rice to see if statement I had collected from Smith was similar to theirs. Both agreed Smith's two statements matched.

At approx. 1130 hrs., AFPD Ofcs. Birk and Glowick arrived at scene. Instructed both to set up perimeter with Tprs. Larkin and Rice. At approx. 1145 hrs., AFPD Ofcs. Lowe and Kolp arrived on scene, instructed both to take statements from minors. At approx. 1200 hrs., ME Ploski and his assistant arrived at scene. Both began to set up equipment for preliminary autopsy of body. Between 1135 hrs. and 1220 hrs., I photographed crime scene, including boot prints around body, body, blood splatter, blood pooling, decapitated head, discoloration of neck attached to both body and head, and perimeter of clearing.

(Will finish report after Det. McDonagh arrives at scene.)

THREE

The body was on its side, knees crossed in a slightly unnatural manner, the collar of the white shirt stained red. Its torso rested on the left shoulder blade, chest open to the sky, the dirt kicked up a little where the shoulders impacted. One arm was cast dramatically behind it, the other neatly tucked against the ground. The watch on the left wrist casually ticked off the seconds, its beat audible in moments of silence.

The head had rolled some few feet away. The eyes were open, the blue pupils still showing a measure of surprise. The lips were parted slightly, though that was likely from muscles relaxing in death. The blonde, straight hair was matted by dirt and blood, the end of the neck purpled slightly from bruising. The skin, normally warm and pink and full of light, was a cold pale marble.

Detective Lydia Pike had already documented every conceivable angle of both the body and the head. She had measured the distance the head rolled and the size of the blood pool below the neck. She even counted the amount of specks in the blood splatter surrounding the body. She could not look at it for one more second.

Stop referring to him as 'it,' Lydia reminded herself.

It wasn't going to be easy. Her instinctive reflex was to objectify the body, to treat it as a thing that she had to work and be around. Somehow it helped her do her job better, let her view the scene with a cold rationality, the clarity of undisturbed ice. But that was going to be almost impossible at this scene.

It wasn't her first. As a detective, this was her sixth scene and fourth murder. She knew what to expect, knew how to handle the scene, how to document every splatter of blood, every unsettled pine needle, every fleck of soil. But she'd never had a scene this quiet before. The patrol officers securing the perimeter were subdued, the Medical Examiner and his assistant abnormally quiet as they began to set up. Lydia couldn't imagine this was easy for any of them. He was Commander Leonid Ellwood, after all, captain of Ash Falls' 14th Police Precinct. He had many enemies in life, but the officers in his Precinct were specially chosen by Ellwood, selected from throughout the force for their bravery, their integrity, and their skill—unique traits in the AFPD. And now he was dead.

Lydia had to stand. She wanted to take a walk, to get away from the body and the State Troopers, the boy scouts two hundred feet down the trail laughing and complaining. But she couldn't leave. She was the only detective on site, and her new commanding officer had told her to wait for Detective Thomas McDonagh. "He'll take over the case," the lieutenant had told her.

Good for him, Lydia thought bitterly.

Instead of leaving, she walked around the perimeter of the clearing, focusing her attention out into the forest. The underbrush was clean and undisturbed, the trails merely dirt. She tried walking five hundred feet in both directions along the path, looking for anything unusual. There was nothing. The boy scouts had seen to that.

McDonagh had better arrive soon, Lydia decided. She didn't want to stay out here much longer. She had half a mind to tell Dr. Ploski to start without him, so they could get this over with. A small part of her thought that was what Leonid would have done.

Crouching at the southeast edge of the clearing, Lydia tried to imagine these woods on a regular day. They reminded her of her mother. She would have loved the trees, which were taller and bolder than any of the dead manzanitas outside of Needles, her hometown. She would have watched the wind sway through the branches and told Lydia they were whispering to each other.

Lydia fingered the necklace that hung from her neck. Her mother's necklace, a charm made of wicker and hair. "Where is he?" she muttered under her breath.

"Your partner?"

Lydia jumped up, stepping into the clearing and away from the edge, turning rapidly, her hand moving reflexively to the handle of her pistol. The ME's assistant stood just inside the tree line. At the sight of her hand, he raised his own. "It's just me," he said.

"Jesus," Lydia said. "You always sneak up on people?"

"Sorry," he said, stepping a little closer. "Seriously, my bad."

Lydia shook her head again, blinking as she studied him. Lydia knew the examiner, Dr. Ploski, but she had never seen this man before. He was a little shorter than her, with brown, wavy hair and an honest face. His nose was a little bent, broken from some childhood injury.

"Are you new?" Lydia asked.

"Yeah," he said, a stammer coming into his voice. "Started last—"

"Okay, word of advice," Lydia said, "don't sneak up on people at a crime scene."

"Seriously, it was my bad," the assistant said again.

"You don't have to keep telling me that. Just don't do it again." Her hand was still gripping her pistol. She needed a moment to slow her heartbeat. Holding the gun helped.

"Fine," he said, his hands still in the air. "I'm sorry." His eyes flicked nervously to her waist, to the hand and the unclipped holster. "I was wondering when your partner was getting here," he said. "We don't have all day."

"When he gets here, you'll be the first to know," Lydia said. She let go of her sidearm and began to stalk off. She heard the assistant mutter, "Bitch," under his breath and nearly whirled back around. *Asshole,* she thought instead. She kept walking, acting like she hadn't heard. Her face was flush, sweat forming on her brow, cheeks, nose, and even chin.

Screw him, she thought. *Screw that goddamn asshole.*

She didn't feel better.

Lydia stopped next to one of the patrol officers. "You took statements from the scouts, right?" she asked.

"Yes, ma'am," the patrolman answered. Lydia noticed the extra formality in his tone, but couldn't tell if it was because he heard the exchange with the assistant or because of Uncle Leo laying seven feet to her—

Nope, Lydia stopped. *At this scene, while you're working, he's just Commander Ellwood.*

In the calmest voice she could muster, she asked, "Can I take a look at them?"

The officer handed her his notepad. She pretended to look through it, asking an occasional pointed but pointless question, only half listening to his response. She took some deep steadying breaths, trying to keep her mind on her anger at the new guy.

Screw him, she thought again, half-heartedly.

"Detective McDonagh," Dr. Ploski called out. "Nice of you to join us."

Lydia turned to see McDonagh walking up the path from the main road, wearing a baggy black suit and a light blue shirt, a white coffee cup in his hand. He was taller than her, with close-cropped grey hair and a long, narrow face. "Sorry," the detective called out as he approached. "I took a wrong turn off 98."

Lydia didn't know much about Detective McDonagh. She had seen enough pictures in the commander's home to know he and McDonagh had once been partners, but she didn't know when or for how long. He never spoke during the daily briefing except to give short, uninspired updates on his cases. She did not know why Lake decided this case would be assigned to him, and she did not care. She was just glad he was here, because now she could go.

"Detective," Ploski said, "I know for a fact you've been down Highland several times before. I find it difficult to believe you couldn't find it again."

McDonagh shrugged as he passed the two examiners. "Get lost every time," he said.

"Well, I don't," Ploski replied, still rooted to his spot near the edge of the clearing, "and I don't have time to wait around for you."

McDonagh was clearly no longer paying attention. Instead, he circled the body, stopping just a few feet from the head. He looked at it, a disconcerted glare on his face. He studied the ground, spinning in a circle twice. Then, he nodded to Lydia.

"Sorry I'm late," he said, approaching her.

"It's alright," Lydia said, though she felt as annoyed as Ploski looked.

"Have you got pictures?" McDonagh asked.

"Plenty," Lydia replied, holding up the camera a little. "Had lots of time."

"Good," McDonagh replied. "Did you get the footprints, too?"

"What I could."

"Can we get started?" Ploski called from across the clearing. His assistant stared at Lydia, though she couldn't quite read his expression.

"One moment," McDonagh said. He turned to stand next to Lydia, surveying the scene. "What have you noticed that's odd?" he asked.

Lydia stared at him. "Besides the head?" she asked.

"Yeah, besides that."

"I don't know," Lydia said. "Lake said you'd be lead investigator," she added when he glanced at her questioningly.

"I am," McDonagh agreed, "but that doesn't mean you're not a detective."

Heat rose up her neck. *First the assistant, now him.*

"Besides the head," Lydia stated, keeping her voice cool, "I can't see anything weird."

"Isn't *that* a little weird?" McDonagh asked.

"Why?"

"It's a murder," McDonagh said, shrugging. "There's always a murderer, always a murder weapon, always some kind of disturbance. As best I can tell, Ellwood simply walked in here and then his head fell off." His eyes scanned around the clearing. "Found any flying saws?" he added vaguely.

"What?"

"Flying saws, like from *Wild Wild West*."

"Are you serious?"

"Seems like a possibility," he shrugged.

"Right," Lydia said. "I'll tell the force to be on the lookout."

McDonagh chuckled. "Found his car?"

"No," Lydia said, "but I did put out a BOLO for that."

"Good. Did you take pictures of this?" He moved back into the clearing towards the body, his fingers pointing two feet left of it. Lydia couldn't see anything.

"The ground?" she asked.

"Yes, the ground," McDonagh said. He stopped about three feet from the side of the body, pointing directly in front of him. "Here," he said.

"Nothing's there," Lydia said.

"Exactly! Absent flying saws, you'd have to assume someone beheaded him, wouldn't you?"

"It's what I was going on," Lydia said.

"Then where are the feet marks?" McDonagh asked. "Or any kind of disturbance? Where is the spot our killer was standing?"

"I've already said," Lydia explained, "I can't figure that out."

"Then document it at least," McDonagh said. "Document that there is nothing, and document when there is something."

"So, document literally everything?" Lydia asked. "Want me to write down the species of trees?"

"It might help," McDonagh said with a shrug.

McDonagh waited patiently while Lydia snapped a few more photos. He even stood closer to the body, arms stretched before him, imitating a spot where the killer might have been. Lydia only pretended to take that one.

Once she was finished, McDonagh indicated that Dr. Ploski could begin, then set his coffee cup on the ground near the edge of the clearing. He came and stood beside Lydia, who had pulled out her notepad. "Ash," she said, pretending to scribble, "that's fir, right?"

"Good thinking," McDonagh said in a whisper. "Except that's pine, not fir."

"So," Lydia said, snapping the pad shut. "If you don't need anything else, I should be going."

McDonagh wasn't looking at her. He was gazing up into the air, studying the branches above them. "I don't know what I need at the moment," he said. "But you can't leave yet."

"Why not?" Lydia asked, stepping to the side a little as he began to shuffle forward. "You're the lead detective. What do you need me for?"

"I don't know if I'm the lead detective yet," McDonagh answered. "This might not be my case."

"Lake said—"

"Besides," McDonagh interrupted, not looking at her, "standard procedure for a murder case is to interview friends, family, and coworkers." He cast her a sidelong glance. "You're two of those, aren't you?"

"So are you," Lydia replied.

"True," McDonagh agreed. He was standing under a tree now, squinting at its trunk. "Let's interview each other, then. You start."

Lydia waited to see if he was joking. He glanced at her expectantly, and Lydia rolled her eyes. "Did he have any enemies?" Lydia asked. "Besides the obvious?"

"I don't know," McDonagh said. He walked up to the tree, put his hand on it. Lydia dutifully noted it was the ash. "He was a commander, and you don't become a commander without breaking a few eggs. And Leonid was particularly good at breaking eggs. But I wouldn't say he had enemies on the force, at least none that are still around."

"What happened to the ones who aren't around?" Lydia asked.

"They got old," McDonagh said. He turned his face to the side a little. He looked like he was squinting, but at what, Lydia couldn't tell. Then his face tensed into a pained grimace, and he let go of the tree.

"Why are you here?" Lydia asked him.

"What, that's the end of the interview?" McDonagh asked, looking across the clearing now. Lydia thought he sniffed. "Not going to ask me about his home life, the kind of work he was doing?"

"I know what his home life was like," Lydia said.

"Ah, yes," McDonagh said. He started crossing the clearing, barely looking down at the ME's work. "He was your uncle, right?"

Lydia watched Dr. Ploski plunge a thermometer into Leo's neck before following McDonagh. "You interviewing me now?"

"Might be. You lived with him for a time, didn't you?"

"Five years," Lydia answered. "While I was in college."

"You grow up around here?"

"No."

"How'd you end up in Ash Falls?"

"He was the closest relative after my mom passed. He and Mariam took me in."

"That was good of them," McDonagh said. He approached a tree on this side of the clearing—an aspen— and put his hand to it as well. After a moment, he let go. His face seemed frustrated this time.

"What are you doing?" Lydia asked.

McDonagh looked at her, confused. Then, he said, "Getting a feel for the scene."

"Right," Lydia said. *What is wrong with him?* she wondered.

"Justin," McDonagh called out. Lydia turned to see the assistant looking up, Leo's head in his hands. A small clump of dirt fell from the neck. "Check inside his mouth, please."

"Why?" Lydia asked, looking back at him. McDonagh was crossing towards a third tree this time—a hawthorn.

"It's about my case," McDonagh explained.

"Your case?"

"I've been investigating two murders," McDonagh said. "Man and woman. Dating. Both beheaded."

"Beheaded?" Lydia asked, surprised.

"That's not even the weirdest part," McDonagh said. "What's weird is that they were killed three days apart."

"Shit," Lydia said.

"Shit indeed," McDonagh agreed. He reached out to the hawthorn, but the moment he touched the bark his hand flinched back. He gripped his wrist, eyes fixed on the ground.

"You okay?" Lydia asked.

"Yeah," McDonagh said. He wasn't looking at her. Deliberately, she realized.

"I want you to go back to the station," McDonagh said. "Go through his office, his notes. See if he was working on anything in particular. I'll stop by his home and interview Mariam."

"I'm not on this case," Lydia reminded him.

"You're not?"

"No," Lydia said.

"Don't you want to know what happened?" McDonagh asked. He jerked his head towards the body. "He'd stop at nothing if it was you."

Before Lydia could say anything else, Justin called out, "I got something."

Lydia turned in time to see the ME pulling a small paper thin object from the mouth. When it was clear, Lydia saw it was small and green, cut to have fluted spikes.

"It's a leaf," Justin said, clearly surprised.

Lydia looked at McDonagh. By the way his face had darkened into a scowl, Lydia could tell it was consistent with his other two scenes.

That's three now, Lydia thought. *More than enough to be a pattern.*

"Bag it," McDonagh ordered.

FOUR

Thomas hadn't been here in nearly twelve years. In the old days, he had often come to see Leonid, to drink a beer and talk about work. Sometimes it was for a social gathering, Leonid playing host in his favorite grey suit, his big, broad shoulders taking up half the room. But the majority of the time, Thomas came when Leonid wasn't home. The majority of the time, he came to see Mariam.

It all still felt the same, like anger and sadness and excitement. These were not good feelings. He had left those feelings behind on purpose, twelve years ago, and he was not happy to have them back.

Thomas took a deep breath. Then, he took off his sunglasses, stepped out of his car, and made the long walk up to the front porch. He climbed the stairs in three steps, crossed to the door in two, and knocked. When he was visiting Leonid or coming for a party, he would always ring the doorbell. When he was coming for Mariam, his knock was a soft tap. This was a sharp rap, three notes on the door's stained window.

For a moment, there was nothing. Thomas coughed. Already the dry heat of the day was beginning to invade his lungs, the sun starting to drain whatever moisture remained in his skin from his morning shower. He had not meant to work today, had not really meant to see anyone. The animal was still in him from last night and it felt wrong. He hated the full moon. And now he had to interview the widow of a dear friend.

Thomas coughed again. *She might not know yet*, he told himself. But Mariam would know. She wasn't a fool and her husband was dead. When he hadn't come home—for the MEs had confirmed that the body had been dead at least a few days, slowly decomposing while Thomas hunted—when Leonid had been gone all weekend, Mariam must have known something was wrong.

He saw movement somewhere in the house. A shadow appeared at the end of the hall, no more than a black drop through the dappled glass of the door. It swelled outward as Thomas heard footsteps approaching. Then a pause, the window entirely dark. Thomas waved.

A chain was pulled, then a latch switched. The door opened and Mariam waited just beyond it, her dark hair tied up into a bun, her face clear and cold and white. She was already wearing a plain, black dress, rigid and formless.

"Tom," she said.

"Mrs. Ellwood," Thomas replied.

Mariam began to cry. She fell into him and he held her there, his arms wrapped entirely around her. She cried into his shirt, her shoulders heaving, her hands balled into fists against his chest. Thomas stayed motionless, watching down the dark hall of her home, feeling the warmth of her small body shudder against him.

"Where did you find him?" she asked.

"In the woods outside of town," Thomas replied. "Long way from here."

"How did he die?" she asked.

"I don't know yet," Thomas lied. Or at least he didn't give her the full truth. "I need to ask you a few questions, Mrs. Ellwood."

"Stop that," Mariam said, pushing away from him. "You don't get to treat me like any other grieving widow."

She turned and started walking back into the house. She left the door open, and after a moment's hesitation, Thomas followed, closing it behind him. "Mariam," he called after her.

"You want some tea?" she asked, her voice coming from the kitchen.

"No, thank you," Thomas said. He followed her in, where she stood filling a kettle with water.

"You sure?" she asked.

"Yes."

Mariam turned off the water and left the kettle in the sink. Her hands were shaking as she pulled a glass from one cupboard, then a bottle of whiskey from another. Thomas watched as she poured two fingers' worth, drained it, then poured another. "I'd offer you one, but I know you're on duty," she said.

"Thanks," Thomas replied.

He waited, watching to see if she would drain this one as well. She didn't, instead taking a small sip while she matched Thomas's gaze. A tear trickled down her lined cheek, but she wiped it away absently.

"When was the last time you saw him?" Thomas asked.

Mariam took a breath, wiping another tear. "It must have been three days ago," she said. "Maybe four. He went into work on Friday, and I haven't seen him since."

"You didn't report it?" Thomas asked. "You didn't call anyone to ask where he was?"

Mariam shrugged. "You know Leo," she said, "you know the job. The life. He was always disappearing for unusual amounts of time. Especially recently."

"So you didn't think anything was wrong?" Thomas challenged.

Mariam didn't answer at first. She set the glass down, her eyes unfocused on the counter. "No," she said, "I could tell. Something felt off."

"Why didn't you call anyone?"

"I felt silly."

"Why didn't you call me?"

Mariam's eyes focused on him. They took a hard edge, a coolness. "You stopped coming by, Tom," she said. "Not me. You stopped being someone I called a long time ago."

Thomas didn't say anything. He wanted to tell her that was ridiculous, that he could have helped. He wanted to argue and to rage, to do anything but keep calm and take her crap. But she was right, even if he didn't think it was fair. *You left those feelings behind,* he reminded himself, his near constant mantra. *Those were not good feelings.*

"Had you noticed anything unusual?" he asked

"Unusual?"

"Was he acting strange?"

"No."

"Did you seen any strange people in the neighborhood?"

"No."

"Any unusual letters or late night calls?"

"Not for twelve years."

"I meant for him."

"Oh. No."

"Did he say he was worried about anything?"

"No."

"Do you mind if I look around?"

Tears were still leaking out of her eyes. Slow tears now, not the weepy fat ones from when she greeted him at the door. She opened a drawer and pulled out a napkin. "What do you think you'll find, Tom?"

Thomas shrugged. "I don't know," he said.

"Then why do you want to look?"

"I don't have to," he clarified. "It seems pretty clear that it wasn't you, at least to me. And if anything comes up, I'll just get a warrant."

"Don't you want to tell me that a guilty person would have nothing to hide?" Mariam asked, holding the napkin to one cheek.

"No," Thomas said. "I want to find out what happened to Leonid."

Mariam sniffed, then put the napkin down on the table. "Good," she said. "Who've you got on it with you?"

"Lydia Pike."

Mariam chuckled, looking down at her glass. "Of course it's her," she said. "Tell her to call her aunt, if you don't mind."

Thomas nodded. "You'll call if you think of anything?" he asked.

"Of course," she said.

Thomas was halfway across the yard when she called out to him from the door. "Tom?" she asked. "Do you want any meat?"

"What?"

"Do you want any meat?" she asked again. "Leo got about a hundred pounds just before he disappeared. I don't know what I'm going to do with all of it."

FIVE

Lydia was at the precinct long enough to find out Ellwood's office was locked. Before she could figure out who had a key, two patrol officers found Leonid Ellwood's car on the westside of town, near the waterfront. Because Lydia was again the only on-duty detective in the station and McDonagh wasn't answering his phone, Lydia's sergeant made her go.

The green Ford Charger was parked on 2nd Street, opposite the river. When Ellwood left it, he had parked under a tree, where a layer of pine needles and bird scum had collected over its polished surface. Lydia tried the doors, but they were locked. She wasn't surprised, but a locked car still presented an issue. She didn't want to wait around for a locksmith—nor did she know how to break into a car. She knew the theory of it, maybe, but not the practice.

"Either of you know how to jimmy a car door?" she asked the patrolmen.

Both of them shrugged.

"Not really," one said.

Locksmith it was.

After putting in the call and telling the officers they could leave, Lydia leaned against the hood of Ellwood's car. She was glad he had chosen to park in the shade. The day was only growing hotter, the summer getting longer. A little of the river's cool breath made it to the streets, but it was quickly overpowered by scorching hot pavement and the reflections of glass and steel. The few parking spots shaded by the city's trees at midday were almost impossible to find open, and when they were, it was only for a minute, two at most. Lydia was surprised Ellwood's car hadn't been keyed or had a headlight smashed for occupying such a prime location for so long. But, at the same time, this was an out-of-the-way street.

That was something to consider—why had Ellwood come here? And, more importantly, how did he get from here to a hiking trail far outside of town without his car? This street was nothing—warehouses, a few parking garages. The city's shipping docks were less than a block away, and the only other reason to come down this street was to get out of town. No houses, no businesses—nothing. What was he doing?

Lydia watched a cargo ship come into view far down river. It rode low in the water, its deck laden with heavy shipping containers. It had probably off-loaded a minor portion of its cargo in Reedsport before making the winding trek up the Umpqua. Ash Falls was a difficult dock to get to. At least one ship ran aground every year, always the biggest accident. Below that were the more usual accidents of sport boats crashing into each other or houseboats inexplicably sinking.

Maybe that was why Ellwood came here. Maybe he liked to watch boats, liked to come and see the ships roll in and out, the dockworkers going steadily about their business, whatever case he was working on mulling around his brain.

Lydia rubbed her temples. It was a simple solution, but it didn't feel right. It didn't sound like Uncle Leo—he was more into motorcycles—and more importantly, it ignored the question of how he ended up out on the far side of town.

She checked her watch. The locksmith said he couldn't come for at least an hour, and he wasn't known for being on time. Lydia rolled her eyes. The cargo ship was making its way around another bend now. Some of the dockworkers were idling, watching her as she watched them. They were the only other people on the street, the only possible reason for him to be here. Lydia pursed her lips, made a high, squelching squeal by sucking air through her teeth.

"Screw it," she said, starting down the road.

When she showed Foreman Shaft a picture of Commander Ellwood, the man instantly recognized him.

"Yeah," he said, jowls quivering slightly as he spoke. "He came in here Friday, wanted to ask some questions about shipments we've been getting." Lydia decided that if he was a type of dog, he was a pug. "I told him he couldn't," Shaft continued, "not without a court order. It's dockyard policy, and that's what I'm telling you too.

"That's fine," Lydia said, giving him a conceding nod.

"I told him he could talk to any of the workers," the foreman continued, "but that I couldn't order them to talk and they could refuse to talk, also dockyard policy. Same goes for you."

"So you wouldn't mind answering some questions about him?" Lydia asked.

Shaft squinted a little. "Why?" he asked.

"He's dead," Lydia replied.

"Jesus," the foreman said, his eyes widening. For some reason, he removed his hard hat, placing it respectfully over his chest. "What happened to him?"

"He died," Lydia replied bluntly. "Were there any specific shipping records he was looking into?"

"Yeah," the foreman said. He scratched his temple a little, his brown, watery eyes holding on the pad of paper in Lydia's hand. "Yeah, he was asking to see any shipment orders placed by some lady. Can't remember her name now. Drank a lot of beer this weekend, you know?"

"Do you remember anything about the lady? Did she work for someone? Was she ordering for herself? Did Ellwood ask about any specific things in the shipment?"

"It was a normal name, I know that," the foreman said. His eyes were a little hazy, no longer directly looking at anything in particular. "Began with an 'M,' I think."

Lydia gave him a moment. "Margaret?" she asked, a stab in the dark.

"No," Shaft said. "Shorter. Megan? Yeah, Megan, that was it. 'Rude' I think was her last name. That one's easier to remember, pretty unusual."

"Do you know who Ms. Rude worked for?" Lydia asked.

The foreman shook his head. "Again," he said, "can't tell you that without a court order."

Lydia bit her lip for a second. "Then what was Ellwood asking about her?"

"Well, he tried to weasel a few questions about what kind of things she was shipping in," Shaft said. "Again, nothing I could reveal. He asked if I've seen her recently, which I hadn't and still haven't. Then he asked if there are any particular dockworkers she worked with." Shaft paused a moment, glancing awkwardly at Lydia.

"You couldn't tell him that either," Lydia guessed.

"Well, I could. At least, I think I could. No one works for any particular company here, but a few of our teams keep to one warehouse and a few companies prefer to ship in and out of one warehouse. The workers I sent Detective Ellwood to are in one of those warehouses."

"Commander," Lydia corrected.

"What?"

"He wasn't a detective."

"He said he was."

Lydia didn't know what to make of that, so she let it be. "I'm guessing Rude's company prefers to ship out of that one warehouse, don't they?"

The foreman shrugged his big, meaty shoulders. "I couldn't tell you."

Lydia squinted a little. "Well, Commander Ellwood wasn't your client, so you can at least tell me who he talked to."

"I suppose I could. One hasn't shown up for work this week, but the other two are over at warehouse six."

Lydia made it five steps before she caught up with everything he'd said. She turned back to Shaft, who was already looking down at his clipboard. "Hey," she called, and he looked back at her. "Why hasn't the one shown up?" she asked.

The foreman shrugged. "I don't know," he said. "She hasn't called in, and her coworkers don't know anything."

"What's her name, just so I have it?"

"Emma Bosk," the foreman said.

Lydia found Kevin Wood and Ian Caldwell at a quay between warehouses taking a smoke break. Or, rather, Wood was taking a smoke break while Caldwell looked on, perhaps a bit disapprovingly. The water behind them was empty—only two ships had come in today, and they were at docks two and four. Wood wore a heavy leather coat, which Lydia thought was odd considering the heat. He had a lined, weathered face, set in a perpetual scowl. Though he didn't quite have a beard, his cheeks and chin were covered with a grey stubble, at least a few days old.

Caldwell was much younger than Wood. He wore a pair of ragged jeans and a white t-shirt which revealed a thin, wiry frame. He kept a baseball cap firmly over his head, the ends of some blonde curls peeking out. The hat had large lettering which read, "I love Weed," followed by an almost minuscule, "California." He gave Lydia a cursory nod when she approached, but remained mostly silent while she questioned them.

Lydia started by asking them if they had met Leonid Ellwood. Wood replied that they had not. Lydia pressed them on this, stating that their foreman had already told her they had. Caldwell shifted uncomfortably while Wood took a long drag on his cigarette. Did she mean the cop, he finally asked. Yes, Lydia had meant the cop. She even showed them his picture.

"Right," Wood said. "That guy. Yeah, he showed up late last Friday, asking us a few questions."

"About what?" Lydia asked.

"You'd have to ask Emma that," Wood said, staring at Lydia coldly. "She did most of the talking while Ian and I kept working." Again, Caldwell shuffled his feet a little, his gaze carefully avoiding Lydia's.

"Do you know where she is?" Lydia asked.

"Why would she be anywhere?" Wood replied.

"She's supposed to be working today, isn't she?" Lydia asked. "Why isn't she here?"

"She's sick," Caldwell cut in.

Lydia looked at him. "Sick?" she asked.

"Yeah," Wood affirmed. "Sick."

"So you can tell me how to contact her," Lydia said.

She could immediately sense Wood panicking. "We don't know where she lives," he said. "None of us are that close."

"But you have her phone number," Lydia said. "Your foreman said he doesn't know why Bosk is out, so she must have called one of you two."

"No," Caldwell blurted out.

Lydia was getting confused, though she tried not to show it. Her brow furrowed as she glanced between Caldwell and Wood. "No?" she confirmed. "Then how do you know she's sick?"

"We saw her on Sunday," Caldwell said.

"You both did?" Lydia asked.

"No," Wood said. "I didn't."

"You just said 'We,'" Lydia said, pointing at Caldwell. "Which is it?"

"Just me," Caldwell stammered. "We hang out on Sundays, sometimes."

"I thought none of your were very close," Lydia said.

"Nobody said that," Wood said.

"You just did," Lydia said. "No more than a minute ago."

A silence fell among the three of them. Lydia waited, her eyebrows raised, gaze flicking between the two men. Caldwell shifted his feet again, still evidently uncomfortable. Wood took another drag, then threw the butt into the river. *I could bring you in for littering, dick*, Lydia thought.

"How long did they talk for?" Lydia asked.

"Who?"

"Bosk and the detective."

Again, Wood shrugged. "Must have been no more than ten minutes."

"And then what did he do?"

"He left."

"He left?" Lydia said, her eyebrows almost disappearing into her hairline now.

"Yup."

"He didn't talk to you two at all?" Lydia asked.

"Nah," Wood said.

"Nah," Caldwell added after Wood.

Lydia rounded on him again. "Where did you and Bosk hang out?" she asked.

Caldwell seemed lost for a second, but Wood spoke up. "It was your place, right?"

"My place?" Caldwell asked. Then his eyes widened a little. "Yeah," he said, "my place."

"Right," Lydia said. "So you two don't know how to contact her?"

"Nah," Wood said. "You'd have to ask the foreman."

"How long have you three worked together?"

Wood paused. "Five years, it must be," he said.

Lydia scratched the side of her nose, her eyes closed tight. "And you don't know how to contact her," she stated. She fished into her pockets and pulled out two cards, handing one to each of them. "Well," she said, "if you think of anything, feel free to contact me."

"Sure," Wood said, taking the first card.

"Will do," Caldwell said, taking the second.

Back on the street, Lydia flipped through her notes a moment. An hour had passed and there was still no sign of the locksmith. Lydia didn't mind anymore. She could spend the time trying to figure out why Kevin Wood and Ian Caldwell were lying to her.

SIX

With each step, the stiff, stretching pain in Lester Phillip's calves grew and grew. He felt his chest constricting, his lungs laboring to inhale enough oxygen as his mind descended deeper into a haze. With each step, he felt the weight of his body.

It was always like this. Lester had run this route every day for the past twenty years. It was a hiking trail to the southwest of Ash Falls. The beginning was a steep climb, but it leveled out on a ridge that overlooked the city. Then it descended again for a time, before rising towards a small mountain lake, where the trail ended. The first climb was always the hardest, but Lester knew that running was about getting over that first hump, working past your body's initial resistance, finding the point where you wanted to give in.

As he aged, that first hump always grew a little longer. Now it was the entire first leg. Only when he reached that mountain lake did he feel relief, and then the run back was always better. He would take a quick rest at the hawthorn which shaded the lake, catch his breath in the serene beauty of the outdoors. But he had to get there first.

It felt like a great, burning stone rested on his chest, choking him and setting his calves on fire. He could barely see, but he knew he was almost to the hawthorn. Then he tripped.

Lester's vision slowly returned. His cheek was pressed into the hot dirt, raw and bleeding. Each exhalation stung like a knife in his lungs, which did their best to pump air in and out of his chest. The old, familiar stitch. Instinctively, he dug his thumb into it, the way he had dug his thumb into a thousand stitches before, and he tried to remember why he was on the ground. The ground was muddy, his legs wet. That was unusual. It was a hot summer's day, and there weren't any feeders on this side of the lake. Lester closed his eyes again, wondering if he would be back up and running when he opened them. His other cheek roasted in the sun.

With a grunt, Lester pushed himself up. He struggled to stand, realizing his left ankle was hurt. His leg struggled to accept his weight, cried out for relief when he leaned on it. He swore. It was probably just a sprain, but he would have to limp back to the trailhead, already more than three miles away. He wiped some sludge from his legs, then turned to see what it was he had tripped on.

A body lay across the path. Chest down, arms by its side, a gun resting in the right hand. Lester did not understand at first. Was the person hurt? Then, his eyes registered the neck, the bloody, jagged stump, the white spine poking out a little. He registered the pool of blood beneath the neck, registered that the blood fed into a mud puddle, the mud that he was currently standing in. The mud he was covered in.

Lester did the following: he threw up; he started walking down the trail, trying to get a signal for his phone; he passed the head of Emma Bosk, which had rolled down a ditch to rest in the shadow of a fern, a final snarl twisting her face. He called the police.

END of Episode One

EPISODE TWO: AXE-IDENT PRONE

ONE

Ash Falls Police Department - Field Report

Rank: Patrol Officer   *Name:* Anne Marie Herrick

Date: 08/09/2017   *Time:* 0900 hrs.

Location: Umpqua State Forest

Report:

Partner and I responded to 911 call at 0725 hrs. Caller identified himself as Lester Phillips, stated he had found a body three miles down trailhead. Arrived at trailhead at same time as AFPD Ofcs. Bradley and Rodriguez. Ofc. Bradley agreed to wait at trailhead to keep perimeter log. Partner, Rodriguez, and I proceeded down trail at approx. 0730 hrs.

Met Phillips half-mile down trail at 0740 hrs. Phillips claimed to be suffering from a sprained ankle and in no condition to hike the trail twice more, so he told us about how far down the trail we had to go. Ofc. Rodriguez agreed to escort Phillips to trailhead while partner and I continued on. Three miles down trail, at 0830 hrs., found decapitated body. Partner informed dispatch, requesting ME and investigators. I inspected the body for identification, found: (1) wallet in back right pocket, (1) .38 caliber revolver, (1) cell phone, and (1) set of keys. Found Oregon Driver's License in wallet belonging to Emma Bosk. With help of partner, established perimeter. After approx. 5 minutes of searching, found head two feet off trail. Used Driver's License to identify head and body as Emma Bosk.

At 0845 hrs., dispatch informed us that AFPD Det. McDonagh was enroute to scene and would lead investigation. Completed report while waiting for arrival.

TWO

In the two days that followed, Lydia did her best to not get roped into investigating Ellwood's murder. The discovery of Emma Bosk on Wednesday seemed to confirm to the entire department that there was a serial killer in Ash Falls and Lydia wanted no part in that. The papers had already picked up the story—some enterprising young intern named the killer "Holly" after the news of his calling card leaked.

So instead of working, Lydia visited her aunt, and the two got good and drunk while remembering the commander. Well, only Lydia got drunk—Mariam just drank.

She was doing her best on Thursday to hide the hangover when Lieutenant Lake called her into his office. Ellwood's office, actually, but Lake had set himself up in there while a new commander was chosen.

Of all the officers in the 14th, Benedict Lake had been on the force the longest. Before becoming Ellwood's second-in-command, the lieutenant had captained three other precincts —the 7th, the 18th, and the 12th. All three suffered drastic catastrophes while under his command—detectives murdered in broad daylight, cruisers getting ambushed and destroyed by gangs. The 12th's headquarters even burned down.

Because of all that, Lake had been demoted. Somehow, though, he still found his way to the 14th. Ellwood once told Lydia that he had the sharpest mind in the Precinct, that if she was ever stuck on a case, he should be her first stop. But he would never be in command of his own precinct ever again—everyone knew that. Sometimes bad luck just followed someone, like a coat that doesn't fit right but still never gets thrown away.

When she filed into the office, she found Detective McDonagh sitting in a chair to the desk's right, perusing a file in his hands. Across from him was a whiteboard, a rudimentary map of Ash Falls drawn across it. Four dots were scattered across the map, each one with a name scribbled next to it. Her eyes were drawn to the green "Leonid Ellwood," not far from a red "Emma Bosk" in the southwest. On the other side of the river north of town, a black dot named "Sean Tanner" seemed lonely, as did the blue "Megan Rude" buried in some southeast suburbs.

"Megan Rude," Lydia said aloud. She hadn't really meant to, but the name sounded familiar for some reason.

Lake closed the door behind them with a smart snap, and Lydia turned around. McDonagh did not look up.

"What about her?" Lake asked, crossing over to the desk.

"Who is she?" Lydia asked.

"Our third victim," McDonagh asked, still not looking up.

Lake took the seat behind the desk, crossed his hands in his lap, and leaned back. Lydia kept her eyes on him, expecting him to speak. When he didn't she asked, "Another one?"

"No," McDonagh said. "The one before Ellwood." He closed the file and placed it on the desk. "Sean Tanner was the first."

Lydia looked at the whiteboard again. "So Bosk's the second?" she asked.

She turned back in time to see that Lake and McDonagh had traded a brief glance, though she couldn't tell what they meant by it. "The second?" Lake asked.

"Tanner's the first, Rude's the third, Ellwood came after Rude, that means Bosk is two?"

"Bosk is fifth," McDonagh said.

A moment of silence followed that statement. Lake had covered the bottom half of his face with a hand, and Lydia couldn't tell if he agreed or not. Eventually, she decided he didn't.

There was a chair to her left, but it would leave her back to the whiteboard. She took one last look at it, then sat in the chair. "You don't say?" she said.

"What can you tell me about Jude Bates?" McDonagh asked.

Another name she didn't know. She was about to say so when Lake cut in. "She hadn't gotten this information yet when she closed the case," he explained to McDonagh.

"His name?" McDonagh responded to Lake. "She didn't even wait for his name?"

"I'm right here, guys," Lydia said.

"He was the floater you filed as a cold case last week," Lake said. "You determined it was an accidental death and ran the vic's DNA in the database with a note to identify his family if a match ever came in."

Lydia remembered the slimy pale body with algae clinging to its limbs as it was pulled from the reservoir. The head was missing and the fingers too riddled with moisture for her to check his fingerprints or dental records, so she took the outside chance someone had his DNA somewhere in the world. If his DNA ever did match up with a name, then she'd open it again to see if she could find anything more, but it could take weeks for that to happen. She had other work to do.

"That ever come back?" she asked.

"This morning," Lake said. "Vic's name was Jude Bates. He did time for drug possession a few years ago."

"And you think it was related?" Lydia asked.

Instead of answering, McDonagh asked, "You never determined how he was decapitated, correct?"

"I didn't see how I could," Lydia replied, defensively. "If I had to guess, I'd say he fell into the river and got hit by a propeller. Happens all the time."

"Right," McDonagh said, opening the file in front of him again. "Except that when something get cuts off by a propeller, it's uneven and jagged. Lot of stray cuts." From the file, he began to pass her a slew of photos—missing legs, arms washed up on the waterfront, plenty of necks. Then at the end was the one she had taken of Jude Bates. It alone stood out from the others, which were all as McDonagh had described. But this neck was a single, clean, cut, no extraneous damage to the torso. She didn't need to see Ellwood's photo to know they were the same.

"And to top it all off," Lake added, "Bates and Tanner worked together for the lumber company."

"And so did Rude," McDonagh added.

"Okay," Lydia said, nodding. "So he's your second victim."

"Our second victim," McDonagh said.

Lydia looked at Lake. "I really don't think I—"

"Your familial relationship with Commander Ellwood is not enough of a reason to keep you off this case," McDonagh said. "You were in charge of the Bates case, you were the first detective on the scene at Ellwood's murder, same for his car.

There's no other detective that knows this case as well as you now, besides me, and you know too much to sit it out." As he spoke, McDonagh stood, crossed to the whiteboard behind her. With a purple pen, he marked a dot in the reservoir east of town and wrote "Jude Bates" beneath it. "I don't like it either, believe me," he added. "But we're at a point now where I don't have the time to bring someone else up to speed. I need you."

Lydia opened her mouth, but Lake interrupted her again. "In case you're wondering, this is an order, so protesting won't matter too much."

"Right," Lydia said. *Except I can just leave*, she reminded herself. *I just lost an uncle. They have to give me bereavement time.*

But she didn't really want that, either. She had taken a day of bereavement already, and all day all she wanted was to work. There was nothing to do except plan the funeral, and Mariam said she would take care of that. Fine for Lydia, except that all that left her was work or drinking all day. She didn't have the stomach to drink all day, and apparently working meant working on this.

Right.

She looked at McDonagh. He was going to be awful to work with, she could tell already.

"Got any leads?" she asked.

"None," McDonagh smiled.

"Theories?"

"None that are any good," Lake said.

"Ouch," McDonagh chuckled.

"Do you know how he's choosing them?"

"Not really," McDonagh said. "Tanner and Bates worked together, Rude and Tanner were dating, but nothing really connects any of them to Ellwood or Bosk."

Lydia blinked. "That's not true," she said. "Did you read my notes from getting his car?"

"Whose car?"

"Ellwood's."

McDonagh shook his head. "I saw you did some interviews at the dock, but I didn't read them," he said.

"Ellwood went to the docks the day he disappeared," Lydia said. "The people he interviewed said he was asking about Megan Rude." McDonagh and Lake both looked up at the same time. "While he was there he interviewed Emma Bosk," Lydia added.

"Jesus," Lake said.

"Did you talk to her?" McDonagh asked.

"No, she wasn't there," Lydia answered.

"She was already dead," Lake said. Those last words hung in the air between them. Lydia was starting to build a picture in her mind, to draw the lines that needed to be connected. But there was a lot left to be answered.

"Did Ellwood say anything when you took on Rude's case?" Lydia asked McDonagh.

"Nothing."

The lieutenant shifted in his seat to look at McDonagh. "You know whose name we keep not saying?"

"Let's keep not saying it," McDonagh answered.

"Whose?" Lydia asked.

"No one."

"Rowan Bale," Lake said.

"Stop it," McDonagh said, a hint of disgust entering his voice.

"Why not?" Lake asked. He started counting off reasons on his fingers. "Your first three victims and your fifth all worked for him in some way. Your fourth was involved with one of them, somehow, we're not sure yet, but he was also an

AFPD Commander. Bale has never been a great friend to the police, especially to Ellwood. What do you think are the chances Ellwood finally had an informant?"

"Pretty slim," McDonagh said.

Lydia disagreed. But she also didn't have to ask why McDonagh didn't want to pursue this lead. Ash Falls Timber was not only the city's largest employer, it was the city's oldest company. To say Ash Falls was built by loggers would be an understatement, and everyone, even a new detective like Lydia, knew that Rowan Bale, owner of Ash Falls Timber, truly ran the city. She also knew that to go anywhere near company property would kick up a lot of dust she liked to pretend wasn't there. Keeping the peace was what she truly cared about, and as far as she could tell, Ash Falls Timber helped keep that peace, one way or another. As long as she didn't have to take a bribe, she didn't care.

"It sounds to me like there's two working theories," Lydia said. "One is that, for some reason, all of these victims were killed because of some kind of relationship to Rowan Bale. The other is that a serial killer just happened to kill four people that worked for the lumber company and a fifth who was somehow involved. Either way, what we don't know at the moment is why they were killed, how they were killed, where they died, and, most importantly, who killed them."

McDonagh was still frowning at Lake, but he nodded to Lydia's statement. "That about sums it up," he said.

"What do we know, then?" Lake asked.

"When," McDonagh answered. "Based on time of death, it seems like each victim was killed every three days. If our killer holds to his pattern—"

"Then there'll be another murder tonight," Lydia finished.

"Then that's what you two need to be working on," Lake said. "I'll see if I can find anything in Ellwood's notes about why he was looking for Megan Rude at the docks and keep you updated. Anything else?"

Lydia didn't say anything. She waited for McDonagh to shake his head, then they both stood and left the office.

"Who did you talk to at the docks?" McDonagh asked.

"The foreman and two of Bosk's coworkers," Lydia said.

"We should talk to them again," McDonagh said. "If the pattern holds, one of them might be next."

"Want to go there now?" Lydia asked, stopping by her desk. The squad room was mostly empty now, just a couple of detectives eating lunch at their computers.

"I have a few CIs I want to talk to first," McDonagh said, checking the watch on his wrist. "The kind that only talk to me," he added, answering her question before she could ask it.

"Fine," she agreed. Confidential Informants could be tricky like that, Lydia knew, even if she didn't have any of her own. "I'll familiarize myself with the case then. Meet at the docks in an hour?"

"Let's do two."

Lydia was seated at her desk and beginning to read Sean Tanner's case file when McDonagh came back again. "You don't have my number," he asked, "do you?" He wrote it down on a piece of paper, then left before she could give him hers.

"Okay then," she said.

THREE

Ian was certain he had never been to this part of town, let alone heard of anyone named "Madame Rosa." How Kevin had picked this place, Ian would never know. The old man had simply shown up at Ian's apartment, woken him with a loud, insistent rap on the hardwood door. When Ian looked through the peephole, he saw Kevin in his usual leather jacket, his eyes bloodshot and nervous.

"It's today," Kevin said once Ian opened the door.

"How do you know?" Ian asked.

Kevin held something up in his hand, then tossed it to Ian. Ian missed. Whatever Kevin threw clattered to the ground, leaving a red mark where it bounced off Ian's shirt. Ian muttered an apology and crouched to pick it up.

"Emma showed up at my door with something similar the night she died," Kevin explained. "She found it in her home, came to me, we went into the woods, and you know the rest."

Ian touched the thing. It was soft, a patch of red fur tightened around a thin frame of bone, muscle, and claw. A paw, Ian thought, but of what he couldn't tell. He lifted it gingerly, eyeing the bloody stump where it had been severed. "So you brought it to me?" Ian asked, fear coming into his voice.

"Who else would I bring it to?" Kevin asked. "You're the only other one who knows what's going on."

"That's not true!" Ian protested. "I have no idea what's going on!" He threw the thing back at Kevin. It thumped against his chest, leaving a red mark on Kevin's white shirt too. "Why bring it to me?" Ian asked. "Why not bring it to the police?"

"The police are useless," Kevin said, waving a hand in a dismissive gesture. "And I came to you because I can't handle it myself. I've got a plan to kill this thing, but I need help. Your help."

"Why me?" Ian groaned. "I just want to be left out of it. This isn't the kind of thing I'm good at." He tried to shut the door in Kevin's face, but the old man stuck his foot between the door and the frame, his fingers curling around the top of the wood panel.

"You being left out is what got Emma killed in the first place," Kevin snarled. "The three of us could've taken it—that's why it didn't fight us at the docks. It's your fault she's dead. Now I've got to make do, and I'm making do with you."

"What if I say no?" Ian said, trying to push the door closed through Kevin's foot.

It was to no avail. Instead of giving way to the pressure, Kevin thrust open the door, advancing on Ian quickly. Despite his age, he was both stronger and faster than Ian. His hand gripped around Ian's throat and slammed him against the wall. Ian prayed his neighbors would hear, but knew this wall was between them and his bedroom. He doubted his neighbors would have done anything, anyways—there were always scuffles in the apartments of Ash Falls. Ian had ignored plenty during his time in the city.

"If you say no," Kevin hissed, his mouth next to Ian's ear, "I'll—I'll—"

And then he let go. Ian coughed, his back sliding down the wall a little. He looked up at Kevin, whose face was still locked in a snarl. "You'll what?" Ian asked, his voice weak. "You're a dead man, Kevin. So am I, probably, whether I come with you or not."

Kevin's hands curled into fists. For a moment, Ian was sure Kevin's anger would get the better of him, that Kevin was about to lay into him, turn Ian into a bloody pulp. Ian wouldn't have blamed him, honestly. Sometimes all that was left was to hurt someone, though it never actually changed anything. He closed his eyes, waiting for Kevin's fist.

But it never came. Eventually, he heard Kevin's breathing slow, then heard his feet move across the hardwood floors. Ian opened an eye.

"Call in," Kevin said.

"I've already used all of my sick time," Ian said after thinking a moment.

"Call in," Kevin said again. "At the very least just spend the day with me. I've got until nightfall and a few things to do in between. Call in."

Ian rubbed his chin, watching his co-worker. He still had to shave, so he'd be late anyways. And alone. Some kind of jobs are never worth working alone, and the dockyards was one such job.

So, he went with Kevin. While Ian dressed, he listened to Kevin pacing nervously in the kitchen, felt his blazing hot eyes as he cast them about the room. Kevin had a nervous energy that seemed to set the whole building buzzing. Too busy focusing on all that, Ian forgot his belt.

Kevin brought Ian far down into the city's southwest. They were definitely outside of the industrial district and well away from downtown. This was a suburb, a place where happy, well-to-do people made their home—at least the few left in Ash Falls. And in this suburb, down a small road off of 34th, was a small home with a small sign hanging out front. The sign was made of a stained brown wood and it read, "Madame Rosa: recently relocated. Walk-ins welcome." Next to the words was painted a small picture of a palm facing towards the reader, an eye placed directly in the center. Ian frowned, pausing outside the gate.

Kevin, who was already inside the garden, turned to look at him. "What's the matter?" he asked.

"How'd you hear about this place?" Ian asked.

Kevin shrugged. "Why does that matter?"

"It matters because I don't want to be seen walking into some whorehouse," Ian replied. "I've still got a girl in Medford, remember?"

Kevin rolled his eyes, turning away from Ian and heading up the stairs. "Right," he called back, "and my promdate is still waiting for me all the way down the Five."

"What the hell's that supposed to mean?" Ian asked, following through the gate. He let it slam shut behind him.

"It means that's a weird thing to be bringing up now," Kevin said, "especially since you never bring up… Annie, right? And don't let Madame Rosa hear you talking like that, she probably won't like it too much." He stopped in front of the door. Ian caught up to him, pulling his pants up as best he could, bitter because he was sure Kevin had remembered Fannie's name wrong on purpose. When Ian was on the porch too, Kevin turned and knocked at the door.

"There's a lot that's weird right now," Ian muttered under his breath.

"It'll only get weirder before it gets better," Kevin said matter-of-factly.

"If it gets better."

Kevin knocked again.

"It says, 'Walk-ins welcome,'" called a voice from the other side of the door. "That means you don't have to knock."

Funny thing, Ian reflected. No one in Ash Falls ever actually said things like, "Come in." He remembered having to get used to it when he moved here. "They don't want to let a vampire in on accident," Kevin had explained sagely, prompting a chittery laugh from Emma.

Kevin tried the handle. It only turned a hair's breadth, and Kevin gave a grunt as he tried turning it harder. Nothing. He jiggled the handle a little, then called back, "Then unlock the damn thing!"

There was a flurry of curses shot back at him from the other side, accompanied by some shuffling and bumping. Eventually, the curtain across the door's window fluttered a little, a young face poking out from behind it. Kevin waved and Ian did his best to appear unthreatening. The face scowled at them, then they heard a chain being drawn and a bolt flipped. The door swung open on creaky hinges to reveal a young woman in a simple dress with a book in her hand.

"Sorry," she said. "Must have locked it behind the last customer."

"Right," Kevin said, stepping in as the woman turned away. "Is she busy then?"

"She is," the woman confirmed, stepping behind a small desk with a computer on it. "But she shouldn't be long. They've been in there about half an hour, so I'm sure she'll be out soon. Will you be wanting separate readings?"

"We each want one," Kevin said, "but we'd prefer to do it at the same time."

"That's okay," Ian tried to say, shutting the door behind him. "Just one will be fine."

"It's my treat," Kevin said.

"Two readings," the woman said, marking it down before Ian had a chance to protest again. "She won't like doing it at the same time, but if you're in a hurry we can always make exceptions."

"No hurry," Kevin assured her, "we just would prefer to do it together."

The woman, who Ian decided was some kind of secretary, nodded, watching them out the corner of her eye. "You know," she said, suddenly careful, "when couples get a reading, it's usually best to do it separately. That way there's no… surprises."

Ian and Kevin looked at each other. Kevin, ever unpredictable, only shook his head and sat down on one of the sofas. Ian gave the secretary a little smile and said, "That won't be a problem."

"Right," the secretary said again, an eyebrow raised. "Well, if you have a seat, she'll be with you shortly."

She sat at the desk, her gaze immediately drawn to the computer. The room had three small couches, each covered with a garish floral print. The walls were mostly a bare white, one painting of an ankh hanging on the wall opposite the door. If it weren't for the white wallpaper all over the room, Ian would have started to feel hemmed in, everything a little too close together. Even with the room as it was, with curtains drawn across all the windows, Ian was a little nervous, the hairs on his arms and back of his neck standing on end. He took a seat on a different couch from Kevin, still glancing around the room. While he sunk into the cushions, his eyes fell on the door. The bolt lock was thrown again, and the chain secured across it. He frowned. *Did I do that?* he wondered.

The room was uncomfortably silent. Kevin shifted a little in his seat, the chair's legs making strange squeaks as he twirled his thumbs. Occasionally, the secretary would type something into the computer, her nails clacking against the keys. Ian thought it was obnoxious. To pass the time, and to take his mind off the strange noises of a silent room, he recited a poem in his head that he had memorized in high school.

> *Then they showed him the shield*
> *That was of bright red*

Click clack clack went the secretary's nails.

> *With the pentangle displayed*
> *And in pure golden arrayed*

Kevin coughed—a loud, hacking cough like he was expelling some demon from his lungs. Eventually he hawked something into his hands, then wiped it on the sofa.

> *For of faithful in five virtues and points five since,*
> *The man's golden deeds were known.*

Suddenly, a man started crying. The sound came from somewhere in the house, a breathy, noisy sob that was slowly getting louder. Ian caught Kevin's eye and raised his brow, but Kevin only shook his head, making a brief sign of the cross over himself. The sobbing had turned into a quiet blubbering, strange and unfamiliar words tumbling over each other. Frowning, Ian tried to understand them, but they were foreign and strange to him, unintelligible.

"Ma-tha," it sounded like. "Lee-ma-tha, ha-bee-bee."

One of the doors to the house opened and a man came through, his head in his hands, wet seeping through his fingers. A woman followed, rubbing his shoulders while also firmly pushing him. "There, there, Mr. Alami, I know, I know. Sandra here will settle you up. I'm afraid I need to see my three o'clock now."

"Kelba!" he shouted, still crying. "Ta-kha-thib, kelba."

"Now now, there's no need for that," the lady said. She smiled brightly at Ian. "Please, do come in," she said, "I'll be just a moment." Both Ian and Kevin stood, and the woman frowned. "Uh, whichever was first."

"Lee-ma-tha," the man sobbed, apparently beginning to crumble. He almost fell into Sandra's arms, but she stepped back with a distasteful scowl.

"We were hoping to be seen together, actually," Kevin explained.

"La-la-la," the man screamed, curling up into a ball on the floor.

The woman seemed relieved. She no longer helped the man, stepping over him to approach Kevin. "Excellent," she said, smiling broadly. "I could use something happy. Good of you two to consult me before you seal the deal, don't want to end up like Mr. Alami here," and she jerked her head at the floor.

"Ta-kha-thib," the man moaned pitifully.

"Yes, yes, that's quite enough," the woman said irritably. "Sandra," she snapped, "do something for him, will you?" Back to Ian and Kevin, all smiles. "Right this way, gentlemen."

"What the hell do you want me to do?" Sandra asked, her voice high-pitched and a little screechy.

Kevin began moving toward the hallway. "Keeeeeeeeeeelllllllll," the man yowled from the floor, "baaaaaaaaaa!" The cry slowly subsided into sobs, his shoulders heaving in great gasping breaths. Ian awkwardly stepped over him.

"Just to the end of the hall," the woman said brightly. Then, in a far more sour tone. "I don't know, give him some tea or something. Just get him out of here."

The hallway was dark, strangely muffled. The farther Ian walked in, following the vague outline of Kevin, the quieter Mr. Alami's sobs became behind him. The woman tutted. "Don't ask questions if you're not prepared for the answers," she said, "it's the first rule of love." Neither Ian nor Kevin laughed.

They reached a room behind a wall of blue beads. They felt oily and misshapen as Ian pushed through them, and though they were hard he noticed they made no noise while clattering against each other. The room beyond was a modest space, cramped shelves lining the walls filled with memorabilia too dark for Ian to distinguish. A large table filled the center, bare and wooden, wax caked in various places, though not enough to cover the scratches and burns that marked the surface. Four candles lit at the center were all that illuminated the room, while several rickety looking stools were placed haphazardly around the table. On the far side of the door stood a sumptuous looking red armchair Ian did not notice until the woman sank into it with a sigh.

"That's better," she smiled. "Much less of a headache. You both know who I am?"

Kevin nodded, already on his stool. "Not really," Ian said. He had not moved from the doorway, was still looking around at the shelves. The candlelight reflected only off of black metal, black leather, black beak, black bone, and black feather.

"I see," the woman said, no hint of annoyance in her voice. "A newcomer. Well then, I am Madame Rosa, fortune-teller extraordinaire."

"Yeah, that I got from the signs," Ian said, "but I don't know anything else about you. Like, what kind of fraud are you?"

Kevin leaned forward. "Please forgive him, Madame Rosa," he said. "You're correct, he's new to all this. He hasn't learned how to find jewels amongst the plastic."

Ian couldn't understand Kevin sometimes. All day, he had been irritable and snarky, demeaning Ian at every opportunity. But for this lady, he was suddenly the most modest, quietest little church mouse that ever existed. Reverent was what he was.

Does he actually believe this? Ian wondered.

Madame Rosa shrugged nonchalantly. "It's not uncommon for me to get doubters. Doubt, itself, can be a very noble trait, in my opinion. So long as ignorance doesn't lie beneath it."

"What did you tell him out there?" Ian asked, jerking his head down the hall. A thin, pitiful wail still made its way to them. "Or in here, I guess. What did you tell him here that made him like that out there?"

She shook her head, tutting. "That is not for me to reveal," she said. "I have no right. His secrets are his own, even if I'm the one who shows them to him." She leaned forward, smirking conspiratorially. "That's my promise to all my customers."

Ian scoffed. "Sounds like an easy way to pull the wool over our eyes," he said.

"That may be true," she said, laughing. "That may be very true. I can tell you that he, like yourself, had a lot of doubt. But underneath his doubt lay the ignorance of fear. He had much fear, and so he buried it in ignorance. Is that what is underneath yours? Fear of what you cannot know? Or fear of what you do?"

Ian did not respond, only making a small noise in the back of his throat, kicking at the floor. Kevin shifted on his stool, a flush of pain crossing his lined face. Madame Rosa stayed motionless, her eyes watchful.

"Maybe," she said, leaning forward, her fingers steepling before her, "maybe it will help if I demonstrate on someone without any doubt." Her eyes flicked to Kevin. "Do you have something on your mind?"

Kevin gulped. "Yes," he said.

Madame Rosa squinted at him. "I was wrong, wasn't I? This is not a matter of love."

"Yes," Kevin said again.

Intrigued, though still conscious of how stupid all this felt, Ian sat.

"What service will you be wanting me to perform today?" Madame Rosa asked.

Kevin shrugged. "I've only got twenty bucks on me," he said.

"I'll tell you what," Madame Rosa said, reaching to somewhere below the table and producing a stack of cards, "since you're bringing me a new customer, I'll perform two tarot readings for you. But," and she flashed a smile at Ian, "you have to promise to come back."

Kevin said nothing. Ian said nothing. They didn't even look at each other. If this made Madame Rosa nervous, she didn't show it.

"Well," she said, "let's just see what comes up."

She babbled while she shuffled the cards, no longer asking anything. Ian could barely follow her hands as she moved the old beat-up deck through them, listened instead to the soft thrush of the cards flipping past her fingers. "We'll start simple for you, sir," she said, bringing the deck back fully together. "Past," one card facedown, "present," another facedown, and "future," a third.

Ian glanced at Kevin. The old man hadn't moved since Rosa took out the deck, his face lined and creased in a deep frown.

"A good one," Madame Rosa said as she flipped the first card. A man stood in a field, resting on a hoe. In a pile before him were seven golden circles, small stars inlaid on the surface.

Madame Rosa let out an audible gasp when she flipped the second—not a fake kind of gasp, the kind a performer might use to let the audience know something important had happened—a real gasp. The card showed a building on fire atop a cold mountain, lightning striking its roof as a man and woman jumped from it. Ian looked up to see Kevin's face was beaded in sweat. Madame Rosa said nothing.

The third had a white horse, a man in black armor sitting atop it, his face a skull. This at least wasn't hard for Ian to recognize—Death.

"Oh, dear," said Madame Rosa.

Four

It took Lydia some time to realize she had parked under the same tree Ellwood's car had been. She hadn't meant to—it was just a spot in the shade, after all. Still, the coincidence struck her.

Unusually, McDonagh was the first to arrive. Lydia saw him waiting towards the front of the dockyard, his perennial cup of coffee in his hand. He waved to her as she parked, but Lydia still took her time getting out. It felt good, keeping him waiting for once.

When she was finally within earshot, she called out, "Small line?"

"It was one of the few times I felt compelled to say I had important police business," McDonagh replied. "Everyone let me cut ahead."

Before she could wonder if he was serious, McDonagh turned toward the dockyard. It seemed unusually quiet and less crowded. The few workers there moved quickly, barely sparing them a moment's glance.

McDonagh leaned towards Lydia's ear. "Do you see anyone you talked to last time?" he asked.

She didn't know, but she felt Wood and Caldwell weren't there. Warehouse six was dark, the area around it motionless. Still, she looked at the face of each person hurrying around them. Maybe responsibilities shifted on the docks more often than she realized.

"Well?" McDonagh asked, insistent.

Lydia bit her lip. "Give me a second," she said. She scanned more faces, recognizing most of them. She had mentally marked them while doing her interview. At the very least, no one new was working.

"Did you forget what they look like or something?" McDonagh asked.

Lydia was about to snap at him when she saw a round, jowly face, rolled up plaid sleeves, and an unnecessary hard hat. Foreman Shaft was glancing at something on his clipboard, flipping back and forth between two pages. Every minute or so, he barked out an order that seemed to have no effect on what was happening around him.

"That guy," she said, walking forward.

The foreman did not seem happy to see her. In fact, once he looked up from his clipboard and saw Lydia standing in front of him, he let out an exasperated groan that felt a little excessive.

"Look," he said, "today is probably the worst of all possible days."

"Why's that?" Lydia asked politely. She felt her partner step up beside her, his looming presence drawing the foreman's gaze.

"Well," Shaft said, his eyes widening a little, "not only is Bosk not showing up, but Wood and Caldwell both called in too. That's an entire warehouse crew, which means everyone else has to pick up the slack. Not to mention they left warehouse six a mess, so there's no chance we're working out of there today. Which means," he started to step away, "I'm busy."

Lydia opened her mouth, but McDonagh was faster. With two simple steps, he positioned himself so that he was in the foreman's way, his chest puffed out but his hands in his pockets. Shaft barely had enough time to notice the movement, narrowly avoiding a collision with McDonagh's bigger frame. A snarl was written onto her partner's face, and it made Shaft shrink away, both hands clutching his clipboard.

"We just have a few questions," McDonagh said, his voice quiet.

Lydia remembered how insistent Shaft had been on he and his employees not having to answer questions. She was sure, even a little worried, that Shaft would stand up for himself now. It was such a clear misstep to Lydia that she was already preparing to cuss McDonagh out. But, to her surprise, the foreman only nodded his head, a polite "okay" escaping his lips.

"Good," McDonagh said, smiling wickedly. "First," he said, "what kind of mess did they leave?"

The foreman gulped, glancing back towards Lydia. She kept her expression blank, her arms crossed expectantly.

"They just left crates laying around," he said. "There's no order, so naturally we don't know where to find anything. Not that anyone's come to pick up anything from there anyways, but still."

"Would we be able to take a look?" McDonagh asked.

Shaft nervously shook his head. "You can't look at the crates or what's in them," he said, "not without a court order."

"You've been awfully trigger happy about wanting a court order," McDonagh said. He jerked his head towards Lydia. "Isn't that right, Detective Pike?"

Lydia considered not answering for a moment. Even started to grit her teeth rather than say anything. But at the last moment, McDonagh's eyes cut to her, sharp but clear. "That's right," Lydia said. "Why is that, Shaft?"

"I know my rights," the foreman stuttered. "I know our clients' rights. You can't just look at whatever you want, you need to have a probable cause, and you need to run it by a judge first."

"Right," McDonagh said, nodding thoughtfully. He crossed his arms, his eyes now back on Shaft. "How about this," he said. "How about you just tell me what's getting smuggled through warehouse six. Just so we know what kind of crap those three were into."

Lydia felt a pang of shock cross her face at the same moment she felt goosebumps rise on the back of her neck. The shock, she knew, was from how suddenly McDonagh had taken them out of standard procedure into the realm of the unlawful. If they found a smuggling operation, they'd be required to report it. She didn't know why the goosebumps appeared, except that it was the same feeling she got when she knew she was being watched. The dockyard, she realized, had gotten unusually still.

"I never," Foreman Shaft blustered. "I can't believe you would even ask such a thing, that's utterly preposterous, I —"

"What harm could it do?" McDonagh asked, putting his head closer to Shaft's. "It'll be our little secret."

The entire dock was definitely watching them.

"There was nothing through warehouse six," Shaft said, finding at last a backbone to rest on. "Nor through any of my warehouses. That's not the kind of dock I run."

"Why can't you tell me?" McDonagh asked. "Do I really look like Special Investigations to you? Does she?" He jerked his head to Lydia, who remained motionless.

"That's not the point," Shaft, puffing himself up. "The point is, nothing illegal goes on here, at least not to my knowledge. If you think Bosk, Caldwell, or Wood know anything, you'll have to ask them."

"Well, we'd certainly like to," McDonagh said.

"Find them yourself then," Shaft said, starting to turn away.

"We did," McDonagh replied. "Or, we found Bosk at least."

This made the foreman pause. Before he could ask the question, Lydia, sensing her moment, answered it. "She's dead."

"Goddamn," Shaft said, taking off his helmet.

"We're investigating both murders as related," Lydia added. McDonagh shot her a glance, but she ignored it.

"Emma's and the detective's?" Shaft asked, meeting her gaze. "Why?"

"We can't answer that," McDonagh said.

Shaft turned to him. Lydia watched the moment that passed between then, the questioning look in Shaft's eyes, the cold emptiness in McDonagh's. She watched Shaft look down, nodding. "What can I do?" he asked.

"Tell us what was going through that warehouse," McDonagh said, again before Lydia could say anything.

The foreman shook his head. "I really don't know," he said.

McDonagh pursed his lips. "Alright," he said, "I believe you."

Lydia felt the dockyards moving again, felt the weight taken off her shoulders. "Then let us at least look around in there," she said.

Shaft seemed to think for a moment. Then, he shrugged. "I guess I can't see why not," he said. "Go ahead."

McDonagh had already started striding away. Lydia waited a moment longer, gently putting a hand on the foreman's shoulder. He looked up, a clear note of surprise in his face. "Where are Caldwell and Wood?" she asked.

"I don't know," Shaft answered. "They both called in sick today."

"Both?" Lydia asked.

"Yeah," the foreman nodded. "Didn't sound very sick though, if you ask me."

Lydia nodded again. "Alright," she said. "Thanks again." She gave Shaft her card before following her partner.

"Look at this," McDonagh said when Lydia caught up with him. He had already gotten to the warehouse and was pointing to the side of one of the crates, where something was written.

"Falls' Brewing Company," Lydia read, bending closer. "Does Rowan Bale have anything to do with them?"

"I think he owns stock," McDonagh said. He was already moving through the crates, all left unorganized, corners sticking out at weird angles. "He owns stock in a lot of these companies," he added.

Lydia crossed her arms, not moving from where she stood. "So tell me something," she said.

McDonagh's head stuck out from behind a crate. "Yeah?" he asked.

"What was that back there?"

McDonagh blinked. "I have no idea what you mean," he said.

"Right," Lydia said. "I couldn't get a peep out of him three days ago. How did you know the whole intimidation routine wouldn't get us kicked out of here faster than a body sinks in the river?"

McDonagh placed a finger on the side of his nose. "You can smell it," he said, "if you have the nose."

Lydia raised an eyebrow. "And how do you get the right nose?" she asked.

"Practice," McDonagh said, his head disappearing behind the crate again. "Lots and lots of practice." Lydia heard him walking farther away from her, deeper into the warehouse.

"What you'd get from your CIs?" Lydia asked.

"Nothing. I wonder what's inside these," McDonagh said.

"Do you think it matters?" Lydia asked. "We need a court order, anyways."

"Not unless we find something," McDonagh called. "Won't know 'til we look."

Lydia thought she heard a snick, felt McDonagh getting farther away from her. "Be careful," she warned, starting to move into the crates. "If Shaft sees you, he'll have us both out of here in no time."

"He'll try," McDonagh said. Lydia glanced out of the front of the warehouse again, didn't see anyone coming towards them. Then, without much more noise, McDonagh called out, "Pike, come look at this!"

Checking again to make sure the foreman wasn't looking towards them, Lydia stole deeper into the crates. "That was fast," she commented, finding McDonagh. He held his flashlight, shined the glow over a large break in the crates, wide enough for seven people to stand shoulder to shoulder.

"Nah," McDonagh said. Lydia froze. The illuminated concrete was covered by a thin, brown powder, spread out in a circle almost ten feet wide. Lydia had seen enough old crime scenes to recognize the substance.

Blood. Dried blood, and a lot of it.

"Looks like a murder scene, doesn't it?" McDonagh said.

FIVE

Ian's feet hurt. The tank of gasoline was heavy, and it was hard to hold the damn thing while also holding up his pants.

Reversed four of cups.

His legs hurt too, and his back.

Upright six of swords.

Even though it was night, Ian still felt hot and dusty, like a sock left outside for too long.

The Tower.

Ian hated hiking.

Kevin was ahead of him, barely visible. The old codger was still wearing his dark leather jacket, which disappeared easily into the shadows of the trail. If it wasn't for Kevin's shock of white hair, Ian would have completely lost him. Not that Ian would have minded. The trail was easy enough to follow back to town.

Not for the first time, Ian asked himself why he had come. Madame Rosa said the future was never certain, that the cards might hold many meanings. Maybe this was only Kevin's windmill, and Ian was Sancho Panza. Maybe if he backed out now, he'd be safe. After all, Kevin had come with Emma, had gone with her on her way to certain doom. Surely it was madness for Ian to go along now that Kevin was cursed with that same doom. Surely it would only be passed on to him.

But no, he reminded himself, that's not how this worked. He wasn't sure how it did work, nor how anything really worked anymore. But escaping this was as unlikely as him ever escaping Ash Falls. As unlikely as the river freezing.

At the top of the first ridge, Kevin stopped. He turned, waiting for Ian to join him. Ian struggled up the last few feet, the gasoline can scraping along in the dirt. Kevin let him catch his breath, then pointed the way they had come.

Ash Falls was laid out before them, a grid of lights and streets like a blanket of stars before their feet. The trail they had followed descended far below them, a strangely bright line through the trees. Ian hitched up his pants.

"Here," Kevin said. "We'll end here. If the bastard is still chasing us this far, we'll light the gas and take off down this hill. Keep your feet and he'll have no chance at catching us."

"The heroes always trip," Ian said.

"What?"

"In horror movies," Ian explained. "The heroes always trip while the monster is chasing them. Every time."

"Well, we're not in a horror movie," Kevin said. "Don't trip and you'll make it."

Ian certainly felt like he was in a horror movie. Everything up until this point had seemed like a bad dream to him. But, on the plus side, if things kept going the way they were, Ian didn't have to worry about himself tonight.

"Come on," Kevin said. "You carried, so I'll dig. Then I can carry the gas a ways and you'll dig."

Ian shrugged. He couldn't say no to a rest. "It's your plan," he said. "You make the decisions."

Kevin had brought a foldable spade that he picked up in an army surplus store. With it, he dug two small foot wide and foot deep holes, one on either side of the trail. Once he finished, Ian filled both, then sprinkled the trail between the holes with gas.

Kevin added twigs to this, the ends sticking out of the holes. The twigs would take a moment to burn, but the real goal was to light the dried pine needles. These hills were covered in a blanket of these resin filled incendiaries. Ian knew, like everyone in wildfire country, that once you get the needles burning the blaze would rip through the woods, almost impossible to stop.

They were putting Ash Falls in danger, sure, but some things had to be risked. What they were trying to kill was much worse than a few buildings burning down. And, as Kevin pointed out, not much could survive being set on fire.

They made three more similar stops, spaced about half a mile apart. A relatively short distance, though neither were particularly strong runners. To Ian's mind, the plan seemed to place a great reliance on fear. It would be fear that spurred them on, fear that made them light the fires, fear that carried them down the hills and back to the city. This didn't worry Ian. He already knew he'd be scared shitless.

At the last stop, Kevin threw the empty can off into the woods, small drops of gas arcing after it, glittering with moonlight. "Won't need that anymore," Kevin muttered.

Ian watched Kevin reach to his hip, watched him take some dark object from his belt, heard the grind of metal sliding across metal, the snap of a spring unloading. "What's that?" Ian asked warily.

"Gun," Kevin said.

"Where'd you get it?"

"Bought it."

"Think it'll do anything?"

Kevin shrugged. "Didn't do anything for Emma, but what the hell."

"Do I not get a weapon?" Ian asked.

"Should have brought one," Kevin said. "Here." He tossed something bright and small into Ian's hands. "You get to light the fires," Kevin said. From the feel of it, Ian could tell the object was Kevin's Zippo lighter.

They set off again, moving slower now, even though they had less to carry. Ian paused every few feet to hike his jeans back up his waist. When they couldn't smell gasoline anymore, Kevin inhaled a deep, steadying breath. "Wish I had brought a cigarette," he said.

"Why didn't you?" Ian asked.

"Oh, you know," Kevin said. "Smokey the Bear and all that. Just ingrained to be careful about the woods."

Ian felt his mouth hang open a little. "You were concerned about starting a fire?" he asked. "Tonight?"

Kevin stopped, turning back to Ian. Then they both burst into peals of laughter, the sound unnaturally loud in the forest. Something ran in fright from the sudden noise, and they immediately cut their voices, nervously glancing around. Ian felt rather than saw Kevin's gun, felt the old man pointing it out into the darkness, heard a metallic click as he pushed the safety off. Nothing happened. Slowly, Ian's shoulders slackened, the tension easing out of him. He pulled up his pants a little.

"Let's stop here," Kevin said. "It's as good a spot as any."

"Why's that?" a voice asked to their left, strange and foreign.

There was only a shadow. A great, looming shadow, a shadow that didn't quite fit with the trees but seemed to be of them. A shadow that made Ian's heart boil and his blood freeze, made his skin stand on end and his hair crawl. And in the shadow's hand, the finely sharpened edge of a huge and awful blade caught the errant stars.

"Glrayagh," choked out of Kevin's gawping mouth, and the gun went off.

Ian did not wait. Down the path he ran—shot—flew— away from that thing as fast as he could. He was faster than he'd ever been, faster than he'd ever be, faster than it was possible for him to go. He ran, spurred on by a fear older than the trees, more primordial than the mountain.

There was another shot behind him. Just in time, Ian remembered the gas, remembered the cool metal in his hands, remembered his missing belt. His pants were practically around his knees by now, so they made him stumble and fall to a grinding stop along the path.

Just to his right, he could see a shimmer of liquid and smell the fumes. He flicked at Kevin's Zippo. It didn't light. He flicked again. It didn't light. A third shot rang out from behind him. Ian flicked again. A small flame burst into life, suspended in air just before Ian's eyes. He waved it close to the ground, pine needles turning to small tendrils in its wake.

And then, a spark flew into the puddle, which erupted, flames engulfing Ian's hand, burning twigs flying through the air. Ian clamped his hand under his elbow, dousing the flames, then tried to stand, grabbing at his pants and pulling them up again. But the needles were already taking, fire already spreading over the carpet in a rush. Ian was almost surrounded.

A hand gripped Ian by the scruff of his neck. Kevin grunted in his ear, throwing Ian farther down the trail. "Run!" Kevin roared, firing behind them, and Ian was off again, his feet thudding and his heart pumping. The fire raced alongside him, licking his shins and cackling in fury.

Run, Ian told himself. *Run. Run!*

He was not sure where the next half mile was, where he had to get to. All he could think about was keeping his pants up, about the thing behind them, about the air pressing on him so hot he was sure his clothes would catch flame. There was nothing but orange fire around him, hot and angry, the only gap in it the path forward. Ahead, he saw two pillars of flame, an explosive gate beckoning him forward.

The gas, he realized. The gas was already alight.

He wouldn't make it. The flames bit at his hands and cheeks. His lungs filled with ash and smoke. His eyes watered and his tears boiled, and Ian's world was becoming dark. Then he was through the flames, bursting into cool, clean air.

Oh thank God, Ian thought.

His foot caught on a root and Ian was flung face forward into the dirt, his flame-brittle skin cracking against the ground.

He scrabbled, trying to find a purchase. "No," he growled, pushing himself into the air. There was a nudge against him, and Ian flung himself widely around, a snarl on his lips. But it was only Kevin, his back to Ian, firing two more shots.

The flames were slower, unable to climb up the hill as easily, giving the pair enough time to try and see through the wall of light into the darkness beyond. It was impossible.

"Where is he?" Ian shouted.

"I don't know," Kevin shouted back.

Nothing for a moment, only the slight creep of the flames towards them.

"I think he's gone," Kevin said.

A foot emerged through the fire, then an ankle, then a calf, and soon a whole leg. More came with it—he could see the whole body behind, face gleaming in the fire's orange glow. All of him unburnt, all of him green. Ian turned and fled.

Three more shots rang out behind him. Three shots and a scream. Ian kept going, refusing to turn back, one hand clutching the lighter, the other clutching where his belt should have been. The fire was behind him now, slow and distant. But the night was not quiet. The fire had already spurred the birds and the beasts, already begun a clamoring exodus. The animals ran beside him, around him. Ian was one of many, escaping the calamity he created.

He sensed rather than knew he was reaching the second to last trap. He slowed a little, trying to look for it on the ground. Something brushed past his knee, another barely missed his head, but he ignored them. He heard a splash ahead, and he sprinted to the noise. He hoped whatever had fallen in was out already, but he didn't have time to check. He crouched just beyond the small puddle, bent low, the lighter ready in his hands. Something four-legged bounded over him, the tip of a hoof barely rustling his hair.

"Kevin!" Ian shouted.

Nothing.

"Damnit," Ian said. He lit the Zippo on the first strike this time and dropped it into the needles. He didn't care about lighting the last set of puddles, just wanted to get out of that forest, get home before that thing found him. He didn't let the fire surround him this time, stood and turned to run while the gas burst alight.

He made it a hundred feet before colliding with something. Whatever he ran into was solid and heavy as a rock, yet still had the slight give of skin, the compression of blood. But that was not nearly enough give for Ian, and the sudden appearance of the thing sprawled him onto his back.

The fire spread around them, but never came close. A small, perfectly even circle, centered on Ian. And on Him.

Ian looked up, meeting the cold eyes made red by fire.

"I have a challenge for you."

END of Episode Two

EPISODE THREE: CROSS

AXE-AMINATION

ONE

At around 2 a.m., word came about a forest fire south of Ash Falls. Thomas was asleep in the front seat of his car under a tree near the docks. Detective Pike sat in the seat beside him, intently watching their suspected murder scene. She woke him up as dispatch relayed the information through the radio. The police wouldn't have to do anything, they both knew. Not yet. But a fire so close to the city meant only one thing—evacuation. And while the firefighters were in charge of delaying the flames as much as they could, the police would have to get everyone out of the city. So, knowing how much work would have to be done the next day, they called it a night.

Thomas dropped Pike off at the precinct, then went back to his one room apartment near 39th. After two hours of sleep, he showered, ate a piece of toast, and drove straight to the station, ignoring his desire for coffee. Pike was already there, chewing a nail at the windows. The hills to the south glowed an angry orange.

"You even go home last night?" Thomas asked, removing his jacket and hanging it on his chair.

Pike nodded. "I swung by the docks on my way here. Nothing. No sign of anything."

"You went alone?" Thomas asked.

Pike didn't look at him. "Something must have happened there," she said. "We should go back, investigate it as a crime scene."

"Why did you go alone?" Thomas asked.

Pike glanced at him, eyebrow raised. "Just in case, I guess. Why do you care?"

Because you're still new to this, Thomas thought. "It might have been dangerous," he said.

Pike raised her chin. "I can handle myself."

"I have no doubt," Thomas replied. He had not meant it sarcastically, but that's how it came out. He saw Pike's mouth become a flat line, saw the way she crossed her arms and set her shoulders. He tried thinking of something to say, to tell her he believed in her, that he just wasn't ready to lose another colleague. But no matter how he phrased it, he couldn't see how to make it right. So, he let it alone. He went to his desk, opened the newspaper, and tried to not look at her.

Slowly, the squad room came to life around them. Officers came in off the night watch, detectives showed up for the day already grumbling about the morning briefing. Everyone was talking about the fire, rumors already spreading. Even the AFPD was not immune to gossip, especially when it was something they didn't understand. "Firefighters from Montana are being mobilized." "They've called up the reserves." "The fire department is doing nothing, we're all doomed." "They'll start the evac any second now." "Everything's fine, the fire has moved off already." No one knew anything, everyone knew something. In the midst of it all, Detective Pike stood at the window and Thomas flipped through the paper.

Eventually, Lieutenant Lake came up the stairs. A hush fell over the squad room. Lake didn't acknowledge anyone while he crossed the bullpen, hung up his jacket in Ellwood's old office, filled a mug with coffee, and walked back in to the still silent squad room. "Briefing, ten minutes," he said. Then he disappeared into his office and a low hum returned to the officers.

The sides of Thomas's lips twitched outward, somewhere between a grimace and a grin. Reluctantly, he folded up his newspaper and joined Pike at the window again. He felt a slight bristle at his approach, or maybe he imagined it. Either way, Pike didn't move.

"The trail is cold," he said.

"You can't be serious," Pike replied. "After what we found? Even if nothing happened there last night, don't we have a pair of suspects now?"

Thomas shrugged. "It's still nothing concrete," he said. "And suspects aren't much good if you can't find them."

"What's your point then?" Pike asked.

Thomas curled his hand into a fist as he thought about how to answer. There was a commotion at the front of the station, but Thomas ignored it. There were always commotions in the precinct's lobby—homeless wandered in, mothers came looking for missing children, winos tried to get released through the miasma of their hangovers.

"Maybe you're right," Thomas began, "maybe Wood and Caldwell did murder all the rest. Maybe Bosk got cold feet, which was why they killed her too. Maybe they even did kill someone last night. Or you're wrong, but they both know something anyways and have skipped town. Either way, there isn't much we can do. Nobody's going to find a body today, or tomorrow. Everyone will be too busy packing or calling families, trying to find a hotel in Eugene or Salem. And there's no point in going after Caldwell or Wood.

Finding them in the city was already a needle in a haystack. Who knows where they'll go."

Pike's jaw was firm, her arms tightly crossed. She no longer stared out the window, but straight at Thomas, her eyes cold. "You still haven't gotten to the point," Pike said.

The commotion in the lobby was getting louder, enough to draw Thomas's attention. It seemed like someone was yelling. Something like, "I need... I need..." but Thomas couldn't tell what else.

"It's going to be all hands on deck for this evacuation," he explained. "Commander's going to pull us, is my point."

The commotion sounded like it had turned into a full-blown fight. Two patrol officers ran out of the squad room, going to see what was happening. Pike didn't answer at first, distracted by the noise.

"And you're okay with that?" she eventually asked, facing Thomas again. "This case you've been working on for nearly a week, just done?"

Thomas nodded to the south hills. Even now, with the sun fully risen and the sky a vibrant blue, the horizon there was a dull orange, great plumes of black smoke rising. At any moment, the wind would shift, blowing that cloud of ash over the city and bringing the flames with it. "Priorities shift," Thomas said.

The commotion, while no longer a fight, was still getting louder. Or, rather, closer. Clearer. "I need bike... I need spike... I need..."

Thomas's eyes widened at the same moment Lydia looked back at him. "Pike! I need to see Detective Pike!"

Pike spun on her heel, looking down the hall towards the lobby. Two officers were dragging a disheveled looking man, his wrists cuffed together, still trying to wriggle out of their hold. He was thin and lanky, almost unhealthy, with a pale grimy face and beady green eyes. A strong smell came with him, like woodsmoke and dirt. "Who the hell is that?" Thomas asked.

"Ian Caldwell," Pike replied after a moment.

At the sight of Pike, the man gave up his struggle and let himself be dragged, feet sliding across the floor. "Detective!" he shouted. "Detective, I need to speak to you!"

"Jesus," Pike muttered.

"He assaulted Crowe," one of the officers called out. "We're going to book him for that. Says he wants to speak with a Detective Lydia Pike," he added unnecessarily.

There was a brief silence as all eyes in the room turned to Pike, still standing at the window. She was squinting, her gaze somewhere between accusatory and inquisitive. She did not appear to notice everyone staring.

Thomas cleared his throat. "Put him in a holding cell," he ordered. "Read him his rights and clean him up. We'll talk to him soon."

Pike didn't react to Thomas, but Caldwell began to struggle as they led him away again. "No!" he screamed. "No! Detective, I need to talk to you now! It can't wait." Thomas had almost lost interest when Caldwell added, "I have information! About Emma! And Detective Elbow, or whatever his name was."

Thomas's ears perked up. *Information?* he thought. *What information? Is he turning on Wood?*

He looked over at Pike who, to his surprise, was smiling. Caldwell's cries quieted as the officers dragged him farther away, out of sight and earshot. "What is it?" Thomas asked.

"Trail isn't cold now," she said.

Two

Ash Falls Police Department - 911 Transcript

Date: 08/11/2017   *Time:* 0030 hrs.

Begin Transcript:

    911: 911, what's your emergency?

    Caller: Fire! There's a (inaudible)

    911: Sir, please remain calm. What's your address?

    Caller: What?

    911: Your address, sir, what's your address?

    Caller: I'm not at an address!

    911: Sir, I need you to remain calm. What's your location?

    Caller: The forest, the state forest!

    911: The forest is on fire?

    Caller: Yes!

    911: I'll dispatch the fire department, sir, please stay on the line until—

    (Call disconnected)

THREE

Ian Caldwell shivered, illuminated only by the cold light of a neon ceiling lamp. Lydia could tell his hair was still wet, but she thought it might be fear that bothered him. She could see it in his eyes, wide and panicky, darting between the observation mirror and the room's only door. The orange jumpsuit, Lydia knew, was uncomfortable, the shoes apt to slip off his heels, the undershirt itchy from being starched again and again and again. To clean him, they had sprayed him with cold water, and the precinct's air-conditioning was always blasting in the summer. But this was Caldwell's fault, Lydia told herself, because Caldwell had turned himself in. So, she tried not to pity him. If he was afraid, it was because he knew he had done something wrong.

Due to the proximity of the Umpqua Wilderness Fire, AFFD had set the evacuation status to two, high alert. Evacuation recommended. When it dropped to one, evacuation was mandatory. As Lieutenant Lake explained in the morning briefing, the 14th Precinct would be responsible for evacuating the industrial and waterfront districts. He also refreshed them on the basic outlines of the plan, warned them to be ready, and dismissed them for regular duties. By then, Caldwell was ready to be interrogated.

Though it wasn't standard procedure, McDonagh decided they would interview Caldwell separately. "He came wanting to see you," he explained. "We can't give him what he wants right away."

"We don't know *what* he wants," Lydia replied.

"We *do* know he wants to talk with you," McDonagh countered.

The lieutenant, distracted and barely paying attention, agreed. McDonagh went first while Lydia watched, listened to the strange story Caldwell had to tell. Honestly, strange didn't cover it. Better to say "improbable," or even "impossible." Caldwell was either mad, lying, or both. McDonagh was just trying to get a statement, the bare facts, but even he couldn't resist openly scoffing at some parts. Caldwell didn't care. Once he started the story, his eyes glazed over and his expression deadened. He told it almost like he was reading from a script, like he had rehearsed what he would say for hours. He didn't sound like the man Lydia had talked to, back on the first day of the investigation. But Lydia anticipated that, once he was questioned more intensely, he would start to shift, show the same ill practice with lying she had seen then. Once Caldwell finished, McDonagh asked a few clarifying questions, then stood to leave. Lydia expected Caldwell to call out, asking when he could talk to Detective Pike, but the dockworker stayed silent, still shivering.

"What do you think?" McDonagh asked, joining Lydia at the two way mirror.

"He's lying," Lydia said. "Probably trying to hide the fact that he killed Bosk. Probably did Ellwood and the rest too. It's a smokescreen."

"So, you don't believe any of it?" McDonagh asked.

Lydia snorted. "Even my mother wouldn't have believed this," she said, "and she believed some weird things." Then she noticed McDonagh's frown, his hand rubbing his jaw pensively. "Do you?" she asked.

McDonagh shrugged. "Probably a lot of it is made up," he admitted, "but he wasn't lying. Caldwell believed everything he said."

"Then he's crazy," Lydia replied. "But it's probably an act. I mean, come on."

"Then why turn himself in?" McDonagh asked.

Lydia thought for a second. "Maybe he saw us watching the docks last night, figured out we were onto him. Maybe he thinks if he spins us some outlandish story he'll get sent to an asylum for a bit instead of doing any jail time. Five months, three square meals a day, and then he escapes to some other town, some other state, goes back to whatever weird game he has going."

McDonagh raised an eyebrow. "That's a pretty elaborate tale too," he said, the trace of a smile crossing his lips.

"Yeah," Lydia replied, chuckling, "but it's based in reality. Everything I just said is possible. Everything he said isn't. The killer walked away after getting beheaded? Stepped through fire? Took bullets to the chest and ignored them?"

"Right, but that's my point," McDonagh said. "I think he believes all of it."

Lydia pursed her lips. "What are you saying?" she asked.

"I don't know," McDonagh shrugged. "Maybe we should get a psychiatrist in here. See if he really is imagining things."

"Really?" Lydia asked, incredulous. "That's playing right into his hands. You can't seriously be buying any of it."

McDonagh shrugged again. "I try to keep an open mind." He kept his gaze away from her, rubbed a thumb along his cheek. "I've seen some weird things on this job, things you wouldn't believe. But this," he nodded at Caldwell through the glass, shook his head, "this takes the cake."

"Let me talk to him," Lydia said. "I'll give him some pushback, see what parts of his story don't hold up to scrutiny."

"You think we can wear him down?" McDonagh asked. "That's going to be tough, if he's planned it out like you say."

"Won't know until we try," Lydia answered, undaunted.

McDonagh let out a short bark of laughter. "True," he agreed. "Good luck."

Lydia took the case file from McDonagh, then left the room. Outside, she took a deep breath, looking both ways up the empty hall. McDonagh hadn't even touched the file, so she didn't need to check the evidence it contained. It would all be there. Another breath. A third. Then, face set and mind steeled, Lydia opened the door.

Caldwell watched her in silence as she entered, his thin frame still shaking. He had a gaunt, hollow look in his eyes, his fear more palpable now that Lydia shared the room with him. She carefully laid the case file on the table. Once she was settled, she looked up and met his gaze. "Well?" she asked. "I'm here. What did you need to tell me?"

Caldwell shrugged. "I already told your partner," he said.

Lydia couldn't repress a chuckle. "Yeah," she nodded, "I heard. Made for a good story, I'll give you that. Maybe you can publish it one day." Lydia leaned across the table, letting her upper body rest on her folded hands. "Why don't you tell me what really happened," she said. "Tell me why you came here, why you hit an officer just to get the chance to speak to me."

"Again, I already went over it with your partner." He kept his eyes level with Lydia's. "I came because I need protection. It looks like that's what I'm getting, so why does it matter who I talk to?"

"Protection?" Lydia asked.

Caldwell raised an eyebrow. "I thought you heard everything."

Lydia leaned back. This wasn't what she was expecting. This wasn't the shifty, evasive young man she had met at the docks. There was still plenty of fear in him, but he wasn't nervous. He wasn't scared of being caught. Either he had gotten a lot better at lying, or McDonagh was right.

"We went to the warehouse," she told him. "Took a look around." Neither of their eyes moved. "There was a lot of blood," Lydia continued.

"Yeah," he replied. "Like I said, I already told your partner about it."

"You really expect me to believe it all came from one man?" Lydia asked, unable to suppress a grin. "A green man, no less."

Caldwell shrugged. "I don't care what you believe," he said.

"You know what I think," Lydia continued, "I think that blood belongs to Emma Bosk. I think it belongs to Leonid Ellwood. I think it belongs to Megan Rude, Jude Bates, Sean —"

"I already told you," Caldwell interrupted, shaking his head, "I didn't kill any of those people. That *thing* must have."

Lydia tutted. "You know, Ian, this may be the worst alibi I've ever heard. It's inventive, to be fair. But honestly, I've always preferred true crime to fantasy."

Lydia had hoped the prodding would get a rise out of him. Belittling, probing, annoying—these were good tactics to get someone to explode in anger, to say something they didn't mean to. Lydia's first partner had used it like a master. But Caldwell didn't respond to any of it. Instead, he deflated, sinking into his chair, his head falling into his cupped hands. "I don't know what you want from me," he said. He almost sounded pitiful.

"The truth."

"I've been telling the truth."

"Then tell it to me again. From the beginning."

Ian lifted his head only a little, enough to rub the tiredness from his eyes. Lydia waited.

"Fine," he said. "From the beginning."

Four

Lester had never seen anything like it before. Not that he had much wildfire experience, but he knew *this* was not normal. Below him, near the bottom of a deep vale, was the edge of the inferno. It covered the opposite hillside, its roaring heat like the open door of an oven, even from this distance. As he watched, the upper parts of an old sentinel of the forest ignited like a torch, the green needles sizzling and popping as the sap boiled. Beyond the top of the hill and for ten miles beyond, it was all the same. The fire raged, burning plant, needle, and creature. It was all normal. Explainable.

What was unexplainable was why this hilltop was fine.

Half of the hill on this side of the valley was a barren wasteland. Tree trunks still stood, but their branches were completely empty. Gaping holes in their bark showed where the fire dug its way through to the sap, the pure sugar that the fire gobbled up like candy. The ground was covered in a foot of white ash, pockets of hot coals still burning underneath. Here and there were the charred skeletons of a squirrel or deer that hadn't made it out of the inferno in time. The bugs and seeds hidden in the forest floor were all dust by now, immolated spontaneously.

The second half of the hill was a lush green forest. Flowers bloomed to greet the few rays of sunlight that made it through the branches. A chipmunk crawled in the swaying tree tops, dropping a pinecone to the ground with a satisfying *thud*. From all he knew of wildfire, it was impossible for any of it to remain. Lester could even see a fern right at the edge of the hellscape, half a frond burned into nothingness, the rest hale and healthy. It was as if someone had drawn a line across the slope, created some invisible barrier that the fire could not pass through.

For some of the crew, it was a miracle. They dropped to their knees, clasped their hands before them, and thanked a merciful God for sparing their city, their families, their lives. Even those that were not religious knew this was outside the realm of the explainable.

After letting his own awe wash over him, Lester stepped before his team. Their eyes flicked towards him, worried, expectant. He waited until he had everyone's attention, until the last prayer died off their lips. "We got lucky," he said. "Let's not waste it. We'll make a control line here, at the top of the ridge. I want it twenty feet across, or as close as we can. Clear brush, then we'll spray the trees with retardant. Other crews will be working all over these hills, but we've got a mile swathe to protect. This is our mid point. Understand?"

Everyone nodded. Lester hoisted his shovel. Making a control line meant hours of work in the unforgiving August heat wearing full gear in case the fire came shooting up the hill. Already, he was drenched in sweat, and that was just from hiking. But Lester didn't mind that. Like he said, they had been extremely, uncomprehendingly lucky.

He hoped it held.

FIVE

"We didn't lie to you about Commander Ellwood," Ian began. "He came, he asked us about Megan Rude, we told him everything we knew."

"Which was?" Lydia asked.

Ian shrugged, his hands raised in the air, palms pointed up and out. "That she picked up deliveries at our warehouse, about once a week. That I thought she was hot. That we didn't think much about it when she stopped showing up."

"Once a week?" Lydia clarified.

"Yeah, something like that."

"Megan Rude disappeared on the first of August," Lydia said.

"That's what Ellwood told us," Ian answered

"That's a week and a half ago," Lydia said. "We found eight crates addressed to her when we stopped by the warehouse two days ago."

"Your point?"

"If she was only getting deliveries once a week, why are there so many crates waiting for her?" Lydia asked, crossing her arms.

She watched his eyes go from hostile, to unsure, to questioning, watched them turn inward and search for an answer there. "I don't know," he finally said. His eyes turned to her again, creased at the edges, slanted up, pleading. "I didn't pay attention to all that," he added. "I just loaded and unloaded crates, put them where Emma told me. Maybe Rude came more than once, maybe other people picked up her stuff for her. You have to believe me."

Lydia stayed still. "What was in the crates?" she asked.

"I don't know."

Bullcrap, she thought.

"What was in the crates?" she asked again.

"I don't know," he said, a wheedle of pained exasperation tinging his voice.

"Fine, what did Bosk tell Commander Ellwood was in the crates?" Lydia asked.

"Nothing. He didn't ask that."

"He didn't ask or she didn't answer?"

"He didn't ask. Maybe. I don't know, lady, I really don't."

"Why?" Lydia stood up, started walking around the side of the table. "It seems like an easy enough thing to remember." She came to a stop by his side, rested against the table. "Why can't you?"

"I got distracted by what happened after." He looked up at her, head tilted awkwardly.

Lydia rolled her eyes, blew out a rough breath towards the ceiling. "Right," she said. She could almost feel McDonagh's disapproval through the glass, could tell the interrogation was getting away from her. "Let's talk about that. The commander questions you, then what?"

"He walked off," Caldwell answered.

Lydia pushed off the table, walked so that she was behind him now, slowly pacing. He remained still, watching her in the mirror. "Walked?" Lydia clarified. "He didn't drive?"

"No, he definitely walked," Caldwell said. "I remember it being strange, because I thought I had seen him get out of a car. But no, he just walked off down the street, into the night."

"You're aware his body was found six miles outside the city?" Lydia asked, stepping around the table again.

"Yeah, your partner mentioned that."

"So you expect us to believe he walked—what, twelve miles? When his car was right there?"

"I don't know if that's what he did," Caldwell said. "I just know he walked off."

Lydia made it to the front of the room again, leaned against the wall with the observation mirror, resting her foot on its toes, crossing her arms. "For the one telling this story, there's a lot you don't know, Ian."

Caldwell flicked his hand a little, a gesture Lydia read as *goddamnit*. "I still know more than you," he said. "That's why I'm telling the story."

"Are you sure?" Lydia asked, a smile creeping onto her face.

"What, you know something I don't?"

"I think we know the same things, Ian," Lydia said, taking a deliberate step forward. "I think we both know this story you're telling is malarkey." She took another step forward. "I think you killed Commander Ellwood—or Kevin did, or Emma. But you were there, Ian," she took a third step, was now standing at the table, her palms resting on the cool metal surface and her face inches from his. "You saw it, Ian. You helped clean it up. You lied about it. That's the story I know."

Ian grimaced, pulled away from her. "I don't know any of that," he said. "Maybe it's the story you need," he added, "but it's not the truth."

"Then tell me the truth."

Caldwell sighed. "Like I've said," he continued, and Lydia rolled her eyes, "we kept working into the night…"

Lydia stepped back from the table. "For how long?"

"Long enough to be the only ones there," Caldwell shrugged. "Maybe three more hours."

Lydia realized she was clenching her jaw, remembered to release the tension. "And then?" she prompted.

Ian looked away. "And then," he paused, collecting himself, "and then a man dressed all in green walks up to us, holding a branch and an axe."

SIX

Before walking out onto the floor, Lilly made sure to tie her black hair into a bun behind her head. With it firmly in place, she took her clipboard off the table, along with the pitcher, measuring glass, and pen. These items in hand, she pushed through the double swinging doors, jotting down the time as she went.

The brewery floor was empty, dark save for the glow from the kettles' heating compartments. The fire beneath the two huge brass structures cast long orange shadows across the concrete. For a normal person, this would have been barely enough light to walk around in, but too dark to see. For her, this was just right.

She ignored the big kettles, walking past them while still making her final notes. Those were for the tried and true lager, the beer that was slowly making the brewery famous. The people of Ash Falls already loved the stuff, drank it by the quart when they could find it. Lilly didn't much like beer herself, but that didn't matter, did it? The beer wasn't for her kind.

Near the far wall, the head brewer had set up six smaller kettles for her, each perched above a large bunsen burner going at full flame. Three batches of the standard lager and three batches of a stout, each started at the same time, fifty-nine minutes ago. Next to them was a table, on which the woman set the clipboard and pen.

There are two important factors to brewing: time and precision. Time collects the yeast, grows the malt, toasts the grains. Time ferments the beer, eating the malt and producing the alcohol. And time brews that alcohol with whatever flavoring added to it.

Precision makes sure all that timing happens the same exact way batch after batch. Precision makes sure all the ingredients are measured equally. It makes sure that the beer keeps coming out the way people like it, the way they crave it, the way they need it. To fail at either timing or precision means failing the people. If you fail the people, why are you making beer?

Lilly still held the pitcher and the measuring cup. With a flourish, she twisted the lid on the pitcher, releasing a softly sweet scent, just on the edge of sour. Instinctively, Lilly felt her mouth water. *No*, she reminded herself. *Not yet.*

She crossed to the first kettle, opened the small glass cover that was hot enough to burn skin. Slowly, she measured a cup of thick red liquid from the pitcher, then poured it into the kettle. For the next, she poured two cups, and in the third she poured three. She did the same amounts with the three stout kettles—one, two, and three. Then she replaced the glass covers on all six kettles, making sure they were tight.

There wasn't much of the liquid left, but that was alright. She wouldn't need any more until these batches were done and tasted. Precision. Time. It mattered what kind of beer she added the ingredients to and how much she used. She needed to know what would taste the best.

Standing at the table again, Lilly poured the rest of the liquid into the cup and set it on the table. She glanced over

her sheet again, added another note, then capped the pen.
The smell of the liquid surrounded her, filled her. She picked
up the measuring cup, about three quarters full, and sniffed.
It was pungent up close. Meaty. Lilly smiled, then downed
the liquid in one gulp. It burned at the back of her throat, its
iron taste coating her mouth and tongue. The small amount
wasn't nearly enough to fill her, but it did for a light snack.
Once the cup was drained, Lilly licked her lips, removing the
last trace of red. She felt warm, like she had just drunk a
strong liquor. Like she could go get in some trouble. The
woods might be burning, but there was still plenty to do in
the city. Ash Falls was like that.

She left the cup and clipboard on the table, taking only
the empty pitcher. She might have been more careful about
leaving things around had she not drunk the liquid, but she
knew the building was empty. She had checked all the
entrances herself.

Well, not entirely empty.

Off the floor, she walked down a long unlit hallway. Past
the tasting room, office, and lobby. Past the restrooms, the
storage closet, the janitor's closet. She walked to the one door
no one else entered, the one that was always locked. She
pulled the only key from her shirt pocket, opened it
unhurriedly, a small smile playing across her lips. Somehow,
this part never failed to give her a thrill.

The room was empty except for a gurney and a machine
beside it. A man was strapped to the gurney—tall, muscular,
ghostly pale. His eyes were closed. Lilly approached him
confidently and slapped the side of his face. He didn't move.

Lilly walked to the machine. A thin tube ran from the
man's arm to the top of the machine, entirely red. She
crouched beside it and opened a small panel. Another
pitcher, identical to the one she held in her hand, waited

inside with the lid removed. In a swift maneuver, Lilly replaced the pitcher in the machine with the one in her hand. She waited a moment, heard a small *splat*, and smiled. The man was still alive. Still providing ingredients, his body trying desperately to replenish what was being drained from him at an excruciatingly slow pace. A battle he was destined to lose, but it was better this way. This way, the woman could extract just a little bit more from him.

Seven

"Yup," Lydia said, trying to hide her frustration. She took a seat again. Caldwell still wasn't looking at her. "So you're sticking to that story," she stated.

"You asked."

"I asked because I want what really happened," Lydia said.

"And that's what you're getting," Caldwell replied, glancing up at her.

"Right," Lydia pinched the bridge of her nose. "Okay. Explain it to me."

After a moment, Caldwell asked, "What do you mean?" His eyes roamed around the room, not meeting hers. Trying not to. "Like I said, a green man walked—"

"Right, right, right, I hear what you're saying," Lydia said. "Explain 'green' to me."

Caldwell gritted his teeth, though his eyes were blank. "You know the way grass looks? In the shade, but lush and healthy? That color green."

"Okay," Lydia elongated the word, rolling it around her mouth while trying to understand. "Wasn't quite what I meant. I get what the color green is. I get what a man is. It's the combination that throws me for a loop. Are we talking like the jolly green giant, or was it just his—"

"Yes," Caldwell said.

Lydia blinked. "So, his shirt—"

"Yes."

"His pants?"

"Yup."

"Shoes?"

"Yes. And his gloves, his cloak, his goddamn undershirt I bet. His hair was green, his beard was green, his skin, his nails, his—"

"Hold up," Lydia interrupted. "It wasn't just his clothes?"

It was Caldwell's turn to put his head in his hands. "No," he clarified. "He was green too."

"So, literally everything was green?"

After thinking a moment, Caldwell said, "Not everything. His eyes were red. When he smiled, he had a row of bright, white teeth. And neither the branch nor the axe were green."

Lydia, for some reason, still couldn't quite understand the concept of an entirely green man, so instead she switched to something that made sense to her. "What kind of branch?" she asked.

Caldwell shrugged. "I don't know," he said. "It had green leaves and red berries. The wood was white where it had been cut."

"And the axe?" Lydia asked.

Caldwell took a long time to answer that. When he did, his voice was a soft whisper. "Awful," he said. "Terrible. A heavy hunk of steel sharpened to the finest edge and fastened to the end of a gnarled wood rubbed smooth by time and use. I have never seen something so beautiful yet so ugly."

A gleam appeared in Caldwell's eyes. Lydia looked away as it became a tear and ran down his cheek.

Eventually she broke the silence. "Okay. What happened then?"

Caldwell took a deep breath. "The guy starts talking shit," he said. "He looked around at us, calling us cowards and children. He made fun of me and Kevin for taking orders from a woman. He made fun of Emma for thinking we actually respected her. He said—"

"Sorry," Lydia interrupted, unable to ignore her question. "Did you tell him Emma was the boss?"

Caldwell hesitated a moment. "No."

"Then how did he know?" Lydia asked.

Caldwell threw his hands into the air, palms facing the ceiling, more tears appearing in his eyes. "How the hell should I know?" he asked. "Look, I've got as little information on this guy as you. I've seen him twice now, and neither time made sense."

"Were you talking about her being the boss just before he got there? Was she giving out orders?"

"Nah," Caldwell said. "I mean, we always followed her lead. But mostly we worked in silence."

"Had you been silent since Commander Ellwood left?"

Caldwell shrugged. "I guess. We talked about how weird it was, getting interviewed by a cop. But three hours went by, you know? We got over it. We had work to do."

"I see," Lydia nodded. "So, then what happened?"

The edge of Caldwell's mouth twitched downward. "He challenged us," Caldwell said. "He told us he had been looking for men, but we would have to do."

Lydia let the silence that followed stretch, let Caldwell live in whatever he was seeing for a moment—memory or fabrication. She knew what he was going to say, had already heard Caldwell's answer to McDonagh. But she wanted to hear it again. She needed to look into his eyes as he talked, see what he believed to be true.

"What was the challenge?" she asked.

Caldwell breathed in deeply. "We could do whatever we wanted to him with the axe," he said. "He would give it to us and kneel at our feet, and then what happened would happen. As long as we agreed to take the same from him in three days."

"Take the same?" Lydia quoted.

"That's what he said," Caldwell agreed, his eyes still on the table.

"What does that mean?" Lydia asked.

Ian shrugged. "I've never seen it, personally. But I'll know in a couple of days. I didn't get all the way through his neck, so maybe he'll go easy on me."

Lydia let that slide for now. "Why did you have to take the challenge?" she asked instead.

Caldwell's brow furrowed a moment. "What?" he asked.

"Why did you take him up on it?" Lydia asked. "Why not just say, 'Thanks, but no thanks, have a nice night?'"

Caldwell looked at her blankly, his mouth hanging open. Absently, his tongue made a soft *cluck*. "I've got to be honest," he began, "I'm tempted to say, 'He had an axe,' but it's not like he threatened us with it. I don't know. Why not throw the axe in the river the moment he handed it over? I can't tell you why, just that it didn't cross my mind. There was just something, you know? Even though I was scared out of my mind, when he laid that challenge down, there was something that made me want to kill him. Made me want to kill him so goddamn bad. The others felt it too, I think." He chuckled, the hollow chuckle of someone who regrets everything that led him to this moment. "Guess I'll never get to ask them," he said.

Lydia slid her tongue across the bottom of her teeth, pausing at the incisors, replaying what he had just admitted. None of this had been in his interrogation with McDonagh. "Do you often want to kill people?" she ventured.

Caldwell thought on that one. "No," he said. "Not really."

"Then why did you want to kill him?" Lydia asked. "What set you off?"

He leaned forward, putting his head into his hands, his eyes staring at the table before him. "I don't know," he said. "You'd have to see him to understand, I guess."

"That's not really a good answer," Lydia growled.

Caldwell shook his head, still between his hands. "No kidding," he grunted, mirroring her frustration. "I know you don't believe a word of this."

Lydia counted to five, waiting to see what else he would say. Then, leaning forward a little, she asked, "What happened next?"

Caldwell took a deep breath, held it. "Emma took the challenge," he said, his body tense. "She took the axe out of his hands. He knelt just like he said he would. Emma took a good heavy swing at him, sunk it straight through his neck." He let out his breath as a slight chuckle. "Honestly, I wasn't sure what came over her. She'd never been violent before. Nothing felt normal that day. Especially when his head rolled to my feet, blood gushing everywhere."

That was the moment Lydia knew it was just a really good act. His gaze was too vacant, too obsessed with details that couldn't be true. Part of him believed it, of course—he needed that. It was that part of him that reached out to her, asked her to believe too. Part of her wanted to. Part of her wanted to believe in the impossible. In fairytales. But fairy tales had no place in her line of work.

McDonagh was right, Lydia decided—they would need to have a psychologist talk to him. Someone to root out what part of him didn't believe this story. The part of him that had cut Detective Ellwood's head from his neck.

"I didn't see him when he stood," Ian continued. "I only noticed his big green hand grabbing his shaggy green hair and lifting his green head off the ground, blood still pouring out of it, still smiling." A shudder ran through Ian—too obvious, again. Clearly an act. "Then he took the axe back, said, 'See you in three days,' and he was gone. His head left a trail of blood behind him."

Despite her decision, Lydia couldn't help asking, "And then?"

Caldwell's eyes focused back on Lydia. "And then, three days later, Emma turned up dead," he said.

EIGHT

During his wildfire training, Lester was taught that
exhaustion was the true enemy of a firefighter. Exhaustion
brought on by the heat of the flames, the lack of shade from
the hot sun, and the weight of the equipment. Exhaustion
was inevitable, and not even the drinking water a firefighter
carried could prevent it. Out on the burned fields, the water
was hot in the canteen and burned the throat. It was
exhaustion that made a firefighter fail to notice the shifting
winds, to see the bed of coals hidden under the ash, to
outrun a swift moving flame. Exhaustion made firefighters
forget to secure their oxygen masks, or fully cover
themselves in their fire blankets, or breathe slowly while the
inferno raged around them. Exhaustion drove a firefighter
wild for fresh air when all that awaited them was hell.
Exhaustion killed good firefighters. Not the flames. Not
asphyxiation. Not dehydration. Exhaustion.

 Their luck held. Whatever force kept the fire from Ash
Falls also drove it away. The inferno was so hot that it
obliterated everything before it, leaving a path of wasted
devastation. There was nothing left to burn in that
devastation, so there was nothing left for the fire to turn back
on. Lester and his crew were never threatened by flare-ups,
never came close to seeing the fire encircle them. Miles away,
deep in the Umpqua Wilderness, Lester knew other crews

were preparing burn lines and that they were in real danger. Lester and the fighters from Ash Falls were the hunters slowly pushing the fields of flame and ash to the cliff's edge. They moved carefully, dousing coal pits when they saw them, cooling the earth with what strength they had. The farther in they went, the longer their luck held.

But no amount of luck in the world could keep exhaustion from exacting its toll. Joanne Clarke didn't notice a coal field in front of her and suffered second degree burns on her feet, losing her boots in the process. Jason Oronski lost his footing and slid down a hill into a still burning patch of fire. He stopped moving by the time they reached him, and last Lester heard he was in critical condition. Rob Albo stopped to rest his hand on a trunk that was still burning inside. He suffered third degree burns, and Lester knew that Albo would never feel in that hand again. Victoria Kamen's legs were crushed when she pushed Kevin Bocek out of the way of a falling tree. Bocek was too exhausted to notice its collapse, had stopped to rest in its slight shade. Kamen would probably never walk again. Still, all-in-all, they were lucky. No one was dead.

If he could help it, Lester would keep it that way. He had his crew take breaks every twenty minutes and made sure they all had fresh drinking water. He asked them how they were, and if they took too long to respond he ordered them to the tree line for four hours, where they could eat, drink, and get a little sleep. Only one of his firefighters refused this order—Bocek, just before he cost Kamen her legs. Lester sent Bocek home after that.

Had he known he would find another body that day, Lester would have stayed home. For that matter, if Lester had ever been told he would find a body on one of his morning jogs, he would have never taken up running. Lester became a firefighter to save lives, not corpses. Their eerie stillness sickened him, the way something was absent. The only thing that made a corpse worse, Lester now knew, was a missing head. He had never seen a burnt body before, but he doubted he would like it very much.

So when Lester brushed aside some ash, looking for coals, he almost walked away when he saw four black sticks and one nub attached to a grizzled length of burnt arm. It was black all the way through, and fragile to the touch, but Lester could still tell it was an arm. With growing trepidation, he brushed away more ash, revealing a bicep, and then a shoulder. The chest followed, then another arm, a waist, a groin, and two legs, almost indistinguishable from burnt logs. All this was enough to fill Lester's throat with bile, but he held it in for the sake of his crew. They had gathered around him, silent, no longer caring about a break. He stayed strong for them, held back the vomit for them. That is, until he realized he couldn't find the head. The neck just ended on a soft layer of ash, a bit of charred bone sticking out. Just like the woman.

Lester couldn't help it. He walked five feet and puked. It made a plume of foul smelling smoke which engulfed his head, and he puked again.

NINE

Lydia had to stand. Caldwell was still going on with his story, saying something about Kevin Wood, about meeting the green man again and trying to kill him. He had already said it all to McDonagh, almost word for word. Lydia stood in front of the observation glass, her back to Caldwell and her expression blank.

"I should have known fire couldn't kill him either," Caldwell finished. "Nothing can." He went quiet. Lydia could see in the reflection that he wasn't looking at her. His arms were wrapped around his shoulders, which were shaking. Every minute or so he would let out a slow exhalation, but he never seemed to breathe in.

Lydia scratched her chin, thinking back on what he said. She would give him one thing—he stuck to his story. Mostly. He had lied to her at the docks, the first day she talked to him. So had Wood. If this testimony was to be believed, the two men knew exactly where Emma Bosk was. But she didn't want to present him with that fact yet. She was adamant now about a psych eval, certain that someone with some training should talk to him. After that, she and McDonagh would hit him with his inconsistencies, question him with their own timeline and version of events. A timeline that they would develop once they compared notes over the next day. A timeline that made sense.

Something niggled at the back of her mind. Something odd. She played the interview over in her mind, all the way from the beginning. She and McDonagh had missed something, but she couldn't place her finger on it.

She watched Caldwell in the mirror. His gaze shifted, starting at the floor, then rising slowly up her back. At her shoulder, his eyes flicked to meet her reflection. His face went red, and he looked away.

"Do you believe me yet?" he asked into the silence.

"Where did you and Wood go?" Lydia asked. "To set your trap?"

Ian licked his lips. "South," he said. "Past the suburbs and into the woods down there."

Lydia's eyebrow lifted quizzically. "And you lit a fire?"

Ian nodded. "Yeah."

Lydia looked into the mirror, towards where she thought McDonagh would be standing. "I want to remind you of your rights," she said. "Anything you say to us is on the record and will come up in court. We can use anything you say to prosecute you. You have the right to a lawyer, and we can provide you with one if you are unable to hire your own. Are you aware of this?"

"I was wondering when you'd put it together," Caldwell answered, his chin lifting in defiance.

She turned. "Are you aware there's a wildfire in the hills south of Ash Falls?" she asked.

Caldwell nodded. "Yes," he said. "I started it. I dug pits, filled them with gasoline. I not only let the fire spread, I made sure it did. I had an accomplice too, but he's still out there."

She stepped to the table again. "Tell me why, Ian." She wasn't sure she believed him, didn't want the natural disaster to get pinned on him. But what if there was some truth in his story, even a small grain of it? Where was it?

Ian met her eyes, sadness tinging the blue. "I already told you why."

"Stop wasting my time," Lydia said, her voice a growl, unwilling to concede in this.

"Look lady, you're asking," Ian replied. "I'm just telling you what happened. Again," he added, spite and anger emphasizing the word.

"You wanted to talk to me," Lydia's voice rose.

"Oh, go to hell," Caldwell's eyes rolled backwards. "Look, I don't want to believe any of this crap, just like you. I preferred my life when it was simple, without any monsters in it. Nothing was trying to kill me then. But I already told you my story, I didn't ask you to come in here and make me tell the whole damn thing again. You asked. I'm just telling it like it happened."

"Yeah," Lydia straightened, "and I don't believe a word of it. It's horse hockey, all of it, and you're not leaving until you give us the real story."

Caldwell opened his mouth, but, instead of words, a weird, guttural growl came out. "Whatever," he said, leaning back and turning away. "I don't need you to believe me. You're going to see him for yourself, real soon."

"Is that so?" Lydia asked. "How do you figure?"

"I lit the fire," Caldwell said. "That's arson, right?"

Lydia shook her head in disbelief, cleared her throat with a small cough. "Something like that," she said.

"Bring me a confession, I'll sign it right now," Caldwell said. "That way you don't have to release me. Plenty of time for my good friend to come around."

Lydia couldn't stop a laugh. "Yeah?" she asked. "What happens then?"

"You'll see," he said. "You can't save me, but you'll believe me." Caldwell smiled, an attempt at bravery, but coated in fear. A pitiable fear, a fear that Lydia could tell was no act. "Hell is coming," Caldwell said, "and when it's done with me, I hope you're not next."

END of Episode Three

Episode Four: Axe-essive Force

ONE

The detectives stand behind the glass, watching the prisoner beyond. He is eating now — some cheeseburgers and a packet of fries, the easiest thing for them to scrounge up at this time of night. He eats slowly, small halfhearted nibbles at the burgers, a fry every once in awhile. You'd think he'd be hungrier, seeing as they've been interrogating him for two days straight. First, it was just the detectives, then they brought in their 'professional,' a waspy elderly man who could only tell them that he detected nothing wrong with the prisoner. Then they went back to interrogating him.

Before they brought the food, he was pacing, hands rubbing at his recently freed wrists. But that does not mean they are letting him go. They've only briefly loosened his constraints, a breath of freedom before the plunge.

I expect he will fail. He surprised me, certainly, by coming here. But surprises are not what wins this game. And trapped in here means he cannot find my gifts when I leave them for him, means he will gain nothing to give me. Not that it will help his chances at survival, it just makes waiting seem so pointless.

"Patient appears to suffer from clear delusions," the male detective reads from a paper. "Spent majority of day with patient, attempting to find origin of delusions in past. Patient appears to have no traumatic event before beginnings of delusions nor any history of delusions."

"That sounds like shrink-speak for, 'I have no idea what's going on,'" the female replies.

"It might be," Detective McDonagh shrugs. "Puts a wrench in some of our theories." He places the paper on a table, then crosses his arms while looking into the room.

"It just means he's lying," Detective Pike says, shaking her head.

"Well, we need evidence of that," says Detective McDonagh. "Because this," he taps the paper again, "says he's not."

"He lied before," says Detective Pike after a moment.

"When?" McDonagh asks.

"The first time I talked to him," Pike answers. "He and Kevin Wood knew where Emma Bosk was the night she died. They lied and told me they didn't."

"Why does that matter?" McDonagh asks.

It's not that he doesn't know. He is testing her. Always testing. Gauging. Teaching. He thinks it's his duty, as the elder. When he looks at her, he meets her eyes with a plain honesty he does not extend to most. He tries not to find her weaknesses, tries not to find what he can exploit. He respects her enough to extend that courtesy—or, at least, he likes to think he does. He watches her eyes, listens to her words, picks up on her thoughts as she is having them. Evaluating. Weighing. Breaking. Whether he realizes it or not, he always looks at her like the predator he is, and it does not matter if he sees a mentee or quarry.

I understand. He is a hunter, like me. The instinct never leaves, no matter how hard he represses it. Of all my prey so far, he is the only one who might pass the test. If only he would take his eyes off her.

"It matters because if he was lying then, what else is he lying about?" Detective Pike says.

McDonagh can't suppress a grin. "That's how most cops think," he says.

"So?" Pike asks, looking at him.

"When you're a detective, it can be an issue," McDonagh replies.

"Bull," Pike says, looking back to the prey. He is done with his cheeseburgers now, his head resting in his arms. He has not touched the fries in some time.

"Listen to you," McDonagh says. "You've already decided that one lie leads to ten more, but you haven't even tried to find out why he was lying."

"Why is it not the right assumption?" Pike asks, keeping on point. "Why do we not think he's lying now?"

"He could be, sure," McDonagh says. "Finding this lie could lead to ten more, or twenty, or a hundred. Hell, it could even lead to a thousand. Or it could lead to nothing, because things have changed since he first met you."

"Doesn't mean we shouldn't try," Pike says, moodily.

"That's true," McDonagh agrees. "Just try to make your conclusions at the end, not the beginning."

I almost don't want to test her. It doesn't really seem worth it. She doesn't see the hypocrisy in her thinking, how she is so certain of what she deems possible and dismissive of what can't be. She'll probably think I'm part of her imagination even as she fails my test. She looks at her partner and sees a grizzled old dog. Patronizing. Slow. Lonely. She could run circles around the work he does, not knowing that he gives her the easy work on purpose—to hide her from what she cannot comprehend, not yet. Not that he's right to, but her assessment that he's a lone wolf is more on the snout than she realizes. As a solitary soul herself, there are definitely things she could learn from him. But each hour is an opportunity lost, and these two have far less time than they know.

"Well, I say we try him again now," Pike says. "While he's full and tired. He'll slip up, I'm sure."

"No," McDonagh says. His hand is curled into a fist before his face, the tip of his thumb sliding across his chapped bottom lip. "We let him stew. Put him back in his cell for the day, let him rehearse the same story again, over and over. We'll do some work tomorrow, then interview him at night. Let him tell the whole damn thing again, not responding to anything."

"And then?"

"Then we take him through it one more time, except we push him on every little detail. Together. On everything. It'll throw him off, and we can use his discomfort to find the truth."

Pike chews on a nail. "Sounds tedious," she says.

"Welcome to the AFPD," McDonagh says. "It'll work though."

It won't, but only because he'll be dead by then.

Pike shakes her head in disbelief. "If you say so," she says. "What do you want me to do in the meantime?"

"Get a court order for the manifest of warehouse six," McDonagh says. "Find out what other companies were shipping through there. See if Rowan Bale owns stock in any of them."

"You're sure?" Pike asks.

"If Rude really was the commander's mole," McDonagh answers with a shrug, "then it's worth exploring Bale. Maybe Caldwell has cracked, or maybe it's just a cover still. He could be a hitman for the company."

"What are you going to do?" Pike asks.

"I've got a lead to track down," he says. "It'll take me most of the day."

"That sounds more interesting than cross-examining the manifest," Pike says. "What if I came along instead?"

"No," McDonagh growls. "We'll cover more ground if we split up."

In the holding cell, the prey stands and starts to pace again.

"Fine," Pike says.

"I'll see you tomorrow evening," McDonagh says. He turns and leaves Pike alone in the observation room. Through the glass, Caldwell pauses and looks up, almost like he can hear the door closing.

Two

Ash Falls Police Department - Interrogation Report
Rank: Detective   *Name:* Lydia Pike
Date: 08/13/2017   *Time:* 1030 hrs.
Location: 14th Precinct
   Report:
   Subject Ian Caldwell turned himself into police custody
on 08/11/2017 at 0730 hrs. After Caldwell was processed,
Detective McDonagh and I interviewed Caldwell over the
course of three days. Caldwell refused Miranda Rights,
agreed to interview without lawyer present.

   After three days of interviewing, Detective McDonagh
and I agreed that Caldwell revealed nothing of substance.
Please see interview recordings 0071486 through 007208.

THREE

Thomas left his apartment early, his badge and sidearm hooked to his belt, a flask hidden in the front pocket of his jacket. He went to the station first, hoping he would arrive before Pike. It wasn't that he didn't want to see her—he was afraid she would notice the lump over his heart. She would know without having to ask. Pike was observant, after all—a trait that made for a great detective, but a bad partner. In his opinion.

Luckily, there was no sign of the young officer. The night shift was still going about their business, pale and sleepy-eyed at the end of their day. Thomas recognized two men that were part of Monya's gang, manacled in front of a dour detective. The two looked up when Thomas entered, but he only spared them a cold glance before moving to his desk. He wrote a quick note to Pike, then looked through their case files. After some consideration, he only took Bates's, though he wasn't sure he'd use it. The file in hand, he walked back across the squad room, the two pairs of eyes following him the whole way. Pleading.

Thomas didn't care. He didn't know how they had been caught, but it wasn't his problem.

After leaving the station, Thomas drove his car to 1st Street, turned east onto it, and kept himself in the rightmost lane. He stayed there all the way out of the city, through the farthest reaches of downtown, then Riverside, then Wilford's Ferry. He drove until 1st Street became Ascension Road. Instead of buildings, this road was surrounded by trees. Instead of straight and broad, it was narrow and winding, climbing into the foothills of the Cascades. He drove until the road overlooked Ascension Lake, the hydroelectric plant, and the small community of homes and buildings there, the very outskirts of Ash Falls. And then he kept driving.

He could have gone west, but that would have brought him close to the fire and his nose would have been so filled up with smoke and ash that it would have been impossible to keep himself safe. Besides, he had already tried that direction in the two days after Ellwood's death. The spirits that way only knew of something strange happening in Ash Falls, but there was always something strange in Ash Falls.

He could have stayed in the city, walked right down to the waterfront. He could have picked a spot somewhere under the bridge and summoned a spirit there, saving all the time this would take him. But he found that the denizens of Ash Falls' otherworld were not as friendly as the fey in the wilderness. Most were downright hostile to him or too concerned with the ongoings of the spirit world to be any use.

He could have tried the lake, but not many spirits gathered in that place, where the water was still. The ones that did were slow, their faces covered in grime and mud, and rarely wanted to say more than a few words. Thomas had heard too many stories of what lurked in the deep to go anywhere near the reservoir.

So, Thomas went east, following the upper parts of the Umpqua that fed into the lake. Thomas knew himself well enough to not go too far. Whenever he climbed these hills, he felt an intense pain in his stomach, a dizziness in his head.

Altitude sickness, he knew. It always made him want to return home and drink a glass of beer. He pushed on now, knowing he wouldn't be going too far.

A mile after the reservoir, Ascension Road crossed a bridge. The green sign at the end called the waterway below "Bear Creek." Just beyond was a small dirt road, which Thomas turned right onto. It was rough, with huge holes where the rain had puddled. Thomas had to take it slowly. The road followed Bear Creek higher into the hills, and Thomas felt his stomach grow thick with nausea, a tight buzzing in his forehead.

Thomas drove until he found a pullout—or at least what passed for a pullout up here. Two of his tires were still on the road, but it would have to be enough for any other vehicle that happened to be in these woods. Thomas doubted there would be a problem. He stepped out of his car and walked around to the other side, taking a deep steadying breath. The day was already warm, and these hills were full of sweet pine and dusty earth. Just at the edge of his senses, Thomas could smell the clear water of Bear Creek tumbling over smooth stones. The wind was so heavy with ash, he could taste its grim char.

Thomas took the flask from his breast pocket, then removed his jacket. He put it on the front passenger seat of his car, along with his badge, phone, and wallet. He kept his gun. Whatever or whoever killed Ellwood was still out there, after all. The bodies had all been found in the woods— maybe it lived out here. If it did, Thomas did not want to meet it empty handed. He didn't know what a gun could do that he couldn't if he lost control of himself, but that wasn't an option he'd like to pursue. Not if he didn't have to.

Nothing up here resembled a path, so Thomas picked a direction and started walking. He followed the gurgle of the water, let it guide him through the trees, over a few hillocks, and down a steep incline. At the bottom was the creek, no more than five feet wide and a foot deep. He stopped on the bank, kicked off his shoes, and stuffed his socks into them. He tied his shoes around his neck by the laces, then rolled his trousers up to just below the knee. Fallen pine needles pricked at his feet and crunched where he put his weight.

He was careful as he stepped into the water. It was cold on his skin, raising gooseflesh in the split second before he fully covered his feet. His right foot found a stone, so he shifted his weight onto it, then stuck his left foot out to what looked like mud. His toes sunk into the dark earth, the water rippling around his legs. Thomas waded farther out to the middle of the stream. There, he opened the flask, took a sip, and let a few drops fall into the water. The whiskey wasn't his favorite—bourbon—but for whatever reason, he'd always had the best results with it. It tasted sour in his mouth, this early in the morning, but it eased the pain in his stomach.

He started to wade up the creek, fighting the firm current and careful to not slip on any rocks. The key was to find someplace secluded—more secluded than a creek bed in the middle of nowhere. Spirits were always very particular about that sort of thing, didn't like being walked up on by surprise. Neither did Thomas.

He didn't know why his process for meeting spirits worked. Many people claimed to know, but they were the people who studied reaching into the beyond like it was a science. Mediums were especially good at it, he'd found, though they dealt mostly in ghosts. The dearly departed always had something they wanted to say, wanted another taste of life this side of the veil. Thomas learned his craft by instinct, without a real teacher or guide. He hadn't even known it was possible to commune with the spirits most of his life. One day, not long after he joined the force, he simply spat some whiskey into the dirt at random. A tree spirit responded to the whiskey, reaching out to Thomas and connecting with his mind. Thomas nearly had a heart attack. It was a short conversation.

Whiskey wasn't the only way to touch the spirit realm, of course. Thomas seemed to have a particular ease with trees, often only having to touch them with his palm. He didn't like it, however. Trees were strange, their minds alien and slow, their thoughts impenetrable. Even worse, they didn't move and didn't like to look at the world around them. When they did, they watched dull and unimportant things, like the wind rustling through the leaves, or the way a single blade of grass grew. More often, he left the tree more frustrated than when he started.

It was like that the day they found Leonid. Without any human witnesses, Thomas figured he might as well ask the trees what they had seen. They gave him nothing.

That wasn't right, Thomas reflected. They knew what was happening when Leonid was killed. And they were afraid of *it*, whatever it was that killed him. They did their best to avoid looking at him, and if he came into their vision he was strangely shadowed. But it had the shape of a man— Thomas latched onto that. His working theory was that Wood or Caldwell suffered from some kind of possession, something so terrifying to spirits that they simply refused to acknowledge it.

Of course, he couldn't share any of this with Pike. Not yet, anyways. From what Thomas could tell, his partner had no knowledge of the supernatural in Ash Falls, was like the many other thousands who simply pretended nothing was strange about the city. Thomas couldn't blame her, of course. He was even a little jealous. Growing up in the pack, he had never known anything but the shadow side of the world. What if he had been normal? Would he still talk to his family? Would he have gotten married? Would he have even become a police officer?

Probably questions not worth thinking about. Instead, Thomas went back to the day they found Leonid. He thought of the hawthorn, the last tree he tried to speak with. In all his previous dealings with that species, he always found them to be pleasant and well-mannered. Still strange, to be sure, but never aggressive. Never angry. They never lashed out at him, as that tree had. It burned him, and while he burned, all Thomas knew was red anger. For the first time, Thomas understood an emotion that a tree showed him.

And it terrified him.

I do not like that emotion, he had told himself while Lydia looked on. *It is not a good emotion.*

Farther upstream, Thomas finally found a good spot. It was at a bend in the creek, shaded by an old fir and a steep slope of rock. The fir's branches hung low above the water and dipped in when the occasional strong wind came. Thomas took the flask from his shirt pocket again and took another small sip. After swallowing, he tipped the flask back and filled his mouth with whiskey, even ballooning his cheeks a little. When the flask was almost empty, Thomas turned his head a little and forced the liquid out, making it into a fine mist that sprayed above him in an arc. After, there was maybe an ounce of whiskey left. He finished it in a single swallow, his feet numb from the cold of the water.

He checked the time. Almost eleven. Getting out here had taken him longer than he planned.

Slowly, imperceptibly, the waters of the creek began to rise. Thomas only noticed because he felt it growing up his legs. He didn't move, just waited with his face to the sun, aware of how leathery his skin was becoming. The water rose from his midcalf to his knees, then from his knees to halfway up his thigh, almost reaching his groin. Still, Thomas did not look. Water spirits were a tricky lot, especially ones that lived in the mountains. The water had barely risen a foot and a half, but he didn't want to do something that scared the spirit and made the water rise another ten. Only when the gurgling stopped, when quiet descended again over the creek, did Thomas take his eyes from the sky.

The spirit was a few feet away from him. A pile of rocks rose three feet out of the creek, water spouting another foot from the top before trickling down the sides. If Thomas squinted, he could just make out a face in the water, though it was fleeting and always disappeared the moment he focused on it.

"Wolf," it called him.

"Hello," Thomas answered slowly. He never knew what to call the spirits. Some expected formalities, disappearing if the proper respect was not shown. Others didn't seem to care, were just bored enough to suffer Thomas. This one did not reply to his greeting. It stayed motionless, water rolling down the rocks back into the creek.

"Something has been happening in the city," Thomas said. "And in the woods. Strange things." Thomas wanted to avoid asking questions as much as possible. Statements always made the conversation longer.

"Yes," this spirit agreed. "Something dangerous, even to wolves." Its voice was like stones clicking together in the current.

"No one I've talked to knows what it is," Thomas asked.

"They all know, in a way, just as you do," the spirit said. "We all recognize something that isn't native. Something imported."

"Imported by whom?" Thomas asked.

"By you," the spirit scoffed. "By wolves and bats and all things that have gathered in the city."

"It's human?" Thomas asked.

The spirit laughed, the trill crash of water descending a fall. "No. It is not even a spirit," it said. "It is worse. Far worse. I am just glad I am up here, where it will not come."

A fairly talkative spirit. Maybe the whiskey had helped. "It won't come where it's not welcome," Thomas said, trying to sound knowledgeable.

"No," the spirit snapped. "It comes where it wants to, and it does not want to come up here. Not yet anyway. May it never."

Thomas frowned. "You're afraid of it?" He had meant to make it sound like a statement, but he couldn't keep the question from his voice.

"We all should be," the spirit answered. "Bodies pile around it, trees burn in its wake. Stay out of its way, and it might not see you. Give it what it wants, and it might spare you. We should all be very afraid."

"Who brought it here?" Thomas asked. "And why?"

The height of the spout dipped momentarily. "Your kind did, wolf," the spirit said. "Whenever you meddle, you risk sparking the unknown."

"How could we have known, if even you don't understand it?" Thomas asked.

The spout dipped again, losing strength as the rocks began to fall away. "That is why I stay up here," the spirit murmured. "That is why I do not meddle. If you knew anything, you might do the same."

"How can I stop it?" Thomas asked.

Again, that trill laugh, though softer this time—distant. "Who knows?" the spirit said. "Give it what it wants, accept what is given. Only you can decide how to accept your fate."

Thomas squinted, not quite understanding what the spirit meant. It was like talking to a tired child, in a way. Sometimes it was as clear as day, others as muddy as the lake. "There has got to be a way," he said.

The plinth of stones had almost disappeared back into the creek. "You cannot put back what you have already chopped down," the spirit said, its voice barely a whisper. "You cannot dam a river unless you know its depths. We have been trying to teach your kind for a hundred years, but you wolves only listen to your own howls."

This was one of those clear as day statements. 'Chop,' 'dam,' 'wolves'—the spirit did not mean humans. It meant Thomas and his 'kind.' He might have time for one more question.

"Is that how Rowan Bale is involved?" he asked. "Did he start this?"

But it was too late. The creek flowed around his ankles. Branches of the tree rustled in the wind, dipped into the cool pool. Thomas was alone.

FOUR

Ben's Antiques & Oddities for the Curious Mind.

Crowley Fine Liquors.

Falls' Brewing Company.

Three companies. Besides the Timber Company, these three were the only companies who received recent regular shipments through warehouse six, where Bosk, Wood, and Caldwell all worked. A few other companies had one or two shipments, or had been regulars but stopped going through the warehouse more than a month ago. Some more companies were still regulars, but only started a month ago —still suspicious, but not quite what Lydia was looking for. Only these three had been regulars for a long time, and the deliveries never seemed to stop. She had her guesses about what the curios shop or liquor store received, though couldn't explain the Brewing Company. Still, they were worth looking into.

These names represented six hours of work for Lydia. Twenty minutes writing the warrant request, thirty taking it to a judge, another fifteen pleading her case to the Honorable William Varano, twenty-five to take the warrant down to the docks; five to find Foreman Shaft, ten for Shaft to take it to *his* boss, twenty to let him look it over, fifteen for him to find a manifest, one for Lydia to realize it wasn't the complete manifest, thirty for Lydia to confront both of them about this, six minutes for her to threaten a raid, another twenty before they finally turned over the whole damn thing, thirty for Lydia to fight traffic all the way back up to the precinct, and two hours and thirteen minutes going blind trying to make sense of the tiny illegible scrawl, cross-referencing entries with notes, notes with details farther down the manifest, and details with her own memory. All of that, only to produce three names in the end. A long, tedious, exhausting, and—in the end—satisfying process.

Before she could get too proud, she got a text message. It was from McDonagh, a reply to the question, "Where are you?" she had sent five hours ago. "Two hours out. Caldwell okay?"

Lydia glowered at the message. He had been gone all day, supposedly talking to a CI again while she did all the heavy lifting. He was using her, Lydia was sure, getting her to do grunt work. He likely didn't want to do it and he didn't think her capable of anything else. When Lydia solved the case and got Caldwell to crack, McDonagh would probably take all the credit. He'd provide some small connection, something that Lydia would realize was part of the bigger picture, and then McDonagh would always say he found the Holly Killer. And, if Lydia tried to say something, it would be her ass on the line for not 'acting like a partner.' For not 'having his back.'

Her mother had warned her it would be like this. Teachers, too, in high school and in college. But it was her mother who had turned to magic and fairies, tried to fight the system with make-believe rather than effort. "We don't need men," Lydia's mother used to say.

In her small home, hooked to an IV drip, hair falling out from the chemo, frail as a chicken bone, her mother wasn't exactly the best example of this. But Lydia had let it go, at the time. Because maybe her mother would be right. Maybe her brain hadn't baked in the desert sun.

Lydia pushed the memory aside, focused back on the text in front of her. Her mother's necklace felt itchy on her neck. "Caldwell okay?" McDonagh had asked.

"Probably," Lydia replied. "Still in his cell."

"Get him to an interrogation room," McDonagh said. "Let him steep a bit before I get back."

"When will you be back?" Lydia asked.

A while later, long enough for Lydia to order Ian Caldwell brought to interrogation room one, Lydia got a reply. "Soon."

"Great," Lydia said to herself. "Fucking typical."

"Is he always late?" a voice asked.

Lydia's hand went to her pistol, only to find that it was gone. Locked away in her desk. She managed to keep herself from jumping a little as she turned, her heart beating wildly from the surprise. As soon as she recognized the voice, however, she was completely unsurprised to see Justin, the ME's assistant. Same curly hair, same ugly broken nose, same curious gaze. He wore a dark blue sports coat, underneath which Lydia could tell he wore a set of scrubs.

"Do you always sneak up on people?" Lydia replied curtly.

Justin grinned apologetically. "At least it's not a crime scene this time," he said.

"Maybe you should just never do it again," Lydia said. She could feel her brows disappearing into her bangs as she glared at him, saw him try to stand up to her gaze before his resolve withered and melted away. He looked around the squad room.

"Seriously though," he said, "where is your partner?"

"Out," Lydia said.

Justin nodded slowly. "Okay. When will he be back?"

Lydia couldn't repress a bitter chuckle. "That's the million dollar question," she said.

Justin, mistaking her chuckle as a sign that he was winning her over, took a step forward. In an instant, the smile was gone from Lydia's lips, but she held where she stood, the glare returned in full force. He stood under her fury three seconds before stepping back again.

"Well," he said, again looking away, "I think I've got something you two'd be interested in."

Lydia said nothing.

"Fire crews pulled in a body," Justin continued. "They found it out in the fire."

"I heard," Lydia said, which was true. She and McDonagh had even texted each other about it, briefly, in the early hours of the morning, debating whether it might be Kevin Wood. Lydia didn't think so and McDonagh was on the fence. Ultimately, the case remained unassigned because nothing remained of the crime scene. Whoever the person was, however they had died, the case would be lumped in with a general investigation of how the fire started. Lydia still didn't think Caldwell had done it, no matter what he said, but that was not their problem now. For now, the force waited while the fire department did their job.

"What about it?" Lydia asked.

Justin chewed his lip a second. "Are you still working the commander's case?" he asked.

Lydia watched him in silence, gauging. Was this really going to be worth her time? Standing in front of him for even one more second?

Eventually, she answered, "I am."

"I think this one's related," Justin said, still bothering to smile.

Lydia leaned against her desk, crossed her arms in front of her. "Why?" she asked.

"Well, for one, the body was decapitated."

Lydia raised an eyebrow but kept her interest in check. It was too good to be true. Even the timing checked out. "Couldn't it have lost its head in the fire?" she asked.

Justin laughed at that, and Lydia grimaced. "You're serious?" he asked, seeing her expression.

Lydia shrugged. "Stray tree falling, random rock rolling over the neck—anything can take a head off, as I'm sure you —"

"I know," Justin interrupted. "However, nothing random takes off a head like this. And besides," he fished into his jacket pocket, "I also found this."

He produced a small plastic bag. Lydia instantly noticed that he had already tagged it properly, that all it needed was to be assigned a case number. But what intrigued Lydia more, what made her breath catch, was the small green leaf inside the bag. It had the same fluted points, the same oblong shape, the same crispness. English holly, somehow preserved from the fire.

"Where did you find that?" Lydia asked, her voice quiet.

"Same place I found it in Commander Ellwood," Justin replied, already confirming Lydia's suspicions.

"On the body you pulled from the fire?" Lydia asked, just to be sure.

"Yup," Justin said. He was smiling again, again took an unconscious step forward. Or maybe it was conscious. Either way, Lydia still stepped away.

"What else did you find on him?" Lydia asked.

"Not much," Justin admitted. "I checked the mouth first, once I saw the neck wound. Then I came to find you."

Lydia spent a moment considering this. Whatever he was supposed to do, stopping in the middle of an autopsy was not it. But, on the other hand, this was the exact leaf she had been looking for the last three days.

"Has anyone else seen this?" Lydia asked.

"Just you," Justin said.

"Can I get a look at the body?" she asked.

Justin's smile widened, and he took a step forward again. "That depends," he said.

Lydia did not want to ask what it depended on. She could see it in his smile, the way his eyes traveled down her, assessing her. This time she did not glare at him.

Instead, she grabbed his arm and gripped it, hard. Whatever he was expecting, it wasn't that. He let out a small gasp as she twisted him, still gripping his arm like a vice, toward the door. "It better depend on whether we can get to the autopsy before Dr. Ploski gets back, because so help me God, Justin, if it depends on anything else—"

"Yup, it depends on that," Justin said, trying to keep his voice quiet while gasping in pain. "Just that, I—"

"And after you show me the body," Lydia continued, "you will continue to treat me with the same respect any other detective would expect to receive, which includes—"

"Yup," Justin groaned, "seriously, I read you loud and clear."

Lydia gave him one last firm squeeze before thrusting him forward. "Which includes," she finished, "not leering at me like a coed at your premed frat parties."

"I gotcha, I'm sorry," Justin said. He walked forward, not looking at her, but Lydia could still see his face was beet red. She also knew all eyes in the squad room were on her.

She ignored them.

Just before she left, Ian Caldwell was escorted in by two patrol officers. He looked tired, dark bags under his eyes.

"Where you going?" he asked.

Lydia ignored him. To one of the officers, a young heavy-set man with yellowy wet eyes, she said, "Put him in room one. If McDonagh shows up, tell him I'll be back soon."

As she left the squad room, Caldwell called after her, his words echoing in her ears. "Don't go far," he said. "Don't want you to miss it."

FIVE

AFPD's 14th Precinct was lucky enough to be in the same building as its morgue, which was two floors below Lydia's squad room, just above the station's parking garage. It was a cold, quiet place, the rows of stainless steel doors set in the far wall full of desperate expectation.

Who knew, truly, what waited in there, coiled like a spring, hoping to be the next rolled out on a slab. How many ghosts waited, thinking they just needed to be let out of their cold cells?

Justin held the door open for Lydia. Three bodies waited on the autopsy tables in the center of the room. Two had white sheets pulled over them, suspended on the high points of their forehead, nose, chin, chest, stomach, and toes.

One was a man, Lydia could instantly tell. Fat. Not yet cut open, by the smell. The other was a woman, recently sewn shut, awaiting a debrief from the detectives on her case.

The third table didn't need the ceremony of a sheet. Nothing was recognizable of the body, just burnt flesh and carbonized bone. Tall, maybe six foot. Well, five three if you excluded the head.

"Firefighters did a good job," Justin said, filling the silence. "I would have expected him to fall apart, he's so brittle."

"Him?" Lydia confirmed.

"Him," Justin agreed. "Size of the pelvic bone gives it away. Too narrow to be a woman."

Lydia frowned. It didn't look like Kevin Wood, but it was hard to tell. She hadn't really gotten a good look at his build, as he had been wearing a thick leather jacket when she met him. But he had seemed thin, wiry. Strong, too. But not some kind of 'roided out hulk.

Her instincts told her, however, that it had to be Wood. The coincidences were just too many. If Caldwell was to be believed, he and Wood had gone into the forest together, where Caldwell started a fire and then left without Wood. If Wood never left, then that would explain why he was burnt to a crisp. But something still didn't quite make sense.

"Did he have any clothes on?" Lydia asked, a thought striking her.

Justin shrugged. "Not when he came in," he said. "Probably burned off in the fire."

"Would they have burned?" Lydia asked. "Or could they have melted?"

Justin was silent a moment, considering the body. "If the clothes were mostly plastic fabrics," he agreed. "I hadn't really gone over the body," he added.

"Do you think you could do that?" Lydia asked. "I'll wait."

"Yeah," Justin said slowly, still looking at the body. He got closer, his nose inches from the torso. "It could be," he muttered. "Looks like there are some irregularities. That's what you get for looking in the mouth first."

"Justin," Lydia said, and his head snapped up. "I'll wait," she said again.

"Here?" Justin asked in surprise.

"Uh-huh," she said. "I want to watch while you look it over."

"Dr. Ploski could be back though," he said, his voice pleading.

"That's fine," Lydia said. "I don't have all day either. So hurry up."

Justin stared at her, then turned away. Lydia was certain she heard him grumble, "Bitch."

"Excuse me?" she asked.

"Nothing," Justin said, crossing the room and taking off his jacket.

"The same respect as any other detective," Lydia said to his back. He didn't respond, but he didn't call her a bitch again either.

While he washed his hands, Lydia crouched so that she was eye level with the corpse, her arms crossed and resting on the edge of the table. The head was mostly black skull now, a weird, crooked smile written into the teeth. The head was separated from the neck by a few inches, enough to make it clear he had been found headless. Lydia's gaze slid down his side, taking in the thick shoulders. There was a line across the top of them that Lydia now saw as an inseam. Strange what could hold up, even in the flames. Lydia continued her scan over the ribs and wooden arms, down to the hip and upper leg. Here she stopped, noticing a small circle.

"What the hell is that?" she muttered.

It seemed to be both raised out of the skin and a part of it. It was an inch wide, with smooth edges. If anything had been printed on it, the ink was completely burned away.

Lydia looked around. A pair of tweezers sat on a table nearby, arrayed amongst a full set of surgical equipment. Lydia grabbed them, then carefully gripped the edge of the small circle with the points. After tugging a moment, the object came away—a full circle, a small chunk of burnt flesh coming with it.

"Justin?" Lydia called. "Do you have an evidence bag over there?"

"Yeah," Justin replied. "Why?" Lydia did not look up, could sense him turning. "Goddamnit," he said, and she heard his feet stepping across the floor. "You're really not supposed to do that," he said.

"Just get me a bag," Lydia replied.

She stood slowly to her full height, waited patiently for Justin to bring a clear plastic evidence bag to her, the same size as the one with the leaf. She slid the circle in, then put the tweezers back on the table. Justin scribbled some notes on the tag.

"What does that look like to you?" Lydia asked.

Justin hesitated. "A poker chip," he finally said.

Lydia nodded. "I can see it," she agreed. "You think you could clean the ash off it?"

"I can try," Justin said. "Want me to do that now? Or, should I get back to the autopsy first?"

Lydia didn't have time to respond. From somewhere in the building came three sharp *cracks*, like the snap of a firecracker. Silence came after, and then seven more, a flurry of bangs deadened by the morgue's thick walls.

"What the heck?" Justin said.

Justin was a doctor, or training to be one. He could not recognize the sounds the way Lydia—who had trained for hours at the AFPD shooting range, who had been in a firefight before—could. It was obvious to her the moment the first noise reached them.

Someone, somewhere in the AFPD headquarters, was shooting a gun. From the sound of it, probably more than one gun. Someone was probably shooting back.

Instinctively, Lydia's hand moved to her hip. There, she found her badge and her retractable baton, but no gun.

"Wait here," Lydia told Justin.

Six

At the top of the stairs, Lydia paused to listen. There was no more shooting, but she could still hear yelling and screaming. Looking through the small window of the door to the stairwell, Lydia saw the hallway was full of people running from her squad room. Civilians mostly, some still manacled for processing, but a few uniformed patrol officers were in the flow, trying to maintain order.

Lydia unhooked her baton. She kept it sheathed as she opened the door and snagged a passing patrolwoman. Officer Rodriguez, she read on her name patch.

"What's happening?" Lydia asked.

"I don't know," Rodriguez replied. "We heard some yelling from an interrogation room, Lee and Rorke went to check it out. Next thing we knew, Rorke is shooting and Lee's flying down the hall."

"Flying?" Lydia asked, then shook the question aside. "Which interrogation room?"

"I don't know," Rodriguez said.

"How do you not know?" Lydia asked, exasperated.

"I just don't," Rodriguez said. A passing person—a man, his eyes wide and terrified—bumped into her, accidentally pulling her along with him. "Lake told me to get them out," Rodriguez added.

Still frustrated, Lydia gritted her teeth and waved her on. "Go," she said. Lydia turned back towards the onslaught of civilians. They must have emptied the drunk tank, too. Some of the people stumbled, obviously still drunk, even with fear burning through them. Another two shots went off in the squad room—Lydia saw flashes of light coming through a doorway. The noise was echoed by screams, a few people in the halls dropping to the floor. They weren't hit, just reacting to the noise.

Lydia bent to help one that had fallen, a vagrant in a plaid shirt and dirty cargo pants. He had his hands over the back of his head, pressing the front of his face into the cold ground. She touched his shoulder, but he shook her away. Lydia realized he was sobbing. "No!" he cried, voice muffled against the floor. "No, I can't go."

"It'll be alright," Lydia said, trying to sound soothing. "Just get up and keep moving."

"No," the man said again. "I can't."

Lydia gritted her teeth. "Come on," she said. She put her hands under his armpits, shifted into a rough squatting position. "On your feet."

"I can't," the man breathed.

Lydia pushed with her legs, pulling the man with her. He made it to his knees. Lydia kept him propped against her, felt him shudder when another shot went off. "You're getting out of here," she said, wrapping her arms around his waist.

"I want to die," the man whispered.

"Well, do it someplace else," Lydia said. Again she lifted, this time getting him to his feet. She pushed him down the hall and he tottered away, shaky but able to keep his feet. She made eye contact with a passing patrol officer, pointed at the man. "Help him," she said, and was surprised when the officer did as she said.

A hand gripped her shoulder, and Lydia, already on edge, jumped straight into a defensive posture. A flick of her arm snapped the baton to its full length, and she held it above and behind her as she turned, ready to crack whoever's skull stood behind her. Before she could swing, a pair of palms thudded into her shoulders, propelling her and the assailant away from each other. She swung anyways, but the momentum had carried him just out of her range, the end of the stick whistling past his face.

Lydia blinked. It was McDonagh, his hands raised now, palms outward, showing her he had nothing. It had been these hands that gripped her shoulders, these hands that pushed her. Nothing malicious, she realized, just trying to get her attention.

"You okay?" he asked.

"Yeah," Lydia said, lowering the baton. Then, "Sorry."

"What's happening?" McDonagh asked. The hallway was almost clear now, the squad room silent after a shout and a strange thud.

"I don't know," Lydia admitted. In another mood, she might have blamed Rodriguez for that, but right now it wasn't foremost on her mind. "Something's up though."

"Yeah," McDonagh said. They both looked towards the squad room. Someone—a detective, Lydia thought—was sprawled in the doorway like a discarded rag doll. "Where's your gun?" McDonagh asked.

Lydia gritted her teeth. "In my desk," she said. "Locked in a drawer."

McDonagh scowled. He drew his own, checked the chamber and took off the safety, then motioned for Lydia to follow. Lydia fell in behind as he started to pad down the hallway, their boots stepping lightly on the linoleum floors.

As they approached the door, Lydia could see that it was indeed a detective, though his name escaped her. He was hurt, but not badly. Breathing heavily, with a cut across his forehead. He groaned as they approached, clutching at his chest. "Goddamn," he muttered.

"Stay there," McDonagh said, stepping over him.

"No problem," the detective muttered. He barely stirred as Lydia stepped over him into the room beyond.

It was a mess, a wake of destruction and chaos. Officers lay everywhere, strewn about like stalks of wheat cut down in a field. They were all alive, Lydia could tell, shifting and moaning, clutching at broken limbs or struggling to stand and failing. Desks had been overturned, some in an attempt at creating cover, while others had broken apart against walls, thrown just like the people. The glass of the break room window was shattered, as was the window of the holding cell, and a water cooler had been shot, the contents spreading over the floor. At the center of all this chaos, Ian Caldwell stood alone, his wrists in chains.

McDonagh's gun raised to point at Caldwell. He wasn't looking at the detectives, was instead looking in fear towards the commander's office. "Caldwell," Lydia called.

The skinny man jumped in the air, whirled to face them. Lydia could easily read the expression on his face as terror, pure and simple. He held up his hands to them, empty palms outward. "No, please," he said, "you can't."

McDonagh slowly advanced on Ian. Behind him, Lydia felt useless with just her nightstick, but she couldn't see any guns within reach, and her desk had been thrown clear to the far wall. "Take it easy, Ian," McDonagh said. "Whatever this is we can talk it out."

"You don't understand," Caldwell said, starting to cry, fat tears running down his cheeks. "Nobody understands."

"Help us understand," McDonagh said.

"I've been *trying* to," Caldwell said. "That's what you don't understand. This wasn't me. This was *him*." Caldwell pointed to the commander's office.

Taking her eyes off Caldwell for one moment, Lydia glanced towards the office door. It was empty, the space beyond still. "Who?" Lydia asked.

"Hiiiiiiiiiiim," Caldwell wheezed, and, as if in answer, a man stepped through the door.

To Lydia, he was like a flash of lightning suspended in time. The air crackled in his presence, froze in Lydia's lungs. A small turn of her upper body to face him fully felt like wading through jelly, all sound and thought muffled. McDonagh turned too, slowly, gun pointed. But as Lydia took in the man, all desire to shoot him left her. Not that she didn't want the man dead—she just didn't want McDonagh to be the one to do it. She wanted to do it with her own hands.

"Please don't try," Caldwell whispered, his voice far away. "It never works."

The man, as Caldwell had said, was entirely green. His hair—curly, even a little bouncy—was green. His face—broad and flat, with a sharp angular nose and a full beard covering his chin—was green. His neck and chest—robust with muscles, old scars showing underneath his shirt—was green. His arms—like thick logs—and his legs—sturdier than the columns in city hall—were green. His bare feet—flat and hairy, with big bulbous toes and sharp old nails—were green.

He wasn't painted. No brush or hand could ever be so even, and no trace of skin seemed to shine out beneath it. He was simply green, in a way that felt so alien to Lydia that she couldn't take her eyes off him. And she hated him, hated him with a rage she had never felt before, an anger devoid of thought or fear or reason. She could no longer imagine a world without him, even though her one desire was to cleave him from this mortal coil. The man looked at her and smiled, his lips still pressed together.

"Please," Caldwell whispered, "just go."

In one hand, the giant held a single wooden pole. It looked like a twig in his huge hands, but Lydia guessed the shaft was as wide as her bicep. Embedded into the top was a broad piece of steel, curved like half of a shovel, with an edge that caught the light and held it. Even at almost four feet long, it looked small beside him. Lydia didn't have much experience with axes, but she could see that this one was of fine make and quality, even if it was hideously ugly. This was not an axe made by an assembly line, fierce but fragile, useful but unwieldy. This was older, more terrible. Made specifically for this green man's hands with the express purpose to kill. And from the way the wood was discolored a dark brown around the head, Lydia guessed it had.

In his other hand, the green giant held a single branch. It was covered in green leaves, small dots of red spread throughout. Looking at the leaves, Lydia recognized them as the same leaves they had pulled from the mouths of the victims, the same leaves that were Holly's calling card. This, on top of everything else, was the most compelling evidence to Lydia that this was their man. This was Holly.

"I'm already dead," Caldwell said.

McDonagh's pistol lowered. Lydia glanced at him, surprised. McDonagh did not look back at her, but dropped the pistol to the ground, then held up his hands. Lydia, for her part, did nothing with her baton. She didn't think it would do much against the man's axe. But he didn't seem to mind. When McDonagh put his pistol down, the man's smile deepened.

McDonagh walked towards the stranger, his steps careful and silent, his palms raised towards him. Lydia realized that McDonagh was stepping between her and the green man, presumably for her protection, though she was not against shoving McDonagh out of the way.

"We can work this out," McDonagh said.

The green stranger's eyes held on McDonagh, red and inscrutable. "Not yet," he said, his voice a deep bass, mellow and familiar but as unsettling as his skin.

The green man stepped towards Caldwell, who had not stopped crying. "Oh God," Caldwell whispered.

"The same stroke," Holly rumbled, "that is what you promised me. Freely given and unhindered. You have already broken that promise by seeking protection, by making me find you here. Now, at least, see this through with honor." Lydia couldn't keep herself from stepping forward, only stopped when McDonagh put an arm in front of her. "Kneel," Holly commanded.

Slowly, his legs shaking and his lips trembling, Caldwell got to his knees. Then he leaned forward, putting his hands on the floor, so that he was prostrate before the green man. Holly's smile vanished, and he slowly walked to Caldwell's side. From this position, he now faced Lydia and McDonagh. The axe rose into the air, loaded with energy.

"Don't do it," McDonagh said, his voice hoarse.

The red eyes looked up, met them both.

"There has to be another way," McDonagh said.

"No," the green man replied, "there isn't."

In one stroke, the axe descended. It bit cleanly through Caldwell's neck. A spray of blood shot across the room from the stump of Caldwell's body in a red arc, then decreased to a heavy ooze in less than a second as Caldwell's body slumped to the side. His head fell to the ground with a crunch, then rolled the opposite direction of the body. Lydia watched it come to a stop at her feet, the face looking up at her, mouth parted slightly, eyebrows raised, as if surprised at how little it hurt. Or at how much.

"Run," his lips said, though no noise came.

END of Episode Four

EPISODE FIVE: L'APPEL DU HACHE

ONE

Ash Falls Police Department - Dispatch Transcript

Period: 1828 - 1829 hrs. 08/14/2017

Dispatch: Be advised, 211 in progress at 27th SW and—

PCT 14-01: Back-up! We need back-up!

Dispatch: Who is this?

PCT 14-01: Sergeant (inaudible)—

PCT 14-02: Jesus Christ, we need someone here now.

Dispatch: Identify yourselves, immediately.

PCT 14-03: Intruder, 14th Precinct—

PCT 14-01: Precinct Four—

PCT 14-02: 14th

PCT 14-01: —teen

PCT 14-03: an intruder in 14th Precinct

Dispatch: 14th Precinct, how many units do you need?

PCT 14-01-02-03: Everyone!

TWO

With a grunt, the green man pulled his axe out of the floor. Blood from his victim's neck pooled around his bare, green feet, as if his gravity pulled it to him. He let the axe rest on his shoulder, gripping it and the holly bough in the same hand. Slowly, his eyes scanned across the room, taking in the damage, the destruction, the chaos that he had wrought. His green knuckles left a smear of red as he stroked them through his beard. Lydia bared her teeth when his eyes fell on her.

"He sought protection," Holly explained, not looking away. "The honorable thing would have been to find me alone, to accept the final term of our agreement. He failed."

The squad room was silent. The wounded, splayed across the floor like ears of discarded corn, made no noise, wondering what the green man would do next. Lydia and McDonagh stood alone against him, a police-issued baton in her hand, nothing in his. They waited, every muscle tense, ready to stop him if he made any attempt to flee.

"I came to this city to see if there were any here who could win my game," Holly said, hand leaving his beard to rest on his hip. "I came to see if any of that old strength still lived, the strength that humanity forged in the fires of battle and strife. To find honor, humility, bravery. I came to see if one who could be held to their word still walked this Earth."

His gaze shifted to McDonagh, who was stepping to the left. "I have found naught but cowards and oathbreakers," the green man said.

"Which was he?" McDonagh asked, nodding to the body on the floor. The green man turned slowly with McDonagh as he walked.

"Both," Holly said.

"And Emma Bosk? Leonid Ellwood?"

"Oathbreakers, as was this one's friend. Megan Rude was a coward, as was Jude Bates."

Lydia began to shift to the right, helping McDonagh to surround Holly. He was following McDonagh with both body and gaze. Soon, his back would be to Lydia. A mistake. Lydia was armed after all, and though she didn't look it, she was capable of doing a lot with that baton.

"And Sean Tanner?" McDonagh asked.

"The worst of them all," the green man laughed. "He was a fool."

"So you admit to murdering them?" Lydia asked. McDonagh had completed a half-circle around Holly, putting the giant squarely between the detectives.

"Murder?" Holly asked, indignant. "I do not murder. They chose this game, as will many more."

"But you killed them?"

Lydia raised her nightstick, readied herself to charge. One good stroke to the back of the head and he'd be down.

"Aye," the green man said. "I killed them. Them, and many more besides. I have killed beasts and demons, giants and men. I have tested kings and served queens. I have spared the worthy, smote the wicked, seen nations fall and castles burn. I have—"

Lydia had heard enough. She pushed herself off her front leg and dashed towards the giant. She moved silently, a scream written on her face though she made no noise. She raised the nightstick higher, her eyes locked on the back of his head, the rage filling her, driving away the fear. She swung.

At the last moment, the green man spun towards her, his free hand grabbing her wrist. In a single move, he continued his spin, lifting her in the air and flinging her over his head. Lydia felt his vice-like grip, felt her body go limp as she was borne into the air. Now she did scream as he released her, flinging her head-first towards the wall.

McDonagh saved her. He stepped directly into her path, and for a moment he appeared huge, larger than Holly even, his body covered in fur instead of clothes, his nose and mouth elongated into a snout. But when she hit him, the force carried both of them to the wall of the commander's office, where they collapsed into a heap. Hitting the brick wall still hurt, and together they slid down it, groaning. Lydia's whole body blazed with pain, her very bones protesting what had just happened. McDonagh, despite a dazed expression, looked entirely normal.

Footsteps approached. For a second, Lydia thought she had gone blind, but realized she was just squeezing her eyes shut. She kept them closed, not wanting to see the axe ready, to see her death coming.

The footsteps stopped.

"Even here, in what should be a hall of chivalry, I find fear," the green man said, his voice booming somewhere above her. "I came looking for warriors, but all I have found are beardless children. Are there none brave enough to stand alone before me? Are there none bold enough to take my challenge?"

"I am," a voice rasped. "I will."

Lydia felt McDonagh stir beneath her, as surprised as her by the voice. She opened her eyes. The green man was standing over them, his axe hanging loosely by his side, the branch in his other hand. His face was turned to the entrance of the commander's office. Lydia looked too. Lieutenant Lake stood there, a hand to his side, the other resting on the door frame. Blood ran freely from both his nose and mouth, and when he gritted his teeth they were red like the berries on Holly's branch. But Lake straightened himself, spat a glob of crimson spittle onto the floor. "I'm up for your challenge," he said.

Holly smiled. "Are you sure?"

"Yeah," the lieutenant grimaced.

McDonagh was pushing Lydia off of him. She didn't move. She couldn't. She didn't want to. Even his hand on her shoulder felt like being stabbed.

"You might not be so eager if you knew what the game is," Holly said.

With what looked like great pain, the lieutenant took his arm off the door frame. He stepped gingerly into the squad room. One of his eyes was sealed shut by blood, a cut above his brow refusing to scab.

"So tell me and we can get it over with," the lieutenant said. "Then get the hell out of my precinct."

With a small grunt, aided by McDonagh's hand on her shoulder, Lydia sat up. Her head throbbed with pain, her back and shoulders and limbs screamed for relief. She put both hands to her forehead, which felt sticky. When she pulled the hands away, blood covered her palms. McDonagh was on his feet—Lydia had no idea how he'd gotten there—and was carefully guiding her to rest against the wall.

"Today," the green man explained, holding out the axe, "you will take this weapon in hand. I shall kneel before you, expose my neck, and let you do what you wish to me with my axe. One stroke, to prove your strength, your will. But you must give me your word that you will find me in three days. In three days, you will submit yourself to receive the same stroke from me. In doing so, you will have proven your honor."

Lydia, against the wall, let out an impotent whimper, hand still pressed against her forehead, unable to take her eyes off that axe. Everything was exactly as Caldwell had described—including the rage, the burning desire to take that axe and kill him. This was the man she had been hunting for a week, standing in front of her in the flesh, threatening her commander. And she could do nothing. How McDonagh was standing, how Lake stayed in control in front of that thing, Lydia couldn't understand. And she couldn't look away.

Lake's frown deepened. "What's the catch?" he asked.

The green man's smile only deepened. "No catch," he said. "Why?"

"What happens if I cut off your head and kill you?" Lake asked. "How will you meet me again in three days?"

"If you kill me," Holly replied, "I won't be able to. But you have only one stroke. That is the test of your strength."

"If you move—"

"I will not move," the green man said. "You shall have a clean chance, one that you'd never be able to get otherwise."

Lake blinked. The room was still. The green man held out the axe, blood covering the handle. Lake took it.

"Wait."

McDonagh stepped forward. "Let me do it," he said.

"Stand down, McDonagh," Lake ordered. "This is my fight."

"All due respect, sir," McDonagh replied, "this is my case."

Lake took his eyes off the green man, glanced towards McDonagh. From where Lydia sat, McDonagh seemed mostly fine, even if she had just been thrown into him. The green man laughed, a low rumble that almost shook the room.

"Besides," McDonagh added, "there might be some trick here. Let me take the risk. The precinct still needs you."

Slowly, Holly went to his knees before the two men, gently laying his bough of leaves on the ground beside him. They soaked up Caldwell's blood. "Decide quickly," the green man said, "or be seen for the cowards you are."

McDonagh held out his hand. With a grunt of frustration, Lake handed the axe over before stepping away. Lydia, using an overturned chair, managed to push herself to her feet. She fell almost instantly, having to catch herself against the wall to stay upright, the sour taste of adrenaline in her mouth.

The green man put his palms on the floor.

"Where will I find you, in three days?" McDonagh asked, circling to stand beside him. His boots squelched on the wet floor.

"Complete your part of the game first," Holly replied. "I will tell you after."

McDonagh grunted in frustration. "There won't be an after," he said.

"Strike true," Holly chuckled, "and pray there isn't. *I* do not miss."

Lydia's breath was shallow as McDonagh raised the axe into the air. Something about it drew the eyes, something bright gleaming through the red stained metal. McDonagh lifted it easily enough, holding it above his head. Then, with a roar, he swung it over and down. It made the same satisfying squelch as it sliced through the flesh and bone, the same satisfying thud as it bit into the floor. Blood sprayed across the room, and the green head fell with a crunch, the curled hair dragging through the gore.

All was still.

"Damn fool," Lake sighed.

Lydia could not take her eyes from the body. Unlike Caldwell, it did not immediately slump to the side. It stayed rigid, still held up by the arms.

"How could either of us have possibly missed," Lake muttered, shaking his head as he took a step forward.

The body moved. It pushed itself onto its haunches, one arm picking up the holly branch. Lake jumped backwards, almost slipping on the slick floor. Lydia's breath caught in her chest. A gasp like the deflation of a tire echoed through the room. McDonagh was still as a statue. The green body rose to its full height, took the axe from McDonagh's stiff hands. Gently, the body stepped and stooped, scooping up its head by the hair. Lydia watched the orb rise, watched as the face slowly spun into view. It smiled at her, the eyes still full of life. Then, the body faced McDonagh.

"You'll find me in the holiest wild you know," the head said, the moving mouth looking unnatural without a body below it. "I'll wait to meet you there." The body turned, a trickle of blood still coming from the head. He walked fluidly to the door of the squad room, stepping over bodies and around furniture. Nobody moved to stop him. Everyone watched him leave.

Lydia pushed herself from the wall, staggered across the room after him. She expected McDonagh or Lake to stop her, but neither did. They were frozen, not quite recovered from the shock of what they had just seen.

Lydia paused at the door, looked down the long hallway. Just at the end, she saw a flicker of green disappear around the corner, followed by screams of terror. A trail of blood marked the way, small drips of red down the middle of the floor. Lydia followed.

She did not reach him in the lobby, but saw the doors swing shut behind him. She did not reach him on the street either. The night was dark, but she could still see the trail of blood. Wincing at the pain in her limbs, Lydia fished out her phone, turned on the flashlight. The blood led down the street. She followed.

The trail lasted for two blocks, then ended on a dark corner overhung by an old tree. Lydia looked for where it picked up again, but there was nothing. He was gone.

"Don't worry," a voice said. Lydia spun towards the tree, which sounded like the origin. No one was there. No one stood on the corner, nor behind the tree, nor in the doorway of the closest building. Lydia was entirely alone. "You'll get your chance," the green man—she knew his voice now—added. It came from a place so close to her, Lydia felt his breath on her ear. But she must have imagined it, for when she whirled around, the street was empty.

THREE

Bocek was the first to see the tree. He reached the top of a ridge, his boots nearly disappearing into the ash as he climbed. Lester, still a few feet below and helping Doss up a steep incline, saw Bocek pause, then shade his eyes with his palm. Burdynski joined him, and together the pair shared a word, Bocek pointing out whatever it was he saw. Then Burdynski turned and called down to Lester.

"You're going to want to see this," she said.

"What is it?" Lester called back.

A moment of silence, followed by, "You really should just get up here."

"Go," Doss said, but Lester ignored him, practically dragging the big man up the rest of the hill. Bocek helped the last few feet, eager to make up for his earlier mistakes. He didn't need to—everyone made mistakes, and Lester couldn't blame Bocek for making the first.

They helped Doss rest against a dead log, then Lester joined Bocek and Burdyinski at the crest. "What do you see?" he asked them.

"Well—" Burdynski said.

"I'm not quite sure, to be honest," Bocek finished.

Lester scanned the valley below. The wall of flames on the opposite hillside made a huge plume of smoke, which rose high into the air and then blew over their heads, obscuring the sun that still rose in the east. Lester couldn't make out anything in all that smoke. He only saw shades of red and black and grey.

"Not sure about what?" Lester asked. "What was it?" The day was already getting to him. He was tired and sore and would be smelling smoke for a year. In three days he'd had little to eat and even less rest. And it was unlikely they'd be pulled from the frontlines any time soon, as the other crews, the ones trying—and failing—to contain the rest of the fire were being relieved first. Lester and his crew were still lucky, but that luck was stretching extremely thin. Of the ten firefighters Lester set out with, only five were uninjured. And Doss wasn't looking too good. Even a rest through the night hadn't been quite enough for him. Exhaustion always took its toll.

"If we did see it," Burdyinski said, hesitant, "it's unbelievable."

Lester felt his temper rising. "You think you imagined it?" he asked slowly.

Neither of the firefighters had the courage to look at him. Bocek admitted, "I can't find it again, that's all," he said.

"You hustled me up here because you imag—" but then Lester saw something. A part in the smoke revealed green leaves and white flowers, a healthy tree nestled amongst the destruction.

Lester took off a glove and wiped his eyes, clearing some of the grime from his face. Then he looked again.

It was still there. Not only that, but the fire seemed to be parting in a small section, leaving a swathe of grass and bushes around the tree.

"What the hell?" Lester muttered.

"So you do see it?" Bocek asked excitedly.

"That's," Lester said, "impossible."

Burdyinski let her shovel fall to the ground beside her. "It's not unheard of," she said. "Fires will go around vineyards or other farms, sometimes, because they're separated from the trees and the vines don't burn so easily."

"We're still in the wilderness though," Bocek said. "Barely three miles in. There aren't any vineyards around here, nor any lakes, I think. And it can't be the river, that just wouldn't make sense."

Lester gritted his teeth, running his tongue over the roof of his mouth. It still tasted like vomit. He checked his watch, then glanced at Doss, who was taking small pained sips from his canteen. "We'll rest here for a bit," Lester said. "The fire needs to move up that hill more before we can work our way into this valley. We'll find out what this is then."

They all collapsed in various places on the hilltop. There was only a little shade, but the smoke made the sun into a harmless orange blob anyways. Lester searched his pack for supplies, passed dry crackers and peanut butter around to his crew. He made them eat the snack, knowing it would make them more thirsty and therefore drink more water. A supply truck would come by soon to resupply them.

Lester didn't want to stay on the hill. He wanted to go home, was almost willing to sprint all the way back to Ash Falls. He could see his crew felt much the same, saw it on their drawn and tired faces whenever they glanced east. They had all fought through their homesickness, sometimes having to physically prevent each other from turning back. No one was immune. Lester kept his mind from the fact that if he injured himself, he'd get to return. He was certain that if he thought about it too hard, he'd do it. Thinking about home, about the warmth of his bed or the comfort of the things he knew—it was dangerous.

They watched the fire ascend the hill, watched it leave the same destruction it had always left. And they watched the tree emerge from it, like a protective mother hen huddled over her nest. Lester counted four bushes, seven flowers, and two squirrels around the tree. The supply truck came, and they ate ham sandwiches from an ice box. They filled their canteens, the truck moved on, and the fire was far enough off for them to approach.

The crew was careful descending the hill, cutting a path directly to the spared tree. Lester, eager to see the tree up close, nearly led them into a coal field, but Bocek stopped him at the last moment. They had to double back, then traverse a wide circle around the embers. By the time they were back on a path towards the solitary tree, they were coming at it directly from the north instead of the east. The tree seemed no different from this side—a hundred buds bloomed along its branches, small trios of petals.

Once Lester stepped into the circle beneath the tree, the air dropped ten degrees. It was like stepping from a hot street into an air-conditioned building, except instead of the air feeling stale and recycled, it felt fresh and new, cleaner than any of the air that lay between them and Ash Falls. Life-giving, instead of merely sustaining. By the expressions of relief from his crew, Lester knew they felt the same.

Burdyinski broke the silence first. "How is this possible?" she asked.

Lester shook his head. He glanced at the tree, set his palm against its trunk. "Anyone know what species this is?"

"Hawthorn," Doss answered. Lester raised an eyebrow, but Doss only shrugged.

"Are they known for being fire resistant?" Lester asked.

"No," Doss shook his head. "They burn just like any other tree."

Slowly, Lester circled the trunk. Doss, still not fully rejuvenated, sat on a root. The others began to shoulder off their packs, recognizing a break when they saw it.

"You know what this feels like?" Bocek said. Lester met his eyes, had been thinking the same thing. He didn't want to say it though, wanted someone else to make the connection. "It's like whatever stopped the fire going towards Ash Falls," Bocek finished. "Not just how this shouldn't be here, but this—" he waved his hand in front of his face. "It *feels* the same," he said. "When you sent me back for the night, I felt this intense wave of relief. Not just from being off the front line, but like the air was lighter."

Lester could tell that each of his crew were beginning to think of home, felt their faces turn there, their feet begin to shift. He understood their longing, knew what was on their minds because it was on his too. Bocek was making them all think about it, even if he didn't mean to.

"I agree," Lester said. "It's another miracle. And this," he patted the tree, "this is the greatest miracle. A sign that even in all this death, life can persist." Lester met the gaze of each crew member, made sure they understood what he was driving at. Doss stood. Bocek looked away.

"We must protect this," Lester said, patting the tree again. "This tree is Ash Falls. Nothing can happen to it. Agreed?"

Silent nods, jaws set in determination. Lester put his helm back on, and the others did the same.

"We'll clear this valley first," Lester said. "No stray spark lights this tree, no moment of distraction leads to its destruction."

They all grunted in agreement. They had six hours of daylight left, and Lester made sure they used it.

FOUR

Lydia sat before a well, a swirling expanse of dark muddy liquid. The warmth of it made her cheeks rosy, brought feeling to her fingers and palms. Staring into the water, Lydia felt the urge to dive in, to drift away on some unknown current, to sink until she was too deep to ever find air again.

There's a name for this, she told herself: *the call of the void.* The desire to self-destruct, to do the thing that will so obviously lead to your death.

Tunnel vision. A separate sensation, but Lydia also recognized it. Focusing on something so intently that it becomes your whole world. In reality, she knew, there was no deep murky lake, only the cup of coffee in her hands. The injured had been removed from the squad room, Caldwell's corpse had been taken down to Ploski's morgue, every square inch of the crime scene had been documented in pictures and notes. Lydia was aware of it all, could trace every moment. But it had only been a dream, happening around her, the movements slow, the voices distant. All Lydia really knew was the coffee, the desire not to drink but to sink.

Lydia did not fight the sensations. She had experienced both, in various ways, throughout her life. She knew enough to know that fighting only made them stronger. It might even be why she was feeling them both so acutely right now —a different Lydia, the one that lived three minutes or three hours ago, had struggled to remain aware. She didn't know. Time was lost on her, now. And she was fine with that. In real time, in the real world, Lydia would have to face something she couldn't explain, would have to accept something beyond the natural. Something she had sworn to not let herself get sucked into again. But here, before the lake of warmth, all Lydia had to decide was whether to give in or not. Whether to answer the call.

"Pike."

Lydia blinked, the lake beginning to shrink.

"Pike."

Clearer now. And closer. A man's voice. The edges of the lake shrank into view, slowly coalescing into the cup between her hands. She felt briefly dizzy, fought it away with a shake of her head.

"You okay?"

Lydia looked up. McDonagh stood beside her, a hand reaching out to her shoulder, unsure if he needed to shake her awake. On a different day, Lydia might have resented that hand. Today, it didn't matter. But when she met his eyes, his hand still twitched instinctively backwards.

"Yeah," Lydia said, her voice muffled.

McDonagh didn't respond, still holding her gaze. Lydia wished he would stop. She was starting to tunnel again, starting to get lost in his eyes, so light they were almost grey. Then, he glanced at the chair beside her, flopped into it, and Lydia was present again. More or less.

"Check this out," McDonagh said, fishing into his pocket and producing something. A small plastic bag, which he handed over to her. For the second time in a couple of hours, Lydia held up a green leaf, studied it's tapered edges.

"Where was it?" Lydia asked, dully. She knew it was English holly, but the green man had been holding a branch of the plant. It could have been anywhere.

"In his mouth," McDonagh said, and somehow that was the least surprising answer. "Did you see him put it in?" McDonagh asked after a moment's silence.

Lydia shook her head. "He never went near the head," she said. She didn't think about what this meant, not yet. There were two options, really—the green man had magicked it in there somehow, or the green man had an accomplice. In an hour—or a day—or a week—Lydia would reason away the possibility of it being magic, would confront whoever the green man worked with then. For now, she didn't care.

"Well," McDonagh said, tucking away the leaf and stretching himself out in his chair, "at least we know the timeline's right."

"Great," Lydia said, not looking at him.

"Every three days," McDonagh said. "Which means we have three to find him."

Lydia shook her head. "Doesn't help us much," she said.

McDonagh took a deep breath. "Yes, it does," he said. "Now we know our deadline. Normally, we never get to know the deadline. We start running against a clock that's been running longer than we'll know for certain, ready to run out before we're ready. From the moment we find a body, it's an impossible game of catch up." He smiled sardonically. "But not this time," he finished.

"You don't know that," Lydia said, her voice tired.

"Yes I do," McDonagh said firmly. "We know so much now." He held out his hand, started ticking off each point on a finger. "We know when the next attack will happen," he said. "Three days. We know who the attacker is—our new green friend. We know who he'll attack—me. We know where he'll do it—wherever I choose. All that leaves is why and how. Why is this happening? How do we stop it? If we figure out 'why,' I bet 'how' will become clear."

"But you're still just guessing," Lydia said. "What if we're wrong? This is your life on the line."

"So it's my call," McDonagh replied, his voice firm. "Trust me. I've got a bit of experience in this kind of thing."

"What kind of thing is that?"

"The magical kind," he said, his voice soft.

Lydia glanced at him again. Did he really mean that? Was this really something supernatural? For a moment, Lydia almost believed it could be.

Mom would be so proud, she thought, *and Uncle Leo would be so disappointed.*

"Why," Lydia said. A statement, not a question.

McDonagh nodded. "Why," he agreed.

"It might have something to do with the first victims," Lydia said. "Bates and Tanner."

"Yes," McDonagh nodded. "I've got a contact in the lumber company. I'll drop by tomorrow, see what he knows."

"We both will," Lydia said.

"No," McDonagh waved the comment away. "It's best if I go alone. Trust me," he said again, meeting her eyes.

"You always want me to trust you," Lydia said.

"That's what partners do," McDonagh said. "Now, what did you find before our friend dropped in today?"

Lydia shook her head, not understanding him. She told him about the manifest, told him how she had narrowed the list down to three names—Falls' Brewing, Ben's Antiques, and Crowley Liquor.

"But I don't think anything with the warehouse matters anymore," Lydia said. "If we think it has to do with the lumber company, Bosk, Wood, and Caldwell likely just got in the way. Wrong place, wrong time."

McDonagh shook his head. "We can't rule anything out yet," he said. "Maybe I'll be barking up the wrong tree, maybe you will. But you should still check out those three businesses, see if there's anything hinky."

"You really think we have the time to guess?" Lydia asked.

"We're not guessing," McDonagh answered. "We're closing leads."

Yesterday, Lydia would have been tired of this. She would have kept arguing, would have insisted they start actually working the case together, because this was the last straw. But she couldn't. She was too tired to do anything. Including argue. She couldn't understand how McDonagh was so cheery, so alert. It was like she had swung the axe, not him.

"What else you got?" McDonagh asked.

Lydia shrugged. "I think Kevin Wood's body is in the morgue downstairs."

"Think?"

"He's too burned to identify."

McDonagh sucked in air through his teeth. "Well, it fits with the rest of Caldwell's story. Anything on him?"

"A poker chip, maybe," Lydia said. "I don't know why. It's not like there's a casino around here."

"Not a legal one, anyways," McDonagh said. Then, after a moment, he added, "Could it be an Al Anon chip?"

"Maybe," Lydia shrugged. "Want me to visit a local AA or NA chapter? Or whatever secret underground casino you happen to know about?"

McDonagh couldn't repress a wry smile. "No," he said. "Not yet. It's not relevant, not right now. That's a question for after we get this guy."

This, at least, Lydia had no argument with. She crossed her arms, trying to keep her mind from wandering over the events of the night. "So, what now?" Lydia asked, to distract herself.

"We sleep," McDonagh said decisively. "And eat something that didn't come out of a vending machine. You visit those businesses tomorrow, I'll go talk to my friend. You should probably stop by Wood's and Caldwell's apartments too, if you can, see what that gets us. Caldwell's probably got a key, and you can talk your way into Wood's. Hell, just break in if you need to. I want to know 'why' by the end of tomorrow. That gives us a day to figure out 'how,' then a day to plan and prepare."

"Prepare what?"

McDonagh shrugged. "Something. But for now, go sleep."

Lydia rubbed her eyes with the heel of one hand. "I don't think I'll be able to," she admitted.

"Nonsense," McDonagh assured her. He stood, held out his hand. "You look like you'll pass out any moment."

Lydia looked at him, knew he was right. His back was straight, his eyes sharp and focused. "How are you so calm?" she asked.

For a moment, his eyes softened. "Like I said," he answered, "I've seen some stuff."

If she trusted nothing else, Lydia trusted that.

FIVE

The refugees from the squad room had already dispersed into the night, using the chaos to get away from whatever judgement awaited them. Thomas was glad. He doubted the AFPD would be able to round them all up again, nor did he much care. Petty crime really didn't seem like much of a priority anymore.

There were two, however, he did want to find. Two he wanted to talk to on his own turf downtown. If he was going to talk to Bale—and he wasn't sure he'd be able to—it was the kind of thing he couldn't do unannounced. No one in Bale's pack would ever talk to McDonagh. So, to get a message to Bale, he would need to go through Monya—and to go through Monya, he needed to find those two that had been in the station that morning, had still been in the station right before all hell broke loose.

Thomas began his hunt on the precinct's front steps, his nose in the air. Below him, the street stretched away, a ribbon as dark as the night's sky. Thomas waited for a wind to pass, inhaled deeply as it brushed his face. Gas. Steel. Asphalt. Ash. Water. And underneath it, the smell he had picked up in the station. They had gone east, the opposite direction of their home. And they were still close. Thomas inhaled again. He could almost see the path they had taken, could follow their scent as well as any hound.

Thomas set off on foot, descending the steps in a rhythmic gait. They had gone up 10th, following a path parallel to the river. So did Thomas, not quite walking and not quite running. It was a bounding, invigorated trot, like a horse just given its head. He stuck to the shadows beneath the buildings, even though the streets were emptier than usual. In Ash Falls, you never knew who might be watching.

He followed them four blocks east on 10th, kept with their scent south on Triflorium, and then west on 20th. They crossed Main, then dove into the maze of alleys and side streets between 20th and 29th. Thomas dogged them the whole way, only stopping to avoid other pedestrians as best he could, pretending to ignore them if he couldn't. Most ignored him back, which suited Thomas just fine.

He caught up with them underneath I-5. Trucks and other traffic still rumbled overhead, but the intersection below was entirely deserted. Thomas could tell as he approached that they were waiting for him there, knew by the way their scent had settled and not moved on. No doubt they had noticed his scent too, felt him following. Probably why they had left the main streets. They would never have lost him though. Not on foot, not downtown. Thomas guessed they just wanted a little time to prepare.

Thomas slowed as he approached the intersection, first from a trot to a walk, then to a meander, his hands raised above his head. When he was in the middle of the intersection, he came to a stop. He had a small comfort from the weight on his hip, the gun he had retrieved in the aftermath of the night. Not that it would do much good, but it still felt nice.

"I need to talk," Thomas called out.

Silence. He counted to five in his head.

"Seriously," he added.

"We don't," one of them called back.

McDonagh nodded. "I guess that's fair," he said. "It's not really you I need to speak to anyways."

Another pause. "I don't think she wants to see you either," the other said. They still had not left their hiding spots.

"Then we're all on the same page," Thomas said. "But wanting is different than needing."

"What do you need then?"

McDonagh sucked cool air through his teeth. "Did you get a look at that monster?" he asked.

"Not really."

"But you smelled it, didn't you?"

Silence.

"I think Bale had something to do with it," Thomas continued. "If he did, then he has put all the packs in danger. But he'll also know things that will help me stop it. I need to talk to him."

"What's that got to do with us?"

"Nothing," Thomas shrugged. "But Monya can let him know I'm coming. I'll also see her, if she wants. I need to pay my respects anyhow."

No answer.

"I'm going now," Thomas said. "You take care of yourselves." He turned and started to leave the intersection. He could tell when he was passing one of them, but he ignored him. The werewolves let him go. Thomas made his way to the nearest big street, then angled his path towards his apartment.

Six

Lydia made it as far as her car in the AFPD parking lot. She was sitting inside of it, key in the ignition, when she lost control. Instead of turning the car on, she leaned her head forward, crossed her arms across the wheel, and rested her forehead against them.

She screamed.

She screamed until it reverberated around the interior of her car, until her emotions echoed back at her, frustration becoming fear, pain becoming exhaustion, and loathing becoming hate. She screamed until her voice was hoarse from it. Until she had lost all her breath. Until she didn't care if anyone else heard.

When she was finished, she stayed in that position a few minutes longer, taking deep breaths of the car's stale air. Her eyes itched, and she wiped them on her forearms. Then she leaned back, resting against the headrest, hands now holding onto the wheel. She thought of her apartment, of her cold, empty bed. She thought about the leftover Chinese food in her refrigerator. And, most importantly, she thought about the one can of Pabst Blue Ribbon she had not drunk yet.

"Screw it," Lydia said. She pulled her keys from the ignition, took her badge off her belt and stowed it in her glove box. She still hadn't found her sidearm or nightstick, but she knew she didn't want either one. She checked her jacket pockets for cell phone and wallet. The phone she stowed in the glovebox too. From her wallet she took a twenty and her driver's license, then threw the rest into the center console, from which she removed a small makeup kit. Her hand shook as she fumbled through the various items, but then she muttered "screw it" again and threw the whole lot back in the console. Instead, she grabbed a set of brass knuckles—not her favorite, but they would have to do. At the last minute, she changed her mind again and grabbed her phone. With that, she climbed out of the car, shut the door, and locked it.

Most of the 14th Precinct preferred a bar called Brenin, an old school Irish pub one block south of the station. It was the kind of bar that still allowed smoking, and the cops still let it happen because most of them wanted a place to smoke indoors. It was where they let off steam, got into fights, or made bets on who would solve the most cases in a week. Lydia had only been there once. Her partner at the time—an older patrolman named Arne who never had a chance at detective—got too drunk and made a pass at one of the waitresses, telling Lydia to watch and learn. The place lost its appeal after that.

Instead, Lydia found Chooski's, a dive three blocks in the opposite direction. She liked its dingy close quarters, its weird wall art, its set of surly regulars who all sat one seat apart at the bar. They tolerated Lydia's presence as long as she came alone and the bartender mixed a strong drink no matter who you were. Nobody talked. Exactly the kind of place she liked after a long day on the pavement when all she wanted was peace and quiet and to not see any other uniforms. Exactly the kind of place she needed tonight.

When she arrived, she noticed it was a little emptier than usual—the regulars had not yet thrown up their shield of indifference, and there were large gaps between the stools. Lydia didn't recognize the bartender either. The woman behind the counter tonight was tall, with pale skin and dark hair tied behind her head. She smiled brightly at Lydia as she entered. Not quite normal for Chooski's, but Lydia still smiled back. She chose a seat one space away from another regular, all but completing the shield.

"What'll you have?" the bartender asked, placing a small glass of water on the counter before Lydia.

"A beer," Lydia said.

"We've got plenty," the bartender said.

"Just a cheap one. Not PBR, though." She drank that enough at home.

It looked for a moment like the new bartender was about to say something else, but then she only shrugged and turned away. Lydia watched as she took a glass, kept watching as she put it under a tap and pulled. A golden yellow liquid flowed into the glass, white foam climbing up the sides.

When the bartender returned, she slid Lydia's beer across the counter without comment. Lydia took a steady drink. The beer was wonderfully cool and smooth, with a yeasty aftertaste that made her want more. For a moment, Lydia literally felt the tension release in her shoulders, and she leaned back contentedly.

"You like it?"

Lydia glanced up at the bartender, who was smiling. She had green eyes, Lydia noticed, and a sharp, angular face that was quite attractive. Her name tag read "Lilly." Lydia couldn't keep from smiling back.

"I do," Lydia said.

The bartender smirked. "Thought you might," she said. She gave a little wink, then kept moving down the counter.

Lydia watched her work, only looking away when the bartender happened to glance back at her. Otherwise, she quietly enjoyed her beer, doing her best to not think about her day. Beer was good for that. Whenever the memory of Caldwell's head rolled through her memory, she simply had to wash it away. It wasn't a good long-term solution, but it would do for tonight.

Lilly the bartender returned. "So do you come here often?" she asked, leaning on the counter.

"Yeah," Lydia couldn't help it. "All the time."

Lilly glanced at the door, trying ineffectually to hide an infectious smile, complete with perfectly white teeth, incisors that were just a tad too long. "Well then," Lilly said, "I guess you know I'm new?"

Lydia shrugged. "I wouldn't have been able to tell otherwise," she said. "You're a natural back there." She kept smiling, but inside she gave herself a sharp kick. *What the hell did that mean?* she asked herself. *Was that supposed to be a compliment?*

Instead of answering, Lilly leaned against the counter and asked, "So, shit day?"

"Excuse me?" Lydia asked, taken aback.

"You look like you had a shit day," the bartender said, tilting her head to the side. "No offense."

"None taken," Lydia chuckled, and Lilly grinned. "Yeah, I had a pretty shit day." She looked down at her glass, tried to focus on the pale foam.

"Want to talk about it?" Lilly asked.

Lydia nodded, her eyes locked back on Lilly's green irises. "Yeah," she said. "But I can't, really. It's hard to explain."

Lilly smiled, showing her incisors again. "Try me," she said.

Before Lydia could take her up on that, a group of ten people walked in. The volume in the bar got immediately louder. The bartender walked around from behind the counter after they were all seated, giving Lydia a small wink as she passed. The regulars all shifted a little uncomfortably at the noise, but they didn't say anything.

"Do you like it?" Lilly asked as she returned to the bar, nodding to Lydia's near empty beer glass.

"Yeah," Lydia smiled, looking up from her phone. "What is it?"

"It's the Flagship Lager from Falls' Brewing," Lilly said. "We're a local brewery."

Lydia raised an eyebrow. "We?"

"I'm an assistant brewer," Lilly said, modestly. "I tend tables as a side gig." She pointed at Lydia's glass. "You want another?"

"Sure," Lydia nodded.

Lilly ventured farther down the bar, taking orders from the other regulars, and Lydia watched her for a moment. When she looked back at her phone, she had forgotten why she pulled it out.

Just as she remembered, her phone rang, the screen flashing "McDonagh" at her. Lydia nearly dropped it in surprise, but she managed to keep her grip, answer, and put the phone to her ear—all while barely keeping a particularly angry curse behind her lips.

"Hello?" Lydia asked.

"Come to my apartment," McDonagh said. "Now."

"Why?"

"He's been here," McDonagh said.

Lydia was gone before her second beer arrived, her twenty soaking up some condensation from the counter.

SEVEN

Thomas missed the lock on his first attempt, heard the tip of his key scratch against metal. He cursed under his breath, kept struggling to find the hole. Though some of his kind could see well in the dark, it was one of the few traits he had failed to inherit. He also failed to inherit his mother's good memory, because he always forgot to turn on the porch light when he left in the morning.

Key clenched between his fingers, Thomas found the keyhole with the pad of his thumb. Once he had it, he kept his thumb pressed against the opening while sliding the key next to his thumb, then shifted both until the key slid in. He had learned this technique on power outlets as a teenager, using it to plug in a lamp in the dark so he could keep reading. Back then, he surprised himself when a flash of blue arced between his finger and the prong of the wall plug. Teenager Thomas's arm was numb for a week after that. He might have learned to never do it again, but instead he only chose to be more careful. He was shocked twice more in his life, but it was never enough to dissuade him.

Mariam hated it, of course. Most of the women Thomas knew kept a casual indifference to the habit, maybe only telling him to not do it if they were sharing a bed. But Mariam actively tried to break him of it, told Thomas to never do it in her home and made him promise to never do it away from her. As with all his promises, he did a poor job keeping it. Old dog, new tricks, and all that.

The apartment's rear window opened just below a street lamp, so Thomas would have light once he entered. It was getting through the door that was hard. Once inside, he always immediately threw the lock, bolt, and chain before moving farther in. He emptied his pockets onto a small table conveniently next to the door before removing his coat and hanging it on the rack. Only after all this did he turn on the hall light.

Something in the apartment smelled off to him. A faint whiff of decay. It filled his nostrils the moment he opened the door. He thought it was probably a dead rat in the ventilation. One of the other tenants would complain soon enough, once the stench was too great for humans to deal with. Thomas would simply suffer in the meantime, not wanting his landlord to grow suspicious.

McDonagh moved first to the bathroom, then into his small bedroom where he kicked off his shoes and undid his tie. He threw it on the bed, then walked back towards his door to check the mail slot. One envelope sat in the tray—a bill. Thomas knew the amount without having to look, so he threw it onto the side table too. Then he flipped on the kitchen light, thinking about what to make for dinner.

He stopped. Very suddenly, he knew what smelled of decay. He reached out carefully. His fingers touched one of the points—hard, covered in a thin velvet. Definitely real. Thomas did not touch the rest.

Six prongs—young, still narrow. But impressive, nonetheless. They grew from two antlers, which rested upright on his table, pointing towards the door, as if someone had arranged them there. A patch of fur connected the antlers, and a line of red blood trickled from it, showing the slight slant of Thomas's table.

Thomas didn't take his eyes off the display. His hand fished into his pocket, pulled out his phone. He dialed the most recent number, then put the phone to his ear.

"Hello?" Pike answered.

END of Episode Five

EPISODE SIX: I LEFT MY HEART IN AXE

FALLS

ONE

Lydia thought his bedroom was small and a little cramped. This in spite of the fact that the only thing in the room was his well-made bed, the blue blanket folded into tight military corners. That was it—no desk, no side table, no chair, not even a closet. The room practically *was* a closet. The room of a man who had been alone for a long time.

Not that Lydia could judge. Her apartment wasn't much better.

She crossed to the small window, lifting up the blinds to look at the locks. She tried shifting the window but was unable to. She couldn't unlock it either—the metal was rusted together, unopened for a very long time despite the August heat. She pursed her lips. No one had gone through here, that much was evident.

Lydia found McDonagh where she left him—in his small living room, sitting at the table that was evidently his desk and dinner table. He hadn't moved an inch, his eyes locked on the antlers occupying the center of his kitchen counter. He looked small, sitting there. Not the tall, lanky man who drew gazes in the squad room and on the street. He looked like the kind of man you would look past, the kind of man you would forget.

"They're all locked," Lydia said, taking the apartment's other chair. "You sure your front door was locked?"

"It was when I got home," McDonagh said, not moving.

"Are there any other keys?" Lydia asked.

"No."

"Your landlord doesn't even have one?"

"He lost it a few years back," McDonagh said.

"Could that—"

"I took it," he added, finally glancing at her.

"Why?" Lydia asked, raising an eyebrow.

"So that something like this couldn't happen," McDonagh said.

Lydia nodded thoughtfully. Seemed fair enough. "What'd you do with it?"

"I destroyed it."

"How?"

"I heated it up over a hot flame, then used a hammer to flatten it into a sheet. I made the sheet into a ball, then threw the ball into the river."

"All that, and yet you only use one lock," Lydia commented.

"There's a fine line between being safe and drawing too much attention to yourself." He put his head in his hands, rubbed the corners of his eyes with his thumbs. "You'll get the hang of it eventually," he added.

Lydia ignored him, still running through possibilities in her mind. "Do you know the keysmith who made the copy?" she asked.

McDonagh thought for a moment, then shook his head. "I haven't the faintest idea," he said. "The apartment's so old my landlord probably doesn't even know. Do keysmiths keep old copies?"

Lydia shrugged. "I doubt it. I don't have any other ideas, though. And without any evidence the lock was picked—"

"Which there wasn't."

"Then I have no idea how he got in here."

"I've got one," he said, now resting his chin on his clasped hands.

"Which is?"

"Magic."

Lydia scoffed reflexively, then caught herself. The image of that green smile came back to her, unbidden, the way that green body had moved with ease and grace. So lifelike it was horrifying.

She met McDonagh's cold eyes. He was watching her intently, his stare probing in a way that made her vaguely uncomfortable, like he was flaying away her skin and bone.

"Do you believe?" he asked.

Lydia was careful not to answer with body language. "I didn't know it was AFPD policy to consider the paranormal in its investigations," she said.

McDonagh's gaze remained fixed. "It's not," he admitted. "This isn't a conversation we could have with the lieutenant. This isn't a conversation you and I could even have at the station. But we need to have it."

Lydia's eyes narrowed. "What conversation?" she asked.

McDonagh waited a beat, then asked again, "Do you believe in magic?"

Lydia waited to see if he would smile, waited to see if he would say it was a joke. When he didn't, she answered truthfully—"No." But no sooner had she said it than that image came to her again, that sickening smile. And as soon as that smile faded, another image replaced it—her mother, sitting in the desert, wearing nothing but a loose white shirt and a bandana to protect her bald head. She and Lydia sat in a circle sketched in sand, the lines of a pentangle traced around them. Her mother was spreading some herbs on the lines, but harsh winds almost immediately kicked them up, blowing them away while Lydia's mother struggled to complete the ritual.

Lydia held her mother's necklace between her fingers. The rough texture of the wicker hurt her fingertips when she pressed too hard, but she gripped it tight anyways, trying to decide what she believed.

"No" was not quite the right answer to McDonagh's question. The right answer was "Not anymore." The right answer was that she used to, but that she had seen it fail too many times, and the few minor attempts she saw work could be easily explained away by natural phenomenon. The right answer was that her mother had, and that her mother's—and Lydia's—belief in magic was what killed her in the end. Believing it instead of her doctors. But all that would be too difficult to explain to him—nor did she want to—so all she said was "No."

Then she asked, "Do you?" though she was a little afraid of the answer.

McDonagh carefully sighed. "I don't believe it exists," he said, and Lydia unclenched the hand by her side. "I *know* it exists," McDonagh clarified.

Lydia frowned, waiting for him to explain. When he didn't, Lydia pushed him. "How do you *know*?"

McDonagh smiled. "Are you just choosing not to remember what happened at the station?" he asked. "Or are you really that dumb?"

At first, she thought he meant when he caught her because, after all, she thought she *had* seen something. Something about him. But even that was too quick to be anything other than her imagination. Besides, he obviously meant what Holly had done. And that was something Lydia could not explain away.

She shook her head in frustration. "That was not necessarily magic," she said, though she wasn't sure she believed that either. She wasn't sure if she believed anything anymore.

McDonagh leaned forward, resting his elbows on his knees. "Then what was it?"

"I don't know," Lydia said. "Some kind of David Copperfield thing? He ever do something like this?"

His lips peeled back into a wolfish smile, a chuckle rattling through his teeth. "You know I saw a Copperfield show once?" he asked.

"Is that why you 'know' magic exists?" Lydia asked, eyebrow raised.

"No," McDonagh said. "It's how I know he's a faker. And no, David Copperfield never picked up his own severed head and walked out of a police precinct—dripping blood the whole way, mind you—before disappearing entirely."

"So, what?" Lydia said. "You've seen magic? Before the little show we got tonight?"

McDonagh's smile faded. He chewed his lip a moment, shifted evasively in his chair. "I really can't believe you've been here this long and haven't seen anything," he said, which Lydia couldn't help but notice was not an answer. She let it pass.

Instead, she leaned back in her chair, crossed her arms. "What am I supposed to have seen?" she asked.

McDonagh shrugged. "More of what you saw tonight," he said. "A lot more."

"Seriously?"

"Yeah," he nodded. "Half the force knows about it, at least. The other half have an inkling."

"Half the force is corrupt," Lydia retorted. "Or at least a little."

"That's because they've seen what I've seen," McDonagh answered. "What you should've seen."

They watched each other as she processed this. Finally, she asked, "So does that mean you're corrupt?" His only response was half a smirk.

He stood and walked to his counter. Lydia listened while he shuffled a few things around, evidently trying to ignore his grisly new trophy as long as possible. She turned to see him uncap a pen and begin to write something on a piece of paper.

"What's that?" she asked.

"Someone I think you should meet," he said. He finished scribbling and tore the paper from the pad. "When you've got the time," he added, handing her the paper.

Lydia glanced at it long enough to see an address from somewhere on the eastside. McDonagh didn't sit again, was leaning against the counter, his eyes on the antlers. Lydia folded the slip of paper and put it into her shirt pocket. When she stood, McDonagh didn't react. She studied his face —pale, even in the warm glow of his apartment. Drawn. Lined. Worried. More creases than there should have been, more than there were yesterday. She guessed she didn't look too good either.

"Want to come sleep at my place?" she offered, tensing a little as the words came out.

"Nah," he said, not turning to look at her. "Doubt I'll get much sleep anyways."

She relaxed just a little, because it appeared he had not taken the offer in a way she had not meant it. "Want me to stay here then?" she asked.

Now he turned, a rueful smile on his face. "You don't have to," he said. "I'm not worried he'll do anything. He said he wouldn't."

Her tension released fully then because she had not wanted to stay here either. She had only offered because that's what good partners do, and he evidently didn't think she was a good enough partner.

Lydia stood and McDonagh pushed himself off the counter. "I should get going then," Lydia said.

"Yup," McDonagh agreed. He led her towards his door and started unbolting his extra locks. "We've both got an early day."

"And a long one," Lydia added.

She waited while he finished opening the door for her. He paused once all the locks were undone to check the peephole. Satisfied, he swung it open and stepped aside to let her pass. The air outside was cool, crisp after the damp of his apartment. Lydia stopped on the step to take a relieved breath, then nodded once to him.

"You know," she said, "if it really is magic, doesn't that mean he's cheating at this game?"

"So?" he asked.

"So if he's cheating, why do you have to even go through with it?"

"Because I can cheat too," McDonagh replied after a moment. Then, "Goodnight, Pike."

"Goodnight."

He closed the door as she descended his steps, troubled.

Two

Ash Falls Police Department - Acquisition Request

Date: 08/15/2017   *Precinct:* 14th

Rank: Lieutenant   *Name:* Benedict Lake

(#) Item(s) - reason:

(12) desks - old desks destroyed or in unrepairable condition

(16) computers - old computers destroyed or in unrepairable condition

(13) desk chairs - old desk chairs destroyed or in unrepairable condition

(2) microwave ovens - old microwave ovens destroyed or in unrepairable condition

(4) tables - old tables destroyed or in unrepairable condition

(7) table chairs - old table chairs destroyed or in unrepairable condition

(3) break room couches - old break room couches destroyed or in unrepairable condition

(1) coffee maker - old coffee maker destroyed or in unrepairable condition - *high priority*

THREE

The stairs up to the apartment were covered in puke. Lydia frowned as she studied them, making sure this was the right place. At the top of the staircase were two doors, one with a 'sixteen' placard nailed to the wall next to it, the other with an 'eighteen.' Ian Caldwell's driver's license listed his apartment as 836 South Francis, apt. 18. So, this had to be it.

At least the vomit didn't look fresh. If Lydia had to step in it, not much would stick to her shoe, and what did would probably come off easily. The smell was atrocious, though, and not at all what she needed after a night of tossing and turning, the image of Caldwell's head rolling through her mind.

She stuck to the edge of the staircase, stepping gingerly on her toes, one hand held over her nose, the other gripping the banister. She almost ran her hand through some vomit that had managed to land on the railing too, but she noticed it just in time. Whomever this belonged to, they had hurled their breakfast from the top of the stairs—there was almost none on the landing. With a grunt, Lydia jumped to the last stair, avoiding the rest of the vomit and coming to a stop in front of Caldwell's door. The smell, if possible, was even worse up here.

Lydia wasn't sure she ever heard Caldwell mention a roommate. To be safe, she knocked twice, waited patiently for an answer or a noise—some indication that someone was in there. Nothing forthcoming, Lydia pulled Caldwell's keys from her pocket, began testing each one on the door's lock. This wasn't exactly legal, but she figured Caldwell wouldn't complain.

She had already been to Wood's apartment. All she found was a lack of alcohol and a calendar with every Tuesday and Thursday marked off, "7:00 p.m." circled below the date. This was enough to convince her, even if it didn't confirm, that the body in the AFPD morgue belonged to Kevin Wood, that the chip she'd found was his sobriety chip.

She found the right key on her fourth try, though the lock stuck at first and she had to throw her full weight behind it. When the door finally opened, it made a loud, slightly ominous creak. Inside the apartment was completely dark, even though it was already nearly ten. Lydia scowled, thinking about the flashlight she had left locked in her desk.

"Why do I never have something when I need it?" she muttered to herself.

Her hand slid to her waist, came to rest comfortably on her pistol. She unbuttoned the holster so she could have a clear draw, then ran her hand over the walls behind Caldwell's door. After a moment, she found two switches. The first did nothing, though Lydia heard a faint buzzing somewhere above her head. The second brought the hallway beyond to life.

The apartment was small enough that the hallway light illuminated the rest—the living room, the small kitchen, the entryway to a bathroom. She guessed the bedroom was around the corner. It was clear that the apartment had been empty for a few days. An almost imperceptibly fine layer of undisturbed dust covered the floors. The smell alone would have driven anyone out. It was like unwashed blankets wrapped around old hamburger—fusty, damp, putrid. Lydia had to keep her mouth covered as she entered.

A quick check of all the rooms confirmed the place was indeed empty. Satisfied, Lydia rebuttoned the holster, checking to be sure that her safety was on, then shut the door to the apartment. This, somehow, made the smell worse, even though the door kept the vomit smell out. The air felt close—warm. Caldwell used blackout curtains, which accounted for why the space was so dark, but Lydia still couldn't quite figure out what made that awful stench. The longer she stayed, the worse it got.

Trying to put her finger on what it was, Lydia turned on more of the lights. All the floors were covered by the same layer of dust, undisturbed except where Lydia walked. The smell was the least pungent in the bedroom, but as Lydia walked back to the front door it became worse again.

Not the front door, she realized. *The kitchen.*

To test this, she walked into the living room, which again wasn't as bad. But when she took two steps into the kitchen, it got so vivid she had to retch.

She looked in the fridge first. Nothing unusual except for some old milk, which Lydia knew from experience didn't smell like this. Nothing in the freezer either. The cupboards, filled with the expected cups, pots, pans, and plates, held nothing that would make the smell. Nothing in the sink, nor below it. Nothing in the dishwasher. That left the oven, which Lydia noticed was unusually large as she opened the

—

"Shit," Lydia spat, slamming the door shut in reflex. All she heard was the pounding of blood in her ears. She needed a minute or two to steady her breathing, a hand placed over her chest to calm herself.

Inside the oven, there were three heads.

She had to look again to confirm they weren't human. On the left was a deer, the eyes still open, a fat, pink tongue hanging from the mouth. In the middle was what looked like a hairy pig, its mouth bloody and strange. And to the right was a small coyote, its fur dyed red by its own blood. At least, that's what Lydia thought they were. She had never been good at identifying animals, was always more interested in plants.

The smell was coming from the deer. Of the three, it was the most decayed, maggots crawling from its eyes and nostrils. The deer also made her think of the antlers in McDonagh's apartment. Unless Caldwell was into some weird cooking techniques, the connection was obvious. But what did it mean? What did it have to do with Holly? Why hadn't she found anything at Wood's apartment, and did the other victims have something similar?

Lydia couldn't concentrate on an answer with the stench clogging her mind. Nor did she have a way to bag the heads as evidence, or even to close off the apartment except to lock it. "Shit," she muttered again, unhappy with all of it. She wished McDonagh had come with her.

She stopped herself. This was her scene. She found it. She could handle this.

A plan came to her in a single flash. She had a camera, so she could photograph all the evidence exactly the way she had been trained to. Then she could use the key to lock the apartment, preserving the evidence until she could come back and document it properly. And, along the way, she could impress upon the property manager how important it was that no one went in there. A flash of her badge would seal the deal, or at least buy her a little time.

And she did exactly that, but not without stepping in the vomit on her way out.

FOUR

Thomas started in the main lobby of the Ash Falls Municipal Dockyards. The secretary who greeted him eyed Thomas suspiciously when he said he was there to see Rowan Bale. She consulted a screen and informed him that he did not have an appointment, which Thomas agreed was true. He said Mr. Bale would want to speak with him anyways. The secretary, still suspicious, dutifully took down his name and asked him to wait. Then she went to find some junior member of the pack who would be interested enough in why Thomas McDonagh had bothered to show up at the dockyards.

He waited for two and a half hours.

He was about to give up when a new secretary came to collect him. Either they talked to Monya, or they had just decided to kill him. The secretary showed him to a small office with one window and a stack of papers on the desk that towered over the werewolf behind it.

This interaction took about fifteen minutes. Thomas was careful to maintain a certain level of aloofness with this wolf, who he didn't even bother to learn the name of. After all, his age and experience put him well above this low-level bureaucrat, even if he was no longer a pack member. The young pup might have felt otherwise, might even have grown angry at being disregarded by Thomas, but that was not Thomas's concern—he would not let his own anger rise with the pup's.

I do not like that emotion, he reminded himself. *It is not a good emotion.*

Eventually, frustrated and a little put off by Thomas, the low-level grunt turned away and made a call one step up the ladder. Thomas didn't know who he called, but he knew by his adversary's suddenly ashen face that whoever it was asked for Thomas to come immediately. It was a simple thing, then, for Thomas to be led past a row of grey cubicles to another waiting room, this one quiet and without any personnel to watch him.

Thomas waited here for forty-five minutes, occupying himself with a copy of *Modern Dog* that he felt was left a little pointedly.

When the mid-level manager finally came for him, Thomas could tell by his expression that he and Thomas had met each other before and that this manager expected him to remember. Thomas, of course, did not. But he acted like he did, and the two were friendly while the manager escorted Thomas back to his office. This room was slightly larger, with two windows and a stack of papers that was neither large nor small. Manageable, Thomas thought, thinking of his own increasing amount of paperwork at the station.

They talked for about half an hour. This time, Thomas was more open with his adversary, maintaining a friendly banter while slowly working his way towards being let farther into the building. It soon became clear that this manager wouldn't just *let* Thomas go any higher, nor did Thomas think he would particularly care that Thomas needed help. So, instead, Thomas referenced some rumors he had heard, rumors he had disregarded because he didn't really care about pack politics and had no desire to join a new one, even if it was threatening Bale's hegemony. What little he did know of this new pack is that they used fear against their foes, jealousy to make friends. He wanted no part in that.

I do not like those motivations, he told himself. *They are not good motivations.*

This manager, however, evidently did care, because as soon as Thomas brought it up and implied he had information, the manager made a call. Before long, Thomas was escorted up to a new floor, where he was unceremoniously deposited into a new waiting room.

Thomas only had to wait here for ten minutes before a completely new secretary came and asked him what he'd like for lunch. Thomas, who hadn't held his breath that he'd be fed, ordered a caesar salad after staring at the secretary blankly for a moment. Then he waited for another hour before being called to an office down a long brightly lit hall.

Of course, this office was again bigger, with four windows wrapped around the corner of the building that looked to the southeast. The desk had no papers on it, just a large computer and two settings, complete with plates covered by silver domes.

Thomas was pleased to see that he knew the occupant of this office well. They had been in school together, were probably even distant cousins. While their paths had diverged, she had always sent him a card at Christmas for the past few decades, while he always replied with a card for her birthday. For the hour he spent with her, Thomas was careful to remain grateful, complimenting her on her magnanimity and thanking her profusely for the meal. When she talked, he listened attentively. When he ate, he was careful to take only small careful bites. When he spoke, he was quiet and gentle, deferring to her when he could. She seemed neither surprised nor annoyed when Thomas admitted he actually knew nothing about whatever pack was muscling its way into Ash Falls, and she couldn't suppress a pleased smile when Thomas said he instead needed help. That he would be eternally grateful did not need stating, but Thomas was sure to mention it anyways.

Eventually, they finished eating. She rose from her seat, and Thomas rose with her. He remained standing while she asked him to wait and stood at one of the windows after she left. She never returned.

Instead, a young wolf—younger than the first he had met with—came for Thomas, looked him up and down while informing him that he'd be taking Thomas to Mr. Bale's office. Thomas only nodded in response. The two remained silent while they walked down another hall, past another row of cubicles, down a second hall, and eventually ending in a pair of unmarked doors.

"Please wait in there," the young wolf said.

Thomas didn't argue. He had been here before, after all. He had also been in the office of the Chief of Police, of the Mayor, of the local representative to the state government. Name an industry or position in the city limits of Ash Falls, Thomas had been there. None of them stunned him like this office.

Two walls of this office were entirely windows. From them, Thomas could see the snowy tips of the Cascades. He could see the beginnings of the Umpqua, could see the way it wound down until it fell into Ascension Lake. He could see the great dam stretched across it, the buildings that cropped up around the plant, the river winding its way into the city, where it seemed to practically end at the base of this building. He could see the two bridges—traffic filling one, a train crossing the other. He could see ships moving into the docks, laden with cargo from all over the world. He could see the sprawl of downtown clashing with the edges of wilderness. He could see the green fields of the Willamette Valley to the north, the desolation of fire to the south. He could see the clot of humanity flowing through the streets of the city, the ordinary people going about their ordinary lives seamlessly mixed with the unordinary going about their unordinary lives. He could see it all, and it always filled his heart with a resentful pride.

Resentful because the message had never been lost on Thomas. He was a guest in this room, and this view was a treat. The room belonged, however, to one man. The view was of *his* domain. Of *his* city. In this way, Bale ruled his dominion, which was why Thomas had left.

I do not like this feeling, he said. *It is a bad feeling.*

"Beautiful, isn't it."

Thomas did not turn. He did not wonder when the old wolf had entered the room—that wasn't for Thomas to know. Nor did Thomas answer. Rowan Bale knew what Thomas would say.

Bale joined him at the window, hands tucked into the pockets of his slacks. He seemed too big for those clothes, just as Thomas always felt too small for his. Thomas watched him out of the corner of his eye—a hyena waiting to see what the lion will do.

Eventually, Bale stated, "Things have been going well for you down there."

Thomas snorted. "Not too well."

"You're alive, aren't you?" Bale said. "That's better than a lot of cops, especially at the 14th."

Thomas shrugged. "Not for long," he said.

"Ah," Bale said, his gaze turning momentarily on Thomas. "Is that what it is?" he asked. "Is that why you bluffed, lied, and groveled your way into my office? Because you're afraid?"

Thomas didn't answer and the two contemplated the city for a moment. On some unspoken cue, they turned away from the window, Thomas following Bale's lead. The rest of the office had a large, empty desk, a pair of sofas occupying the middle of the room, and statues arranged around the edges. Bale settled into one of the sofas, crossing his legs and spreading his arms languidly. Thomas sat opposite him, careful to maintain a straight back, to resist the urge to spread out like Bale. That was *his* right. This was *his* office.

"Is it that phantom you've been hunting?" Bale asked casually.

"Phantom?" Thomas asked.

"It's this morning's headline," Bale said. "'Phantom lays waste to AFPD HQ.' The paper hasn't put it together that it's this 'Holly' you've been chasing, but there's enough information to make the connection. Besides, it's *you* that's come to me in the wake of this tragedy, not anyone else."

Thomas met Bale's gaze evenly. "It's departmental policy to not comment on current investigations except through approved channels," Thomas said.

It wasn't that he couldn't say anything, or even that it mattered if he did. He just didn't feel like admitting anything to Bale.

"I see," Bale said, a knowing grin spreading across face. "Then what are you here for?"

Without peeling back his lips, Thomas ran his tongue over the top of his teeth, counting each as he passed them. He did not break his gaze from Bale's, nor did he reciprocate the wide, gleaming smile the multimillionaire was flashing at him. They both knew, of course, why Thomas was there. The key for Thomas was to ask his question without saying 'current' or 'investigation.'

"Do the names Sean Tanner, Jude Bates, or Megan Rude mean anything to you?" Thomas began.

Bale waggled his eyebrows. "Just what I read in the *Gazette*," he said. "That you're *investigating* their deaths."

"So you don't know they worked for you?" Thomas asked.

Just a smidge of Bale's smile faded. He broke eye contact too, his gaze losing focus for a moment. "No," he admitted. "I know that too."

"Did you work with them closely?" Thomas asked. When Bale's eyes sharpened on Thomas, a cold question in them, Thomas shrugged, spreading his hands apologetically. "Treat me like I know nothing," he said. "It'll help."

Bale drew in a rattling sigh. "No," he said, flatly. "Non-pack members rarely rise very high in this company, and those three were not exceptions. Sorry," Bale caught himself, "Is that still assuming you know too much?"

Thomas waved the question aside. "So, they weren't werewolves?" he asked.

"Obviously," Bale said. "No member of my pack would ever be taken so easily by whatever idiot you're tracking."

Thomas smiled, not sure how pointed that comment was. He asked, "What did they do?"

"Tanner and Bates were woodcutters," Bale said. "Ostensibly part of a larger crew, but their manager tells me they were good enough to take side gigs, just the two of them."

"Side gigs?" Thomas asked.

"Specific trees," Bale explained, "specific lengths, specific thickness. People who need a special piece of wood and have the money to have us find it."

A little intrigued, Bale asked, "What kind of things would they need it for?"

"Furniture restoration," Bale said. "Mostly that. Other things too, like," and here Bale's lips curled into that knowing smile again, "weapons. For specific foes."

Ah, Thomas thought. He was well aware of the underground politics of Ash Falls. Well aware that, no matter how publicly powerful Bale was, not every creature in the city bowed to him.

I rebel, Camus wrote. *Therefore, we exist.*

The maxim applied to monsters too.

"Were Tanner and Bates working one of these specialized jobs when they disappeared?" Thomas asked.

Bale thought for a moment. "They were," he eventually conceded. "In fact, they were working several."

"Who for?" Thomas asked.

Bale's smile took a slight edge. "You know I can't tell you that," he said.

"Surely, in light of everything surrounding this case, you'd be willing to make an exception," Thomas said. "To ensure no one else is hurt."

"I'm afraid the confidentiality of my clients is, as always, paramount," Bale said, his tone excessively polite. "If it is so important, get a judge to sign a warrant."

Right after hell freezes over, Thomas thought. No judge in the city would sign anything with Rowan Bale's name on it.

"Could you at least tell me what they were looking for?" Thomas asked. An offering of compromise.

Again, Bale thought about this more a moment. Eventually, he said, "They had three species on their list. Northwest hawthorn, ash, and elm."

"Oddly specific," Thomas commented, though his memory instantly flashed to a vision of red fury, of a tree lashing out at his touch. "Pine's the only common tree around here, isn't it?"

"True," Bale agreed. "But those two would've had no trouble finding what they were looking for. Everything I've learned since they disappeared shows they were excellent foresters. A shame they weren't born to the right mothers, or they might've done excellent for themselves."

Thomas ignored the way Bale's eyes bored into his. "What about Megan Rude?" he asked.

Half of Bale's face smiled, the other half remained still. "Officially, she was someone's secretary," Bale explained. "In practice, she was our mole. The person we employed who we knew talked to the police, passed the information we wanted passed."

No use hiding that then. "So you knew she passed information to Ellwood?" Thomas asked.

"Oh yes," Bale nodded. "We thought she was a corporate mole for a while, which was why we let the relationship build. I only put it together she was an AFPD mole when the late commander started beating every bush and shaking every tree in sight once she went missing."

Or a little earlier, Thomas thought. *Makes no difference.* "So, what did you do?"

Bale shrugged. "Does that really matter?"

Thomas grimaced. "Yes," he said. A little distracted, he rubbed his earlobe. "We haven't confirmed how Ellwood was killed," he explained. They had. Or Holly had. But he wanted to know what Bale would say. It was just his training leading him on, his instinct to find every scrap of information.

Bale slowly nodded. "I'll have my secretary give you my schedule for the last two weeks," he said. "It's the one she keeps, both what was planned and what actually happened.

We had no desire to lose this relationship, even if it was with the police. And we also want to know what happened to one of ours, just like you."

"Thank you," Thomas nodded, genuinely grateful. "Is there anything else you can tell me?"

Bale shrugged. "What else do you want to know?"

There wasn't much. What Bale had been able to tell Thomas was interesting, though he wasn't sure if it answered any questions. And it wasn't like Thomas could press Bale for more information. If Bale was to be believed, whatever happened to the woodcutters—Thomas stopped himself. He knew what happened to them. But *why* they drew Holly's ire would, for now, be a mystery. Maybe Thomas could ask the culprit himself.

Thomas ballooned his cheeks, wondering if he should bother asking the other question on his mind. Finally, he managed, "How are my parents?"

Bale's face remained impassive. "It's pack policy not to comment on inquiries made by outsiders," he said.

Fair enough.

Thomas stood, reflexively patting his pockets to make sure he still had everything. "Well, thank you for your time," he said, no longer meeting Bale's eyes. "This has been helpful, even if there wasn't much you could tell me."

"It's my pleasure," Bale replied. "Do reach out if you need anything else."

Only half of Thomas's mouth curled into a smile. "I will," he said. "Shall I just go out the door then?"

"Yes," Bale said. "Someone will be waiting to show you out of the building."

Thomas was almost at the office doors when Bale added, "Tom." Thomas turned, watched the side of Bale's head. The wolf was not fully looking at him. "Whatever this 'phantom' is, you would be doing the pack a great favor by destroying it."

"And how do you suggest I do that?" Thomas asked.

"You know how," Bale said. "You've always known how."

I do not like this idea. It is not a good idea.

"Tell my dad hello for me," Thomas said. He opened and stepped through the door, nodding wordlessly to the wolf that waited beyond it.

FIVE

Lydia grimaced as she stepped into the deepening dusk of Crowley Street. Nothing, again. McDonagh had probably guessed it was a dead end. Lydia thought that was why he made her come here. She had found nothing at the antique store either. The elderly man who ran the store did his best to avoid every question she posed. At least the manager at Crowley Liquor had been happy to talk to her, had even started to show her the invoices before she lost interest. On any other case, she would have investigated further, but neither had even the faintest whiff of the green man about them. Or anything odd, for that matter.

Which left the brewery. It so happened that it only was about ten blocks from the liquor store, a walk that cut along the edge of downtown. Lydia set off, running through every stage of the two interviews, making sure she hadn't missed anything, that she would remember enough of the finer details to satisfy McDonagh. She didn't want to have to return to Crowley needlessly or make the even longer trek out to the antique store again.

She wasn't worried about remembering what she found at Caldwell's apartment.

Lydia did try to keep from thinking about who could be waiting at the brewery. Lilly had seemed sad when Lydia left Chooski's, had tried to hide that disappointment behind a warm smile and a confident "See you later." She hoped that Lilly wouldn't be there tonight, that Lilly wouldn't learn she was a cop. Not yet. That way, Lydia could hold out hope of mildly flirting with her while Lilly didn't have the impression that Lydia was only doing so to learn more about the brewery. Flirting is never the same when one person involved is a police officer.

Was Lilly even flirting though? Lydia could never tell. Her only experience with it growing up had been awkward boys in the hallways of Needles High, and there were many reasons Lydia had no interest in them. Everything since had been a lot more forward, a lot less vague. Quick, painless, without any attempts to hide. Lydia hadn't been a cop then. She was free to ask without it being weird.

But that didn't answer if Lilly was interested. Lydia didn't know. She wanted to find out, though. Just not tonight. Not when they were both working.

Lydia had never been to a city in the northern hemisphere that was pleasant in August. The concrete and asphalt soaked up the heat, releasing it back onto the pedestrians as they passed. Add to it a few thousand engines releasing their dirty smog, and you have the perfect concoction to make people pass out in the streets. This summer was even worse because ash was literally falling from the sky, clogging the people's throats and covering the sidewalks in a white powder finer than snow. When Lydia moved to the city, Ellwood told her the place was named for a nearby waterfall. She never thought something like this could happen, but nothing surprised her anymore.

Walking ten blocks, however, proved to be harder than Lydia thought it would be. She wasn't really sure what she hoped to accomplish from it, wasn't sure what she'd find on the streets that had anything to do with her case. She regretted leaving her car at the HQ's garage, missed its air-conditioning and tinted windows. When she arrived at the brewery, she was covered in a thin film of sweat, which had soaked through her shirt at the armpits and back, and an even thinner layer of ash clung to the sweat, making her grey and dusty. The setting of the sun was not enough to cool her yet. When Lydia stepped into the brewery—a large converted warehouse with outer walls bleached white—she groaned in pleasure to discover they had air-conditioning.

The main entryway was a small corridor with black, empty walls. The desk at the end was also empty, while just beyond the hall split into three directions. Lydia waited a moment, wondering if anyone would come along. When no one did, Lydia cautiously stepped to the intersection beyond the desk. Nothing.

It was night, but the front door was open. Lydia hadn't thought they'd be closed. But then, where was everyone?

To the right, the hallway went farther into the building, a few doors on either side, some windows in the walls showing the rooms beyond. To the left, the wall was much smaller, ending in a single door with a prominent wooden handle. Straight ahead the hall came to an abrupt stop, two doors on either side without any handles. When Lydia ventured a little farther towards these, she saw that the door to the right had a blue placard, the white outline of a person stamped into it. The door to the left was the same, except it also had the pointed edges of a dress.

"Hello?" Lydia said, hesitantly, moving back to the intersection again. No one answered. Lydia was thirsty. She ventured a little farther down the right hallway. "Hello?" she said again, louder.

The front door opened. Lydia spun quickly, saw a figure move through it and shut the door with a firm snap. Then the woman turned, glancing at Lydia.

She recognized her instantly by the soft angles of her cheeks, her cool, slightly sunken eyes that stared at Lydia confidently, the thin, red lips that had so easily smirked at Lydia behind the bar. In the harsh industrial light of the brewery, her skin seemed paler, almost translucent, and her hair was tied into a tight bun instead of loose. None of this weakened her effect on Lydia.

Lydia didn't know what to say.

That was fine. Lilly started for them. "Can I help you?" she asked.

Lydia had trouble talking for a second—the ash was clogged in her throat. "Sorry," she eventually managed, "there was no one at your desk."

"We've met, haven't we?" Lilly asked, and Lydia smiled. She let the memory come, let Lilly see past the ash and sweat and exhaustion. When Lilly made the connection, her face brightened a little. "At Chooski's," she said.

"That's right," Lydia said. She held out her hand. "We were never properly introduced."

She took Lydia's hand without hesitation, and they shook firmly. "Lilly Soren," she said. "Assistant brewmaster."

Lydia couldn't quite keep the smile on her face from growing a little wider. "Detective Lydia Pike," she said as they let go. Again, she thought of how terrible she must look, how sweaty and dirty. She reached to her belt and unclipped her badge, showed it to Lilly, and added, "AFPD."

Lilly's smile faded at that. "Ah," she said. Her body tensed, and she crossed her arms. Her tone confirmed every fear Lydia had about meeting her again like this. "Is this a professional visit, then?"

"Yes," Lydia answered, trying to keep her smile friendly.

"Then you shouldn't be beyond our front desk," Lilly said coldly, stepping smoothly past Lydia.

She shrugged. "No one was there," she said, keeping her turmoil hidden. This was definitely not going how she wanted it. It was stupid to have walked past the desk, she told herself. Lazy.

"Well, someone's here now," Lilly said, her arms still crossed while she glared at Lydia. "Please tell me why you're here, or I will have to ask you to leave."

Lydia took a breath. She had one shot at learning anything. Come off wrong here, and Lilly would insist Lydia leave immediately. She took another breath, trying to steady her nerves. Lilly still glared, her stony eyes boring into Lydia's.

Lydia opened her mouth, and in that first moment, nothing came.

I'm so thirsty, she thought.

After another moment, Lydia blurted, "Can I use your restroom?"

Lilly blinked. "What?" she asked.

"Your restroom, would it be alright for me to use it?" Lydia asked. "Before I tell you why I'm here and we get into all of it."

Lilly's mouth dropped a little. "I..." she said, more a rasp than a sound.

"Look at me," Lydia said. "Look at what it's like out there. I walked here. I just need to wipe this grime off, splash some cool water on my face."

Lilly's eyebrows were now halfway up her forehead, while her mouth was only dropping lower. "You're serious?"

"You can wait here for me, or if you need to go I'll wait on that side of the desk until someone else comes. I just need to ask a few questions, and then I'll be on my way." Lydia held her breath a moment, wincing already at the impatience surely about to boil over into anger.

But Lilly started to laugh. She put her forehead in her palm and rubbed it a little, shaking it from side to side. Lydia didn't know what to say. "It's on the left," Lilly managed. "Would you like a glass of water?"

Lydia felt relief wash over her, refreshing as any air-conditioning. "Thank you," she said with a smile.

The women's restroom was empty, the floors clean and the stall doors closed. Lydia turned on the water in one of the sinks, listened to the cool, clear liquid splash against the basin. For a moment, she was tempted to bend over and drink from it, even if it would taste like vinegar. Instead, she dampened a paper towel with it and began to wipe the ash from her face. It smeared at first, making her skin even darker, but Lydia kept at it. The cold water felt excellent against her skin, her pores soaking in as much moisture as they could. Lydia let herself have this moment, let herself bathe in the delicious quiet of the bathroom. When she was done, she turned off the faucet and gave herself another once over in the mirror. She looked better, though she still felt like a fool.

She did know one thing now: she really liked the way Lilly laughed.

Lydia pushed open the door and stepped back into the cool hallway. Lilly, Lydia was surprised to see, was not there. Lydia looked down the long, deserted hallway. Everything was, again, still.

"Hello?" Lydia called out a third time.

Nothing.

Odd, Lydia thought. She took a step down the hall towards the rest of the brewery, then remembered her promise to Lilly. She would wait at the desk. That was the right thing to do.

She heard a noise from the door at the end of the hall, the one that Lilly had stepped in front of. It was a low bump, soft enough that Lydia might have imagined it, but loud enough that it drew her attention. She turned to stare at the door, waiting to see if the noise would come again.

It was a plain enough door. Wooden, like the handle, and painted a dull brown. There was no sign on the door, unlike the others. Nothing to show its purpose, to tell you what lay beyond. Lydia wouldn't have looked twice at it had it not been for... she wasn't sure.

She was about to write it off when something caught her eye. A liquid was oozing from underneath the door. Lydia watched it, frowning, a strange pain throbbing in her temples. She took a step towards the door. Then another.

She recognized the substance. She had seen it plenty of times in her work, had gotten used to its color, its metallic smell, even the way it moved. It was exactly like the red that had oozed from Caldwell, that had dried all over Bosk, that had formed a strange puddle around Ellwood. Why was it here?

The smell of it filled Lydia's nostrils, and in her mind's eye she saw Holly, the green man, hefting his awful and terrible axe. Just the thought of him made Lydia's mind go blank—blank from the terror of beholding him, blank with rage to hide behind, blank with lust for the blood that came from just beyond the door—because, in her mind, it was suddenly his blood, seeping from his freshly severed neck, and she wanted to bathe in it.

Her hand turned the door handle slowly. Lilly had left it unlocked. Lydia pushed, and the door swung easily to reveal the room beyond.

There was a table. Cold and metallic, like the autopsy slabs in the AFPD morgue. A man lay upon the table, asleep and shackled to it. There was a machine sitting beside the table, small and squat, a strange sucking noise coming from it. Tubes ran between the machine and the man, sticking out of his arms, his neck, and his legs. One of these tubes had come loose, and the blood covering the floor spurted from the wound in his arm. Lydia processed all of this, her rage vanishing.

"Holy shit," she said.

She ran to his side, immediately putting her hand over the open wound in his arm. She barely registered the warm liquid seeping against her skin while she tried shaking the man to wake him. She got nothing at first. He was obviously alive, she didn't have to check for that. Was he drugged?

"Shit shit shit," she said again. There wasn't much else to say.

With as much force as she could muster while still holding the arm, she slapped the man across his face. "Wake up," she said when nothing happened, slapping him again.

She thought his eyes might have fluttered.

"This is gonna hurt," she whispered, getting a better grip on his arm. She squeezed below the wound, pressing her finger into the gaping hole. Her finger worked past the flesh, and she felt the blood trying to slip past. She only squeezed harder. It wouldn't help him live, but it was painful. Painful enough for the man to gasp, his eyes flying open. He tried to sit up, but the tubes and his constraints held him down. He started trying to scrabble against them, but that would only make his situation worse. Lydia threw her weight on him, forcing him back on the table, making a shushing noise as she did.

"I'm here to help," she said, trying to break through his panic.

Thankfully, it only took a moment. Maybe two. But he was so weak from blood loss that he wouldn't have been able to struggle long. "I'm going to get you out," Lydia kept repeating. "I'm going to get you out, my name is Detective Pike and I'm going to get you out."

When he stopped moving, she looked back at his face. His eyes, colored a dull, muddy green, were open, faint but aware. They locked onto hers. He whispered something, the faintest "Help" Lydia had ever heard.

"That's right," Lydia nodded. "Help."

His eyes widened, he inhaled, whimpering and trying to struggle away from her, terror plain on his face.

Something struck Lydia across the back of the head with a loud *thwack*, and everything went dark.

SIX

Thomas opened his apartment with relative ease, mostly because he hadn't bothered to lock the door when he left. What did he really have to lose, after all? The green man was going to get in anyways, and since Thomas was so thoroughly in his sights, Thomas doubted he would let anything else happen to him. Sure, someone might try to hurt Thomas. Someone might even come very close. But that someone would surely meet a very grisly end, or, at least, a horrible disfigurement. Holly was hunting *him*, and it wouldn't be right for someone else to steal Holly's prize.

Even thinking about it made a spot just above Thomas's eye throb. He rubbed at it as he walked through his apartment, casting off his effects as he went. Only once he had kicked his shoes off did he remember to close his front door, and this he did with half a bemused smile on his face. He still didn't lock it.

That pain would not go away—that throb. It had been with him all day, even if he hadn't always noticed it. Maybe that was why he hadn't figured anything out. Maybe that was why he'd be dead in two nights, his blood spraying everywhere while he shit himself like the disgrace he was. Maybe it was his headache's fault that he was a failure.

I do not like these feelings, he told himself. Only part of him believed it. Only part of him listened.

Still in the dark, Thomas found his glass. Not *a* glass, not *a* cup, not *a* vessel. *His* glass. The one he drank from every night, the one he left in the same spot always so he could find it later. Next to it was the most recent bottle of whiskey —barely touched—from which he poured himself two fingers. It burned when he sipped it.

He knew the real reason, of course. The reason he had found nothing tonight. It wasn't because he was a failure or worthless or any of the reasons that brought him to the bottle. He had failed because he guessed wrong, and because he guessed wrong he was no closer to understanding *why* than he had been the night before. Which meant he didn't know *how*, which meant he didn't know *what*.

Anyway you looked at it, Thomas was soon to be dead— which was what really brought him to the bottle.

He didn't turn on the lights because he didn't want to see what Holly had left for him tonight. He had smelled it, whatever it was, the moment he walked in. It was a taunt, a reminder of Thomas's failure. Holly's way of saying, "One day closer, detective."

His hope lay with Pike. He hoped that she had found something useful. That wasn't likely, of course, because he had sent her to close leads, not uncover new ones. But maybe she could make sense of what Thomas had found. Maybe she could draw the connections he could not.

Not a particularly inspiring thought, but it was his only faint glimmer in the dark soil of despair.

With a heavy sigh, McDonagh reached to the lamp beside him. By sense of touch, he found a small chain dangling from it, pulled it in a sharp motion. The light *clicked* to life, illuminating his living room.

Sitting on his counter, very near where the antlers had been, were two bones.

The bones were naturally sharpened to a fine point on one end, broad and powerful at the other. Red liquid still oozed from the broad end, marrow staining his white counter. Thomas wracked his mind for what animal native to the northwest would have something like these, but he couldn't place them. They looked like elephant tusks, only shorter. As if they belonged to a wild boar.

From where he sat, it seemed plausible, though thoroughly unlikely.

But then again, nothing about this case was likely.

END of Episode Six

EPISODE SEVEN: AXE-EPTABLE LOSSES

ONE

Ash Falls Police Department - Competency Evaluation
Rank: Commander   *Name:* Ruby Hammerick
Date: 08/16/2017
Rank of assessed: Lieutenant   *Name of assessed:* Benedict Lake
Cover sheet:

Due to circumstances beyond his control, Lieutenant Lake was placed in temporary command of his precinct on 08/08/2017. Within a week of him taking this temporary command, an unknown force assaulted his precinct and managed to put 7 officers in intensive care, took another 4 off active duty for a week, and left the rest of his unit injured in some way. In addition, most of the precinct's office supplies, investigative equipment, and sidearms were damaged, most having to be replaced. It will take weeks, if not months, for the 14th to be back on its feet again.

This is, quite frankly, not an exception for Lieutenant Lake. At this point, it has become a pattern. It is my opinion that, for the good of the force, Lieutenant Lake should not be placed again into any position that could lead to him captaining a precinct again. His history and past failures make it clear that Lake, no matter how competent an officer he has proven himself to be in the past, does not have the necessary temperament to be in command.

For full assessment, please read following report.

TWO

Lydia walked a path she had never seen before in a forest she did not recognize. The trees were all barren, their summer leaves cast off and buried under a foot of snow. At the edge of her senses, Lydia heard the faint babble of a happy brook.

She was barefoot, but her feet were not cold in the snow. In fact, they felt heavy, like they and the rest of her body were covered in cold iron instead of soft nylon. She was neither tired nor alert, neither hungry nor full, neither thirsty nor satiated. The only thing she felt was itchy. Itchy in one particular spot on the side of her neck, which she scratched at as she walked. When she pulled her fingers away, they were daubed in blood.

Eventually, she rounded a corner into a small clearing through which a stream cut a crooked line. On the side closest to Lydia was a large mound, distinct from its surroundings because fresh, verdant greenery covered it. No frost touched any of the flora atop the mound, and not one looked wilted by the cold or lack of sun. In fact, the mound looked touched by spring about to turn to summer, sun-kissed and resplendent.

Lydia slowly circled the mound. At both the northern and southern sides, she found a small hole, barely large enough for a person to slip through. When she crouched at either of the holes, she found a small set of stairs. At the bottom was a space large enough for a human to walk around, but there was something about the place that made a mortal dread grip her heart and she refused to explore farther.

While she knelt at the northern entrance with her back to the creek, a strange scratching noise broke through the happy babble of the water. It was high and drawn, like sheets of metal sliding over each other. Lydia jumped up, backing away from the mound and looking into the empty woods. The sound continued, patient and inexorable.

"Where are you?" Lydia called out, unable to keep a tremor from her voice.

"Abyde," came the reply, a deep boom carried on the forest wind, "And þou schal haf al in has þat I þe hyȝt ones."

The sound of metal scraping across metal continued and Lydia stood rooted to her spot, barely able to think, let alone move. After a time, she summoned the courage to lift her left foot. Slowly, steadily, she carried it behind her, then deftly placed it back in the snow. The moment her skin touched the white powder, the noise abruptly ceased and all was quiet in the woods again.

"Hello?" Lydia said, her voice barely above a whisper.

The Green Knight emerged from the woods, looking exactly to her as he had the first time she saw him. His eyes glowed red beneath a mane of curly green hair, and his broad shoulders were like mountains muscling through the trees. The haft of his axe was longer now, standing about as tall as him, but the head was the same—wicked, magnificent, and sharp.

He planted the haft in the soft dirt by the stream, then vaulted himself over the water as easily as a fisherman casts a line. When he landed on Lydia's side, he continued his gentle stride as if nothing had broken it while locking his fearsome eyes onto hers.

He said her name and then, "God þe mot loke!"

Lydia opened her eyes. It took her a moment to register the dappled white of the ceiling, even longer to recognize the warm comfort of a bed. *Her* bed. The one she had woken from every morning for the past four years.

She sat up slowly, wincing as her head throbbed. She rubbed her brow, though she knew it wouldn't do her much good. She recognized a hangover when she felt one.

She covered her eyes with her palm, trying to remember details from the night before. It was mostly blank. Had she blacked out?

Starting to feel embarrassed, Lydia looked around for her phone. After a minute of searching, she found it piled amongst her other personal belongings near the doorway to her bedroom. It was nearly out of battery. The time, she read, was 7:10 a.m. Lydia opened her banking app, feeling a little more nervous by the minute. She scratched at her neck absently. With relief, she saw that her bank accounts were all where they should be. She checked her wallet, too— everything was there.

That was unusual, even if it made Lydia happy. She scratched at her neck again.

Lydia stood, still checking her phone to see if there were any messages. She had missed a few calls from McDonagh, but he had not bothered to leave a voicemail. Lydia plugged the phone into her charger, deciding to call him back when she felt a little better.

She went to her window next and gazed out at the shaded street below her. It was empty, save for an occasional passing vehicle. Some morning fog wisped about at ankle height and there was still a faint layer of ash fall, grey now—

the grey of cold char kicked up by winds and spread for miles in every direction.

The ash, they were saying, would finally stop falling in a few days. By next spring, some small amount of plant life would return to that section of wilderness, growing stronger every year after that. But to be the fine forest it had once been would take a century, at the minimum. At least the city was surrounded by forests. Only a small section—small being a relative term—was gone.

Absently, Lydia covered her eyes with her palms again. Last night was still a blank and the harder she tried to think about it, the more it slipped away. That persistent itch at her neck wasn't helping anything. Lydia took one hand from her face to keep scratching, but she kept her eyes squeezed shut. It felt like there were two bug bites on her neck, though whatever bugs they were had to have been pretty big.

Lydia remembered going to the apartments; remembered going to the liquor store and antiques shop. She remembered walking through the hot streets, ash coating her hair and face. She remembered getting to the brewery as night fell, seeing Lilly—

Lydia flinched at a sharp pain in her neck. Her nails had dug too deep, had bitten through the puffy flesh of the bug bite. Lydia drew her hand away and saw her own blood covering the tips of her fingers. The bite only itched more with the pain.

Without thinking, Lydia put her fingers in her mouth, licking the hot blood off with her tongue. Her initial reaction was disgust, wondering what in the hell had possessed her to do that. This was immediately replaced by surprise, pure surprise, that the blood tasted… good. Really good. When she pulled her hand out of her mouth, now entirely clean, she found herself wanting more.

She shook the thought away, wincing again as pain flashed through her neck. She walked quickly to her bathroom, grabbing a wad of toilet paper and pressing it against her neck. She held it there while she looked at herself in the mirror. She had lost weight, she realized. Her skin looked stretched over a tired and worn face; thin lips near the same brown as her skin, dark bags under her brown eyes; weary shoulders, the thin form of muscles in her arms and hands. Even her white tank top seemed wilted.

She turned a little, so she could better see the wound. When she lifted the paper away, it came with a few splotches of blood, tiny, bright roses that drew her eyes. Then she saw the bites.

There were two holes—round, bigger than she had expected. She frowned as she looked at them, suddenly glad that her bed wasn't covered in blood. Whatever did this, it happened long enough ago that it had scabbed. Her scratching broke the scab, hence the blood.

She studied the holes, a little more liquid oozing out. She winced, then covered the holes with a fresh side of the paper. At least she wasn't bleeding as much as that man.

That was when she remembered.

At least, everything until she was hit on the head.

"Shit," Lydia whispered, lingering on the hiss of the *sh* before spitting out the *t*. "Shit shit shit."

She ran to her phone, then threw it down and instead went to her closet, throwing on a fresh shirt and pants. She had to find McDonagh.

She had to find him *now*.

THREE

Everything is calm at Detective McDonagh's apartment. He is sitting in his chair, his glass in his hand, his bottle beside him. He is not asleep, not really. He is just enjoying the calm of the cool grey morning, trying to ignore the sight his eyes cannot turn away from.

Detective Pike comes. She is a rush of energy in the still air, a crackle of lightning over an empty plain. She does not fit. Her mad rush will destroy his carefully constructed fugue, will jolt him out of his reverie, will make him confront his problem.

I feel for him. Sometimes alcohol can cast a spell on you, can bring you away from the problems of the world. When I am that problem, any spell will do.

Detective Pike breaks the spell by pounding on McDonagh's door as hard as she can. She knocks three times, the firm command that she normally uses to enter buildings with a warrant.

Like dust settling, quiet returns to the complex. In a tree nearby, a woodpecker starts its machine-like hammering, which echoes off the building. Pike barely hears it, but still looks up at the sound—assessing whether it's a threat, I think. She's on edge. McDonagh does not move.

Pike tries again. When there is still no answer, she calls, "McDonagh!" and tries to turn the handle. It responds to her command. The door even pops open, revealing a sliver of the darkened hallway beyond.

She stares at the open door, still gripping the handle. Does she think I am beyond it? In a way, I suppose I am. She at least knows McDonagh is too private to leave his apartment unlocked. Too careful. The McDonagh she knows would never have left it this way, which must mean something awful has happened.

Nothing has happened, of course. This is just not the McDonagh she knew. This is a McDonagh without hope, a McDonagh who is about ready to accept there is nothing he can do to stand against me. It's sad really. I was expecting more from him, but I've been wrong before.

Detective Pike carefully removes her hand from the handle. Slowly, holding her breath, she moves her other hand to her hip, unbuttons her holster, and gently draws her gun. She holds it in one hand long enough to nudge the door open farther with the other. Then she firmly grips her sidearm, holding it the way she was trained, and enters the building.

McDonagh does not move when she sees him. For a moment, she stares. He's sitting in his chair and wearing the same dark suit as the last time she saw him, though he removed his tie at some point. He's slouched forward, looking like a single gust of wind will topple him over. Her eyes take in the glass, the near empty bottle, the sheen of sweat on his skin. She wonders, for a moment, if he's dead. Wonders if this is how my hunt will end, or if I will just move onto a new victim. Then he snores loudly.

"Goddamnit," Detective Pike says, holstering her weapon and closing the door behind her.

Not God, I want to tell her. Gog. But that's a joke from a different age.

Four

Thomas showered quickly, conscious of Pike's presence in his kitchen. He brought a clean set of clothes into the bathroom with him so he could dress without having to dash into his bedroom. His foresight impressed him, even made him chuckle a little. "Good job, Tom," he said, patting his own back while looking in the fogged up mirror.

Perhaps he was still a little drunk.

He smelled coffee once he opened the bathroom. Pike had apparently taken the time to find his coffee maker, the old rusted thing he had left below his sink. He was surprised that it still worked.

"I hope you cleaned that thing before you used it," he called to her, throwing yesterday's clothes on his bed. He would clean it up later he told himself.

"Should I have?" Pike answered.

Thomas stopped himself, went back into his bedroom, carefully moved the clothes from his bed and into the hamper where they belonged.

"I haven't in months—years, probably," he replied, finally leaving his bedroom and walking back into his living room.

Pike stood across the small counter, her expression grim. She pushed an orange mug across the counter to him. "Tastes alright," she said.

Thomas put the mug to his lips and took a careful sip that burned his tongue. He tasted a round fungal flavor beneath the acrid crispness of the coffee. Whether the fungus was in his old as dirt coffee grounds or the machine, he wasn't sure. Either way, he should probably throw out both.

Pike, he realized, did not have a mug.

"Tastes great," he said, raising his towards her.

Pike's expression did not change. "You sober yet?" she asked, a little coldly.

"More or less," Thomas answered, returning the mug to the counter. With a quick surreptitious glance, he noted that she had hidden the whiskey.

He went to the chair she found him in earlier and sank into it, putting his palms on his knees, rubbing them a little. His eyes roved around the room, stopping for a moment everywhere except the trophies on his counter—the old and the new. He had been watching those all night, didn't need to keep watching them. When he was ready, his gaze returned to Pike—who still had not moved—and nodded.

"So," he said.

She started at the exact place he hoped she wouldn't. With a jerk of her head, she indicated the pair of tusks sitting next to the antlers. "Looks like you had another visit," she said.

"Very observant," he replied.

"When was it?" she asked.

Thomas shrugged. "Sometime during the day," he said. "They were here when I got back."

"Got back from where?"

"The Ash Falls Municipal Docks," Thomas replied, the hint of a smile crossing his face.

Pike's chin raised a little, considering this. Deciding what to ask next. Thomas waited patiently, knew that he too would get a turn.

"What time did you get back?" Pike asked.

"Must've been eight or nine-ish," Thomas said. "Later actually. It was full dark."

"Did you notice anything odd—besides the obvious," her hand gestured towards the tusks again. Thomas refused to look.

"No," he said.

"Anyone unusual in the area?"

"You mean anyone big, hairy, and green? No."

"I mean anyone unusual," Pike said through gritted teeth.

Thomas clenched his own jaw, had to look away from her for a moment. He had forgotten what it's like to be interrogated, was used to being where Lydia stood. He understood why they were exchanging information like this —he was still a little out of it. He might omit a detail without meaning to, or just forget. Like this, Pike would force every drop of information out of him, piece by piece, squeezing where he needed to be squeezed, prodding when he needed to be prodded. That she had to take an adversarial stance to do it was just part of her nature. But no form of being interrogated would ever be comfortable for him.

It had to be done though, so Thomas set his expression and met Pike's gaze. "No," he said. "No one unusual." Then, he added, "He had been gone for a while."

Pike raised an eyebrow. "How do you know that?" she asked.

"I couldn't..." Thomas paused to find the right words. "I couldn't feel him."

It was obvious that Pike didn't understand that. She tried her best to keep her expression blank, but her brow furrowed by a fraction of an inch. Thomas waited to see if she would move on to something different. She did not.

"You can't have forgotten it," Thomas said. "You've felt it too."

"Tell me anyways," Pike replied simply.

Thomas drew in a slow breath. "The anger," he said, not looking away from her. "The fury. The malice. The hatred that drove you to your feet, bruised and broken, to pursue Holly's headless body out the door. The rage that made Lieutenant Lake, half-blinded by his own blood, want to hack away every piece of him with his own axe. The ire that inspired a room of well-trained detectives to have a gunfight with an unarmed assailant and lose."

He had nearly let it consume him. Every last inch of his self-control went to keeping the anger in check, and what little was left went to keeping himself and Lydia alive. During the whole ordeal at the precinct, Thomas was barely aware of what was happening, only that he could not let the anger take him, transform him into something he had not been for twelve years.

I loved those emotions, he said, *but they were not good emotions*.

Except now, he wasn't sure he believed it anymore. Now that his life was actually on the line.

She did not answer him, but the confusion left her eyes. She remembered too. She understood.

"It must be his magic," Thomas continued, finally looking away. "It must be how he gets his victims to cooperate. It's easy to hate what you don't comprehend, and he is incomprehensible." Thomas stood, walked to the window of his living room. He didn't have much of a view, but just over the tops of a tree he could see the tall buildings of city center. "Try not to give into it next time," he warned her. "If you can."

He let Pike process this, let her ask the next question. While he waited, he put his hands in his pockets and rocked on the balls of his feet. The drunkenness was almost gone, the dull ache of his hangover actively replacing his stupor. It was about to be a rough day, he knew. He wasn't young enough anymore to finish an entire bottle of whiskey and be fine in the morning.

"What did you find at the docks?" Pike asked.

Thomas ran his tongue across his bottom lip. It did not really matter what she knew, he decided, so Thomas told her everything.

"Rowan Bale knows nothing about who Holly is," Thomas said, "so, by extension, nobody in his organization does. He does not know what Bates and Tanner did that might have drawn Holly to them, just what their assignment was when they disappeared. He knew that Rude was passing information to Ellwood, but it did not bother him. He used it as an opportunity to pass fake information, probably to throw Ellwood off his trail."

He turned around in time to see Pike press against the linoleum counter with her knuckles, her brow now deeply furrowed and her mouth a sharp scowl. "You talked to Rowan Bale?" she asked.

Thomas only shrugged. "I've got an in," he said.

"Okay, but—again—what happened to not poking our noses where we don't need to poke them?" Pike asked.

Thomas raised an eyebrow. "What do you mean?"

Pike rounded the counter, and as she did so, Thomas noticed a sharp red blotch on her neck for the first time. "Day three," she said, holding up that number of fingers for emphasis, her voice beginning to rise, "day *three* of this investigation, we stood in the commander's office and you said you didn't want to involve Bale. That it would be dangerous."

Thomas held his ground, hands still firmly in his pockets. "So?"

"So why the change?" she asked, her voice rising.

"What's it matter?" Thomas asked in return, his voice only marginally calmer than hers. "I'm dead anyways."

Pike was inches from him now, her fingers in his face, but those last words caught her short. She curled her hand into a fist, shakily lowered it to her side. Her nostrils flared as she calmed herself. Thomas watched her, a little wary.

"You're not dead yet," she eventually managed to say. "And even so—I'm not, Lake's not. He's got enough on his plate without the lumber company breathing down his neck."

Thomas shook his head, smiling gently. "My conversation with Bale won't bring anything down on you or anyone else in the department."

"You don't know that."

"Yes, I do," Thomas said, and he knew by his own calm certainty that he was right, that she would believe him. "What's between me and Bale and anyone else at that company is personal," he added. "It won't come back to you."

Pike looked like she wanted to spit on him. Instead, she momentarily bared her teeth—somehow a little sharper than he remembered—and growled, "You better be right."

She turned away. Thomas watched as she paced around the room, her anger venting off her like heat from an engine. She stopped at his bookshelf, started to read some of the titles. This gave McDonagh a better chance to study the mark

—marks—on her neck, to see their size and width, to remember his many, many cases with similar marks on similar necks. Eventually, she took down an art book and threw herself into his one other chair, still not looking at him. His turn, that meant.

"Where did you start yesterday?" Thomas asked, his gaze still lingering on her neck. As if she sensed where he was looking, Pike turned her head, hiding the marks from his view.

"The apartments," she said. "Wood's, then Caldwell's. There was nothing at Wood's, but I found these at Caldwell's." She pulled out her phone, frowned at it while she unlocked the first screen, then handed it across to him.

Thomas already knew, somehow, what it would be but still accepted the phone wordlessly. He kept his expression blank while he flicked back and forth through the photos, each a closeup of the heads in the oven. When he didn't say anything, Pike added, "I could tell one was a deer."

Thomas nodded.

"And these antlers you have look like they came from a deer," Pike said.

Thomas nodded again. *Do you want any meat?* Mariam had asked him. *Leo got about a hundred pounds just before he disappeared.*

"And, now that I look at these," Pike said, "these two pieces of bone look like they might fit in the pig's head."

"It's a boar," Thomas said. He locked her phone and tossed it back to Pike.

She caught it deftly. "What's the difference?" she asked.

"Not much," Thomas admitted with a shrug. "The third one's a fox," he added.

Something about this all felt familiar to Thomas, but he wasn't sure from where. It was as if he had read it once.

Pike flipped the book to a Velazquez. "So you've been getting these," she said, "and Caldwell got those. Why didn't Wood get anything?"

"We don't know he didn't," Thomas said.

Pike pursed her lips thoughtfully. "I suppose not," she agreed. "We don't really know if anyone else did either."

"Leo did," Thomas said, then corrected himself. "Ellwood."

Pike raised an eyebrow. "And you didn't think to bring it up?" she asked.

She was not as good at being interrogated as Thomas. He tried to give her a look that said, *Not now*, but he wasn't quite able to muster it.

"What happened to trusting each other?" Pike asked, her arms crossed. "You said you found nothing at Mariam's."

"I didn't think it was important," Thomas said.

"Of course you didn't," Pike said.

He nodded at her neck. "What happened to you?" he asked before she could say anything else.

He already knew. He recognized the marks, recognized the way her hand twitched to her neck, covering the marks by scratching nervously. The question was, did she know?

"I went to the antique store first," she said, her voice a little softer. She didn't look up from the book. "Then the liquor store. Neither knew anything, both checked out. Then I went..." she trailed off. The scratching grew more intense.

Carefully, so as not to break her reverie, Thomas took a step closer. "To the brewery?" he asked.

"Yes," Pike said. The scratching was harsh, her nails digging into her skin. "I don't think I had a chance to ask about the case," she said.

Thomas took another gentle step. "Why didn't you?" he asked.

"I got distracted," she said. Her voice was softer now, almost a whimper. "Saw someone I'd met before."

Thomas took another step, was standing above her now. Slowly, ever so slowly, he descended to a knee. "And did you find anything?" he asked.

Pike opened her mouth, but no sound came out. Blood was running down her neck now, but still she scratched. "A room," she managed. "With a man inside. He was..."

Thomas reached out and took her hand. She did not react, but let him guide her red stained fingers away from her neck. The two holes stared back at him, oozing their red liquid onto her shirt collar. Thomas gripped her hand harder.

"They were torturing him," she said. "Blood was coming from everywhere, but he was... he was alive."

Thomas closed his eyes. *Oh Lydia,* he thought. *Now you've seen the fire, and it has blinded you.*

"I think it is best we do not go back to that brewery," Thomas said.

"What?" Lydia's eyes snapped open. "No," she said. "No, he's still alive, we can save him."

"No," Thomas said, still holding her hand. "We can't."

"But..."

"I know what this is," Thomas said, and he tapped Pike's neck. "And I know why they had him. Believe me, we cannot save him."

"Then we get more officers," Pike said. "We get in there, we shut it down, we get that man out. It can—"

"Pike," Thomas growled.

She stopped talking.

"We cannot save him," Thomas said, not looking away. "The department cannot save him. No one can save him. That's the price."

"The price of what?" Pike asked, tears starting to form in her eyes.

Thomas gripped her hand all the tighter. "Of living in Ash Falls," he said. "Right now, we need to focus on saving me," he pointed to his chest, "and on saving you," he pointed to her neck.

He felt her hand twitch toward it, but he held it firmly, caught the other hand as it tried to resume the scratching as well. This was the closest they had ever been physically, his face inches from hers.

"It itches," she whispered.

"I know," he said.

"You said you know what this is," Pike said.

Thomas nodded.

She started crying fully then, the tears running down her cheeks. "Well?" she asked.

"It's best for you not to know," Thomas said, after thinking for a moment. *Best for you to not know you're compromised,* he thought.

At first, Pike looked like she would protest. Her hands shifted in his, and this time Thomas let them slip out. She did not immediately start itching again—instead, she stared at her palms a moment, eyes flicking from the red that stained her hands to the red that now covered his. All her blood—not a lot of it, but the liquid spreads easily.

Thomas stood and went to his counter. He pulled a sheet from his roll of paper towels, folded it, then handed it to her. She took a moment to accept it, then pressed the towel against her neck. "Can you help me?" she asked.

"Only a little," he said. "I don't know how though. Not really. I do know someone who will be more useful, however."

"Who?" Pike asked. When she pulled the towel away, there was blood all over it. Thomas took it from her and gave her a new sheet, already neatly folded.

"Do you still have that address I gave you?" he asked.

Pike again had to think about this. "Yes," she eventually managed.

Thomas nodded. "She might know a way to make it itch less. Go and see her, today."

Pike didn't move. "What are you going to do?" she asked.

Wait, he thought.

"I don't know," he said. "I have a few other CIs who might know something. And who knows what else she might tell you. We need to shake every tree we can."

"You put a lot of stock in this person?" Pike asked, rising to her feet. They both checked her neck—the wounds hadn't fully scabbed again, but the blood had stopped, the skin around the edge of the holes throbbing a bright red.

"She has seen more than I ever will," Thomas said. "Though I hear she's been a little distracted lately."

Pike, who looked a little distracted herself, gave a nod. "Can she cure me?" she asked.

There was no distrust in her face as she looked at him. Just earnest hope, hope that her suffering would end. Thomas only knew two ways that would happen though. He didn't want either.

"Maybe," he said.

FIVE

For a moment, Lydia considered not even pulling into the parking lot. Once she found an open spot, she again considered not turning the engine off—just throwing the car into reverse and rolling her way back out onto the road. She watched the building entrance through her rearview mirror, saw no one coming in or out. Twenty feet to her left, at the entrance to the parking lot, was a sign with all the residents of the professional building listed down the front. At the very bottom, on a sign so slapdash it could only have been put up yesterday, were the words, "Madame Rosa: Recently Relocated."

The building itself was small, with wood paneled walls and small windows painted shut. The entrance was a tinted glass door, but Lydia found she could still see through into the sad foyer. The slip of paper McDonagh had given her said the person was in suite 302, the one apparently occupied by this Madame Rosa. Lydia seriously doubted the building had an elevator.

Eventually, Lydia felt a twinge in her neck. She resisted the urge to scratch it, as McDonagh had told her, and reminded herself that this person could help her. *Maybe*, McDonagh had said. Her neck twinged again—insistent, like a longing for sweets. Lydia would do anything to make it go away.

So, she turned off her car. She stowed her keys in her pocket, climbed out of the car and locked it. She made her way across the hot pavement and reached the cool shade of the building. The ash was not so bad today. Lydia could not see anyone in the foyer, so she entered carefully, looking around as she did. An elevator waited at the end of the hall, an 'out of order' sign taped to the front. She was half-right.

It took Lydia five minutes to find the stairs, climb them, and find suite 302. It was at the end of a long, vacant hallway. She paused for a moment, hand in front of the door, studying the 'walk-ins welcome' sign. All the other residents of the building had D.D.S. next to their names, or M.D., or Ph.D., and even a J.D. Nothing for this Madame Rosa—which wasn't even the name McDonagh had given her.

Before she could knock—before she could decide—the door opened in front of her. A man stood there—straight, black hair, red-rimmed eyes with a speckle of green in them, and dressed in a fine suit. He seemed just as taken aback by her presence as Lydia was by his. They stared at each other a moment before the man stepped aside to let her pass. Lydia, hesitantly, stepped through.

Through the door was a small waiting room with blank, white walls and filled with green upholstered chairs. There was a window to another empty room. A woman stood in the room's only other doorway, her hair black and curly, a bandana tied around it. She smiled at Lydia, then waved at the man, who had stepped into the hall but was still eyeing Lydia with something that bordered on disdain. "Goodbye, Mr. Alami," she said. "I'll see you next week."

The door swung shut on its own before he could respond.

Lydia turned back to face the other woman. She was tense, whoever she was. The smile on her face was forced, her eyes wide and fixed directly on Lydia's. They both stared for a moment, until Lydia managed to say, "I'm looking for Cheryll Wagner."

If it was possible, the woman's posture became even more rigid. Lydia thought the room smelled rank with cheese, and it was somehow getting even more intense. It was almost as if it was coming from this woman.

"Why?" the stranger eventually asked.

Lydia thought for a moment. "I don't really know," she admitted. "Thomas McDonagh said she'd be able to help me."

While the woman's relief was not immediate, it did eventually come. She took a deep, steadying breath, still looking at Lydia, then nodded. "Why?" she asked again.

Lydia, not quite sure how to explain, turned her neck towards the woman, lowering her collar to show the two marks that had been annoying her for so long. "He said Cheryll Wagner might know how to help me with these," she said. "That she might know what they are."

The woman let out a small laugh. "Of course I know what those are," she said. "Don't you?"

Lydia blinked, her hand letting go of her collar and falling back to her side. "No, I don't," she said.

The woman frowned. "You weren't offered a choice?" she asked.

"What choice?" Lydia said, her face scrunched up a little in confusion. "What are you talking about?"

The woman held out her hand, clearly indicating Lydia's neck again. "Do you remember getting bitten?"

Lydia shook her head. "No," she said. "I woke up this morning and they were just there."

This made the woman pause. She put both hands on her hips, eyes now searching Lydia's. Whatever tension left in her body was gone now. Instead, she started to shake her head. Eventually, she seemed to reach some kind of decision and turned to go farther into the office. "You best come in," she said. "I'll see what I can do."

"I think I'd really rather talk to Wagner," Lydia said, still hesitating at the door.

The woman turned back, eyebrows raised. "You are," she said.

"What?"

"I'm Cheryll Wagner."

Lydia's brow furrowed. "Then who's Madame Rosa?" she asked.

Wagner smiled a little, started to shake her head. "I'm guessing Thomas didn't tell you anything," she said. When Lydia didn't answer, Wagner added, "I'm Madame Rosa. It's my business name. It's a little more mystical than 'Wagner,' gives me a little more authority. I tell fortunes, not opera."

She didn't wait for any further response from Lydia, just turned to go into the next hallway. After a moment's hesitation, Lydia followed.

Wagner led her deeper into the confines of the building, through a long hallway lined with art and shelves of strange artifacts. Not many of them drew the eye—they mostly just looked like junk—but Lydia couldn't stop herself from studying a few objects. A glass eyeball. A small statue. A book bound in leather that was open to two blank pages. When Lydia paused too long at this last one, Wagner coughed, drawing Lydia's attention away.

Wagner was waiting at the doorway to a small room. Unlike the rest of the office, this room's walls were painted a matte black. It had no windows, and the only light source was a candelabra on the middle of a large round table. A few old, bent chairs were stationed around the tables, while at the far end was a plush, red chair. Once Lydia had hesitantly stepped into the space, Wagner closed the door behind her and settled into the red chair.

"Please, sit," she said.

With the door closed, the candles barely gave off enough light to illuminate the room. The walls seemed to suck it away, making Lydia feel like they were in a vast space. Only the candle smoke, which Lydia now noticed hung low in the ceiling, retained any of the room's form, reminded her that she was in a tight, closed space. It didn't bother her outright, but her breathing still got a little shallower.

Lydia settled on a chair against the wall to the right of Wagner. Wagner never took her eyes off Lydia. She kept her fingers steepled before her face, hiding her mouth. When Lydia was ready, Wagner nodded.

"Tell me how you know Tom," she said.

Lydia shrugged. "Does it matter?"

Wagner kept her silence, though her eyes narrowed a little.

"We're partners," Lydia said.

"In the AFPD?"

"Yes."

"So you're a detective," Wagner stated.

Lydia nodded.

Wagner touched her neck at the place where the marks appeared on Lydia's. "Do you think these have anything to do with the case you're working?" she asked.

Lydia bit her lip for a moment. "Look," she said, slowly, "can you help me or not?"

Wagner sunk farther into her chair, fingers still steepled before her. "I probably can, in more ways than you think." She reached for something beside her chair, and Lydia tensed, her hand reaching instinctively for her sidearm. But all Wagner produced was a small deck of cards, which she began to shuffle on the table. If she noticed where Lydia's own hand had gone, she did not show it. "What did Tom send you here for?" she asked.

"A way to make the itching stop," Lydia said.

Wagner paused long enough to throw Lydia an incredulous glance. "Is that all?" she asked.

"It's as much as I care about," Lydia said.

Lydia's host pursed her lips but kept shuffling the cards. "I know ways to reduce the suffering," Wagner said. "But I cannot guarantee it will work well. People with this affliction rarely get better. At best, they learn to ignore it, to suffer in perpetual silence."

"Will it not heal on its own?" Lydia asked, a little confused.

"No," Wagner said flatly.

"What kind of bite never heals?" Lydia wondered, now trying to keep the worry out of her voice.

Again, Wagner paused. "Tom didn't tell you?" she asked.

"No," Lydia replied, frustrated. "He said it didn't matter, that you'd be able to help."

Wagner finished shuffling the cards, shaking her head a little. The curls of her hair bounced as she did, one lock getting caught in an earring. "The best I can tell you is to wash the wound everyday," she said. "Maybe rub some lotion into it. Aloe vera works best. And don't scratch it."

Lydia blinked. "That's it?" she said.

Wagner shrugged. "What were you expecting? Magic?" she said. "Lotions work for a reason."

"But don't you know what did this?" Lydia asked.

"I do," Wagner replied.

"Will you tell me?"

"Do you want to know?" Wagner asked. Before Lydia could answer, Wagner held up a single finger. "Think very carefully before you decide," she added. "This is not the kind of thing that will get better when you know what it is. In fact, knowing will very likely only make your suffering worse."

Lydia stopped, her mouth half-open in response. "Why?" she eventually asked.

Wagner smiled knowingly. "I can't answer without telling you everything."

Lydia was caught. On one hand, her innate curiosity made her want to know—made her want to crack open this woman's head and learn every secret she had in there—like opening a coconut and drinking all its water. On the other hand, the itching truly was nearly unbearable, and Lydia did not want to make it worse. If there was any lesson for Lydia to learn from her past few days, wasn't it that there are some doors she should not look through?

Wagner took up the deck again. She split it in half, then put the bottom on the top again. In rapid succession, Wagner drew three cards and placed them facedown on the table between them. "While you consider it," Wagner said, "a simple reading. On the house."

Lydia blinked, unsure what to say. Because Wagner seemed to be waiting for her, Lydia nodded.

Wagner pushed forward and then flipped the card on Lydia's right. "Your past," Wagner said.

To Lydia, the card showed a man standing on one leg, his other bent, folding his arms behind his back. A tree of some kind grew behind him, and it looked as if he was resting casually against it. It wasn't until Wagner said, "Hanged Man, reversed," that Lydia realized the card was upside down. The man did not stand, he floated. Hung by a single bit of cloth wrapped around his ankle and the tree branch.

Wagner let Lydia observe the card in silence for a moment, then pushed forward the second card. "The present," she said.

A relatively simple card. An old man in a blue tunic standing against a dark blue sky. In one hand he held a lantern, a staff in the other. On his downturned face there was an almost sad look, though it was truly hard to tell through his thick flowing beard.

"The Hermit," Wagner commented, then added, "unusual to get two of the major arcana in a row."

"What do they mean?" Lydia asked, looking up at Wagner.

"I have an idea," Wagner replied with a smile, "but I won't know for certain until I've seen all three."

Lydia glanced at the third card. "Is that the future then?" she asked.

"It is," Wagner said. "Are you ready?"

"Yes," Lydia said. *I swear to god,* she told herself, *if I even see the color green...*

Wagner flipped the card, then flinched her hand backward as if she'd been burned. She stared at the card, eyes wide, nostrils flared. Then she looked up at Lydia. "What case are you investigating?" she asked.

Lydia did not answer at first. She was too engrossed with the card. It showed a barren mountain topped by a single, imposing tower. Flame and smoke poured from its windows, while a bolt of lightning literally blew the roof off the building. Two people, a man and a woman, leapt to escape the destruction, though they only fell to their death down the sides of the mountain.

"What is this one called?" Lydia asked, reaching out to tap it.

"The Tower," Wagner said. "Now tell me, what case are you working?" There was an urgency in her voice, almost threatening.

Lydia met her eyes. "Why?" she asked. Then, "What does it mean?"

Wagner took a breath, holding Lydia's gaze. Then, slowly, she looked back down to the cards. "This one," she said, pointing to the first card, "indicates stagnation. That you were lost, stuck in one spot, with no way to go forward or back. This," now she pointed to the second, "was a good sign. It indicates introspection, wisdom, deep thought. It shows that you are looking for the right answers, that you are using your time well. And this," and here Wagner pointed to the future, to the Tower, "this shows that some great change is coming for you. It will be violent, it will be earth-shattering, and I cannot tell you how you will fare after." Wagner kept her hand on this third card, but leaned closer to Lydia. "I've been doing tarot for nearly twenty years," she said. "Only rarely does it come up, this card. Twice a year, if it's a bad year. I've drawn it three times in a week now. You're the third."

Lydia frowned. Something in the seer's voice betrayed fear, but of what Lydia could not tell. "Who else did it come up for?" Lydia asked.

"Two men," Wagner said. "They came in together, and I gave each a reading. For one man, the Tower was in his present. For the other, it was in his future. I did not hear anything from either man again afterwards, until this morning."

She stood suddenly, pushing past Lydia's chair and out into the brightly lit hall beyond the little room. Lydia was left blinking in the new light, unsure of what to do. Before she could decide, Wagner returned, throwing a newspaper down in front of Lydia. It was from yesterday—"Phantom lays waste to AFPD HQ," declared the headline. "Holly claims next victim."

"There," Wagner said, pointing to a line in the paper.

Lydia read. "Despite the wreckage and amount of injuries, only one death has been reported—Ian Caldwell, a man the police were holding on suspicions of being the Holly Killer."

Lydia was initially too distracted wondering how the *Gazette* had gotten hold of Caldwell's name and the fact that he was a suspect to understand what Wagner was trying to tell her. Then Wagner added, "Him," pointing to Caldwell's name with a single finger, long nail nearly poking through the paragraph. "I did a reading for him," Wagner said. "The Tower was in his future and now he's dead."

Lydia furrowed her brow. *Caldwell was here?* "Who was the other?" Lydia asked.

"A friend I think," Wagner said. "I'd seen him before. His name was Kevin."

"What day was this?"

"Monday."

The day before the fire. The day before Kevin Wood disappeared.

"Do you know anything about this case?" Wagner asked. When Lydia did not answer, Wagner shook her head and sat down again. "What about Tom?" she asked.

"Do your readings ever come true?" Lydia asked hesitantly, still avoiding Wagner's gaze.

"All the time," Wagner said. "They came true for Ian Caldwell, didn't they? I'm guessing for Kevin, too."

Lydia, trying to collect herself, fixed Wagner with a hard glare. "Seems a little suspicious," she said.

The two women stared at each other a moment longer. Then Wagner laughed, a light, sad little trill that didn't reach her eyes. "You really think I have anything to do with this?"

Lydia didn't answer. Instead she stood, checking her pockets to make sure she had everything.

"What do I owe you?" Lydia asked, pulling her wallet out of her pocket.

"Nothing," Wagner said, still seated.

Lydia pulled a ten-dollar bill from the wallet and laid it on the table. "Thank you for your time," she said. "I'll be in touch if we think of anything else."

Wagner did not move as Lydia showed herself out. Just before the door closed behind her, Wagner called, "Be careful, Detective Pike."

Lydia gritted her teeth. She was nothing if not careful.

Six

Thomas left his car on the side of the road at the bottom of the hill. He also left his jacket, badge, and gun. He tucked his keys in his pocket, but apart from that brought nothing. Before starting up the hill, he rolled his shirt sleeves to above the elbow, loosened his tie, and undid his top button. The effect certainly wasn't enough to make him not look like a cop—it wasn't just about the red and gold star, after all. But he did look like he was off duty, out for a stroll in a seedier part of town. Someone to be watched, but not confronted.

When he followed the two wolves from Monya's pack, he had not really meant to talk with her. He hadn't considered yet that she might know something, or have something that he could use. But during the long hours of his second to last day, he realized that of all the people in Ash Falls who could help him, Monya could help him the most. And she might just be the only one who would talk to him.

No one disturbed him as he climbed the hill. At the top was the entrance to a trailer park, "Timber Pines" written on a small sign beside it. A white piece of paper was stapled to the wood between the two words.

The street was empty. Thomas pursed his lips, glancing around him. He could feel the eyes watching him but wasn't sure where they were. Nor was he sure why they were watching him. Why they weren't talking to him.

Slowly, Thomas approached the entrance to the trailer park. He kept his eyes fixed down the long gravel road running between the mobile homes, as empty as a ghost town. The moment he stepped onto the gravel, Thomas knew, he would be entering the pack's territory and would be at their mercy.

A sudden shift in the wind stopped him short. It came directly from the park and it tasted of malice. It smelled of old blood dried on a menacing muzzle, of fur wet with rain, of nights hunting beneath a glorious moon. It smelled like a warning.

I do not like this smell, he thought, *and they know it. To them, it is a good smell.*

His eyes fell on the small sheet of paper stapled to the sign. He could see, now that he was closer, that it was folded in half and on the part facing him was scrawled a single word: "McDonagh."

Thomas ripped it from the sign and unfolded it. In the same hand was a short note, which Thomas read carefully.

Thomas,

Don't use my boys to send your messages again. If you want to talk to your alpha, do it on your own. And if I wanted to talk to you, I'd let you know. Take your respects elsewhere.

The note was signed with a simple, spiky M.

So much for that, he thought to himself.

He crumpled up the note, threw it into the park, and turned away.

The sun was starting to set. This little outing will have been enough, Thomas was sure. Enough time for Holly to leave whatever present he wanted in Thomas's apartment. Thomas took a deep breath, then started down the hill, feeling, for the first time in a long time, well and truly alone.

Seven

It was not normal for Lydia to want to go out twice in one week. There was nothing particularly abnormal in the act, it just seemed a little out of place to Lydia. It was like a small voice, not her own, telling her to go get a drink at her favorite bar. The lotions Wagner had recommended certainly helped the itch on Lydia's neck, but it didn't fully go away. The voice suggested—told—ordered—that a nice drink was really what she needed, that one sip of a good dark beer would make all her troubles disappear.

So, once Lydia finished up some paperwork at the station and could no longer pour over her notes about the Holly killings, Lydia decided she should go back to Chooski's. McDonagh wasn't answering his phone and Lydia figured he was safe for tonight anyways. She filed away her papers, locked her gun, nightstick, and badge in her newly restored desk, and left the precinct through the front lobby.

The weather had cooled off a little. The faintest brush of a storm made landfall farther north the night before. City officials hoped the storm would come south, would put out the Umpqua Wilderness Fire for them—but they had no such luck. Still, the ash fall was significantly less since much of the fire had moved farther away from the city. The fire department reported the blaze to be eighty percent contained now and the city was breathing a collective sigh of relief. No one was going to be evacuated.

Uncle Leo's funeral had been earlier today. With everything else that had happened, she simply forgot about it. Mariam called and left a voicemail once it was done, said that she understood not wanting to show up. "You don't have to feel guilty, though," the voicemail said. "It's not like I expect you to avenge him."

Lydia's lip curled unconsciously at the thought. Avenging Ellwood meant killing Holly. She thought of slicing off his head. Of ripping out his heart. Of dumping his green body in the river. All of these thoughts made her smile deepen, her fist clench, her gait speed up with nervous energy.

This was quite unusual, she knew.

It was lucky the streets of Ash Falls were empty, that no one gave her any trouble. She wasn't sure what she'd do.

Chooski's was a little more crowded than usual and Lydia saw immediately that she'd have a hard time finding a seat. The bar was almost full but still quiet. The stone-faced and silent alcoholics sat in a row at the bar, only broken by two couples that were having nervous conversations. The tables were mostly taken too. She could have found a space at one of these except that she didn't feel like talking or making new friends.

However...

A table at the back of the bar was occupied by only one person. A woman with black hair tied into a bun behind her head and skin as pale as new fallen snow. Lydia felt her breath catch as she realized it was Lilly. A warning in Lydia's mind told her to get out, to run, to put as much distance between Lilly and her as possible, but this was drowned out by a profound desire to touch Lilly. To hold her. To kiss her. The thought of it made Lydia warm in her stomach.

Lydia approached slowly, unsure of how to begin. Lilly was reading, a half-full beer glass beside her and two empty glasses pushed to the end of the table. The beer in the glass was dark and foamy, exactly what Lydia had been craving. The mere sight of it made her mouth water.

Did Lilly want to be alone? Would she be upset at being disturbed? Or would she be happy to see Lydia? Lydia did not know and not knowing was Lydia's least favorite state of being. The inherent uncomfortableness of it made her shift uneasily, pause just outside of Lilly's periphery. Lydia felt her stomach thrum with anxious uncertainty. What should she do?

Once again, Lilly made the decision for her. She turned, looking towards the bar, and must have seen Lydia out of the corner of her eye because she kept turning until she could stun Lydia with the brightness of her smile.

"Well, well, well," Lilly said, "look who's here."

Lydia grinned back. "I didn't mean to disturb you," she said.

"You didn't," Lilly replied. "You just get in?"

"Yeah," Lydia replied. Her mind was focused on Lilly's smile, on her just a touch too long teeth that somehow made her even cuter, on how good her hair looked tied up in a bun, on the glimmer in her eyes, on the soft rosiness of her cheeks. Lydia, tired and wilted and staring like an idiot, knew she couldn't compare.

"Well, as you can see, I've been off for a while," Lilly said, filling the silence between them. "Would you like to join me?"

"Sorry?" Lydia asked, blinking.

Lilly raised an eyebrow. "A drink?" she asked. "Would you like one?"

"Yes," Lydia said, not quite believing it. And then, because it seemed the thing to do, Lydia took the seat across from Lilly.

"Try this one," Lilly said, pushing her half-finished pint across to Lydia.

Lydia needed no more encouragement. She lifted the glass to her lips, sniffed it once—malty and metallic—then took a small sip. It had a nice fungal flavor—heavy on the tongue and an extra meatiness that reminded Lydia of eating pork. It was, somehow, exactly what she was looking for.

"Damn," Lydia said breathlessly.

Lilly waggled her eyebrows at Lydia. "It's good right?" While Lydia took another sip, Lilly got the bartender's attention and ordered two more.

"I've never had it before," Lydia said.

"I should hope not," Lilly replied. "We just released it."

"Falls' Brewing?" Lydia asked.

"Yes," Lilly said, smiling.

Something about the company name was a warning bell in Lydia's mind, something that she knew she was supposed to remember but couldn't quite. It was like somebody was ringing a bell just outside of earshot.

But as soon as Lilly spoke, Lydia forgot all her concerns.

"It's one of my creations, actually," Lilly said, smiling casually.

"Is that so?" Lydia asked. "What's in it?" Should she hold Lilly's hand? Would that be too forward?

Lilly's smile deepened as the beers came. "Can't tell you that," she said, teasingly. "I've got to keep some brewer's secrets."

Lydia giggled, mostly because Lilly was giggling. She took a long sip from her fresh glass, and the warmth of the beer washed over her. This was *exactly* what she needed.

She barely noticed when Lilly's foot touched hers. She did notice—became more interested—as the foot slid its way up her calf to her knee—gentle, tender, inquisitive.

"What are you calling it?" Lydia asked, her voice growing quiet.

She couldn't focus on the answer. She couldn't focus on her phone buzzing in her pocket, probably McDonagh, finally. She couldn't focus on the Holly case or any of the other happenings in Ash Falls. She focused solely on that foot touching her knee, gentle as a kiss. Lydia had worked hard the past week. She deserved a night off.

"Sorry, say it again?" Lydia asked, smiling sheepishly.

Lilly giggled, just as excited as Lydia. "Vampire's Delight," she called it.

END of Episode Seven

EPISODE EIGHT: DIES SECURIS

ONE

Ash Falls Police Department - Request for Re-evaluation
Rank: Lieutenant   *Name:* Benedict Lake
Date: 08/16/2017   *Evaluation Date:* 08/16/2017
Evaluation Number: 2017-08160045
Evaluator Rank: Commander
Evaluator Name: Ruby Hammerick
Reason for Re-evaluation: Evaluation was unfair and unwarranted
Explanation:

Commander Hammerick was ordered to perform competency evaluation by Major Curtis Brown. Both Cmdr. Hammerick and Maj. Brown have evaluated my performance previously, each with consistently unfavorable outcomes. Cmdr. Hammerick wrote her evaluation after visiting the 14th Precinct for 20 minutes. At the time, the precinct had just been attacked by unknown entity and in general disarray and repair. I was in the midst of an effort to reorganize Precinct and establish what occurred and what would need to occur before Precinct could perform normal duties again, an effort not aided by the arrival of Cmdr. Hammerick.

As I've stated, the Cmdr. performed her evaluation over 20 minutes without interviewing me or any of my officers. I believe this evaluation was based solely on the Cmdr.'s previous evaluations and had no basis in the reality of the situation. As such, I would have received a failing grade regardless of precinct's condition.

Because of this, I must formerly request that a re-evaluation of my competency is performed by someone who does not report to Cmdr. Hammerick or Maj. Brown. I am willing to provide references from amongst the 14th and the AFPD.

TWO

There was nothing new in Thomas's apartment when he returned. Dark had not quite fallen, but Thomas was still expecting something. He spent an hour searching through his apartment, looking in every cabinet, under every pillow, and behind every piece of furniture. There was nothing out of place, at least from that morning. He still wasn't used to the antlers and tusks.

Though he was anything but satisfied by this search, Thomas gave up close to eight. He spent some time finishing his gift for Pike, drinking as he did so, then tried to read a book. His mind wouldn't let him. Ever present was the knowledge that this was his last night on Earth, that tomorrow would be his last day.

He wanted to talk to someone. He wanted to see Mariam. He wanted to be alone. He wanted to kill, to make sure something left the world with him. He wanted to end it now.

A little sad, a little lonely, and more than a little drunk, Thomas drifted off to sleep around eleven, still sitting at his kitchen table.

When he woke, his eyes fell immediately on the patch of fur occupying his kitchen counter, the antlers and the tusks placed to the side.

It was red. Red like his own hair in younger days. Red like the blush of a cloud as day turns to evening. It was a patch about a foot by a foot, cut with jagged edges and a little blood still clinging to the underside. Someone had skinned this animal quickly, not caring if it was precise. The message did not have to be precise, after all. Thomas already knew what it meant.

Get ready.

It was the skin of a fox, Thomas guessed.

He didn't waste too much time over it. Nor did he waste too much more time in his apartment. For all intents and purposes, he was already dead to this place, no longer its tenant. He took one last shower in the bathroom that took too long to get hot water, shaved one last time in the mirror that fogged up with steam, and dressed one last time in his too small bedroom with his too small bed. He clipped his gun and badge to his belt, slipped his wallet and phone into his pockets, and laced up his boots. Armed and armored, he made ready to leave.

His last act in his apartment was to pull out a piece of paper and a pen. *Lydia,* he wrote,

If I see you again, then you owe me a beer and I owe you an explanation. If I don't, then I hope this doesn't become your problem. Or if it does, I hope you find a way to end it.

-Tom

He folded the letter into thirds, wrote "Detective Pike" in large letters on the outside, then left it on top of the fox skin.

He hoped he had done the right thing for her. The second and third bites were hard for any dhampir to resist, even if they did know what was happening to them. Maybe Lydia had already given in, had become a blood-sucking lady of the darkness, the latest of many on the force.

Thomas hoped not. He didn't think it would matter to Holly, though.

He sent Pike a text asking her to come by his apartment. Then he turned out the lights and left through the front door. He didn't bother to lock it behind him.

THREE

There's a kind of waking up that feels like being pulled from deep water. The submerged—the sleeper—the drownee— has become used to their state, has accepted that, for them, there is no longer anything but the deep darkness of the water. Air and water, after all, are just different forms of atmosphere. Sleep and wakefulness are, in the same way, different forms of consciousness.

Lydia's sleep was a form of consciousness she had never encountered before. It was deep, deeper than the darkest depths of Ascension Lake. She didn't want to come out, struggled against whatever force was dragging her to the surface. Her sleep comforted her like a cocoon, and her mind wandered over the rootless moments of her life, happily ensconced away from the reality of her present.

But the surface was there, and no matter how Lydia struggled to stay asleep, the bright spot of morning grew closer and closer. Only when she broke through the surface and gasped, sitting bolt upright in bed, did she stop struggling.

It was her room. The same white walls, the same sparse decoration. The same window overlooking the same distant street, the same door leading out to the same living room. But something about it all felt different to Lydia. Something about Lydia felt different.

She felt good. She felt stronger. Everything seemed brighter, too, and she could smell the scents of her room more keenly than ever before.

Lydia got out of bed. She walked to her closet mirror. Nothing *looked* different about her. Maybe her arms were a little more toned, a little more muscled, but it was hard to tell. She turned herself to look at the bug bites—or whatever they were—from yesterday. They still marred her neck, seemed to have even grown worse. The flesh around them was redder, punctures in her otherwise brown neck. She touched one gingerly. When she pulled her hand away, the fingertip was again covered in blood.

Just as instinctively as yesterday, Lydia sucked the liquid off her own skin, reveling in the taste of it. Then she realized what she was doing and practically spat her finger out of her mouth.

What the hell is wrong with me? she asked herself.

Absolutely nothing, replied another voice, a voice that did not belong in Lydia's head. *You are perfect.*

Lydia shook the thoughts away. Almost immediately, her neck began to burn, calling attention back to it. Lydia found the ointment Cheryll Wagner had recommended and began to rub it on her neck again. It helped lessen the burning, at least to something she could ignore.

What happened last night? Lydia had trouble remembering. She could remember running into Lilly again, could remember enjoying herself even though something felt off. Lydia couldn't quite figure out what it was, what her memory was trying to warn her about. She could almost grasp it, but the moment she wrapped her mind around it, something else whisked it away.

Whatever it was, Lydia decided McDonagh would know.

She checked her phone. She had missed a few calls from him, but she was starting to expect that now. This morning he had also sent her a text. Lydia opened it and stared at the message a little nonplussed.

"Come by my apartment whenever you have a chance."

Lydia checked the time and groaned. It was almost noon. She had slept in so late, and McDonagh had sent the text at around 8.

Lydia hurried through getting dressed. She was careful to check that her shirt had a high enough collar to hide her neck. She threw on a jacket as well, even though she could already tell it was going to be hot. Her gun and nightstick were still locked in her desk at the station, so all Lydia had to grab was her wallet, phone, badge, and brass knuckles. At the last moment, she remembered how much walking she had been doing the past few days, remembered how sore her feet were from her work shoes. She decided on a pair of hiking boots instead, and was relieved when her feet slid into their gentle cushion.

So armed and armored, Lydia left her apartment, sure to lock it behind her.

FOUR

Thomas had to admit, as much as he didn't really care one way or the other about the comforts of technology, there was something inherently satisfying about the purr of an engine coming to life. Starting his day in his car always felt right, and he could think of no better way to begin looking for 'the holiest wild he knew.'

That statement had been bothering Thomas since he first heard Ian Caldwell mention it. He considered it as he pulled his car out into the streets of Ash Falls. For Thomas, the idea of a 'holiest wild' was alien, as if his hunter did not quite understand how the wilderness worked. Nobody did, but that was the point. Thomas, whenever he wanted, could wander into some place where things grew, whether it was the endless tracts of woodland that surrounded Ash Falls or a small, slightly overgrown park, and would be able to find a spirit to commune with. Raised in a pack of werewolves, Thomas was taught that where there is a spirit, there is something divine. In his own practice as an adult, he discovered that there is divinity everywhere. There was no 'holiest wild.' All the wilderness—all the world even—was equally holy.

Where, then, could Thomas find Holly? Everywhere? Anywhere?

With no clear path, Thomas decided to leave the city. He followed the route he travelled to meet the water spirit, except that, once he was past the inky, mysterious waters of the reservoir, Thomas drove without direction. Five miles after he crossed Bear Creek, he took a left, using a narrow, wooden bridge to cross the Umpqua. Even without calling to them, Thomas could sense the spirits beneath shrinking from him, turning to avoid whatever tainted his soul. Whatever mark Holly left upon him.

Across the bridge, the road was no longer paved. Thomas's car handled the bumps well at first, but there was still a distinct rattle whenever he hit something deep. He did his best to steer away from the worst of the potholes, at least at first. But the farther he got into the woods, the less he began to care, electing instead to just slow his car a little. There wasn't much room to maneuver anyways. The trees grew so close around the gravel road that Thomas had to take greater care avoiding them than the holes. Even this concern vanished, and Thomas just drove. He was thoroughly in the woods now, and getting his car out would be a quest all its own. Depending on how this night went, it probably wouldn't be his quest.

Finally, one of his tires popped. He heard it immediately and slammed on his brakes, barely keeping his car from crashing into an old pine. When the car stopped moving, Thomas turned off the ignition. For a time, he let the silence of the midday wood wash over him, watching the trees around him sway in the mountain breeze.

He left his keys on the dash. Stepping out of his car, he looked around for anything familiar. All he could see were endless woods. The ground sloped downward to his left, so he guessed that was the way back towards Ash Falls.

He checked his phone, fighting the wave of nausea that always met him at altitudes like this. There was no service up here. He locked the phone, then tossed it onto his front seat. He tossed the wallet there too, and his badge. He forgot his sidearm on his belt until after he shut the door. He didn't think he would need it, but kept it anyways.

He had drunk the rest of his whiskey. Not many spirits would answer his request without some kind of offering. However, he had always been able to communicate with the trees with just a touch of his hands, so they would have to do.

He started with the pine. It was about a hundred feet tall, he guessed, with a broad and powerful moss covered trunk that would have shrugged off whatever his car had thrown at it. Thomas approached slowly, wandering around to its other side so that his car was out of sight. This side, the side that faced uphill, was dry, not a trace of moss clinging to it.

Thomas closed his eyes and reached out his hand, letting his palm rest against the rough bark.

Darkness. Thomas waited, keeping calm. Nothing happened. *Hello?* he asked the tree.

There was no response.

It wasn't that he wasn't communing with the pine, he knew he was. He could still feel the tree's presence, could sense its energy around him, in him. But the tree revealed nothing. It said nothing, refused to show him what it saw or felt.

It *ignored* him.

Please? Thomas asked it.

It was like looking at the face of a large, blank stone, knowing there was a painting on the other side. When

Thomas tried to look for it, the stone only turned farther away. It was enough to drive him mad.

I do not like this feeling, he tried to remind himself. *It is not a good feeling.*

Thomas let his consciousness slip away from the pine, though his palm still rested against the trunk. He opened his eyes and looked up into the highest branches. They cracked and whispered in the wind, way high above. Then, Thomas heard a *snap*, two *cracks*, and a loud, rushing *thud* just to his left as a pinecone crashed into the ground beside him.

Rude, Thomas thought.

He turned away, leaving the tree to its own deliberations. Wandering farther into the woods, Thomas tried to decide which species would be more likely to talk with him. He could almost feel the pines shrinking away, the rattle of wind dropping more pinecones around him as he passed.

He decided to try the next species he saw, an old Douglas fir, one half of its foliage browned by disease. Thomas had to grit his teeth and push his way through the branches, the needle-like leaves stinging his arms and face. When he reached the trunk, he took a deep breath before closing his eyes and touching his palm against the smoother, slicker bark.

Silence.

Thomas furrowed his brow, let his consciousness brush up a little firmer against the fir's. It only shifted away a little, like a parent doing its best to ignore a bored child.

Please, Thomas asked it. *I need help. I can't be alone right now.*

The fir only responded with more silence at first, but, after a moment, Thomas realized that he could still see around him, even though his eyes were closed. The fir showed him the land as it was, with all the trees and beasts and insects about him. Then they began to fade, each organism in its own way, until all that was left was Thomas and the fir. Then the tree faded as well, so that Thomas had only the earth beneath him and the sun above. Then those faded, and Thomas was alone in a void. Far beneath his feet, he saw the full moon, silvery and comfortable. But the fir took that too.

You are never alone, it whispered.

Thomas turned in the void, feeling the hairs on his neck stand. He did not see anything behind him, not truly. But there seemed to be a green smoke in the darkness, which took the shape of a man.

You make a companion of death, the fir told him.

Thomas let the vision fade before opening his eyes. He resisted every urge to peek behind him, to see if Holly was waiting just there. Instead, he showed the fir his gratitude by patting it once, then finding a spot to sit at its base. The fir did not directly tell him to leave, but neither did it acknowledge his presence.

Thomas leaned his head against the tree, stared up through its branches at the sun. He caught his breath. There was still plenty of time until sundown.

Thomas had a hunch about which species of tree would talk to him. The trick would be finding one up here. Maybe he should have enlisted a forester or two, like whoever hired Bates and Tanner.

He would be fine. He just needed to rest a moment. Communing always took a little out of him, and that had been a particularly unsettling vision.

When he felt ready, Thomas stood again. He gave the fir one last pat, then struggled his way out of its branches and needles. Once in the open, he sniffed the air, decided on a direction, and followed it.

Bale had told him there was something wrong in the woods. Pike had found a hawthorn branch on a sidewalk in Ash Falls. The spirit of Bear Creek was frightened of whatever haunted the city. Bates and Tanner had been looking for a hawthorn, amongst other trees. And Thomas had already interacted with a hawthorn, knew that something was not right. He had not bothered to commune with the hawthorn then. If a tree was angry, it was best to leave it alone. But *now*, now Thomas wanted to have a word.

It took him a full hour to find one. When he did, Thomas noticed the tree was in full bloom, its flowers a pale white in the afternoon sun. He approached it carefully, and as he grew closer, a great wind shook the tree, dislodging some of the petals. The ones that touched him stung as if dipped in acid. When he reached the trunk, Thomas hesitated a moment longer. Then, because he had already told himself he should, Thomas placed his palm on the tree.

Red seared through his mind, and, instinctively, Thomas flinched away. It all ended for a moment—the pain, the gale of wind, the petals falling on him. Thomas checked the palm of his hand to see if he had been physically hurt. His skin seemed normal, though pain still rippled up the nerves in his arm.

Thomas took one deep, steadying breath, then closed his eyes. Fortifying his mind, he reached out again to touch the hawthorn.

The anger seemed greater this time, the red that flashed through his vision like staring into the sun. Thomas was an ant compared to the well of energy that churned within the organism, a mote in the eye of a giant. It tried to crush him, to smother him, to burn him away, but Thomas held on, even though every fiber of his being hurt, even though every instinct he had told him to run. Thomas held on, firm in his hope that the tree would reveal something to him.

After a time, after the pain began to feel interminable, after the anger began to feel like it would swallow Thomas whole, he began to notice a difference. Two holes appeared in the field of red before him, green as Holly's skin. They grew as Thomas focused on them, and, as they grew, the pain lessened somewhat.

They were eyes, Thomas realized. A pair of eyes looking at him. Trees do not have eyes.

What do you want? the hawthorn asked him.

Thomas thought. He was not sure. When he did not answer immediately, another blaze of pain crashed through him, a rebuke as sharp as a winter breeze.

What do you want? the hawthorn asked.

To understand, Thomas answered.

FIVE

The squad room was beginning to take on its old energy, though it still fell quiet for a moment when she entered. Lydia did her best to ignore the looks.

Lieutenant Lake barely spared Lydia a glance when she entered his office. "Have you found him yet?" he asked before she had a chance to say anything.

The question caught her off guard, and her mind was still too full of McDonagh's note to understand what he meant. "Who?" she asked.

The lieutenant stopped what he was doing long enough to look at her, a glare crossing his face. "Who the hell else?" he asked. "Holly. The maniac who destroyed my squad room, put half of my officers in the hospital, and murdered someone right before our eyes. And did I forget to mention he murdered our commander. The dirtbag *you*," he emphasized the word by pointing a bandaged finger at her, "are supposed to be hunting. You and McDonagh—who I haven't heard a peep from, by the way, in three days. Who else would I be talking about?" He let the folder he had been reading drop to his desk. "Have you gotten anything?" he asked, standing now. "Anything at all? McDonagh insisted you two could handle it. I wanted to take you off this case. I wanted the whole damn department looking for this guy. But McDonagh said no. So, what have you gotten?"

Lydia waited to see if he was done. He arched an eyebrow at her silence, which she took as a sign to talk. "Which question do you want answered first?" she asked. "There were like six."

Lake bared his teeth for a second. "Have you caught the bastard?" he asked, slowly enunciating each syllable.

"No," Lydia answered, not taking her eyes off Lake.

His brow twitched, just for a moment. "Are you any closer to catching him?" he asked.

Lydia shrugged. "Not really," she admitted.

She watched as his hand closed into a fist, still pressed firmly on his desk. "Where is your partner?" he asked.

"That's why I'm here," Lydia said, carefully. "He's missing."

Lake frowned, and Lydia felt some tension in the room ease. "What do you mean?" he asked.

Lydia held out the note she had found in McDonagh's apartment. While he read it, Lydia explained most of what had been happening the last few days—or at least what she knew of it. She left out her neck, left out her and McDonagh's discussion about magic. She stuck to the facts, the information that would tell what progress they had made on the case. Which wasn't much, she quickly realized. At the end, she added, "His apartment was empty except for the trophies and that note. He's not answering his phone, either. I don't know how to find him."

Lake read the note a second time, returning to his seat as he did. "Where do you think he went?" he asked once he was finished.

"I don't know," Lydia said. "To find Holly, maybe. Tonight's the night, after all."

"You didn't think to run this plan by me before committing to it?" he asked. He drummed the fingers of one hand on the underside of his desk, his eyes locked on Lydia.

She held up a hand defensively. "It wasn't my plan, sir," she said.

Lake rubbed a palm across his face, his eyes closed for a moment. "You're sure?"

Lydia waited until he was looking at her again. "You know how he is," she said by way of an explanation.

Lake tapped his lips, then nodded. "Then what the hell was he thinking?" he asked. "We could have laid a trap. We could have had the bastard surrounded."

"We had him surrounded here," Lydia countered. "Look what good it did us."

"But we could have been prepared this time," Lake shot back. "We could've gotten him."

Lydia shrugged. "Maybe," she said.

"So, what, you agree with his plan?" Lake asked, gesturing towards her again. At least it wasn't aggressive anymore.

Lydia shook her head. "I don't know if he has a plan or not, Lieutenant," she said. "I think we just need to find him. Even if it's only to save him, instead of catching Holly."

"We can do both," Lake replied. "It's just a matter of setting the right trap."

Lydia wasn't so sure.

"So, how do we find him?" the lieutenant asked.

"McDonagh?"

"Yes."

"I have no idea," Lydia said. "His phone's off, so we can't trace it. He didn't say anything about where he was going. We can put out a BOLO, but if he's left the city already he might be impossible to find."

Lake leaned back in his chair, steepling his fingers before his face. "What happens if he never comes back?" he asked. He kept this question quiet, but his eyes never wavered from hers.

Lydia shook her head. "I don't know that either," she said, resisting the urge to grit her teeth. "We won't know until Holly takes his next victim, which wouldn't be for another three days."

"If he sticks to his pattern," Lake commented.

"Did that guy seem like the type to break his routine?" Lydia replied.

Lake didn't respond. Instead, he tapped his fingers together a moment, then checked his watch. "You have until tonight, right?"

"Theoretically," Lydia agreed.

"Then figure it out," Lake said. "That 'theoretically' gives you about seven hours, I'd say."

"Any advice?" Lydia asked. "Or help?"

"I can't give you anyone else, the unit's stretched too thin already. If you know for a fact where he is, we can be there."

"If not?"

Lake shrugged. "You're a detective," he said. "You'll figure it out."

Six

Thomas lasted as long as he could with the hawthorn. The pain it caused him was like a minor ache at the back of his skull, worming its way towards his eyes while setting off every nerve along the way. He told himself to hold out until the pain reached the front. He told himself that it would kill him when it hurt there, but that meant he could hold out until then. He told himself it was for Mariam.

While communing with the tree, Thomas learned seven things. He learned that his father was dead, and that his mother forbade anyone from telling him. He learned a spell to make any man fall in love with him, and he learned that moss on the side of a tree tickles. He learned that a group of gods had made his city into a sacrificial death trap long before he was born, and he learned the Hebrew word for fire. He learned that the fury of the hawthorn and Holly were connected. Or, put more accurately, related. Related in the way his left arm was related to his right leg.

Then, Thomas could take no more. He released his consciousness from that of the tree, brought himself back into the dry August heat of the forest. He practically collapsed against the trunk, had to be careful not to touch his palm to it again. He was drenched in sweat and his mouth felt dry. Thomas closed his eyes.

"My father is dead," he whispered, and the wind whispered back.

And Bale didn't tell me? Thomas asked himself. *I stood in his office and asked him, point blank, how my family was, and he wouldn't tell me?*

McDonagh could've ripped Bale's arms from his body.

This is not a good feeling, Thomas told himself. But that wasn't right. That wasn't the mantra.

He was so thirsty. He didn't know why he hadn't brought any water. August was too damn hot.

Was dad thirsty when he died? Now he'd never know.

Thomas waited against the tree, wondering if he should just stay there until Holly showed up. He kept his eyes closed, letting himself smell his own sweat, the dusty air, the bugs crawling over the plants. His strength slowly returned, even if his thirst did not abate. He listened to his own breathing, to the wind rushing through the trees, to the small animals crashing their way through the underbrush. He decided that he would be able to move on, to survive, if only he could have something to drink. He tasted adrenaline coursing through his veins, the dry cotton of his thirst, and water brought faintly on the wind.

The water was close, he realized. He could smell it, too. Clear, fresh, mountain water, running in a stream not far from him.

Thomas opened his eyes, determined to find it. He pushed himself up onto his haunches, then rose to his full height. The water was not far. He would be able to make it.

A deer stood in the trees not far from Thomas. He noticed it almost as soon as he left the tree behind. It was a large animal, with a great pair of antlers almost as big as the trophy Thomas had received. Thomas did not pay it much mind, nodding to it once before setting off to find the water.

He initially thought the stream was uphill, but as Thomas reached the top of a rise, he realized it was actually farther to his left. He could hear its gurgle now, and it made his mouth water with anticipation. He corrected his course, following the noise instead of the scent carried on the wind.

A twig snapping behind him made Thomas turn wildly. To his surprise, he saw the same deer following him. It too had paused, though it only looked at him. When he made eye contact with it, the deer started looking around as if it was also trying to determine the source of the sound. Thomas knew it had been the deer, however. He could see the broken wood underneath its hoof.

For a moment, Thomas wondered what to do. It's not as if the deer would be a problem, he assured himself. But why was it following? What if the green man sent it? Had the others had similar encounters? Thomas couldn't remember a rash of deer around the station while Caldwell was there. But, then again, he had been gone on the last day. Who knew what strange things happened and were then forgotten, outmatched by the strangeness of Holly.

What Thomas did know is that he wanted it to leave him alone. He didn't need to see anyone other than the trees tonight. He would meet his fate alone.

Just like his father.

He chose to ignore the deer for now. There was a difference in the air, the temperature dropping as he approached the water. When he found it, he saw that the stream sprung from beneath two rocks, a small trickle that wound its way into the valley below. A small pool formed five feet from the spring, barely deep enough to cover Thomas's head, but with enough water for him to drink. Relieved, Thomas knelt, put his dry lips to the surface, and slurped the cool water down his throat.

The deer watched him. It stood over him on the other side of the creek, its great antlered head giving him shade. Thomas arched his head up towards the beast, meeting its eye. The two, wolf and deer, watched each other a long, tense moment, neither blinking, neither moving, water still dribbling down Thomas's chin. Then, as if released from a hold, the deer turned and cantered off into the woods.

Thomas blinked, unsure if he believed what he just saw. Not the deer's presence, nor the way it looked at him. All of that made sense somehow—checked out in his brain. What was odd was the way the deer moved. *It really did canter*, Thomas confirmed to himself. *Deer don't canter. They sprint.*

He looked for it again. It had disappeared.

Something wasn't right, he knew. He could no longer remember the words of his mantra. So much had happened —he had spent too long with the hawthorn. It broke something in his mind, some lock he had forged long ago. Thomas only felt like this on the full moon.

That's not how this is supposed to go.

Thomas got up from his knees. With a quick jump, he crossed the creek and landed on the far bank. He took a moment to find firmer ground, then he looked again, straining to see deeper into the growing darkness. It must still be near.

There! He saw a movement, deep in the woods. A flicker of a white tail, a flash of light reflected in the dark pool of an eye. The deer trotted farther off, but Thomas knew where it was.

Why? he wondered. *It has antlers. Antlers like the ones I got.*

Thomas followed the deer, moving at a steady pace. He would grow close to the animal, then it would gallop away again, its head held high despite the low branches around it.

Thomas knew this game. This was the game human hunters had played with their prey since the dawn of the species. Humans were endurance hunters. As Thomas pursued the deer at his same brisk but steady pace, the deer would tire. It would allow Thomas to grow closer and closer, either unwilling or unable to keep running away. Eventually, it wouldn't run at all and Thomas would be able to catch it.

That was all he wanted to do. Catch it. See if there was anything strange about it that he could detect with a touch of his hand. See if there was a spirit inside of it for him to connect with. He didn't want to harm the deer, nor to kill or maim it. Just to touch it.

Nothing was right tonight, though. No matter how far he chased it, the deer didn't seem to be getting any more tired. There was no sheen of sweat on the beast's coat, no lagging tongue or panting breath. It didn't show any of the myriad signs of tiredness that existed in the animal kingdom. It always trotted away at the same stately pace the moment Thomas drew too close. Then it watched him, the same bored look in its eye, the same challenge for Thomas to show any real desire to catch it.

Thomas didn't have the time for this. Nor the patience. And he was starting to get thirsty again. His feet dragged a little through the dirt, his breath became ragged. He wanted to go back to the creek, but he could no longer remember the way. No matter how hard he tried, the deer was always just ahead of him, its dark eyes taunting.

Eventually, Thomas had to stop. He paused beside a large boulder, leaned against it while he caught his breath. The deer waited for him.

I know one way to get him, a voice in his head whispered. Something from the place he had locked away.

Thomas undid a few more buttons on his shirt. He wished he had drunk more water, wished he hadn't come out here at all. He was drenched in sweat, a salty layer forming on his upper lip. His gun chafed at his hip.

My gun, Thomas realized. He had forgotten it was even there. He didn't have to use the other way.

Thomas unholstered the pistol, flicked off the safety. Humans may have evolved as endurance hunters, but they certainly found more efficient methods.

Carefully, Thomas took aim. He breathed once, then fired.

The deer moved at the last moment. Thomas's bullet whizzed past it, burying itself in a tree not far beyond.

Damn, Thomas thought.

He moved closer towards the deer, thinking that he would do better with the animal in range. He squeezed off another round, but the animal still dodged it.

Die, Thomas thought.

His father had, after all.

He fired again. The deer glanced at him, bellowed a taunt.

Die, Thomas whispered.

So had Leonid Ellwood.

Another shot, followed by the crack of a tree limb being shorn from its home.

"Die," Thomas commanded.

So would he.

Another miss.

"Die!" he screamed.

So would they all, because he would fail.

He fired again and again and again, until he emptied his magazine, shouting obscenities at the deer as he did.

When the last echo of his last shot finished reverberating off the mountainside, the deer still stood. It was only a small distance from Thomas, serene and regal, its head held upright. In exasperation, Thomas threw his gun at the deer too, but even that missed.

I won't fail you, a voice at the back of his mind whispered. *I can do anything.*

A part of Thomas still knew this was a lie. He had sworn away from that choice, vowed to never use it willingly again. But he didn't care anymore. Bale was right. Thomas knew how to end all of this.

The deer stayed motionless while Thomas transformed.

It started in his chest. His body expanded, tearing through his shirt and exposing the growing fur beneath. Then, his hands changed, growing long claws while forming into dense, sensitive pads. His feet changed this way too, breaching through his boots and pants, elongating to give him greater speed. His mouth and nose grew from his face now, his teeth sharpening, his nose gaining an exquisite refinement. His ears shifted as well, so that now he could hear every sound in the forest, and a tail grew from his back, long and muscular. There was more fur, everywhere, growing all over him in thick brown tufts, warming his naked body while also protecting him from the sun. He did not feel like Thomas McDonagh any longer. He didn't know what he felt.

I do not like this feeling, he remembered. *It is not a good feeling.*

No, it was not.

As if released from a spell, the deer sprang away. The wolf followed. He had never failed to kill his prey before.

This would be no different.

SEVEN

When Lydia was seven—long before her mother's illness and long after her parents's divorce—she found herself, very suddenly, alone. Being alone wasn't anything she particularly disliked. She had her own bedroom, after all, and no siblings that she knew of. While her mother was certainly loving and doting, she couldn't be around all the time for Lydia, nor did she make enough to get a sitter. So, at age seven, Lydia knew what it was like to be alone. It didn't unsettle her. That was being alone in the house, though, or in her room, or in the yard when the Needles' sun wasn't brutal. This time—this one time—was different. This time, Lydia was alone and it made her scared.

Even as an adult, Lydia could never remember how she had gotten lost. They might have been at the mall, or they might have been at a park.

Where Lydia was alone changed too. Sometimes Lydia was alone in the woods, sometimes it was in a building she didn't recognize. Sometimes it was in her home.

What never changed was how long she was alone for. A long time. Long enough for a child to get thirsty. Long enough for a child to get hungry. Long enough that she started crying, wore herself out from crying, then started crying again all over. Too long for anyone—let alone a little girl—to be alone.

What also never changed was the moment her mother found Lydia. At her wits end, covered in her own sweat, tears, and filth, thirstier than she had even been, hungrier than she would ever be again, Lydia looked up from the ball she had curled into and there was her mother, kneeling beside her. Little Lydia cried even more, as did her mother, who pulled her daughter into her arms and held her against her chest, frail and thin even before the cancer.

"Oh momma," Lydia wheezed. "I'm so thirsty."

"I know, sweet thing," her mother whispered back, kissing the top of her head.

"Where were you?" Lydia asked.

"I was lost," her mother said. "I lost you. I didn't know how to find you. I was so scared, my dearest love."

Lydia only nestled farther into her mother's embrace, dry sobs heaving against the faint lavender of her mother's familiar scent.

"But I found you," Lydia's mother said, kissing her again. "And now we're going to go home, and neither of us will ever be lost again. Does that sound good?"

Little Lydia sniffled between two sobs, a small break in the tears. "Can I have water there?" she asked.

"You can have whatever you like," her mother said.

It wasn't until after, perhaps a year later, probably less, that little Lydia thought to ask how her mother had found her.

She was kneading dough at the time. At first, it seemed like she hadn't heard the question and Lydia wasn't sure she would ask again. She had almost given up on knowing when her mother said, "Just a trick I know."

"What's the trick?" Lydia asked, always curious, even then.

Taking a break from her work, Lydia's mother wiped some sweat from her brow with her wrist before pulling at a necklace of yarn around her neck. From under her shirt came a small figure made of wicker and twine. She showed it to Lydia. "This," she said.

Lydia was afraid to touch it, and her mother didn't seem like she wanted to let her. "Is it a voodoo doll?" Lydia asked.

Her mother frowned. "Where did you hear that word?"

"TV," the pair said simultaneously, then Lydia burst into a fit of giggles while her mother smiled. She hid the small doll in its spot under her shirt, still held around her neck.

"It's not quite a voodoo doll," Lydia's mother explained as she returned to the dough. "Not really one at all, actually. But it's also similar, in a way."

"What is it?" Lydia asked.

"A charm," Lydia's mother said. "A way to feel where someone you love is. A way to find them."

"Can I have one?" Lydia asked.

Her mother paused. "You'll have to make it," she explained, her voice careful.

"Why?"

"It doesn't work if someone else makes it for you. You have to want to find the person you're looking for."

Lydia ran this through her child's mind while her mother returned to the dough. Eventually, she concluded that there was only one thing to do.

"You can teach me how to make it," she said.

Though her mother didn't turn to look at Lydia, she could still see her smile. "Would you like that?" she asked, fingers buried in the gooey pre bread mess.

Lydia nodded.

"It starts with who you want to find," her mother explained. "Have you decided that?"

"Yes," Lydia said.

"And?"

"I want to find you."

It was the first spell Lydia ever learned. Like all the others, it never worked for her. Lydia's mother told her it was alright.

"You can have mine," she said, taking it from around her neck. "Let me have yours. That way, you'll always be able to find me."

"I will?"

"Yes. It works both ways. So, if you ever get lost again, you can find your way back to me, and I'll build a new one to find my way to you."

"What if I lose mine?"

"Then you'll just have to build another one. So don't ever forget the spell, okay?"

She never lost hers. Not even after her mother died and her uncle helped her move north. He was itching to be back so quickly, she almost left everything behind. But even he made sure of a few things.

"The rest of it isn't worth much, but you should keep this," Leo said. "It has your name on it. Looks like something your mom would've made."

She never forgot the spell either, no matter how hard she tried.

She rehearsed it to herself as she drove home from HQ. McDonagh had told her that magic was real, that they needed to consider it while investigating these murders. While hunting for the murderer. Why not use magic to find McDonagh? Wherever he was tonight, the green man was sure to be there as well. Even if McDonagh wanted to face him alone, Lydia reasoned they would have a better chance together. If he didn't want her to come, that was too bad.

She needed to start with supplies. Most of the ingredients were easy to find—a wax candle, willow branches, twine, flax. Though it took her to some strange shops, these were all things she could procure with a little patience and a little cash. She needed dirt as well, which she got for free from her apartment complex. Her own blood was the most macabre ingredient on the list, but it was also the most readily available. That left the last and trickiest ingredient. The one that could make or break the charm.

The old spell book Lydia's mother used called it, "Piece of Mind."

"Something that is on your subject's mind a lot," she explained to Lydia as they constructed her doll. "Something that she loves and will think about often. Whenever I am thinking about that thing, even in passing, the charm will show you how to find me."

Lydia, using her child's wisdom, took a flower from her mother's garden, where she spent much of her free days. Her mother smiled at the decision but said nothing. It was Lydia's spell, after all.

Lydia had no idea what would be on McDonagh's mind.

With the rest of her supplies gathered, Lydia returned to McDonagh's apartment, hoping for inspiration. She did her best to ignore the grisly trophies left on McDonagh's counter and the stain of dried blood beneath them. Instead, she started searching through the desk and bookshelves of his living room, trying to find out what it was her partner cared about.

The only answer she could come up with was "Not much." There was no obvious theme to the books he kept except that they seemed long and boring. No letters to one particular person or organization, just the bills that everyone accumulates by being alive. There weren't even pictures of loved ones or family, just the occasional newspaper clippings. He had no medals, no accommodations from the force.

Like at Leo and Mariam's, however, there was evidence they and McDonagh had been friends in a different time. Several of the clippings referred to Leo and McDonagh as partners, and Lydia found a picture at the bottom of his desk of the two men as fine young officers, Mariam's dark, curly hair standing out between them. Even then, McDonagh looked lean and wary, a cautious glint in his eyes despite the strained smile. On the back, McDonagh had scribbled, "Last day in Portland with Leo and Mariam."

None of this was helpful, Lydia thought. Maybe they had been friends, but Ellwood was dead now. However their friendship ended, it hadn't effected McDonagh enough to distract him from the case. And Lake had assigned it to him in the first place. Lydia replaced the picture and closed the bottom drawer.

Getting a little desperate, Lydia took a book from the shelf, opened it, and flipped through the pages. Then she opened another. And another after that. When she was done with a book, she tossed it on the floor, not caring if McDonagh had a system. None of the books had anything anyways. Then she opened a fourth and a picture slid out from the pages. Lydia frowned at it a moment. It was of a woman, taken at a close angle, her face turned away from the camera. Intimate. Even a little sexy. Her dark curly hair bounced playfully over a bare shoulder. It took Lydia a moment to realize it was the same woman in the photo from the drawer. Aunt Mariam.

She started at the bottom shelf. *The War of the Worlds* by Wells. Nothing. *The Color Purple* by Walker. Nothing. *Sir Gawain and the Green Knight* by Waldron. Nothing. All names she had heard, perhaps, but didn't know anything about. Lydia started to go faster, barely giving each book a moment before flinging it down. After eight she found a letter. Lydia only read the first line of it before she knew what it was. The neat "Mariam" signed at the bottom confirmed for Lydia that her partner and her aunt were having an affair. She almost wanted to scream but couldn't. She could deal with all this after she found McDonagh. To do that, she needed something other than the letter and picture, of that she was sure. For this to work, she needed something that was a part of Mariam.

She kept searching. So much of this day had slipped by and she still didn't have a way to find McDonagh. There had to be something in these books. Something more than letters and pictures.

Then, she spotted one with a bookmark. Or, at least, it looked like a bookmark, except that the longer Lydia looked, the more she realized it didn't.

Lydia pulled the book from the shelf. It fell open to the pages marked by the something. Those pages didn't matter. What mattered was that the thing Lydia had noticed sticking from the top of the book was a lock of human hair. Black. Curly. Just like Mariam's.

This was exactly what Lydia needed.

Fingers trembling, Lydia went through the steps of the spell. She wrapped Mariam's hair—it had to be her hair—into a ball, then covered it in the flax and dirt. She dropped a bit of her own blood from her neck onto this, then held the small ball over the lit wax candle while muttering the incantation. Once she was done, she wove the small doll around the ball using the twine and willow branches. When it was fully formed, she kissed it, and whispered the incantation again. Then she waited.

It had to work.

Lydia held the doll to her chest, to her mother's own necklace, wondering where McDonagh was, hoping he still cared about Mariam as deeply as Lydia's mother cared about her. She sat at the same table he drank his whiskey at, surrounded by his things, staring at the trophies left for McDonagh by Holly, the terror of Ash Falls.

She waited. She hoped. She even prayed a little.

Nothing happened.

Frustrated, Lydia stood, ready to give up on McDonagh. Without him, the case was as good as done. She couldn't find Holly on her own, and no other detective would ever understand the case as well as Thomas.

It was over, she told herself. *Leo was right*, she added, *magic is a joke*.

Then she felt it.

END of Episode Eight

EPISODE NINE: AXE OF GOD

ONE

Ash Falls Police Department - Workplace Satisfaction Poll

Precinct: 14   *Commander:* Lieutenant Benedict Lake

Date: 08/17/2017   *Number of respondents:* 147

Questions 9-12

9. Do you feel safe in your work environment?

    (70) Not at all safe

    (29) Unsafe

    (1) Unsure

    (0) Somewhat safe

    (0) Yes

10. Do you feel you commander is aware of your concerns?

    (33) Not at all aware

    (14) Unaware

    (10) Unsure

    (19) Somewhat aware

    (24) Yes

11. Do you feel you commander has taken the right steps to ensure your safety?

    (22) Not at all

    (11) Not really

    (47) Unsure

    (8) Somewhat

(12) Yes

12. Do you feel your commander is capable of his position?
    (2) Not at all capable
    (14) Incapable
    (23) Unsure
    (32) Somewhat capable
    (29) Yes

TWO

With each bite, blood filled Thomas's mouth. There was more than he could swallow, more than seemed possible from a single body. It leaked from the sides of his mouth, spilling over his jowls and down his neck, matting his fur and cooling his skin. The deer lay motionless on the dusty ground, three ribs exposed by Thomas's teeth. Its fat, pink tongue hung limply from its mouth, the eyes open and glossy.

Nearly full of the beast's flesh, Thomas reached his claw under the ribcage. With a single grunt, he cracked open the sternum, then reached in and found the still warm heart. It emerged easily from the cavity and Thomas had only to rip the veins around it. He bit into it like an apple, more blood flowing down his muzzle.

When he was young, his father had always given him and his siblings a piece of the heart. "The heart is sacred," Thomas's father told him. "We might save the flesh for later, or use the hide for clothes, or the bones for jewelry. But we cannot keep the heart. The heart is the root of love, and love left to fester will fuel a vengeful spirit. If you cannot eat anything else, eat the heart."

Thomas hated the heart. It was tough and sinewy, the most defined muscle in any body he had ever eaten. It tasted bad, like licking a bar of iron, but Thomas never forgot his father's words. Considering everything, he thought this might be a fitting way to honor his memory.

While he held the heart in his paw, Thomas sat back on his haunches, chewing slowly. He took in the scene around him, the mess he had made. A deer like this would have been enough to feed most of a small pack. This might have even been one of Bale's, a stag prepared for an eventual lunar hunt. To kill one of these beasts was to invite destruction, to invoke the wrath of the most powerful werewolf pack in the world.

Thomas couldn't help but chuckle. He doubted he would have to worry about that, even if this was Bale's chattel.

The thing looked sad to Thomas, the more he watched it. Its glossy, black eye stared back at him, a fly crawling over the glass of its surface. Thomas, the heart still in one paw, slowly reached out and punctured the cornea with a claw. The juice leaked out and flowed down the deer's cheek until all that was left was the ruin of the deer's face. Thomas licked his claw between bites of the heart. He felt better now that his victim wasn't watching him.

A single hoarse snort came from somewhere behind him. Thomas did not turn, didn't need to confirm that something was there. Something powerful and singular. There was another snort, followed by a low grumble and a cruel grunt. Slowly, Thomas rose to his full height.

The boar slowly walked into his view. It ground its front hoof in the dirt as it circled Thomas, its eyes red with malice and anger. The tusks of the beast were long and sharp, a pale gleam to them in the sun's dying light. Its hide was dark, the bristles along its spine a rail of fine spikes. It was more muscle than beast, and fat. Fatter than anything Thomas had ever seen in nature. A beast like this does not grow to such size and strength without fending off a few would-be hunters. It had scars along its flank, calluses on its brow and snout.

The thing snorted again, still marking the ground with great, powerful strokes of its front hooves. Thomas slowly backed away from it. He needed distance, no matter what.

Thomas's paw tripped against a slippery root, and he stumbled for just a moment. The beast let out a screechy, angry bellow. Thomas tensed every muscle in his enormous body, feeling his own fur stand on end, to show this creature that he was not intimidated.

In the instant before the creature charged, it went silent. It planted its hooves, glaring at Thomas with its fierce eyes. It didn't bother flexing its back, its ridge of spiky hide. It stopped breathing too, for one moment. To the untrained eye, this might look like the boar was about to back off, to leave Thomas in peace. But Thomas knew better. His instincts told him better.

He let his lip curl into a low snarl.

The boar sprang forward, covering the distance between them in a second. Thomas held his ground, claws like knives protruding from his paws, his eyes locked onto the two tusks, white spears approaching him. At the last moment, Thomas dove to the side, lashing out as he did so.

The boar missed. Thomas did not. His claw opened a thin line on the boar's side, and a small amount of blood seeped out. The boar barely seemed to notice.

It didn't lose any of its momentum, turning instead in a wide arc, eventually bringing itself around to face Thomas, then renewed its onslaught with even greater speed. Again, Thomas held his position. Again, he dove away at the last moment. Again, he barely made a scratch in the boar's thick hide. They repeated this dance over and over. Thomas mostly struck the boar, but sometimes he did not. The boar mostly missed Thomas, but sometimes it did not.

Its tusk caught his leg once, making a long, sickening gash up his thigh. Thomas howled in pain while blood splattered across the boar's satisfied face.

The boar caught his arm once, was nearly able to pin it to a tree. Thomas was able to kick the beast away with his good leg, but the pain was worse than an iron brand.

The boar caught his side once, and Thomas thought he was done. Only by using the opportunity to gouge out one of the boar's eyes was Thomas able to escape. It was his first real blow against the boar, and it squealed before retreating from Thomas's body, his blood marring its tusk.

Thomas knew he was getting tired. He was bleeding and injured, his breath ragged and hoarse. The boar barely seemed to care about any of its injuries. Nor was it tired, its only disadvantage a missing eye. If Thomas did not do more to the boar soon, it would do far worse to him.

He placed himself against a tree. *Give me strength*, he pleaded with it. *Make me strong*.

The boar was nearly upon him again. Thomas held his breath, tensed his body, and stared into the wild, raging eye of the approaching beast. As it closed, Thomas did not budge, dared it to reach him, to have its way with him. He let out a roar as it got closer, his every muscle tensed for the defining moment.

As it came, Thomas thrust out his paws, gripping the tusks. At least, that's what he tried to do. One paw managed it. The other was skewered by the tusk. Thomas howled, all while pushing forward with his own body to stop the boar's momentum. The prey squealed as it tasted Thomas's blood in its mouth, bellowed as it realized Thomas was stopping it.

The two fell together, crashing to the ground in a murderous heap.

In the moment he had, Thomas did the only thing that came to mind. Letting out another roar, he broke the tusk of the boar. As it realized what was happening, the beast began to thrash and heave, trying to extricate itself from Thomas. But he did not let go, and though it sent waves of pain coursing through his arm, he managed to break the other tusk—the one stuck in his paw.

Now that it was effectively defanged, the boar's only defense was its thick hide. But Thomas did not care about this either. He had only to reach into the boar's throat, even as it howled, even as it screamed, even as it thrashed. With a single grunt, Thomas ripped the boar's jaw away from its body, then tore at the insides of the beast's head until his fur was matted with bone and brain and gore.

When it stopped moving, Thomas let the corpse fall to the forest floor. There was a ringing in his ear, like it was clogged with something. No matter how Thomas tried to shake it away, the ringing stayed.

Thomas slumped against the tree.

After sucking in as much fresh air as he could, he crawled to the side of the boar. He positioned the beast on its back with a few easy maneuvers. Then, using a single claw, he cut through the thick, fat skin of the beast's chest, spreading it as he worked. Once the beast's sternum was exposed, he reached a paw under it and gripped the slippery bone tightly. With a single grunt, Thomas pulled the sternum away from the rest of the flesh and left it beside what remained of the body.

There, nestled between the lungs, muscle, and fat, was the beast's heart.

THREE

Each time Lydia was about to give up, there was another pull.

She would have never been able to explain it. A 'pull' truly was what it felt like, like there was a string attached to her heart and every now and then—every quarter hour, actually—something yanked on that string from the other end. It made her feel like a dog led on a leash.

It had to be the charm. *Her* charm, the one she had made. The first time she felt the pull, she had been so excited that she accidentally left the little doll behind. She had driven around for two hours, feeling nothing, before she realized it was gone. Only when she returned to McDonagh's apartment to retrieve it did she feel the pull again. Before leaving the second time, she added the charm next to her mother's, hoping that somehow helped.

The charm drew her out of Ash Falls, out past the reservoir and into the Cascades. As she drove higher, Lydia began to get a little nauseous. Eventually, she went so far that she felt the charm pull her backwards. She immediately turned around, then drove more until she felt the charm pull her backwards again. She kept repeating this process until she realized the charm was trying to draw her across a narrow bridge. The road beyond was made of gravel and full of potholes. Lydia drove at an easy pace, careful to avoid the dangers of the road.

The farther she went, the closer the trees got. Eventually, Lydia didn't think she'd be able to drive her car out if the road dead-ended, so she pulled it off to the side as best she could. She sat there for a moment, her headlights illuminating the woods ahead of her, deciding what to do. Then she felt the 'pull' again—the charm telling her to go onward.

Lydia cursed silently under her breath, then turned off the engine. She checked her belongings—gun, brass knuckles, baton, badge, wallet, two definitely-not-voodoo-dolls dolls. She left the wallet in her car, along with the baton and brass knuckles—she was so far in the woods, her gun wouldn't have a chance of accidentally hitting someone. Her phone had no service, so she didn't bother bringing it. That left her badge—which would make any situation with a gun perhaps a little easier—and the charm—which she needed.

Once she felt ready, she locked her car and set off down the road. The sun was just starting to set, but Lydia realized that it wasn't an issue. She was having no trouble seeing in the dark.

Every now and then, she felt a strong, almost overwhelming desire to turn back. She kept thinking of Lilly, of her soft lips, of her little trill of laughter. A part of her wanted deeply to forget all this, to go home and find Lilly, to spend the night with her again. But every time, as she was about to turn away, the charm called to her again, pulled Lydia farther into the forest. There would be plenty of nights with Lilly, Lydia told herself. McDonagh needed her help tonight. Right now, possibly.

After thirty minutes of walking, Lydia saw something ahead of her on the gravel road. As she approached, it began to take shape, to form itself into something she could recognize. A car. McDonagh's car. She knew his plates.

Lydia approached slowly, her gun drawn as a precaution. As she got closer, she saw it was empty. She tried the front door, found it unlocked. A quick glance showed her most of McDonagh's effects on the front seat.

A loud, sonorous howl drew Lydia's attention. It had come from somewhere deep in the woods, though not close enough that she could see what had made it. It must have been a coyote—wolves were so rare these days. But coyotes did not sound like that.

Lydia checked again that McDonagh had left nothing she would find useful. His phone, like hers, had no service, and was nearly out of battery anyways. She wouldn't need his wallet or badge, and his sidearm was missing. Lydia glanced in his trunk for good measure, but found nothing.

Frustrated, Lydia stepped away from the car, glancing around her to see if there was some hint for her to follow, some clear clue like a beacon through the trees.

Nothing.

She slipped the charm from under her shirt and held it in both hands. She let her eyes close, pressed the wicker to her forehead.

Please, she begged. *I'm so close.*

Lydia remained frozen like that, praying to something she didn't know or understand. The wind tossed her hair, kicked up the fallen needles, swayed the tree trunks around her. It carried the ash of the Umpqua Wilderness Fire with it, the death and life of her city. Her adopted home. The place she was only just beginning to understand.

The charm did nothing. Lydia felt nothing.

There was another howl. It broke her reverie, made her open her eyes again and scan the distant woods. Nothing moved. Nothing was still.

Lydia slipped the charm back into her shirt. To replace it, she unholstered her gun, checked to make sure the chamber was loaded and the safety on. Then she set off in the direction of the howl.

Only once she had followed this direction for ten minutes did the charm tell her she was on the right path. Not that she needed its help anymore. The howls kept coming, more and more regularly. Lydia was certain it had something to do with McDonagh.

FOUR

A wolf cannot spit.

Nor could Thomas. He wanted to while he recovered from his battle with the boar. Its heart was sour and Thomas was getting tired of the taste of his own blood as he licked his various wounds. As a man, he'd be able to use his tongue to scoop his saliva into the front of his mouth, then pucker his lips and propel the fluid as far as he wanted. There's something uniquely satisfying about a good spit, especially after a fight. But he couldn't as a wolf, and he couldn't transform back into a human.

As a man, he would die from these wounds. As a wolf, he could lick them, and his saliva would already begin the healing process. It would clot his blood so that it no longer flowed, and it would kill the germs trying to fight their way into his body. This was not magic. His saliva did the same as a man. But as a wolf, he could stand the blood loss for a time. As a wolf, he could survive.

Besides, he did not want to change.

A shift in the wind made his ears prick. It reversed direction and brought a smell of fur, drool, and dirt, similar to a dog or the coyotes that roamed the hills outside Ash Falls. But there was something new to it, something strange and familiar. It was not a smell that belonged in the woods around Ash Falls, and yet Thomas knew it.

Whatever it was, the creature was no doubt aware of him. The wind would have blown his scent right to it. Maybe the stinking carcass of the boar would have masked some of him, but Thomas didn't think he'd be that lucky. Besides, everything else he'd encountered tonight had known about him before he knew about it. Why would this stranger be any different?

Thomas stood. He was still lightheaded from the blood loss, and his injured leg was still weak, but he could run. And he could fight, if he had to. He licked the wound on his limb one last time, then set off north of where the scent came from. He went stealthily, making no noise and listening all the while.

The other was just as stealthy. As he ranged farther north, Thomas began to wonder if he had imagined the scent. Then the wind shifted again, and he caught it a little south of him. Thomas hunkered beside a tree, keeping it between him and the direction of the wind for a time. He watched. He waited. He listened.

It made the first noise. The slight rustle of some needles on a slope knocked loose, tumbling over each other while a paw flinched and resettled. It was closer than Thomas had thought, which was good. Quietly, he padded west of it, then waited until its smell came again. When he knew for certain where to find it, he walked directly into the winds towards it, hoping to catch it unawares.

He did see it before it saw him. A long, red tail with a single spot of black on the tip. An angular, rakish face. A coat so red it might have been tinged with blood. All at once, Thomas remembered where he knew the smell from—the pelt left on his counter. He was so surprised that he knocked a stone loose, and its sudden tumble startled the fox. Its black eyes met his once, briefly, and then the creature slipped off into the night.

There's only one way to catch a fox. Thomas could not use his strength to take it, as no matter how he gripped it the fox would wriggle out of his arms. He could not run it down or outlast it, because the fox was naturally faster and had better stamina than him. Nor, truly, would he be able to sneak up on it as his first attempt had just shown. Even if he moved with the stealth of a shadow, used the wind with the grace of a bird, and made less noise than air sliding over stone, the fox would still sense him before he could make the kill. The only way for Thomas to catch it was if he could outwit it, trap it in some space it couldn't escape from. Even then, he would have to be swift enough to kill it in a single blow. Thomas was not sure of a place in these woods where he could corner it.

But he would have to do something. Even if he lost the fox's trail for a time, he couldn't let it lead him on indefinitely. He would never win that way. Instead, he began to lope uphill, climbing his way to the top of one of the higher foothills. It was a ways, but the hill had a clearing at the top, like a monk's tonsure, and he could see for miles in every direction. To the southwest, he could see the lights of his city, like the warm glow of a candle, and over the hills beyond it he could see the red smoke of the fire—mostly contained, but still burning. To the east, the white caps of the Cascades still glowed in the moonlight, their deep roots stretching down and around him into these very hills and valleys, the silver ribbon of ice water flowing through them. He could see where Sean Tanner had died, where Jude Bates died, where Megan Rude and Leonid Ellwood and Emma Bosk and Kevin Wood and Ian Caldwell all died. If he had to guess, he'd say that he could probably see where he was going to die.

But that wasn't his concern at the moment. At the moment, he wanted to see where the fox would die.

He scanned the valleys below him, not knowing what he was looking for but certain he'd recognize it when he saw it. He wanted somewhere deep, somewhere ominous, somewhere the fox could not climb to freedom from. He knew this the way a fish knows to jump to catch the fly, the way a bear knows to stand in the waterfall. He knew it as a hunter, born and bred, even if he was no longer part of a pack.

He saw it to the south of him. A shadow in a hillside where there should have been no shadow, even in the dark. The sides of that cleft would be too steep to scrabble up, the floor too open for it to hide. Thomas would drive the fox there.

As if sensing his decision, the wind blew the fox's scent to him again. It was north, and Thomas let out a deep howl. "I'm coming for you," that howl told the fox. "You better run."

Over the course of an hour, he drove the fox towards this trap. He made his howls echo from the hills and trees, confusing his prey as to where he was. If it ever tried to backtrack, Thomas sprang towards it, making the fox bolt in the other direction. He was no longer tired, no longer felt his wounds. This was the joy of a hunt, a hunt he was winning, would win. He was both the baying hound and the mounted hunter, everywhere at once that the fox thought he wouldn't be. At last, he chased the fox into the valley he knew held the cleft, so he sent up one last mighty howl that echoed all around them, adding more and more so that the fox began to think it was entirely surrounded. It saw a way out and darted into the craggy vale, exactly where Thomas wanted him to go.

He followed the fox to the end of the cleft. Seeing it was trapped, the fox made one last jump for freedom. Thomas was surprised by how high it jumped, how it was able to propel itself just a little farther up the rock wall. For a moment, he was afraid his prize was about to escape from him again, his triumph pulled from his grasp at the last moment. But then there was a scrape of claw on granite, a disconsolate yelp, and the fox fell to the dark ground before him with a soft thud.

Thomas let it rise to its paws, giving the beast one final dignity. The fox faced its death bravely, baring its teeth and growling at him, even as he drew closer. Thomas only growled back.

It finished quickly after that. It was no match for his strength, and, though it tried to fight, Thomas landed his killing blow in the first few moments. He wasted no time finding the heart and devouring it, ending the fox's life. The heart was chewy, but slid down his throat easily.

When Thomas finally emerged from the gully, the first thing he noticed was the clouds obscuring the moon. It was darker, there on the valley floor. So dark that Thomas could barely see.

That was why it took him a moment to notice something moving in the woods, just beyond the edge of his vision. He became very still, every muscle working towards finding this newcomer. He didn't have to wonder what it was, though. The faint scent of his new foe had floated down towards him, filling his nostrils and mouth and the pores of his skin. He had smelled this before—in his own squad room, on the night his life changed forever.

"Is now the time?" Thomas asked, his voice hoarse and unnatural.

"Now is the time," replied the deep, familiar boom.

The clouds shifted, revealing a single form in a shaft of pale moonlight. Even from a distance and in relative darkness, Thomas recognized him. It wasn't the shaggy hair or the bright, menacing smile, nor the green skin or the green clothes. It wasn't even the holly branch in one hand that Thomas recognized. It was the axe held in the other, the head polished to a bright sheen, shining so much that the reflected moonlight nearly blinded Thomas for a moment.

Holly took a step closer. "If you're ready," he said.

FIVE

So, the scene is set. Thomas McDonagh has arrived to face his test, and I am there to deliver it. All that remains to be seen is how he will do—if he will rise to the occasion.

I don't know what to expect. The test, after all, is not really whether you will come. Nor is it if you can hunt and kill as I do. The test is to see how you fare before the axe, if you keep your word and face it as I do. As I have. As I will. We will not know if Thomas can for another moment or two. It depends on what he decides. On who decides.

If the man decides, he might have a chance. If it's the wolf...

If it's the wolf then it's good Detective Pike is so close. I prefer my next victim to be nearby.

Six

During the long three days that Thomas had to contemplate this moment, he had been working through the issue in the back of his mind. Not consciously, really, or with any effort. But he had always wondered if he could choose how he faced this moment, and if his choice might make all the difference.

He had two data points to work with. Ian Caldwell had tried to hide from Holly, and for that, his punishment was swift death.

Kevin Wood, on the other hand, resisted, according to Caldwell's testimony. Or, more accurately, he set traps. But in the moment, when Holly appeared to Kevin for the third time, the stevedore fled, even if with some greater purpose.

The hearsay from Caldwell was that Emma Bosk tried to fight, that she stood her ground before Holly with a gun and tried to kill him that way. For whatever reason though, it appeared that bullets had no effect on him, and Emma had still ended up dead.

What did Leo do? Thomas had wondered. Holly called him dishonorable, which didn't sound like the Leo Thomas knew. His body was left on its side, as if he tried to run.

But these animals, these three that he killed tonight, the trophies left in his apartment. The meat left in Ellwood's home. The heads in Caldwell's. A deer, a boar, a fox, and a green man. Thomas the man knew he should not fight.

Thomas the wolf did not care. His foe stood before him, and the beast had never lost a fight before. He would not start tonight.

Holly took another step closer to Thomas, who bared his teeth and planted his feet firmly, ready to spring forward.

"Did you forget our game?" Holly asked, his voice deep and melodious.

"I forget nothing," Thomas answered, his voice a rasp in his throat.

"Then kneel," Holly commanded.

Thomas did not move, only bared his long fangs and growled.

If this surprised Holly, he did not show it. Nor did he seem dismayed or nervous. If anything, his smile only widened.

"You made a promise," Holly reminded him. "A stroke for a stroke. Fair is fair. Will you really go back on your word?"

"We're not going to do any of it," Thomas snarled. "I'm going to kill you right now."

Holly smiled. "That is your choice. You are certainly a fool, Thomas McDonagh, and you have no honor."

With that final pronouncement, Holly placed the branch at his feet and hefted the axe in both hands. He did so carefully, though relaxed. His body appeared loose, his manner casual. Only a hint of wariness remained, around his eyes, which locked on Thomas.

Thomas growled with all four of his paws planted. He wanted Holly to charge him like the boar had, but Holly did not look like he was going to move anytime soon. He was waiting for Thomas to make the first move. Thomas was coiled like a spring ready to burst at any moment. The tension was almost unbearable.

Without warning, Thomas sprang forward, his blood pounding in his ears. Two feet before Holly, Thomas came to a dead stop. The axe head whistled past his jaw, missing. Thomas growled in satisfaction as he sprang again, ready to rake his claws across Holly's chest.

But the green man's boot got in the way. He kicked Thomas squarely and firmly in the chest. Thomas had no chance to recover. The blow was too strong and completely knocked the wind out of him. He could only watch in horror as, even as Thomas flew backwards, Holly re-angled the axe head so that its sharp edge pointed at him. Then, in the space of half a second, Holly brought the axe crashing down into Thomas's chest.

He knew he was dead before he thudded to the ground, before the pain of the axe splitting his sternum reached his brain, before he involuntarily shifted back into human form, a convulsion from the sudden shock to his system.

He lay in the dirt of the valley floor, naked, blood oozing from his chest and mouth. There was nothing to say. Holly had won. He had let his emotions get the better of him. He had broken his promises. This was his reward.

With a grunt, Holly pulled the axe from Thomas's chest. "A noble effort," the giant said, stepping to the left of Thomas's body.

Blood poured from the chest wound. Thomas would be dead momentarily no matter how you cut it, but Holly needed his head.

Thomas let his neck relax, let his cheek rest against the forest floor so that he was looking away from his executioner. He did not want to see it. He was ready, but he did not want to see it coming. He closed his eyes, willing it all to be over.

"Ho ho ho," Holly chuckled. "What have we here?"

Reluctantly, Thomas let his eyes flutter open again. Someone was approaching, slowly. Thomas squinted, trying to make out who it was in the darkness.

The figure stepped out between two trees, letting the moonlight fall on her. It was Lydia. Foolish, brave, clever Lydia. Thomas couldn't believe it. She had found him, despite everything. She truly was Leonid Ellwood's niece.

I like this feeling, Thomas realized, looking at Lydia. *This is a good feeling.*

Her gun was out, leveled directly at Holly. "Drop it," she said.

Holly said nothing. For a long moment, the valley was silent.

"I'm doing him a kindness, at this point," Holly eventually replied.

"I said drop it," Lydia hissed.

"No."

Thomas was surprised at his own croak too. He managed to hold up a hand, directed it at Lydia.

"Listen," he said to her. "Don't fight him. Trust me."

Lydia held his gaze. For one moment. Thomas did his best to plead with his eyes, but he didn't have the energy anymore. His hand dropped.

The last thing he saw was Lydia lowering her gun. The last thing he heard was Holly saying, "Good." The last thing he felt was the air above his neck part for the coming axe.

SEVEN

There was a lot about tonight that Lydia did not understand. For instance, she did not know how to explain the mutilated deer she had come across, nor the strange tracks that littered the forest. Nor did she know how to explain the feeling that led her through the hills, the urge that drove her over miles of wilderness. And most of all, she did not know how to explain what happened to her partner, how he seemed to emerge from a strange body, part wolf and part man, that moved with all the intelligence of a human and all the ferocity of a beast. She understood one thing only. Thomas McDonagh was dead. His head, severed from his body in a single clean stroke, was enough to make that clear. And his killer still stood over them, perfect smile written in his ugly green visage.

Holly watched Lydia, his axe blade still stuck in the ground beside Thomas's prone body. Lydia had no doubt that the wrong twitch on her end would send that muscular form into motion, would bring about her own incapacitation faster than she could say, "Stop." She had seen him in action. She knew what he was capable of. So, she waited, her knuckles white from gripping the handle of her pistol.

He did not move either. Blood pumped evenly from Thomas's neck, forming a small puddle between the two forms.

"What was his sin?" Lydia asked. Her voice shook, despite her best efforts to keep it steady, and her vision was growing bleary.

Holly considered her in silence for a moment. "Pride," he eventually answered. "The same as all the others."

"Is pride really so great a sin?" Lydia asked.

Coming to some decision unknown to her, the green man hefted the axe out of the soft dirt. "It is," he said, "when you play my game." His voice sounded, of all things, tired.

Taking his cue, Lydia flicked the safety on and holstered her weapon. She wanted nothing more than to shoot the bastard, to rush across the empty space between them and tear him limb from limb. To kill him, is what it all boiled down to. To hurt him, as she had been hurt.

But Thomas's last instruction was, "Don't fight him." He even asked her to trust him. Despite herself, she did.

Holly took a step over McDonagh's body, careful not to step in the blood pooling around him. Lydia waited, trembling in a mixture of fear, anger, and loathing. On Holly came, approaching until he was within an arm's reach of her, until she could smell his stench of sweat and blood, could make out the curly green hairs on his chest.

He held the axe aloft, pointed towards her heart.

Lydia stared at it mutely.

"You know the game," Holly said patiently. "Now you must decide whether to play it."

A great wind rustled through the trees around them.

"How do you do it?" Lydia asked.

"Do what?"

"Survive the game."

Holly smiled broadly, then touched his forefinger to the side of his nose. "That's for me to know," he said.

"Then how do I survive it?" Lydia asked.

"That's for you to find out," Holly answered.

Lydia almost wanted to kick him in the shins. But she refrained, for Thomas.

"Is there a different game," she asked, "that we might be able to play?"

It was a long shot, but in the moment, Lydia was willing to try anything.

Holly tilted his head to the side, his amused eyes fixed on Lydia's. "Different?" he asked.

"Yes," Lydia answered.

"Different how?"

"Something that involves less chopping off of heads and more of you leaving me the hell alone."

Holly seemed to take genuine pleasure in that statement. "I'm afraid," he finally said, "that the head chopping will have to continue, and that I won't leave you alone until the game is completed."

"I can't refuse?" Lydia interrupted.

A silence then stood between them, a gulf as wide and terrible as the plunge from a mountain. And, into the gap, Lydia felt her anger pour. The deaths of Thomas McDonagh and Ian Caldwell, the bodies of Emma Bosk and Leonid Ellwood—these were the fuel upon which she built the flame of her anger.

The flames slowly grew, filling the silence between them. When Lydia was so angry she could almost no longer see, he began to laugh.

A deep, hearty laugh that pierced through the flames into the depths of Lydia's heart. She laughed too, at the absurdity of her question.

"You can," Holly said. He flipped his axe in his hand, caught it by the head and extended the handle towards her. "But will you?" he asked.

McDonagh's body lay in the dirt behind him. For Lydia to get it, to bring it back, she would have to go through Holly somehow. And she knew the way she wanted to. The handle of the axe was long and inviting, perfectly suited for fingers to wrap around.

"Three days?" Lydia asked.

Holly nodded. "At the place of your choosing."

Lydia reached out and gripped the handle. Again, Holly chuckled, then let go of his end.

"It's that simple?" Lydia asked.

Holly paused, one knee in the dirt, the other still raised. "Unless you want to add another element?" he suggested.

Lydia frowned. Holly's face was a mask, impossible to read. "Another element?" she quoted.

"Oh yes," Holly said. "I've done this before, even. Agree with me that at the end of these three days you shall give me whatever you have gained, and I shall give you the same."

Lydia blinked. "Whatever…" she said slowly, "I've gained?" The green man's face filled with longing—hope, even. A childish grin had spread across his cheeks. "What if I 'gain' nothing?" Lydia asked.

"Hmm," the green man murmured thoughtfully. "True," he said. "I might gain nothing too. Well then," his face brightened again, "how about whatever we've gained since I arrived in this city, we'll exchange that?"

Lydia's mouth hung open slightly. "After I strike you with this axe?" she asked.

"Yes," Holly nodded. "When we meet in three days, we'll exchange what we've gained, then I'll give you the same blow." He sank to his other knee. "Agreed?"

Lydia took a moment to respond. During that moment, she hefted the axe high, then swung with all her might, bringing the blade down into the middle of Holly's head.

It split in two, his brains and bone parting before her like waves split by a rock. Only when the blade had forced its way down past his neck and into his chest did the axe stop, unable to sink any farther.

"Yeah," Lydia panted.

END of Episode Nine

EPISODE TEN: AXE-STINGUISHED

ONE

She sat vigil the whole night.

That's what it was, she decided. A vigil. An observance. Similar to the one she and the other officers gave Ellwood the day they found him. It felt right, somehow. Like it was something Thomas would want. There would be a funeral with full honors, his star would be added to the memorial outside HQ, his friends would mourn, his dead friend's wife would cry, Lieutenant Lake would shut himself in his office for weeks, nursing a new obsession that would eventually kill him. But none of that would have mattered to McDonagh. What would have mattered was this simple act, Lydia staying beside her friend's body while his soul left the world. To have one moment of peace.

If that was the reason, then Lydia could still tell herself she was brave. She wouldn't have to admit that she was unable to move, that a paralysis had come over her. That she was terrified.

The axe had sunk three inches into Holly's chest, embedded between his clavicles. Lydia had tried to yank it free, but it wouldn't budge. Panting, she let go, stepped away from the body and dropped to her knees.

In the silence that followed, even the trees seemed to listen. The soft patter of blood dripping from the axe handle was the only noise. Lydia's breathing slowed, softened, then became almost still.

Holly's eye twitched. One of his arms reached up and grabbed the handle. With a stiff tug, the axe came free. Slowly, Holly stood. The sides of his head flopped onto his shoulders, his strange eyes staring at her with an expression somewhere between mirth and scrutiny.

He held up three fingers. A part of his brain began to slip out of his skull, but he caught it deftly, then held out the three fingers again. She knew what he meant.

Three days, and then it would be her turn.

Holly disappeared after that. Lydia watched him walk into the woods until she could no longer see him.

She did not move until morning.

When the sun finally came up, Lydia realized she was sitting close to McDonagh's head. The ruin of his body seemed deflated and shrunken, almost as if it wasn't him. But his face was unmistakable. It was his nose, his hair, his eyes, his mouth. He had a peaceful expression, despite the blood and dirt that covered his skin.

Lydia was glad she hadn't noticed the head before. Who knows what she would have done to it during the night when her brain was not quite working correctly. What if she tried talking to him? What if he talked back? Lydia shuddered at the thought.

Now, she needed to decide what to do. She wasn't quite sure how far away her car was, but she was certain she could reach it. She didn't feel tired after her ordeal—not hungry or thirsty, even. But she wasn't sure if she could carry him. The thought crossed her mind to just bring his head, but an equally strong part of her wondered if she should even bother.

Her training as a police officer told her no, of course. She needed to preserve the scene of the crime, preserve the location so that other investigators could come out here, could document every piece of what happened and try to determine the killer. They would need to interview her too, of course. Before she had her own meeting with Holly. Before the same thing happened to her.

A week ago, Lydia would have been afraid of no one believing her. She hadn't believed, after all. Not when Caldwell sang his song, nor when they brought in that headless body from the ash fields. She hadn't believed it when she heard the shooting in the squad room and she hadn't believed it when Caldwell lost his head. But then she saw Thomas remove Holly's head, saw him stand and leave, chuckling as he did. They all had seen it. They all believed it then, and they'd believe her now.

So, why bother preserving the scene? It was obvious what had happened. And Lydia wasn't sure she wanted to leave him here like this. She wanted to show his body some respect, for him to have a proper burial. She didn't want him to decay or for coyotes to find him and eat him. He didn't deserve that, did he?

But then, the coyotes had left Leonid Ellwood's body alone—and Emma Bosk's. Maybe they'd do the same for Thomas in the time it took Lydia to get back to town, report what had happened, and then lead a team back to the scene of the crime.

Lydia closed her eyes a moment. It all sounded so exhausting. And she only had three days.

Three days.

Did she even want to go back?

Of course you do, a voice in her head told her. *Don't you want to rest? You could see Lilly again, couldn't you?*

It didn't sound half bad. There was a warmth in Lydia's stomach when she thought of Lilly, and an urge to return to Ash Falls. What was she doing, so far from home?

Go back to her, the voice told Lydia. *Go back to Lilly right now.*

The urge was so strong, Lydia almost forgot about McDonagh's body. It would be so easy to just leave—to make her way back to Lilly and ask her to leave the city with her. For them both to run as far and as fast as they could. Lydia would give Lilly whatever she wanted in return, just as long as they could outrun the green man.

Something fluttered in her chest. It was so sudden, Lydia glanced down, certain she'd see something attached to her shirt.

Nothing was there. Just the charms. The wicker men her mother taught her to make.

The flutter came again. She almost thought she saw the charms jiggle.

Thomas's body was still. The blood had ceased seeping from it hours ago. The head was turning blue around the edges of the neck, where it had been cut. Just like Ellwood's head.

Why is it still happening then? she asked herself.

The sensation came again. And it didn't pull her back towards Ash Falls but farther into the wilderness. In the direction of the one snow capped mountain that filled the horizon.

Lydia took a hesitant step.

No, the voice commanded her. It was sharp suddenly, slicing at Lydia's mind. *Not that way. To the city. To Lilly.*

The charm's tug was nearly constant now. It had not pulled this strongly at her all yesterday. Nor had she ever had quite so terrible a headache, like lightning bolting through her brain. She took another step towards the mountain, and the pain only intensified.

No, the voice commanded.

At her next step, Lydia collapsed to her knees. A hundred hands pushed and pulled at her, a thousand fingers prodding her on top of that, with ten thousand voices screaming around her. But through it all, the charm told her to go onward.

It was too much for Lydia. Something was going to have to give, she knew that. And she didn't know how it was going to give until, quite suddenly, she burped. A small, round belch that jumped from her mouth with an audible pop. The pain lessened for a moment, then renewed its vigorous attack. But burping, for some reason, worked.

She tried to make herself burp again. She took a gulp, swallowed, and then tried to force it out. Nothing came, and the pain worsened. She tried again—still nothing. She filled her lungs with air and tried to swallow it all before heaving it out.

But this time, she heaved too hard. And it wasn't just air that came out, but liquid. And the remains of yesterday's lunch. All the contents of her stomach, really, dumped out before her, a red mush that coated the rocks and dead branches. Her mouth filled with the acidic taste of her own stomach. The vomit kept coming, too, for what felt like longer than should have been possible. When it stopped, she felt much better.

Lydia waited a moment. She swished the bile around her throat a moment, spat out a little more. She wanted water, badly. But the pain was over.

Slowly, Lydia stood. The charm gave her another little tug, the wicker now visibly moving under her shirt. Lydia carefully stepped over the vomit, then looked one last time at McDonagh's body.

"I'll come back for you," she promised him. And then, she set off.

No, the voice inside her head pleaded. *No*.

Two

Ash Falls Police Department - Missing Person Report
Date: 08/18/2017   *Time:* 0800 hrs.
Rank: Lieutenant   *Name:* Benedict Lake
Name of individual filing report: Lieutenant Benedict Lake
Name of missing person(s): Detective Thomas McDonagh,
Detective Lydia Pike
Last seen location(s): AFPD 14th Precinct
Last seen date:
McDonagh - 08/14/2017   Pike - 08/17/2017
Description:
McDonagh - male, 57, white hair, 6'2", last seen wearing
brown suit, red tie
Pike - female, 34, black hair, 5'8", last seen wearing AFPD
windbreaker
Interview:
N/A
Action taken:
    Put out BOLO for both detectives' vehicles and
descriptions

THREE

Lydia vomited several more times as the day went on. There was always a slow buildup, the voice growing louder and more insistent that Lydia should not continue on, should not press farther into the wild and dense forest, but should turn back and head for safety. As the voice grew stronger, so did the pain, until Lydia was having trouble walking, then standing, then staying upright. Eventually, she would black out, only to wake again a moment later in a puddle of her own red vomit. The pain would be over, the voice no more than a faint whisper, and Lydia was able to press on again.

Each time she woke, Lydia would remember something she hadn't remembered before. At first, it was little things, things she was surprised she had forgotten. She remembered rubbing her hand over Lilly's thigh. She remembered the taste of Lilly's first kiss. She remembered how sharp and pointy her teeth were. And she remembered pain. Pain she was unable to place.

There was something else, too. Something following her through the woods, waiting with her while she vomited, remembering with her what she hadn't realized was forgotten. At first, she was certain it was Holly following his prey, ensuring that she would uphold her end of the bargain. But it didn't feel like him. It didn't feel like anything, really. Just a presence at the back of her mind, accompanying her.

She tried to catch glimpses of her follower. As it got on towards noon, she stopped to rest by a stream that ran through a mountain meadow. After she drank from it what she needed, she waited in a crouch, concealed by the tall grass. It was peaceful in that field.

Lydia had gone home with Lilly two nights ago. She hadn't meant to go home with her—it had just happened. They had kissed. They had explored. Lilly's bright white teeth gleamed in the darkness, sharp as knives, and then the pain. The next morning, Lydia was awake in her own bed.

Lydia stood abruptly, facing the way she had come. Her follower froze mid-step, halfway through the meadow between her and the edge of the forest. Its moist, round eyes were locked on her, cautious. Even a little nervous maybe. But not scared.

In the moments before the pain, Lydia had started to kiss Lilly's neck, wandering from her mouth to her cheek and then down her jaw until she was at Lilly's throat, her arms wrapped around her, somehow in both each other's laps simultaneously. Not yet one, but almost. Lilly asked something. Lydia didn't remember what, but she knew she said yes. Then teeth, pain, and waking up alone in her bed.

It was a deer, standing across from her in the meadow. Large and majestic, a full set of antlers held high above the grass and fur a soft brown. It did not menace her and it did not comfort her. It was simply there, as if it had been there for quite some time.

Lydia bowed to the deer. It nodded its head in return. Lydia turned and kept walking. An hour later, when she stopped to look for it again, the deer remained at a distance, picking its way along the path behind her.

Lydia's lips found Lilly's neck and Lilly sighed. Lydia pulled her onto her lap, kept kissing her neck while Lilly moaned in pleasure. Then Lilly pushed herself back so the two could stare for a moment, marvel in being with each other in a way they had never expected to. It was like they were seeing each other for the first time.

Closer to three, Lydia realized she hadn't thrown up in several hours. Nor had she heard the voice, the voice that she was beginning to realize sounded nothing like her own. All she had known was the dirt and the grass, her feet taking one step after another, trudging through the endless woodland that led her upward and upward. Nor had she felt the charm's pull. The only presence she knew of was behind her —the deer, getting closer, but not in any hurry to join her.

"Do you want it again?" Lilly asked, her legs straddling Lydia on her couch.

Lydia thought she knew what she meant. "Yes," she said.

Lydia stopped at the crest of a small hill. She thought she'd be able to see Ash Falls from it, but when she reached the top, there were only more crowns. Not all of the hills were forested—some were fields of grass or craggy cliffs. One even had a house on it, with smoke coming from the chimney. But Ash Falls was gone. Lydia would only be able to see it from the side of the mountain.

Lilly's canines had suddenly lengthened until they were full fangs. Before Lydia realized what was happening, Lilly lurched forward, the fangs sinking into Lydia's skin, her legs holding Lilly down, her arms keeping her from thrashing. Lydia felt her blood being sucked out, felt it replaced by something else. It felt good and terrible at the same time, but the small amount of pleasure it gave Lydia was not enough to cover her scream.

Towards nightfall, Lydia stopped to build a fire. She was careful to dig a small pit with her hands. She surrounded the pit with stones, then built a small pyramid of sticks and branches. She vaguely remembered watching an ex rub two sticks together to start a fire, but it didn't work for her when she tried. That didn't keep her from trying again. She had nothing to cook, but she could go another day without eating. She knew how to recognize a few berries that she could eat. But she would have appreciated a fire's warmth. She was already looking forward to falling asleep beside it. She might not be hungry, somehow, after a day of hiking, but she was tired. At least that was normal.

Before long though, Lydia gave up. She didn't feel too cold anyways, and figured she could survive an August night. She tried to remember if there was anything in her car that could have helped her, but there was nothing she could remember. *Oh well*, she sighed to herself. She wouldn't have wanted to go back anyways.

As darkness fell, the deer approached her camp. He even bent his knees and sat beside the pit, across from Lydia. She didn't do anything to acknowledge his presence, but she was aware of him. For a time after his arrival, all was silent in the woods. The stars, one by one, peeked out from behind their veil. Wind rustled the branches of the ash trees around them.

"Lilly attacked me at the brewery," Lydia said. She remembered, though she hadn't a moment before. When she spoke the words, they became true.

The deer remained unmoving, starlight reflected in its blank eyes.

"I remembered it at the beginning of the next day, but not by the end." Lydia stared out over the forest, watched the treetops sway in unison. "Lilly used that to attack me again."

The deer remained. The stars turned on their wheel in the sky, immortal and fleeting.

Lydia tapped the side of her neck, where the two bites used to burn and itch but were now only a dull ache. "She did this," Lydia said.

The deer leaned forward, touching one antler to the pile of sticks Lydia had piled in her pit. Where the antler touched, flame broke, until the whole pile ignited into a small, cozy fire. Then the deer rose, turned, and left. Lydia stared into the ripples and curls of heat, unsure if she was dreaming.

FOUR

When relief finally came, Lester shrugged off the weight of not knowing when this all would end. A truck bearing a new contingent of firefighters roared over the hill, dodging between the wasted skeletons of trees. When it reached Lester's team, the new fighters hopped out, Lester's crew climbed in, and off they went.

When they crossed out of the ash fields, back into the green forests untouched by flame, Lester shrugged off the weight of missing his home. He was finally answering his body's six-day-old demand—he was returning to Ash Falls.

When they finally reached the safety of the fire station, Lester shrugged off the weight of protecting his team. They were their own responsibility again, after he had kept them alive through the long nights and even longer days. They had done their job and they had done it well. He was proud to be their crew chief.

When he saw his family again, he shrugged off the weight of missing them. He held his wife, kissed his children on the forehead, and knew that they were safe.

When he removed his equipment, he finally shrugged off the weight of his job, the air and water and flame resistant fabric that had bent his back. He stood naked in his bathroom. Ash Falls was finally safe. Lester was finally safe.

The fire was ninety-five percent contained, and that number had risen steadily every hour for the past two days. What was left of it would burn itself out in some remote corner of the wilderness. A few cabins had been burned, a dozen firefighters injured, uncountable acres of land destroyed. The effects of the fire would be felt for years, and there was no guarantee another wouldn't start tomorrow or in the next month or the next year. But that was not Lester's job.

They had only pulled one body from the fire. *That* was Lester's job. To make sure it was only one. When Lester turned on his shower and stepped into the still-cold water, he shrugged off the dirt and sweat and grime that had accumulated all over him. He washed away the ash, let it disappear down the drain.

For this year, it was over.

FIVE

Lydia woke to the dense smell of ash covering her. At first, she couldn't understand why—the fire appeared to have burned out hours ago. The morning dew should have washed the rest of the smell away. It was only when she sat up that she realized she was on the opposite side of the fire from where she went to sleep. She had rolled through the ash pit in the middle of the night, covering her clothes and her skin and her hair. It was sheer luck that the fire hadn't been lit, though she supposed she would have woken a lot sooner if it was.

It took her some time to get ready. She had to find a stream first, to try and rub off some of the ash. When she did, the ash ended up smearing more than anything, so that her hands were soon covered in wet black. Eventually she had to move to a deeper part of the stream, where she could sink her hands into the frigid depths. She used fistfuls of sand from the bottom to scrub her hands, to skin the ash from them. After a time, they began to sting.

She let her clothes dry on a rock for a time while she sat by the creek, her feet submerged up to her calves. When she judged it to be around nine, she dressed quickly, tied her boots tight, gathered the rest of her effects, and set off. She didn't need the charm to tell her where to go anymore. The mountain loomed heavily before her.

She was famished. Sleeping had helped her to be less tired, and the fire kept her warm. But there was nothing to fight the hunger. Most of the day, Lydia managed to push it away, though she wasn't sure how. She just knew whatever she found out here wouldn't be enough.

At least she wasn't throwing up. Nor was she hearing the voice in her head, ordering her to go home. It had faded long ago, though not her desire to turn back. That sprung up every mile or so. Her stride would catch for a second, and she'd find herself almost spinning in place. Each time this happened, she forced herself to come to a complete stop. She'd take a few deep breaths, then press onward again. But Ash Falls never left her. It never would, she was sure.

At around noon, she stopped for a brief rest beside an ash tree. It seemed especially vibrant to her, and offered more shade than many of the other trees. She didn't want to stay long, but she didn't want to pass up a moment to gather her strength, either. She needed all she could get.

Sitting with her back to the tree, Lydia couldn't help but think of Lilly. Two sides of her memory were having trouble reconciling with each other. On the one hand, Lydia had genuinely good memories of Lilly. She was attractive and witty, and Lydia thought she had enjoyed their time together. On the other hand, she had hurt Lydia, had preyed on her the way a lion hunts antelope. And if Lydia knew anything from being a cop, she knew that predators like Lilly never stopped hunting.

A strange grunt broke Lydia's momentary reverie. She opened her eyes to find herself still by the ash tree. Before her, no more than twenty yards away, was the same pig she had seen in Ian Caldwell's oven.

The same kind, anyways. It couldn't have been the exact same pig, could it?

Nevertheless, it had the same tusks protruding from its mouth, the same hairy skin, and the same beady little eyes. Except now the tusks dripped with saliva, and the points gleamed in the mid-day light. The hair was bristly, rippling with life and power. And the eyes were no longer dull and milky but red, a furious anger simmering just beneath.

Lydia did nothing. She had the stray thought to pull her gun, but her hands weren't moving for some reason. All she could do was stare down the pig, and she wasn't sure how much longer that would last. She didn't want to find out.

Neither did the pig, it seemed. It ground its hoof into the dirt, grunting and snorting with increasing anger. Then, all at once, it sprang towards her, covering the distance in a speed she would have thought impossible. Lydia had no time, her gun was clipped into its holster, she'd never clear leather. The tusks approached, death brought by an animal power greater than anything she had ever faced before. Lydia hid her face, curling herself into a ball.

The pig came to an abrupt halt just before her. Lydia couldn't breath. The thing stared at her, panting and stinking. Then it turned and trotted back into the trees.

Only then did Lydia scream.

When she was ready, she continued on. She still had a day and a half to climb it, she knew. But she didn't know how high she wanted to go up the mountain. And that pig was still out there. She heard it as she walked, grunting and rooting around in the brush along her path.

What Lydia could not understand was how she had forgotten about the first attack. She and Thomas had talked about it that very morning. He had even told her to avoid the brewery for now. How did she forget it the moment she saw Lilly again? Why had she wanted to go for a drink in the first place?

It had been that voice, hadn't it? A voice had told her to go get a drink and she hadn't thought to disobey. Couldn't. And it was the same voice that had told her to go back to Ash Falls the day before. It was a voice she had been hearing for a while now.

When the boar came again—that sounded right, all of a sudden—Lydia was still walking. She came around the side of a boulder and there it was, twenty yards ahead of her. Again, it dug its hoof into the ground, its eyes fiery and its voice guttural. Lydia knew now that it would charge, but again she was unable to move. She stayed motionless as the beast chose its moment, sprang forward and covered the ground in a single mad dash. Lydia closed her eyes, ready for the impact. But again, at the last moment, the boar veered away, leaving her in peace.

"Oh, come on!" she yelled after it. "Do it already!"

But the boar had disappeared into the trees, once again a presence felt rather than seen.

"The hell with you then," Lydia spat.

Dark took longer to fall the higher Lydia climbed. She could see the sun setting over the western hills—a mountain range in their own right, but not nearly as large or expansive as the Cascades. She would need to find a camp again, and soon. And she would need to figure out how to build a fire.

Do I? she wondered more than once. She didn't feel particularly cold. Nor was she tired, really. Just hungry. A raw hunger that she could barely keep from her mind. She couldn't explain these discrepancies. It wasn't as if she was unaware of a need for food or sleep or warmth. Her stomach still grumbled, her feet still dragged through the dirt. When she stopped, she still felt the shiver of cold seeping in. But it was like these things were happening to somebody else, to someone standing right next to her. They did not affect her, did not lessen her drive.

She could go a little farther, she knew. Each step today was a step closer to her final destination tomorrow, wherever that was.

The boar stayed close by her. It was quieter now, to be sure. But Lydia could hear its grumble, could even smell its sweaty scent. Lydia was not sure whether it would attack her in her sleep or not. If it would do what Lilly had done.

Eventually, she had to stop. Something told her she'd kill that other part of her if she kept on tonight, that the her which felt hungry and tired and cold would simply give up and be left behind.

Good, the voice whispered in her ear. *Leave it behind.*

Lydia sat against a tree again, an ash, willing her eyes to stay open a moment longer. She could make a fire again, she knew. She could survive the night.

Don't, the voice commanded. *Just go to sleep now. You'll be so much better in the morning. So much more powerful.*

Lydia thought she had left that voice behind. It was faint now, but there. Seductive in its ministrations. Lydia almost missed it.

Come back, the voice whispered. "Don't you want to be like me?"

Lydia actually heard that last question. It was physical, vibrating in the molecules around her and in her. Lydia's eyes flew open and she jumped to her feet, hand flinching unconsciously to her holster. She knew now where she recognized that voice from. It wasn't just a voice in her head —it sounded exactly like Lilly. It *was* Lilly. Lilly was here.

Lydia's eyes flitted to the spaces between the trees, looking for something to dart between them. Her right hand gripped the handle of her pistol, while her left moved towards Thomas's stick. She expected Lilly to come rushing out of the darkness at any moment, and she was prepared to fight. She wanted to.

Something did come through the trees, but it was not human. Nor humanoid, for that matter.

It was the boar, of course. Lydia watched it approach. She did not relax her hands away from either weapon, but neither did she use them. She only watched as the beast approached, her eyes locked on its fire.

It was not quick, and it was not slow. Steady. That was the word. Nor did it grunt or seethe, and all the menace had gone out of its bristly hair. But the tusks were still dangerous, Lydia could tell. They still glowed in the vanishing light.

Lydia told herself not to be afraid. She told herself that she was supposed to meet the green man tomorrow, that nothing bad had happened to any of the others before then. She told herself nothing would happen now.

Telling yourself something is the easy part. Believing it is harder.

The boar sauntered right up to her, so that she could feel its sticky breath hitting her stomach. She wanted to recoil, to jump away from this unnatural presence standing before her. But she was transfixed now, and any sudden movements would surely mean her death.

She could not see the boar's face. Just its strange, muscular back. She wondered what it wanted, what it was doing, what it was waiting for. She wondered when it would leave.

The pig grunted. Before Lydia had time to react, it jerked its head to one side. She felt a slice of pain across her knee. In the time it took her to realize that it had cut her with its tusk, the boar was already trotting off into the woods. Lydia watched it go, feeling the rip in her pants, the wound beneath it.

It was superficial, not much more than a scratch. When she touched her hand to it, only a small amount of blood came away on her fingers.

Perplexed, Lydia set to building a fire. It didn't work. Eventually, she gave up and settled down to sleep in the cold. Much, much later in the night, she realized she was getting hungry.

Six

The brewmaster of Ash Falls' Brewing was a pear-shaped man pushing fifty who looked like he was well into his sixties. Lilly found him in one of Ash Falls' gutters drinking rainwater mixed with engine oil. He looked up when he noticed the strange figure above him—a tall, luminously beautiful woman standing under an umbrella that was more accessory than tool. He smacked his lips unapologetically, his scraggly hair plastered to the side of his skull by the rain.

"Not as fine as the brews I made in Portland, I must say," he sang jovially, "but it will do in a pinch."

Lilly had stopped to drink his blood. *Why not?* she thought. They were on an empty street in the middle of a rainy day. No one would notice the body for several hours and, even then, what's another of the homeless found dead? More paperwork for the cops, more busy work for the morgue, and more labor for the gravediggers. Lilly would have forgotten about him in a few nights.

But she had already eaten, truly, and was not angry enough to demolish an entire man alone. And his statement had struck her as so unusual, so delightfully chipper in an even more delightfully somber city. Back then, she had only just lost her master and become one of the free. The beginnings of her plan were only starting to formulate, but she knew she'd need help. That she'd need servants.

So, she took the gutter rat in, brought him back to her apartment, fed him, clothed him, and let him shower. Within a week, she had found him his own apartment, and he was beginning to have a life of his own again. More than once she fought off the urge to bleed him dry, to fill her stomach with his life. She also fought off his advances more than once, when he got drunk or lonely or assumed that the only reason a woman like Lilly would take in a bum like him was loneliness. It was easy to fight him off—he was only human, after all—but her patience grew a little thinner each time.

Slowly, she began to learn his story. He was from the Midwest, originally—the son of a factory worker and a seamstress. He migrated west for college, ending up in Portland just in time for the microbrewery boom. He did his stint at several of the breweries in the city, working his way up from bottler to brewmaster of his own brand in ten years. That was 2007. That same brewery was one of the many casualties of 2008. Though he got out of it okay, he still ended up jobless in a time when there weren't many jobs. He started looking outside his adopted city for work—first in Oregon, then in the rest of the Northwest, and eventually in California. It was on his way back from an interview in Paso Robles that he stopped in Ash Falls for the night. He hadn't left since.

No source of income, no market for his skills, and no home, the brewmaster was eventually forced into the streets. He survived there for eight years, living mostly on luck until luck brought him to Lilly. As her plan gestated and grew, his place in it became increasingly apparent. He would run her brewery, would be the human face on a business that needed as little scrutiny as possible.

He, of course, was more than willing when she gave him his old life back. All he really had to do was listen to her behind closed doors and not ask any questions. Not a bad deal. And he fulfilled his duties admirably—the brewery was doing far better than Lilly could have imagined.

She never bothered to learn his name though. Nobody knows what the pet cat calls itself, after all, and nobody cares. Lilly called him Falstaff, and even if he didn't quite fit the mold, Falstaff fit the bill. He never corrected her on the name. At least, not that Lilly noticed.

Part of their arrangement was a weekly meeting, just the two of them. Ostensibly this was just business practice. It was good for the workers's morale to see their brewmaster and his assistant discussing the issues of the week, planning the events of the next few days. It made them feel like the ship was on the right course, like the company was in good hands. It meant they were less likely to go snooping where they shouldn't. In practice, these meetings were beyond boring for Lilly. Falstaff gave her a rundown on how the brewery was doing, what he was planning to do next, and then asked what Lilly needed. Lilly always needed something, and, like the good pet he was, Falstaff didn't ask why she needed it. All exactly as Lilly wanted—but that didn't mean it wasn't boring. The stages between major elements of a plan, Lilly was discovering, were the worst. It was in the midst of these doldrums that she began to lose sight of the distant shore towards which she journeyed.

"Does that sound good?" Falstaff asked, his words cutting through her memories. Lilly blinked at him a couple of times, realizing that he had asked the same question more than once. He didn't exactly fear her—he didn't know what she was, after all—but everything she had done for him afforded her a queen's respect.

"Yes," Lilly said, though she had no idea what he was talking about. "Perfect."

In moments like these she almost wished she had made him a dhampir, or even a ghoul. It was hard for her to read his mind if he was independent. If she had bitten him, it would have been a simple matter to sift through his thoughts. She couldn't now—not without giving him a severe headache, anyways. And every vampiress needs her underlings. Falstaff might have made a great first. But she knew waiting had been the right choice, knew that the brewery needed to have a truly 'human' front to keep her from scrutiny. Lydia was the right choice. Even if she was so far away that Lilly could barely sense her—it didn't matter. Lydia would be back—they always came back—and wrapped around Lilly's finger again in no time.

"How was the soft release of Vampire's Delight?" Lilly asked, interrupting whatever Falstaff was babbling about now. This was what the meeting was really about, after all. Her latest creation.

"Ah," he said, not looking up from his papers.

Lilly couldn't suppress a wry grin. "Ah?" she asked, twitching her head to the side. "Is that a good 'ah' or a bad 'ah?'"

Falstaff shuffled through the papers now, still doing all he could to avoid her gaze. "A bad 'ah,' I'm afraid," he said.

"Nobody likes it," Lilly stated.

Falstaff gave a little shrug. "Not *nobody*," he said, emphasizing the second word, "but not many bodies. And certainly not anybody that matters." He finally mustered up the courage to look at her, and when he saw her little half smile he broke out into a relieved grin of his own. "Nobody's first creation ever turns out the way it should," he assured her, his voice carrying the weight of a promise. *Try again,* his voice said, a mentor taking a student under his wing. *It'll turn out better next time.*

"Damn," Lilly said, still smiling. "I had such high hopes for it."

"I did too," Falstaff lied—he was such a bad liar. "Using the stout instead of the lager was a good touch too. But the people like what they like and all we can do is try again, no?"

"I suppose," Lilly said lazily. "You willing to give me another shot, brewmaster?" she added.

"Always," Falstaff said, smiling broadly and adjusting his glasses. He enjoyed the charade a little too much, sometimes. Maybe Lilly should go poking around in his mind while he slept, help him remember his years on the streets, barely surviving until she had come along.

"Thank you," she said. Only a hint of ice had crept into the statement, but Falstaff noticed it.

He tried to press on. "So," he said, flipping a page, "that's it for Vampire's Delight."

"Actually, no," Lilly interrupted. His eyes flicked to hers again, which she kept wide as she continued to speak. "Let's just keep it out there, in a small batch. Sell to only a few bars, the ones that will take it."

Falstaff was transfixed by her gaze, his own eyes equally wide, eyebrows nearly disappearing into his badly cut bangs. "I don't know if any bars will take it," he eventually managed.

Lilly winked. "I think I know a couple," she said. "Besides," she added, "I think I've thought of a way to improve the flavor."

Falstaff opened and closed his mouth several times before taking off his glasses, setting them on the papers, and leaning back in his chair, bridge of his nose pinched between his forefinger and thumb. It must be maddening for him, Lilly knew. But they both know he had only one alternative.

"Alright," he said, taking his hand away from his face. "Hit me with it."

"We could age it," Lilly said.

Falstaff's mouth crooked itself thoughtfully, half pursing half frowning. "That might do it," he said. "Barrels?"

"Yes."

"Wooden?"

"Yes."

He thought a little longer. "It certainly wouldn't hurt," he said. "Want me to order some oak from the nearest winery?"

"No," Lilly said. "I don't want to use oak."

Falstaff blinked. "Everyone uses oak," he said.

"I'm not everyone."

"But the whole point is you use barrels that have already had wine age in them," he said. "That way you get some of that fruity wine flavor in there."

"I'm not everyone," Lilly said again.

Falstaff's tongue clicked inside his cheek. "No, you are not," he agreed. "What kind of wood then?"

"Hawthorn," Lilly said firmly.

Falstaff blinked. Lilly waited, smiling. "A fairly unusual choice," he eventually managed.

"I know," Lilly waggled her eyebrows. "Just imagine how it will look on the label. Bottles will fly off the shelves for the pure novelty of it."

"Uh-huh," Falstaff answered, his voice clearly unconvinced. That was fine with Lilly. She didn't have to convince him. "I wouldn't know where to even begin finding enough hawthorn," he continued, "let alone figure out how we would make the barrels."

Lilly pulled a small piece of paper out of her pocket, checked it, and slid it across the table.

"What's this," Falstaff asked.

"The number for a cooper in south east," she said. "You'll handle all of the business with him, though right now he just needs to know where to send his invoice."

Falstaff looked down his nose at the number, his mouth hanging open slightly. "And he knows where to get all the wood he'll need?" he asked.

"Don't worry about that," Lilly said, standing to leave. The meeting was done, she decided. "I've already made the arrangements."

SEVEN

It took Lydia a long time to wake on the third day. She didn't realize it was a long time—to her, it felt like she woke suddenly, her eyes bursting open as she sat upright, her jacket falling from her shoulders where she had used it as a makeshift blanket. But the sun was high in the sky at the moment of her waking, well past its zenith and beginning to descend into afternoon. She had slept in the shade of an ash, a particularly leafy one that had kept her well shaded in the brightest part of the day. It had only been her dreams that woke her.

The last one was already slipping from her memory, even as she blinked and looked around her, stifling a yawn. She tried for a moment to grasp the dream, to see what secrets it held. But it was only a dream in which she died before Holly's axe, waking as the axe found flesh. All she could remember of it was the executioner's leer, the swish of the descending blade. Lydia did her best to shake it away. The reality was already fast approaching.

Slowly, she stood, stretching out the stiffness and soreness in her skin and muscles, working out the kinks in her spine from sleeping on roots and rocks all night. It was slow work and the day was already mostly burned away, but Lydia did not care. She didn't want to go far. She was almost to the tree line already.

Nothing except a dull ache pulled her to Ash Falls anymore. No voice in her head commanded her to go back, no force felt like it was dragging at her feet. The charm, too, seemed to have finally worn off, though she still felt some vague tugs from it. These tugs were what told her to go above the tree line, to keep pushing farther into the wilderness.

When she fell asleep, her stomach had been growling and grumbling, though she still didn't feel hungry. Nor was she too thirsty, but that didn't mean there wasn't something she needed. It was something halfway between hunger and thirst, something she craved yet didn't quite know how to define. Whatever it was, it grew ravenously within Lydia, though she still didn't feel any weaker because of it. The itching was back too—the two spots on her neck felt inflamed. With no ointment to put on them, Lydia could only dig her nails around the two holes, wincing the harder she dug.

She heard a scurrying on the branches above her head, watched the small animal dart along one of the highest branches.

It was a squirrel, small and fat, its tail brown and bushy. She was transfixed by it for a moment. She could see, suddenly, how easily she could catch it. If she wanted, she'd be up the trunk faster than the woodland animal could blink, would catch it in her hand before its tail could twitch. It wouldn't have much blood, but pouring it down her throat would sate her, even if only for an hour. Then she'd be able to move on, full and content.

She had never done anything like that before, but Lydia nevertheless knew she could. She could feel the raw strength in her arms and hands, could feel the sharpness of her teeth.

And she could sense how good it would feel, all of it, how blood was the answer to her strange craving.

Eventually, the squirrel stopped making noise. And although Lydia knew it was still physically there, it was the absence of noise that allowed her to ignore it. To let herself be distracted from the certainty of its presence, the certainty of the relief it could provide.

She left the tree. When she was fifty feet away from it, she heard an acorn drop and that was almost enough for her to turn around. She pressed on.

When she was a hundred feet away, she heard it scramble down the tree. It was too far away for her to even see it properly, yet the creature scrabbling down the bark was as deafening to her as thunder. It would be on the ground soon, she knew, and even easier to kill. But she kept going.

At two hundred feet away, Lydia heard soft paw thuds, a low snarl, a minute shriek, and then the ripping of fur and flesh. Lydia did turn around at this, but she kept her distance. Back underneath the tree, a fox tore at the carcass of the squirrel.

Lydia knew what it was now. She had not recognized it in Caldwell's oven, but now that she could see the rest of it Lydia remembered what a fox was. But that made its presence all the more confusing. She had lived on the west coast all her life—more than thirty years—and somehow had never once seen a fox. Now they seemed to be popping up everywhere.

Lydia left it to its meal. She had slowly grown to accept all the other unbelievable things about this case—that a giant green man could walk away from a beheading or that her mother's magic was real or that Lilly drank blood and that Thomas could transform into a wolf. All of that could fit into

Lydia's rapidly changing conception of the universe. So could a fox.

By mid-afternoon, Lydia reached the tree line. The last tree she passed was a dwarf maple, more shrub than tree. There were still shrubs, but they were thinly spread across the mountainside. Lydia navigated through them easily. The air certainly felt thinner, but she still breathed easily.

She stopped for a break not far past that last tree, at the spot she came across snow for the first time. It was a small dirty patch of ice, clinging to the side of the mountain underneath a bush. Lydia spent a long time considering eating it.

Everything she had ever been taught told her she shouldn't. The snow would use up too much energy melting in her stomach. The bad always outweighed the good. But Lydia didn't feel cold. She just felt thirsty and she was willing to try anything.

She knelt in the dirt by the ice. Using a rock, she smashed the ice into a couple small fragments. She took the smallest one she could find into her hand.

A twitch of movement caught her eye. She scanned the mountainside, ice freezing to her fingers, watching for the movement again. When it came, it surprised her by how close it was. A flash of red between two bushes.

The fox was following her.

Lydia popped the ice chunk into her mouth. As she expected, it didn't take long to melt but had little to no effect on her thirst. It was like holding up a leaf to protect against the winds of a summer storm. It just blew away.

The fox might work, Lydia wondered.

She took a larger chunk of ice, just to give her mouth something to do, stood, and moved on.

By evening, the entire mountain was covered with snow. It was like stepping into a separate world, one independent of Ash Falls or the troubles of the forests. Where everything was a soft white, the dangers hidden. Lydia tripped more than once.

Around each bend, it seemed, the fox was closer. Lydia willed for it to stay away, unsure of what she would do if it got too close. She was almost fearful of it, its calm demeanor and its red fur like a splotch of ink on the snow's white page. Whenever she looked around it was always the only thing that drew her vision. It made her hungry. But she hadn't killed the deer and the boar and she didn't intend to start now.

As it was beginning to get dark—or, rather, when the sun was going down—Lydia had her first real tumble. She slipped facing forward, her hands landing on a sharp rock that made bright red welts in her palms. Lydia lay there in the snow for a moment, trying to understand how she had gotten to this point. How she was still alive and how she would survive the night. Whether it was even possible. If it wouldn't be better for her to just die where she lay.

Soft footfalls in the snow crunched beside her. Lydia felt something wet touch her hand—a nose, sniffing at her motionless form. The nose moved up her arm, then touched her hair. She twitched. The nose jumped away for a second, and then there was more scuffling in the snow. The nose touched her hand again, then something thin and dry dragged itself along her knuckle.

Lydia lifted her head. The fox was nearly nose to nose with her, its tongue hanging lazily from its mouth while it panted. It almost looked like it was smiling.

Now she really could have it if she wanted. Her hand slowly lifted, snow clinging to her fingers. She placed her palm upon the animal's head, then gently stroked it backwards. She stopped with her hand resting on the fox's neck. A single squeeze and she'd have enough blood to last her through this ordeal. The fox stopped panting, stopped smiling.

The fur slipped through her fingers. The beast trotted back down the mountain. Lydia, unsure whether to be ashamed or proud, stood.

At the crest of the next rise, Lydia had to pause. The ground flattened here, the blanket of snow covering it pristine and untouched. About a hundred yards away from her was a hawthorn tree—large and in full bloom.

Sitting in its shade, a man sharpened his axe.

EIGHT

I still have a headache from where she split my head in two. An unusual idea that, for a moment, I was afraid would work. Axes are so good for beheadings, that's all anyone ever thinks to do with them. Wouldn't that have been my just desert? Killed because someone did the unexpected.

That's probably how most people die, to be honest.

Detective Pike is approaching this tree. She has already seen me, knows that her time is at hand. She hesitated for just a moment when she crested that rise, saw what the plateau held. But now she is coming steadily, head bowed against the effort.

She is the first challenger in a long time to make an actual journey to see me. A long, long time. In those days, I had a whole castle to play my games in, and an unusual little hollow not far away that I called my chapel. A green chapel for a green knight. That's where I would tell them to meet me, not the cryptic little riddle I put before them now. In the old days, they had to make the journey.

But that's all gone now. Or, at least, it's across a continent and an ocean. I didn't really choose to come here, after all, I just make do. Change the game to fit the new environment, the new age. Thankfully, these results have been satisfying.

The ground from the ridge to the tree is slippery and uneven, even as the snow makes it appear flat. I'm not surprised Detective

Pike is taking her time. She looks tired, though I know she won't admit it.

That's alright though. This will all be over soon, one way or another.

I wait for her, sitting on one of the tree's roots. When she finally makes it to me, she collapses onto another one, gasping. I say nothing, continuing to run my whetstone gently along the edge of my axe.

"Couldn't have chosen some place less remote?" she asks, once she's gathered herself.

I shrug. "It was your choice, not mine. You could've gone anywhere, but you came here."

She has no answer to that. I can't help but smile a little, though I hope she doesn't notice.

I think my blade is sharp enough. I run my thumb along it, feeling for any imperfections. There are none, and it feels thin enough that I might start bleeding if I apply any pressure. Satisfied, I set down my whetstone and stand.

After thinking about it for a second, I set down my axe as well. We are to do gifts first, after all.

She is eyeing the axe. No doubt she's wondering if she could make a grab for it, if the effort would pay off. She could, but her only reward would be a swift end after so clear a failure. I let her consider it a moment still. Give her the opportunity to fail.

She does nothing. Eventually, her brown eyes flick to meet mine.

"Are you ready?" I ask.

"Yes," she says.

NINE

Something seemed to have a hold on Lydia Pike. She no longer knew what she would do next, or why. It was like she had floated five feet into the air to rest amongst the leaves of the hawthorn tree and watch as some other woman dealt below with Holly.

She moved to a kneeling position, her knees resting in the hardscrabble of the mountainside and pressed against the roots of a tree that should not have been there. She curled her neck, tucking her chin in a way she imagined presented Holly with a good view of her neck. She took a deep breath, waiting for him to take up his weapon.

"Not yet," he told her, almost a whisper. "Have you forgotten the first part of our bargain?"

Lydia closed her eyes now. "I have no gifts to give you," she said.

"Maybe you don't and maybe you do," answered Holly. "Let me give you mine first."

Lydia looked up at him. He held out a meaty green hand to her, just below her chin. When she hesitated, he flexed his fingers once, pulling the tips back towards him. Lydia put her hand in his, and he pulled her to her feet. He was warm —not just his hand, but all of him, all of him that was within a foot of her. Lydia didn't notice at first when he pointed down the mountain behind them. She turned.

Below her, at the lip of the nearest crest, were the animals. On the left was the deer that had followed her. In the middle was the boar that attacked her. On the right was the fox that helped her. All three meandered in their own way about the slope, ignoring each other as they looked for food. But they were all watching her. Watching *them*. Lydia could see it in the way the deer would stop to arch its long neck, its eyes cast directly towards her, the way the boar would stop digging in the dirt and shake its wild head, or the way the fox would stop to taste the wind. They were waiting for some command, and Lydia knew in her heart it was a command from her.

"These three joined me on my first day in the city," Holly explained. "They each appeared in their own way and made themselves known to me in their own time, but they are mine. They do as I command, when I command. Should you walk away from here, they will be yours as well."

"Mine?"

"To command," Holly nodded. "May they aid you as they have aided me."

"And how, exactly, do I command them?"

Holly gave a little chuckle. He sat again, placing his hands on his knees. Lydia did not laugh with him as she turned. Before she looked at Holly fully, she made eye contact with the fox. It licked its lips, then trotted down the mountain. "It will come to you," Holly said, "when the time is right."

A cold wind blew on top of that mountain. It kicked up some of the loose powder, blew it around them in a wild flurry. Lydia would have covered her eyes if she thought she could take them off Holly for a moment. The cold stung her cheeks and lips, minuscule diamonds as sharp as daggers cutting her.

"What have you brought for me?" Holly asked.

"I've gained nothing," Lydia answered. "Not even knowledge of you."

"Well, that is a hard thing to come by," Holly said, shifting on his root. "But are you sure? There isn't any way that you've changed?"

The marks on her neck winged, the old itch returning again. The wind and the necklace that her and her mother's charm hung on irritated her skin, reminding her of what Lilly had done to her.

She said nothing while absently rubbing at her neck. He was asking her what she had gained, and apparently he had a very broad definition of 'gained.' Hadn't she 'gained' these bites? Hadn't other things come with it?

"I…" she started, then closed her mouth.

Holly watched unmoving. His expression had softened, somewhat. She knew that look for pity, though she was not sure what he pitied. A flush of embarrassment crept up her neck and Lydia had to turn away.

"You said you've played this game before?" she asked.

"A long time ago," Holly answered.

"What did you get out of it?"

"A full belly, a good friend, and three kisses."

"Kisses?"

"Yes. The man I was playing this game with kissed my wife while I was out hunting. When I returned, we feasted on my kills and I gave him the pelts while he returned that which he thought he had stolen."

Lydia turned again. "How do you know that's all they did?" she asked.

Holly's smile widened. "He was a man of great honor," Holly explained. "He only ever lied to me once, and I forgave him for that."

"So if he and your wife had…" Lydia was not sure she wanted to say it out loud.

She didn't have to. Holly laughed heartily, winking at her as he did. "Then I think he and I would've had our own fun as well," Holly said. "After all, I was not what was bothering him at the time. Or, at least, he thought I wasn't." He leaned forward, lowering his voice to a confidential tone. "I used to paint this on, did you know?" he asked, rubbing a hand through his green beard.

Lydia did not answer.

"But I'm talking too much," Holly said, leaning back again. "Did you gain anything else, or should we get on with it?"

"No," Lydia answered slowly. "There's something else."

Holly nodded. "I'm waiting then."

"I need you to hold still though," Lydia said. *What in the goddamn blazes of holy hell are you thinking*, she asked herself.

"I can do that," Holly answered.

Gently, Lydia did as Lilly had done. She slowly approached the green man, screaming at herself to back away. She walked behind him, stepping over the root and the axe, and knelt in the ice. He did not move. Still standing tall on her knees, her head was level with his shoulders.

"Could you get a little lower?" she asked.

Holly complied, shifting so that he sat on the ground now, his legs tucked over the root and his back almost pressed up against her. His neck was covered by locks of his green curls. Lydia brushed these aside to expose the green skin beneath, the muscles like cords of rope beneath. He smelled of earth and blood and leather, his scent filling her nostrils like a thick smoke. She let out a breath and saw the small hairs of his nape stand rigid, so the gooseflesh crossed his veins. There was blood in those veins. A lot of it. "Hold still," she whispered, and then bit.

Her teeth sunk into his neck surprisingly easily. For a moment, she felt nothing, and then a burst of blood spurted into her mouth. She swallowed before she could think to do anything else, then drew back from him in shock.

But that's not what Lilly did, she reminded herself. *Lilly stayed.*

So Lydia bit again, letting his blood fill her mouth before swallowing. Holly did not wince, but a sigh rattled from his mouth as Lydia drank. And, as she drank, Lydia started to feel something leave her. It was like a splinter being drawn from skin, though it left through Lydia's mouth even as she drew in his red liquid. Her limbs suddenly felt weak, and she could no longer stomach the raw blood pouring into her. With a gag, she pushed herself away from him and vomited all over the ground.

She stayed that way for a while. She was cold, shaking, and struggling to breathe in the thin mountain air, a ravenous hunger and thirst coursing through her. It was dark, too—it had been dark for hours. Before, Lydia's world was illuminated by the endless wheel of the stars in the sky and the bright stars of the city below her. That had been enough then, but now she could barely see. She felt empty but whole. She hurt now in a way only the living could hurt.

Snow crunched beneath Holly's feet as he stood. "Thank you," he said. Lydia looked up. The wound in his neck was no longer bleeding, had healed faster than the sun slipping below the horizon. "Is there anything else you've gained?"

The charms, she told herself.

But they were just childish things, and after what she had just done—after what she had just lost and gained—

what else mattered? They were hers and her mother's, and the thought of giving them to Holly made her sick.

She shook her head. "Nothing," she answered.

Holly waited for a moment. Lydia could feel his eyes boring into the back of her head and neck. Lydia raised her gaze to look into his red eyes. It was dark still, but the snow had a pale gleam to it, illuminating him.

He nodded. "Very well," he said, lifting his axe from the ground. He brushed slush from the blood-stained handle, then gripped it in both hands. "Now is the time, Lydia Pike."

Lydia closed her eyes and bowed her head. She kept her arms behind her, resisted the urge to grab her gun and start shooting. "Don't fight," McDonagh had told her. She wasn't sure if she'd even be able to. But that didn't mean she could just sit and wait, either.

She felt a cold kiss on the back of her head—a line of steel, starting at the base of her skull and stretching up the skull, all the weight of doom behind it. Holly was lining up his stroke, resting his axe against her head. He wasn't going to cut it off—he was going to split her in two, just as she had done to him. Lydia held her breath, a hot tear dropping from her cheek into the snow below.

The axe lifted. Lydia involuntarily drew in a breath, jerked her head backwards and away from him, from death. She expected to hear the swish of the axe crashing down into her, parting her skull and brain and nose.

Instead, she heard a strange *tut* from the green man. She looked up, saw that the axe was by his side again. "The deal was," Holly said, "the same stroke I received. Did I flinch, Lydia Pike? Did I cower away and make it harder for you to complete your stroke?"

Lydia's mouth opened and closed. "No," she eventually whispered.

"No," Holly agreed. "And neither must you. You're not a coward, after all. Are you?"

Holly did not wait for an answer. He lifted the axe again, resting it gently now on her upturned forehead. *This*, Lydia thought, *is far worse*. But she did not move while Holly lifted the axe above his head, did not blink as they made eye contact one more time. Then Holly grunted and arced the axe over his head directly into her.

It stopped at the last moment, inches from her head. Lydia's eyes crossed as she stared at the bright edge of the weapon inches from her nose. She almost screamed, except that she had forgotten how.

"Just getting a feel for it," Holly said.

Now she did scream. "Go to hell," she spat. Holly lowered the axe to his side, laughing. "Did I play with you, asshole? Did I test it out a few times?"

"Doesn't mean you couldn't have," Holly said, still chuckling. "You should see your face right now."

"Are we done here?"

Holly's expression grew serious. "No," he said. "The game is not complete."

"Then stop being an idiot and get it done," Lydia snarled.

She bowed now, pressing her fists into the ground, her gaze trained on the snow below her. Her hair fell around her face like a veil keeping her contained, protected. *Finish this*, she thought. She might have even said it out loud. She wasn't sure.

Again, she felt the axe rest against her head. Again, she felt Holly lift it into the air, high above his own head. This time, she did not cry. She did not watch. She did not flinch. She gritted her teeth and waited for the blow to fall, to end her right then and there.

She felt a sharp, singular pain at her left ear. Then, there was the wind against the skin on the side of her face—the chill of the axe's blade gliding past.

Lydia opened her eyes. In the snow beneath she saw a shape—a round half-moon with three circles around it. She could barely see it in the dark. Then another circle was added, a millimeter below the lowest. It was blood, she realized, dripping from her cheek. She touched the half-moon and felt brittle flesh, like a nose or an ear. *My ear*, Lydia realized.

She felt it now—the sting of exposed flesh against fresh air. Her ear was cold while the rest was warm, cold because the ear was gone, warm because her own blood covered her face. He had cut her ear off.

He had taken his stroke.

Holly took a step back, his foot crunching in the snow.

Lydia sprang to her feet, flying backwards as she did, putting distance between her and that axe. She drew her pistol in an instant, brought it to bear on him. All she saw was his wide, white smile plastered over his ugly, green face before she squeezed.

The bullet never found its mark. In the moment after the crack of gunpowder igniting and before the smack of metal crashing through blood and bone, the green man vanished. Lydia looked for him, but she was alone on that mountain save for the rustling of the wind through the hawthorn beside her.

TEN

Lieutenant Lake's back was beginning to hurt. It wasn't so uncomfortable yet that he would have to get up and walk around, but it was getting there. He shifted his position in the small, green-backed hospital chair, crossing his legs and resting his newspaper on top of his right knee. He was halfway through an article about fixing the cracks in the dam, but in the shuffling he had lost his place. It didn't matter—he wasn't really reading anyways. At all times, at least half of his attention was on the woman in the bed before him, on the monitors that meant nothing to him, on the shallow rasp of her breathing.

It had taken two days for him to realize she was missing too. No one had seen her at the station and he had no calls or messages from her. Lake put out a BOLO for her and McDonagh, but nothing came in. No one saw and no one heard anything about them.

On the fourth day, a ranger with the parks and rec department found two cars abandoned in the woods on the eastside, not too far north of the river. The dispatcher immediately noticed that the plates matched the BOLOs and rang up Lake's office. Within an hour, he and several officers under his command were at the scene. Even though there was no sign of foul play with either car, Lake ordered a sweep of the area. Three hours later, they found McDonagh and his head, the holly leaf still in his mouth.

On the fifth day, Lake was placed on paid suspension. Two of his detectives were dead, after all, with a third missing. It had been his squad room that was breached, his officers that were torn apart by the Holly Killer. The Chief of Police told him to take some time to clear his head and get some sleep. His return date was left unstated, as was the fact that he and his team still had not managed to catch Holly.

By the tenth day, Lake realized that there had been no more killings. Or, at least, no more beheadings.

On the fifteenth day, a businessman who owned a hunting lodge and some land about six miles outside of the city decided he wanted to get away for the weekend. When he arrived at the lodge, he found the door open, pine needles strewn across the threshold. Inside, he found a woman wrapped in a blanket, blood covering half of her face and an ear missing. According to his statement, he checked her pulse first and, upon finding she had one, immediately called an ambulance.

The hospital called Lake soon afterward. She had her badge, after all, and the hospital took her fingerprints just to be sure. She had listed her aunt as her emergency contact, but when Lake called the late commander's wife did not answer. So, on the sixteenth day after she disappeared, he arrived at the hospital.

She didn't look like her. Lake almost didn't believe that it was Lydia Pike in the hospital bed. She was deathly thin, her face more like a skull than a living head. The missing ear made her look lopsided too. The other one seemed to stick out from her head even larger, as if making up for its missing sibling. Her skin was pale and broken, scabs covering most of her cheeks and forehead. But, beneath it all, Lake could

almost see the ghost of the Detective Pike he knew. He
wanted to be there when she woke, so he could make sure.

Another three weeks passed. The doctors ran their tests
and scanned her brain, but apart from the obvious, they
couldn't find anything wrong with her. "She'll wake when
she wakes," was all they eventually told Lake.

In the meantime, her ear healed, skin growing over the
stump. The marks on her neck had gone away too. Lake
finally got in contact with Mariam Ellwood, who visited
several times but was otherwise busy planning McDonagh's
funeral. The Umpqua Wilderness Fire was officially declared
contained, and the Mayor held a special ceremony for the
firefighters. Lake's precinct, despite his absence, began to run
smoothly again. One world leader called another "Rocket
Man" in a tweet, and even the Ash Falls media got caught up
in wondering how quickly the bombs would start flying.
Slowly, everyone forgot about the beheadings, about the
green man who killed a man in police custody and was never
caught. Life returned to normal in Ash Falls—or as normal as
life ever got in the city.

A woman came, once or twice, to see Lydia. But Lake
did not know her, and it seemed clear to him that this
woman did not really know too much about Lydia. He asked
for her name, told her Lydia would call her when she woke,
but the woman wouldn't give it. After she left, Lake asked
the nurses to keep an eye out for her. They only rolled their
eyes.

That didn't matter to Lake. He wasn't really leaving
anyways. His wife brought him whatever he needed—
clothes, food, new books to read, or the day's paper. A
couple of his officers stopped by on occasion, claiming they
wanted to see Lydia but really to give Lake updates. Another
Acting Commander was appointed in Lake's absence, a

young man whose career was on the rise. He was the kind of Acting Commander that expected to soon become the Next Commander, and everyone in the precinct agreed. What would happen to Lake when his endless suspension was over was unclear, but the officers wanted to assure Lake they wanted him back.

No one ever asked Lake why he was there—not even his wife. This wasn't the first hospitalized officer Lake stayed beside for a time, after all. This was a very old story, both for Lake and the world.

Which meant that when Lydia Pike woke on the thirty seventh day after her disappearance, Lake was sitting beside her, his nose in a newspaper. First, her heart rate increased. Lake heard the pips speed up, so he folded his newspaper and put it beside him. Her breathing picked up next, almost as if she was having a panic attack, except that her breathing went from nearly non-existent to a normal, steady tempo. Lake leaned forward, placed his hand over hers.

"Lydia," he said. "Lydia, is that you?"

END of Season ONE
Discover more great fiction at
www.fvpress.com

Aknowledgements

No book is the work of one person alone.

First and foremost, this book would not exist without Jeremy Schofield. Beginning with his conception of Ash Falls, he has been a part of *Holly* every step of the way. The fact that five other writers set their books in his world is a testament not only to his creativity but his generosity, as are the countless hours he spent working with us. For all of that, and more, thank you, Ash Father.

Thanks are also due to the folks at Fiction Vortex, without whom this kind of collaboration would never have happened. Thank you all for making this possible.

I owe gratitude to the writers and editors of the Ash Falls' storyverse. Cindy Hess and Melissa Schofield both put a lot of work into the early episodes. Jeanette Koczwara, Joe Mankowski, Keith Fritz, Charel Kunz, and Steve Cotterill gave more of their time and expertise than I could have anticipated. *Holly* belongs to all of these people as much as it does to me, and I have been extremely grateful for their help.

I cannot go too much further without thanking Pauls Toutonghi. Sometimes all anyone needs to follow their dreams is a simple push. It was Pauls who gave me that push, and it will be Pauls who gives that push to many.

It would be impossible for me to list all of the friends and family who have helped me along the way, but there are a few that I cannot leave unmentioned. Ryan, for being the friend I needed. Allison, for being so much more than a friend. Dad, for making sure I grew up with a love of stories. Mom, for teaching me how to tell them. Baby Gran and Big Gran, for all the love and support. I would not be who I am without you. Thank you.

GREETINGS FROM FICTION VORTEX

IF YOU HAVE GOTTEN this far, hopefully you are looking forward to reading more of Ash Falls and other Fiction Vortex™ StoryVerses™. You're in luck! We have an official butt-load of episodes available. Head on over to www.fvpress.com to get all the latest.

Fiction Vortex is all about episodic fiction like the stuff you just read. We are powered by the collaborative writing software known as StoryShop (a project we have helped birth in order to spread our fiction faster!) Thus far, our StoryVerses™ have been a crazy stupid success, but our baby is still so young and frail!

It's time to suckle the milk of brilliant genre fiction until our bones grow strong enough to withstand the slings and arrows of traditional publishing's lumbering giant. At Fiction Vortex™, we are so brazen to assume we can, nay WILL, pioneer the future of digital storytelling. We scoff at the idea of ebooks being the end all of digital publishing.

Let's work together to restore the intimate bonds and direct collaboration between storyteller and audience. Let's use the technology at our fingertips to do so. Become an integral part in discovering the new balance in written storytelling—a balance forged by reader and writer together.